This Family Lies

J.M. Cannon

This Family Lies.

Table of Contents

Break-In

Iris watched them from the second-story porch. They didn't say a word to one another as they walked. There were three of them, she thought. Three figures that were little more than shadows in the weak light of dawn. She lost sight of them as they slipped between the oaks. The birds kept chirping, the sound cheery, sharp, as if this was just an ordinary morning. As if Iris wasn't about to be murdered.

The lights were off in her house, and from where they were in the yard, she knew they couldn't see her where she stood.

Not that it mattered. There was no way out.

A bit of Spanish Moss swayed on an oak branch on the opposite end of the yard. Her eyes darted to it to see another man coming from the old barn. She was surrounded.

She needed to run. But it was spring in the south, and the fields of sugarcane on all sides of her were just sprouting green stubble. There were no tall stalks to hide in. No stand of trees close enough to make a run for.

If she did run, she'd be found by their floodlights in the fields. The trucks would circle her like wolves. If she hid, she'd be yanked from a muddy culvert like an animal.

She left the porch and went to her bedroom. She locked the door behind her.

"It's over, Iris."

She wasn't alone. There was a shape on the bed. Her husband sat with his head in his hands. Long afterwards, in the hospital, she would hear his humid voice like a hallucination. "It's fucking over."

These were the words she remembered. While so much else about this night was a haze—was up for debate in her head—this sentence was not. It was said.

She had to fight the urge to panic. To bounce off the walls like a rat in a trap. To die with dignity, she decided, was the best thing she could do.

"I know," she responded but couldn't keep her voice from shaking.

Her hands trembled, too. She set them gently on the cherrywood of her vanity. She tried to focus on her surroundings as she heard them enter the house. They couldn't be so silent inside. There were the sounds of searching. Their footsteps creaked and doors whined as they opened them.

She stared at her dark reflection in the mirror and sat in the chair. She moved her hands carefully in front of her. Her fingers found lipsticks, foundations, a dozen different shades of blush.

There was the thump of boots on the stairs, steadily timed. One man after another like the ticking of a clock.

Suddenly, she saw her future. She lay on the marble, her body becoming the same cold temperature as the stone. The room smelled of gunpowder. Of blood.

She watched the ivory doorknob turn as someone attempted to open it. She felt a tear race down her cheek. She turned in the chair to face the door. The handle stopped turning. There was a second of silence followed by the splintering crack of the door being kicked from its hinges.

There was no hesitation. The moment the door opened there was a gunshot, and her husband screamed.

Iris stared in horror at the doorway. She couldn't even make out the shape of someone in the darkness. She thought she could best it. That she could stay stoic until the bullet, but she had to scream, too. Just as her lungs filled with air, she saw the brief star of a muzzle flash erupt from the black, and the world vanished from in front of her eyes before she could even hear the shot.

Carats

Iris's memory of the night she was shot is the same every time she thinks of it. There are no new details. No crumbs from the life she lived before those panicked moments. Her would-be death is burned into her brain like a fever dream.

It's the first time Iris sits in front of a vanity since that night. She used to be in the small bedroom on the first floor of the Sweet Blood estate. The doctor gave the greenlight that she's had a near full return of her motor skills, and now she's in a grander guest room upstairs.

It's been more than three months since that night, but she hasn't had an occasion to dress up for. The array of cosmetics in front of her is just as decadent as it was in the house of her memory. There are sixty-dollar primers and bronzers and concealers that are used once or twice and replaced by the maids.

Iris reaches up to her hairline and gently touches the scar left by the bullet. It has shrunk week by week, down to the size of a quarter. It can't pass as a beauty mark. The skin is patchy and textured. It has that burned flesh look of Freddy Kruger. She puts a concealer down. She's not going to cover it up. Not when everybody is going to be looking for it anyway. Their eyes will only linger on her forehead longer, searching.

Iris is supposed to give a speech in front of more than a hundred strangers, and the anxiety isn't all that dissimilar from watching someone come to shoot you in the head.

They're supportive, sure. But all still come from Southern money. The people in her life have been trying to convince Iris that she is a miracle, but she looked up the statistics and found that a surprising 10% of people who are shot in the head survive. Which isn't quite miracle territory, to Iris.

It makes sense, she thinks. She knows a couple women who are famous for bearing the wound. There's Malala and

Congresswoman Giffords. Women who were shot championing politics and girls' right to education. Iris was not doing either. She was in her house on a Tuesday morning when she was shot execution style in the head.

There's a soft knock on the door, and Iris turns.

"Hey, hon."

It's Augusta. Her mother-in-law pushes the door the rest of the way open.

She's a large woman—six feet tall, and in her heels, Augusta has to duck to keep her head from clipping the top of the doorframe. As intimidating as she is, Iris likes to look at her.

Every woman would be happy to look like Augusta at sixty. Her hair is as white as snow. It rolls just past her shoulders and shines even brighter, as it's contrasted by her tan face.

She's kept up with the Botox, but the work she's had done is subtle. Her forehead is flat, and her cheeks are full and taut, but she has two deep lines that run from the sides of her nose to the corners of her mouth. Augusta looks her age. She's just a very pretty sixty.

She walks towards Iris. "You look darling."

The dress Augusta is wearing is a little tight for the occasion, but it is an appropriate black. Her shoulders are broad, but then her body tightens like an hourglass before widening at the hips once more.

Iris looks away. She's embarrassed she let her eyes linger in envy. Iris used to be told she's pretty. Now with the scar, she's not so sure. Her pale skin against her dark-brown hair makes the wrong kind of contrast. Her small nose and ears used to have a nice proportion that was easy on the eyes. But now she thinks they're dwarfed by the warped skin on her forehead.

Iris smiles. "I'm glad you think so."

"Are you sure you're up for this?"

Iris's mouth opens, but no words come out. She's far from sure. Her husband, Joseph, was murdered right next to her. Now she's supposed to give a speech at his memorial dinner.

The problem: she doesn't remember anything about the past. Not her husband or herself. There are spare memories here and there. A kiss. A road trip with her mom. Tumbleweeds, she's grown to call them. Her childhood is there, but the last decade is simply gone. Her doctor says her memory may come to her in time or it might not.

Smells help. She'll catch a whiff of fried food and remember a fair. Anything can send her flying back. Even a dead fish sent her back to a beach date in her teens.

"Do you like it?" Augusta nods towards the vanity, and Iris is slow to realize what she's referencing.

"Like what?"

"Your speech?"

Iris looks at the white sheets on the vanity.

Right. The speech. The one commemorating a man she doesn't remember, written by an intern at the Adler Corp. If she tries, she can picture Joseph's smile—wide, white, and kind. She loved him, she thinks. At least, that's the story she's been told, both by others and the pictures she's seen of them together.

Cheek to cheek. Happy love.

"I can read it."

Augusta looks away from Iris and nods slightly. Her eyes dance around from the vanity to the four-post bed. This was Joseph's room as a child. Now it's just another guest room in Sweet Blood—one of the oldest and grandest plantation homes between New Orleans and Baton Rouge that's still a private residence. The style is quite similar to the house Iris was shot in and her husband murdered, but her old house lies empty on the market, twenty miles to the north.

Augusta's eyes are wet for a moment, and then they steady. "I don't want to speak of him after today."

"What do you mean?"

"Joey. I don't want to hear his name. I don't want to see his picture. Not for a few weeks, at least. That is the only thing that's going to get me through this dinner. I will think about nothing but my son for the next few hours, but then I need to heal."

Iris doesn't think that will be possible. Someone is always talking about Joseph. His brothers, business associates. The police.

Augusta glances around the room nervously, as if afraid of the memories it holds.

She gently touches the back of Iris's neck, and their eyes meet again, only this time in the mirror. They stare at each other. With such loss between them, the gaze says plenty and the silence is not awkward.

"You're not a daughter-in-law anymore to me, okay? You're family."

Augusta unfurls her fist, and Iris feels something cold against her skin. A diamond necklace glitters in the mirror. It's so bejeweled that even in this solemn moment, Iris's brow raises in shock.

Augusta clasps the necklace around her neck and bends down so they're cheek to cheek. "We're going to get through this. Everything. But we have to do it together."

Iris nods and touches the diamonds delicately. They lace over each other and twinkle like stars in the vanity lights.

"The car is out front. Meet me on the porch when you're ready to go."

Augusta leans back and starts towards the door, while Iris is frozen, staring at the diamonds. She touches the necklace again.

This is what she likes, isn't it? Iris thinks. Diamonds. A quarter-million dollars wrapped around her neck. But she feels nothing. She wonders if her greed, the ambition she must've had to be rich, were erased by the bullet.

"And I know. That thing is horrible." Augusta gestures at the vanity with her head from the doorway. "But it's a reminder of how horrible this world can be, don't you think? A reminder of the things we can do to each other..." Augusta doesn't finish her thought and disappears down the hall.

Iris doesn't know what she's talking about. She backs up from the vanity and looks at its woodwork. This room is always dark, and she hasn't stayed here long enough to notice it.

6

The wooden legs of this vanity are delicately carved. There are tiny figures in the woodwork. Women bend towards bushes. Cotton sacks are carved at their hips. It takes Iris a moment to realize that she's looking at slaves.

Her eyes widen, and she grasps the diamonds. Below her feet is the same style of checkerboard marble she was shot on. Was her husband such a great man that she was able to put aside how this family originally made its fortune? That they kept such furniture? Or was she really the kind of woman who just didn't care?

The last question is her greatest fear. She's not sure she's the same woman she was before she was shot. She might've been mean. Vain. There is no doubt she was ambitious.

Iris stays in her seat, staring at her scar. All these things leave her with a vague anxiety. She can't help but think she's not as innocent as everyone thinks. And that maybe, in some way, she deserved to get shot.

Dirt

Iris rises and walks down the hall. An oriental runner stretches from her bedroom's doorway all the way to the top of the stairs, muffling her heeled steps. When she gets to the staircase, she pauses. The hall continues past the stairs to the opposite end of the second story, and here she can see the door to the master bedroom.

It's always closed.

Her husband's father, Joseph Senior, has been bedridden for the last eight years from a stroke. A nurse comes around once a day to do the heavy lifting. She gives him a sponge bath, administers prescriptions, and takes his vitals. Other than that, Augusta takes care of him with the help of the housemaid.

He's nonverbal and bound to a wheelchair when he's not in bed. He's a ghostly figure in the house. A presence Iris can feel when she passes the oil painting of him that hangs in the living room, but she rarely ever sees him. Apparently, he wasn't as proper as the painting might make him out to be. His stroke was the result of a life of heavy drinking and smoking. Business was his pastime, she's heard. Getting hammered was his true passion.

Iris turns to the staircase. This is probably the most beautiful part of the entire house, but it's not easy to navigate in heels. The balusters that run the length of the stairs are carved to resemble sugarcane stalks, and its wide wooden steps shine, buffed. They spiral a couple dozen steps down into the entrance hall, where they spill onto the marble.

She walks slowly, hiking her black dress up in one hand and grasping the railing with the other. There's a round table at the bottom with a towering bouquet of fresh flowers. She strolls out the front door and onto the porch.

Augusta is waiting for her here, and so is Iris's sister-in-law, Annabelle. The two are talking while standing close to each

8

another. Their jeweled brooches and bracelets and rings all glitter in the orange light that illuminates the open porch.

Annabelle is married to Augusta's middle son, Jamie. The couple is living in the guesthouse on the property while their house in Baton Rouge is being remodeled.

"Oh, Iris. Look at you all gussied up." Annabelle strolls towards her. She keeps her back erect as she walks and leans in stiffly to plant a faux kiss on each cheek. She takes high society very seriously. "How've you been this week?"

Annabelle's belly sticks out. She's seven months pregnant, but her dress has been altered perfectly. She tilts her long head at Iris, waiting for an answer.

Iris has always thought Annabelle's face is shaped like a crescent moon. Her forehead bulges over her eyes, and her chin narrows sharply to a near point. She can imagine the teasing she took from boys growing up. *"Hey, Annabelle, why the long face?"*

"I'm fine, thank you," Iris says, softening her voice. Making it formal. "And yourself?"

"Oh." She pats her bump. "Just trying to stay off my feet."

Iris glances down to see that she's wearing heels. She has learned quickly that Annabelle's life revolves around status. She wants to be like Augusta. Powerful. Respected. But there's a fake, forced quality to her attempt. She works for the Adler Corp as a manager, but Iris has heard she's the kind of boss that whips from behind while Augusta leads from the front.

"Oh." Annabelle follows Iris's gaze to her feet. "I know what you're thinking, but I had these broken in by a friend. She has the *exact* same size feet as me. I gave her a hundred bucks to wear them around her house for a day. Now they fit like a glove. Don't worry. I made her wear socks."

Iris has no idea what to say to this. She just smiles.

Annabelle is the kind of woman Iris struggles the most to relate to. The kind that tosses out her entire wardrobe with each new season and winces when a friend purchases a newer car than her. Everything is about hierarchy. And every action is about signaling to others her place in it.

Iris is grappling with the thought that she used to be exactly the same. Always playing the game of high society. Going through money like tissue paper to try to make a statement.

None of it comes naturally to her, while with Annabelle even her voice is expert. Around other society women her tone is always kept in line. Never too casual. Never too excited. Iris has relearned quickly how the rich like to play warden over their tongue. A woman Iris considered fun in these circles would be labeled brash.

"Those diamonds look gorgeous on you, Iris. They really distract."

That is another talent of Annabelle's, Iris thinks. Every compliment must have its catch. By distract she means from the scar. Is that why Augusta gave the necklace to her? So people's eyes will linger on *it* instead of the wound?

"Thanks, Annabelle," Iris says somewhat sarcastically, but Annabelle just beams, oblivious to her tone.

"Are you remembering things any better? How are you feeling?" Annabelle narrows her eyes at Iris, like she's ready to judge her answer.

"The same. To both."

Annabelle tightens her lips and rubs Iris's shoulder.

"It'll come." Her eyes dart to Iris's scar for a moment. "If tonight is too hard, it's okay to leave early. No one's going to judge you. Just say the word, clack your heels, and you'll be back at Sweet Blood."

"Thank you, Annabelle." It's all she can say. Iris isn't sure if she has always been a quiet person, but she is now. She almost wants to ask if she was, but she's awkward around these women. She doesn't feel like their peer. She can't relate to them either, with their money and glamor and perfect social manners.

It didn't used to be this way. The photos Iris has seen suggest they were all close. She'd been married to Joseph only six months before that final night, but in the two years they dated before, she was friends with Annabelle and Augusta.

10

There must've been countless brunches and lunches and fancy dinners like this that Iris can't recall.

When she looks back at posts on her social media, she sees herself with these women. They're posing in bikinis next to a pool in Aruba. Dressed to the nines in jewels and gowns in front of the colonnaded façade of Sweet Blood. Doing an antebellum photoshoot on the grounds of a *plantation*.

This life isn't new to Iris. Apparently, she liked it. Yet now it feels foreign. *Wrong.* Maybe it's because Joseph is gone now. Was he what had tethered her to these strange people?

Annabelle takes her hand, and they walk together down the steps. A black Cadillac sedan idles on the gravel driveway. A bald man in a dark suit appears from the driver's seat and opens the door to the back seat. There are no "thank yous" or eye contact with him as Augusta and Annabelle step into the car, and Iris does the same.

Its back seat is spacious, and Annabelle and Augusta sit next to each other in the two seats that face the front, while Iris sits opposite so she faces them.

The three are silent as the car whisks them away. It's not until they're off the crunch of the gravel and gliding down the smooth highway that Iris finds the strength to speak.

"I've been thinking. I'd like to review my case," she blurts out. She's afraid if she didn't say it now, she never would.

Augusta and Annabelle look at each other. There's disappointment between them, like they were always afraid this new Iris might ask something so silly.

"I mean with the police. You know?" she continues. "Go over how I was shot... and everything."

Augusta physically cringes. Annabelle is the one who speaks.

"Don't you remember going over all that in the hospital?"

"My memory wasn't the same then. I think I've healed more. The doctor says I have. Wouldn't you agree?"

Annabelle ignores her question. "You might just forget it all over again. Waste their time."

Augusta reaches over and puts a hand on Annabelle's knee to silence her. "I can arrange for the sheriff to be at the police station in Preston tomorrow morning. It's where they have all their files on the case. They didn't get many answers when you were in the hospital, so I'm sure the police would be happy to have you in again."

"Great." Iris is nervous yet relieved. But Augusta and Annabelle are silent now, and it seems they don't plan on saying anything more. "I didn't think the sheriff would be workin' Sundays," Iris says to fill the air.

"He's not," Augusta says. From her tone alone, Iris can tell what she's trying to say—*The sheriff does what I tell him.*

Annabelle and Augusta both look out their windows as if Iris has dug something up and dropped it between them and neither can stand to look at it.

It's a couple minutes before anyone speaks.

"You haven't met half these characters, Iris," says Augusta. "Or, sorry. I mean you *have* met some, but you probably won't remember them."

"To be honest, I don't think I'm ready to really mingle."

"You won't have to. Just stay at the table. You're seated by us. A lot of these people may stare at your scar. They may judge you for this and that. Everyone has their own theory as to what happened to you and my son. It's all ludicrous."

"Do they?" Iris asks. Of course there has been gossip, she realizes. But she hasn't heard any of it herself. Whatever it has been, neither Augusta nor Annabelle have relayed it to her. It probably is just that. Ludicrous.

Augusta continues, "One thing to know about these folks is that they're not as prim and proper as they appear. Don't blush under their judging eyes. As far as I'm concerned, you're the purest one of them, Iris."

"What would they be judging me for?" Iris is suddenly anxious. She'd thought she had everyone's sympathy. She's a victim, after all. Her husband has been murdered, and the police can't even figure out who did it.

Augusta looks her in the eye. "Now people just think you did the same things that they picture would get themselves into trouble."

"They say kinks come from a want to go against what you've been told is wrong your whole life," Annabelle chimes in. "So, if the Bible says not to do it, you can best believe they're doing it."

"Like what?" Iris asks.

"Like adultery," Augusta says.

So, they think she was having an affair, Iris thinks. Of course. Double murders are seldom random. So those are the rumors. A love triangle. The idea spurs nothing in Iris's memory.

Annabelle leans forward and cups her hand like she's telling a secret. "Or homosexuality. Congressman Overman is a little close with his college aides. I wouldn't be surprised if he brought one tonight."

"Enough, Annabelle."

Annabelle purses her lips and leans back, and Augusta looks back at Iris. "I'm just trying to say, don't be intimidated by anyone, and if somebody makes some dumb hint at it, you let me know. I'll put them in their place."

"Okay." There is something these women aren't telling her. It's felt that way since she left the hospital. But what Iris struggles to tell is whether Augusta is simply protecting her like she says or if she's keeping her in the dark.

If there's another rumor as to why Iris and her husband were targeted, tonight is her chance to find out.

Black-Tie

The memorial dinner is in an old armory turned event venue. Iris isn't ready for the giant pictures of her husband that sit on easels in the short entrance hall. She stops and stares at him. Joseph had a strong, square jaw and arresting green eyes just like Augusta. For a moment, Iris has to stifle a sense of pride for landing a man so handsome, but of course the pictures chosen for tonight are the very best of him.

The three of them are all late, and once they pass the pictures into the main hall, there's the sound of silverware clinking a glass. Augusta and Annabelle step to the side and gesture for Iris to take the lead.

The chatter dies slowly, as if someone is turning down the volume. Everyone is standing and turning to face the entrance. They're turning to face *her*, Iris realizes with dread.

This is the exact scenario Iris wanted to avoid. She's the dead center of attention. Augusta plans events meticulously. Nothing slips past her. She knew this would happen. If she thought Iris would find this a pleasant surprise, she was wrong. The support from strangers means little. She wants to crawl into a ball.

Two hundred or more people are here. The men are all in black or charcoal suits, and the women wear black dresses. Most of them stare at Iris curiously, like they all had their bets on how the girl who got shot in the head would look.

Cross-eyed and crippled. Dumb and drooling. Iris is none of those things, and her eyes are just as intelligent as they always were. She can see they're somewhat surprised by how normal she looks. Maybe even disappointed. Perhaps they wanted a freak show. Something to pity.

Augusta begins to clap, and then so does the entire room. People cheer and whistle, and as the applause thunders, Iris bows her head slightly with an awkward, tight-lipped smile.

On the far side of the ballroom, a banner, nearly twenty feet long, hangs from the ceiling. It reads, *Iris Strong.*

Her cheeks burn, and thankfully Augusta notices she's uncomfortable and starts walking next to her. "Our table is closest to the stage," she whispers in Iris's ear.

Augusta shakes a few hands and bends to speak to her again. "Not everyone you see is a friend of the family. There's two people you need to be wary of."

Wary of? Iris thinks, trying not to frown. *Like they may have shot her?*

"I'm not going to look," Augusta says, "but the old man to your left with the neck like a turkey? He's been trying to sell his plant to Dow Chemical on the condition they can do an expansion. Joseph was holding up the sale in court around the time of his death. The worry was the waste runoff from a bigger plant would get in our crop."

Iris makes eye contact with the man. His face is emotional. His eyes are squinted as he claps.

"Jerry Morris," Augusta says his name, and Iris forgets it almost immediately.

With his oval-lens glasses and liver-spotted hands, he looks like he'd rather bounce his grandchildren on his knee than pay for hired killers, but then again, for a deal worth hundreds of millions of dollars, Iris has to remind herself that some of these people are capable of anything. But do the people in this room have connections like that? She wonders.

The military culture in the south is strong. Everyone knows somebody who was in the Marines, or Special Forces, or Navy SEALs. It was possible.

"The woman in the lighter shade of black. Ugh. It's almost gray," Augusta whispers. Iris sees who she's talking about. The woman's lips bulge fishlike with fillers, and her breasts, too, press against the tight fabric of her dress.

"She's the widow I've been telling you about. Alanis Barnes."

Augusta had mentioned to the police that this woman might have a motive. Joseph had fired her husband, Will, from the

15

Adler Corp. It was just last fall after hearing he'd exposed himself to his daughter's soccer team. Will was blacklisted by most outfits in the lower valley. Not long afterwards, he drove off a bridge into the Mississippi.

Amy… Alyssa… Iris tries to remember the name Augusta told her, but again, it's already gone. She tries to catch it, like she's diving to return a tennis serve, but it bounces right past her. The applause, the dozens of eyes sizing her up, make it impossible to focus. She tells herself it doesn't matter.

Iris feels like these names are distractions. The old man and the plastic widow do not look capable of arranging what was supposed to be a double homicide. It takes true hate to do something like that.

The women get to their table and sit. The clapping dies down and the chatter resumes, and Iris feels like she can finally exhale.

She's thankful to see people she recognizes at the table. Jamie, Annabelle's husband, is standing and greeting her. He's a chubby man. His fat cheeks would look just like a baby's if it weren't for the short beard that covered them.

Then there's Augusta's youngest son, Gideon. Tall, gangly, and at twenty-four, his expression is still that of a sulky teenager. His hair is nearly to his shoulders and cut in a mullet. He doesn't hug Augusta or say hi to Iris. He crosses one leg on top of the other and looks back to his phone.

There's only one face at the table Iris doesn't recognize. There's a man with a bird-like look. He has a sharp Adam's apple, a long beak of a nose, and small eyes.

"Iris, you've met my nephew, Nick."

The man extends his long-fingered hand to Iris, and she shakes it.

"I'm sure we've met, but—" Iris starts.

"Don't you worry about that at all." He holds her hand for a moment too long.

"Oh," Augusta says loudly now. "I need a drink."

They all sit, and waiters appear around the table.

Iris is fine with water, but the rest of the table orders cocktails. When they're done, Gideon is the first to speak. He looks up from his phone and across the room. "What the fuck is he doing here?"

"You watch your mouth," Augusta snaps. She's no stranger to cursing, but perhaps not in public and not by her sons, Iris thinks. Then she and the whole table turn to gaze where Gideon is looking.

The others only glance and then turn back, but Iris's eyes linger. She doesn't know who she's looking for.

"Who invited him?" Annabelle asks.

"He's still at the company." Augusta shakes her head. "His invitation was automatic."

Gideon huffs and puts his phone away. "You didn't think of crossing him off the list?"

"Believe it or not, I had a lot more on my mind."

Everyone is quiet as the waiters come back quickly with their drinks. When they leave, Iris speaks.

"Who are we talking about?"

No one says anything. Jamie widens his eyes and shakes his head. The others just pay attention to their cocktails.

"Dominic," Nick says finally, but the name means nothing to Iris, and suddenly an older couple appears behind Augusta. There's a flurry of greetings, and soon the whole table is talking with them. Iris is silent.

Augusta stands to greet the couple, and Nick leans over to Iris. His sharp Adam's apple bobs as he swallows. "They're talking about Dominic," he says in a quiet tone. Not loud enough to be heard by the others.

"I don't know who that is," says Iris.

"He's the black kid. Short hair. Glasses. He's at your six o'clock."

Iris turns and sees him right away. Dominic looks a couple years younger than her—twenty-six, maybe. His hair is shaved close to his skull, and he wears a pair of round eyeglasses. Most men his age here have a flaw in their outfits. Their bowties are a little crooked or their belts are dark brown instead of black, but Dominic wears his tuxedo like he was born in it.

"Who is he?"

"He was your husband's assistant."

Iris is still looking at Dominic while she talks. "And why wouldn't he be invited?"

"Um... Ha." Nick runs his fingers over his mouth nervously. "He cried at his funeral."

"My husband's?"

"Uh-huh."

"Is that a crime?"

"Well... sobbed is the better word. He was pretty emotional. Too emotional. It was awkward to say the least. A married man's assistant bawling at his funeral. It started a lot of rumors."

Iris shifts in her seat. "Like they were lovers?"

Nick coughs in discomfort at the very sound of the words. "Your husband... Look, Joseph was straight as an arrow. He wasn't queer. Okay? All the boys knew that. *You* knew that. I'm sure."

"Of course," Iris says uncomfortably.

Dominic is talking to an older man, using his hands emphatically to make some kind of point as he speaks. When he's done talking, he turns his head towards their table. Iris looks away quickly. Too quickly, and she notices Augusta's eyes burn into her. She sits back down next to Iris.

"What are y'all talking about?"

Nick leans back and flicks his nose like he's been caught.

Iris just shrugs. "People who may have shot me."

Augusta doesn't like the blunt language. She puts her hand on top of Iris's. "You mean Dominic?"

"Yeah."

"Oh, Iris. He's just a sensitive man. Remember..." Iris can see she's looking at Nick as she speaks. "Don't believe any of the bullshit rumors."

Augusta pats Iris on the shoulder and picks up her cocktail.

18

Iris knows she loved her son. She'd want nothing more than to get his murderer alone in a room. But still, she can't help but look at Augusta, with her jewels, her posture, her fortune, and think this is a woman whose life was built upon secrets.

She's not just good at lying.

It's a part of who she is.

Scent

Iris grows nervous as the time for her to give her speech gets nearer. Other people have spoken already. Joseph's college roommates, both brothers—Jamie and Gideon. Golf buddies from the country club. It's a kind of second funeral.

Joseph is remembered as a kind man. A rarity in the cutthroat world of industrial agriculture. He was humble and helpful. Loving and kind. Iris recycles these words through her mind, hoping they'll project an image, a memory, anything of the man she spent more than two years with. But they do nothing. There's that same blank space, that black hole, where a great man supposedly loved her.

There are jokes told on stage, and Iris wonders if the funeral was more a subdued, shocked affair. She was still in a medically induced coma during that time. There would've been no laughs for Joseph then. This dinner, with its light tone, buoyed by the silver lining of her survival, seems like a success.

No one prods Iris to talk, which she appreciates. She's trying to hold herself together, but she's not sad or overwhelmed; she's growing angry. People are getting loosened up from the liquor, and the chatter is growing boisterous. It's the questions that are eating at Iris. Everyone knows more than her. About the Adlers. About her husband. About herself.

She hasn't drunk since the injury, but now she raises a finger and requests a glass of champagne. When she gets it, it's gone in two big gulps. Her thirst surprises her, and she looks at the empty glass with a frown.

Despite being Baptists, heavy drinking is a fixture for many of these ladies, and it appears she was no stranger to it either. It's been so long that she has a little buzz, but she instantly wants more. It's almost time for her speech, and another drink to dull her nerves sounds so good that her foot bounces anxiously, but before she can signal a waiter, the room quiets.

Augusta is on stage, and Iris is next.

Augusta pauses in front of the microphone for some time. She lets the crowd watch her in silence, building emotion as she looks through her notes.

"I'm not sure if I can get through this whole thing." Augusta lets out a desperate laugh. She is already crying. "You know how much I loved Joey." She wipes her face with the back of her hand. The informal nickname is all Augusta's. For friends and all other family, he had the same name as his father—Joseph.

"He was a special person. I could go on and on about Joey, but everything that comes out of a mother's mouth is going to be a little biased. So I just want you all to know that your speeches, the things you've said about Joseph, they are the most a mom could wish for. They show me that my son was as special to others as he was to me."

There's applause, and everyone at Iris's table is crying, but she feels nothing. She widens her eyes and stares at the floor so anyone looking will think she's just too overwhelmed for tears.

"And if Joseph had lived, by the end of his life, he would've taken this family far. Even from its heights of today."

Jamie suddenly shifts uncomfortably. All the sons, Jamie and Gideon included, worked for the family business, but it was assumed Joseph, the firstborn, would be the one to take the reins.

"I don't mean to overshadow my son's memory and the strength of my daughter-in-law. But if you knew Joseph..." Augusta looks at Iris for a moment, and then she quickly darts her eyes away. "Then you know he would want us to be as *efficient* as possible." There are a few chuckles at this. "While so many close friends and business associates are in one room together, I'd be foolish not to tell you now." Augusta takes a deep breath. "My son's death has proved to be too much, and in the next few months, I will be stepping down as CEO of the Adler Corporation."

There's a collective groan from the crowd.

Augusta holds a hand out. "Being the first woman to lead this business has been among the greatest pleasures of my life..."

Augusta makes like she's going to keep talking, but the room suddenly starts to applaud. It starts slow and then erupts. She steps away from the microphone. The cheers don't quiet. They only grow as people stand. Soon, everyone is on their feet, even Iris.

Augusta has been CEO since her husband, Joseph Senior, stepped down after only leading the company for four years. Apparently, business was never his passion. He was happy to let her become CEO herself. Augusta had butted her way to the top of this family.

"Run for the Senate!" someone shouts into cupped hands, and the applause dies some as people stop to whoop and laugh.

Augusta smiles. A waiter with a single champagne resting on a tray walks across the stage to her. Augusta plucks the glass off and raises it high.

Everyone in the crowd jostles to raise their drinks.

"To my son, Joseph. And the *daughter* he was able to leave me in his place." She's looking right at Iris, and everyone else in the room follows Augusta's gaze. Iris doesn't have a glass. Hers is empty. She stands still and stares back at Augusta.

"Cheers."

"Cheers!" the crowd echoes back, and then there's silence as everyone drinks.

Augusta brings her glass down, and Iris takes the opportunity to shake her head ever so slightly at her.

She can't go next. She can't stand on stage and speak in front of these strangers. Not about a great man she'll have to pretend to remember.

Augusta seems to understand. She doesn't introduce Iris. She walks off stage and is quickly at her side.

"Do you need to go home?" Augusta asks.

The room never got loud again after the toast. Everybody is looking at them. Looking at Iris. She can feel their eyes on her back like spiders.

"Come on." Augusta doesn't wait for her to answer. She takes Iris by the hand, and she and Annabelle both walk her through the ballroom and out a side door into the parking lot.

It's quiet out here. Most of the parking spaces are still empty, and Iris sees a news van at the far end of the lot. The people inside start to chatter again, but the sound goes mute as the door clanks shut.

"Do you want me to call the car around?" asks Augusta.

"No." Iris closes her eyes as she's hit by a breeze. "I'll be fine."

She is able to compose herself quickly. She's distracted by what she sees a hundred yards away by the news van.

There is a big camera set up on a tripod with a floodlight behind it. A line of about two dozen people, most with picket signs, start to yell and jeer.

"Are they yelling at us?" Iris asks. She tries to make out what they're saying, but it's all jumbled.

"Goddamn vegans." Augusta opens the clasp of her little purse that hangs around her shoulder and pulls out a cigarette.

"They're protesting the slaughterhouse," Annabelle says. "The big pig plant just a little north of us has *Adler* in big letters hanging on the side. Maybe it's time we take those down, Mama. Let 'em think we sold it to the Chinese."

Iris has always found it strange how Annabelle will call her mother-in-law *mama*. Her use of the word is not endearing. There's something sycophantic about the way she says it. She's always sucking up.

Iris finally catches something the protestors are saying.

"Murderers!"

Another voice echoes across the parking lot. "Fucking killers!"

The door to the party suddenly opens again and three men step out. The same three who were at the table. It's the Adler boys, Jamie and Gideon. Nick trails behind them.

23

"We just heard they were out here." Jamie looks towards the protestors like a bull ready to charge. "How about y'all come back in?"

"Then they *win*, Jamie," Annabelle says like he's stupid. "Come on. Join us."

They let the door close behind them and Iris watches Gideon pull out a vape pen. She watches his shoulders rise as he hits it deep, and a skunky smell of cannabis wafts into her face.

The cloud hits Augusta, too, but she either somehow doesn't notice or doesn't care.

Nick walks close to Iris. "See that black truck?"

She does. Close to the protestors, a big black pickup is parked a little crooked. Iris thinks he's about to brag that it's his.

"What about it?"

"There's four sheriff's deputies in there with Billy clubs ready to jump those clowns."

"The protestors?"

"Yep."

"How do you know?"

"You don't know what I do for a living, do you?"

Iris is annoyed. A half hour ago, she didn't even know who he was. "No."

"I'm with the State Police," he says proudly.

"Homicide," Gideon adds while blowing out another cloud of vapor, as if this means his dab pen is safe from confiscation.

"You're a detective?" Iris asks. Now she's actually curious.

"Yes ma'am."

"How much do you know about my case?"

"I want to see these fruits get theirs," Gideon suddenly interrupts everyone by yelling. "Come and get me!" he cups his hands and shouts. "You malnourished *fucking* pussies!"

"Gideon!" Augusta snaps. "Knock it off!"

"I don't suppose you have any want to be the next CEO," Nick quips at Gideon.

"He gave that up when he tried to start his rap career," Jamie adds.

The others chuckle, and Gideon barks, "Shut up!"

Jamie puts a hand on his shoulder. "It's one thing to say the N-word, but another level of stupid to record yourself doin' it."

"It was in a musical context." Gideon pushes his hand off him. "I was being hip, not racist, dumbass."

"There's your problem—"

"Boys!" Augusta shouts. "Please. Gideon..." She steps to him and speaks in a quiet tone. Iris can't hear her at all as the wind blows warm across the parking lot.

Nick and Jamie have begun talking, and Iris is left with Annabelle. She crosses her arms and rests them on top of her pregnant belly. "I'm sorry, Iris. I know tonight might've been a bit too much."

"It's okay, really."

"You know," Annabelle begins. "If it's a boy, Jamie and I were thinking of naming him Joseph."

Iris feels a little flutter of panic. She had thought they already knew the sex of the baby. She thought she remembered Annabelle telling everybody it was a boy. Her lapses in memory make her heart jump. How intact is her brain, really?

Annabelle is silent, looking at her expectantly.

"Are you... asking for my blessing?"

"We just want you to know."

So, Iris doesn't get a say, she sees. It's not like Annabelle to give anyone power over her decisions. Even if it's the polite thing to do.

"But don't tell anyone. We want it to be a surprise."

"That's sweet."

"Thank you."

Iris shifts on her feet. "I don't want to worry anyone. We can head back in."

"Are you sure?"

"This isn't supposed to be about me. People should be thinking of my husband."

"Iris, he wouldn't give a shit. Joseph would just want you to be taken care of."

"Still. I mean it. I'm good," Iris says while making eye contact with Annabelle every other word. She hates the way Annabelle tries to stare through her. It's like she's always practicing a power move she learned from a class on 80's business tactics.

"Alright." Annabelle puts her arm through Iris's, like she's elderly and delicate, but Iris is too polite to shoo her off. They start back towards the door.

Augusta is talking to all three boys now. She turns from them, holding a white handkerchief she'd gotten from one of their suit coats.

She holds it out to Iris.

Iris takes it, and the two go back into the ballroom. She wipes the corners of her eyes and then her nose, when she suddenly freezes.

"Come on, Iris. Back to our table."

She has to force herself to nod and walk. Her brain is doing something it doesn't usually do—remembering. The handkerchief smells of cologne. The scent isn't overwhelmingly macho. It's tasteful. Not a nostril-flaring fruit bomb. It's pleasant and strong but still sexy.

And that's exactly what it reminds her of. Sex. The smell makes her groin buzz.

Iris has to will herself into the ballroom. Her face is perplexed, and she knows it. She quickly tries to look appropriate. She decides on a sad smile, but she's certain to any close eye, it looks as fake as it feels.

She takes a hard right to go back to her seat instead of weaving around the white-clothed tables, and she runs into somebody.

"Shit. Sorry. So sorry," the man apologizes, even though his drink spilled onto himself.

It's Dominic. He had moved from the far side of the room to be next to the door. To do what? Eavesdrop? Iris wonders.

"It's okay," she mutters but doesn't slow down. She's lost in other thoughts. Augusta had gotten that handkerchief from one of the men—Gideon or Jamie, or her nephew the cop, Nick.

She crumples the handkerchief so it's hidden in her fist.

None of those men are her husband, and yet from the memory of the scent, she's certain she's slept with one of them.

Maybe Augusta was wrong about the rumors. Or lying. Her heart thumps. Words appear in her head. Duplicitous. Ambitious.

Iris's idea of the wicked woman she feared she used to be becomes clearer. She learned something new about herself tonight.

She'd been having an affair.

Corpse

The ride home is quiet. Iris doesn't have much to say. She's trapped in her own head, gritting her teeth, willing herself to remember. She pictures the faces of each man, but she's not attracted to any of them. Not in the slightest.

Gideon is too young.

Nick gives her the heebie-jeebies.

And Jamie, well... Jamie is married to Annabelle, Iris thinks. There's obviously something wrong with him.

Iris's pulse has been racing since she smelled the handkerchief. Ever since she woke up after being shot, she's been trying to piece together the person she used to be. It's looking like her fear is coming true. She was like her sister-in-law. Vain. Money motivated. A socialite and social climber.

Of course she was just like Annabelle. Iris wouldn't want to be a part of this world unless she could play the game. Now she has to add unfaithful wife to the list. The worst part is she can't even remember who she slept with. The smell of the cologne reminded her of passion. Guilt. But there is no face to accompany these feelings. She pictures herself being kissed on the neck by a man whose face is just out of sight below her chin.

Just as badly as she wants to understand what happened to her, Iris wants to run. She should have access to Joseph's money soon and his life insurance. The doctors weren't sure she'd ever be mentally independent again, and the family lawyers were quick to tuck the money that would have been Iris's away. But her recovery has been better than expected.

She closes her eyes tight. She'll buy a cabin in the mountains, a thousand miles away from this swampy heat. She'll get a couple of big dogs. Maybe rescues. She'll read books and start a garden. She'll—

"Oh, Christ," says Augusta.

Iris leaves her daydream. They're on a country road not far from Sweet Blood, and there's a swirl of red and blue police lights filling the air. She thinks they're getting pulled over. Then she realizes the lights are ahead of them, and there are *lots.*

"Pull over, Arthur."

"Yes, ma'am."

"What's going on?" Iris asks.

"Stay here." She gets out of the car quickly, leaving Iris and Arthur in silence.

The outfitted Cadillac is so well insulated that Iris can't hear a thing from outside. She scoots towards the window. There are sugarcane fields on either side of the dirt road, and Augusta is talking to a police officer. Iris doesn't even think. She opens the car door and gets out.

Augusta looks over her shoulder. "Stay in the car."

Iris pretends like she doesn't hear her. She crosses her arms and tucks her head towards her chest as she walks against the wind.

The cop Augusta is talking to must be the sheriff. He wears the authority of one, and the age. His body looks like it's trying to spill out of his uniform at his hips, and the skin of his face and neck droops like a bloodhound. The sacks beneath his eyes, too, look as if they're losing their battle with gravity, giving him a tired expression.

Augusta gestures to him. "Iris, you've met the sheriff. I believe you were still in the hospital."

She remembers, albeit vaguely. "Nice to meet you again."

The sheriff looks at her grumpily and she doesn't bother to offer her hand to shake.

"So, what's going on?"

"Overdose," he says confidently.

Iris is confused. She turns to look where two other officers are bent over in the ditch. She's looking at a dead girl. The two cops are wearing latex gloves. One holds a camera, while the other is inspecting her.

Iris can't see her face from here, but her body is somewhat bloated. She's wearing a faded pink tank top the color of chewed bubblegum. Her denim shorts leave little to the imagination of what they hide.

"Prostitute, probably," the sheriff says, as if this fact makes the dead girl mean much less.

"You don't know who she is?" Augusta asks.

"She got no ID on her. Jane Doe. We'll ask around. Shouldn't be difficult to figure out. But you two get on your way now. No need to see this."

Iris is too busy watching the girl to respond. One cop holds her limp right hand by her wrist while the other takes a picture of her fingernails. This scene doesn't have the appearance of an overdose. They're definitely not treating it as such.

"If it was drugs, why is she out here in the middle of nowhere?" Iris asks.

"She might have been out with a John when it happened. He panicked. Dumped her. Happens. But look here, speculation is our job. Don't you worry about this."

"You should've called me, Fred," Augusta suddenly says coldly.

"Sorry?"

"We're a half mile from my home. You should've called me to let me know what was happening on my property."

"Oh." The sheriff perks up. Now there's emotion in his droopy eyes—panic. "I'm sorry, Mrs. Adler. I figured you were home this evening. I thought I'd let you know once we'd cleaned this up."

Iris is torn between watching Augusta and the sheriff interact and looking at the dead girl. She has bright-blonde hair that moves in the wind like wheat. One of the cops pulls her tank top down a few inches to show a tattoo just above her breast. Iris can make it out from where she stands. It's of an eagle. Its talons are exposed like it's about to catch prey. The other cop snaps a picture.

Iris hears another vehicle crunch the gravel as it pulls up behind them. It's a truck, and the three of them all pause as someone gets out.

It's Nick. He has his phone in one hand. He's still in his suit with his necktie crooked and undone. "I'm sorry, Augusta," he says as he walks closer. "I tried calling you. I heard about this just after you left." He pauses briefly as he sees the body. "I didn't want you to see this."

Unlike the sheriff, Nick's tone is casual. He doesn't seem to act like he's done something wrong by failing to reach Augusta.

"Is this a homicide?" Iris asks suddenly, confused. If it were an overdose, why would Nick be here? she wonders.

"No. No. We're just being thorough," says the sheriff. "We had another case somewhat similar to this several months ago. It was round the time you were shot, actually. A girl's body was found burnt to a crisp in the woodlands not far from here." He suddenly looks embarrassed and coughs into his hand. "Pardon my language."

"Who was the girl?"

"That was the mystery," says Nick. "We still don't know. But this here looks like any old overdose."

Nick is at Augusta's side, but she looks away from him, acting like he's not there. It's like she's shunning him for something, Iris thinks.

"We should get going," Augusta says, but she's not looking at anybody as she speaks. She's staring at the girl's body with sorrow in her eyes. She suddenly spins away and walks back towards the car. "Come on, Iris," she calls after her like a dog.

The sugarcane stalks sway and rustle in the wind. The sheriff and Nick are both quiet. Iris can tell they're waiting for her to go before they speak to each another.

When Augusta is out of earshot, Iris speaks. "Did she mention I want to talk to you about my case? About Joseph?" she asks the sheriff.

"Tomorrow, yeah," he sighs heavily, as if to emphasize he's already lost his weekend to work. "I told her we can do that tomorrow."

"Great." Iris takes a step backward.

Nick is smiling at her. He looks her up and down, from her scar to her feet. She feels like he's hitting on her with his eyes, and with a dead girl just a few feet behind him.

"Will you be at church tomorrow, Iris?" Nick says. "I haven't seen you there since the injury."

She looks away from him. "Um... No. I sleep pretty late ever since."

"Course. Well, you get your sleep."

"Yeah. Thank you."

She walks back to the car and shuts the door behind her. Augusta says nothing. As they pass by the body, neither of them looks out the window for another glance.

Overdose. No identification. Nick was called to the scene on a Saturday night. It doesn't add up. They don't think this was an accident, Iris thinks. She's been a part of one well enough to know.

This was a murder.

Ghosts

The next morning, Iris sits at the writing desk in her bedroom. She had already searched all about the burned body the sheriff mentioned. The case had little information. It mentions a woman's charred remains were found on public land about two miles from the town of Port Vincent. Police are still investigating. No mention of potential age. No mention of the initial cause of death.

It's strangely underreported, but perhaps that's because the police know as little as the article suggests they do. Iris closes out of the article.

She's not sure she can keep anything secret in her mother-in-law's house, so she writes her thoughts on the notes in her phone instead of paper.

She's trying to remember as much about herself to not get blindsided by the police. Her memory has had her look like an idiot before. The excuse of the brain damage doesn't help her keep her pride. Iris burns with embarrassment when she's reminded of basic things about her past that she should know.

Her injury has made her think of time as linear, a straight timeline. Her memories were not destroyed randomly. There's a neat gap, like the bullet pulverized everything her brain stored from age fourteen to the day she was shot. She's yet to find any stray memories adrift from this time.

She can remember things she learned. Vocabulary. History. But the events of her life are absent. Still, she knows she's lucky to be as lucid as she is.

Her survival wasn't completely luck. Iris held up her hand to fend off the shot, and the doctors say that's what saved her life.

The bullet nicked the side of her palm, about an inch down from the start of her pinky finger. It changed its trajectory so when the bullet hit her skull, it bounced up and out the top instead of burrowing all the way through and out the back of her head. She'd be dead, or little more than a vegetable, if it weren't for the ricochet.

The scar on her hand is hardly noticeable. It's just a little patch of skin that's pinker than the flesh around it.

What the bullet did hit was her prefrontal cortex. It didn't get much of it, but the brain is fragile. She was told it was the part of her mind that relates to self-thought. Her entire identity could be altered. When some of the teenage Alder cousins visited and heard about this, they thought her injury sounded cool. Like something a spy would have.

But now Iris puts the coffee creamer in the cupboard nearly every time she takes it out of the fridge. Her mood swings can come out of nowhere. And of all things, sometimes she can't tell the difference between gas and a bowel movement.

No, there is nothing sexy about brain damage, she thinks.

Iris is making a list of everything she knows about her husband and the Adler family. She has the basics, the things everybody in Louisiana's high society is bound to know. She's even writing what she knows about herself.

She was born in 1995 in Memphis, Tennessee. She came from a poor family with just one other sibling. A half sister, Lanie.

Her mother and sister visited her in the hospital while she was in a coma. They didn't stick around long. They texted later when Iris was conscious, saying Augusta made them feel unwelcome. That she didn't offer them a place to stay in Sweet Blood when they couldn't afford a hotel for more than a couple nights.

Meanwhile, Augusta said they wouldn't stop hounding her about Iris's inheritance from her husband.

Both accounts are probably true. Iris knows that she didn't move from Memphis for no reason. The memories she does have of her childhood are all boiled hotdogs, holey T-shirts, and yelling. Always yelling.

Iris can remember wanting out. She was a good student in middle school and the half of high school she can recall. She must've been, since Augusta told her she was enrolled at LeBlanc College in New Orleans, where she had met Joseph at a party on campus. He was in graduate school but attending a function hosted by his old fraternity at the time. Epsilon Delta Phi. Iris has the name written down.

She's looked for hints of what their relationship was like. She didn't journal, unfortunately. Iris did have an Instagram, but for a socialite, she wasn't very active on it. She'd post something generic—a southern sunset, a photo of Joseph with a sweet caption—once every other month. It didn't paint much of a picture about the woman she used to be, except, perhaps, that she was private.

There's a light knock, and Iris turns to the door. "I got Saturday's mail for ya, Iris." It's Aurelia, the house's maid. She's a sweet woman. Her face is always warm and readable, and talking to her is a reprieve from the all-seeing eyes of Augusta or Annabelle.

"Thanks, Aurelia."

"Mrs. Adler would like you to be down in fifteen minutes to head to the station."

"Perfect."

Aurelia sets a few letters on a short end table that sits just inside the door. "How're you today?"

Iris smacks her lips before she speaks. "Still just trying to get one foot in front of the other. Trying to remember."

"You'll get there, love. Baby steps."

Aurelia turns to go, but Iris stops her. She's feeling brave today. She wants answers, even if it means being nosy.

Aurelia is black, which Iris has always thought was poor taste for hired help at a plantation. It's a private question, but she wants to know what it's like to work for Augusta. What it's like to work at Sweet Blood.

"Aurelia, do you like your job here?"

Aurelia turns back to Iris slowly. Her face is somewhat skeptical. Like she's trying to figure out what Iris is *really* asking.

35

"I've worked here for twenty-seven-years, so I hope so. It'd be a sad life if I didn't." She smiles, and so does Iris.

"I guess I meant... Um..."

"If it's strange working on a plantation?"

Iris chuckles, embarrassed. Her cheeks burn as she talks. "Yeah, I guess that's what I'm asking."

"Want to know a secret?" Aurelia leans forward. "My friends give me shit for it. All in good fun. The thing is, I get paid. And *well*. Mrs. Adler is a fair woman to work for."

"But is she a *good* woman?"

Aurelia narrows her eyes. She looks left and right down the hall quickly, as if out of instinct. "Can I ask you something?"

"Yeah."

"What *do* you remember?"

Iris is about to lie, but she stops herself. "Nothing, really. I remember nothing."

"Oh, hon." Aurelia sighs, like there's so damn much to tell her. "Mrs. Adler values one thing: loyalty. I give it to her, and she gives me Christmas bonuses big enough to send my grandkids to college. You understand me?"

"Yes."

"You used to be loyal to Mrs. Adler. *Very* loyal. But it seems you've forgotten who you were. You're startin' fresh."

"What does that mean?"

"It means she doesn't trust you. And that's..." Aurelia doesn't finish her sentence. Her face is suddenly frustrated. She thinks she's said too much. But Iris doesn't need her to finish her sentence to know where she was going.

"Dangerous?"

Aurelia looks at her and smirks. "I see you're just as sharp. But you're too quiet now. I know that doesn't sound sensitive to a woman with a brain injury and a freshly buried husband. Though it's something you needed to hear. Your silence is very... different. But I see you in there. You weren't shot stupid. Just different. You used to be *loud*, Iris."

36

"Loud?" Iris says, perturbed. She can't picture herself loud with Augusta and Annabelle. Cackling on the porch, mojito in hand.

"Oh yes. The life of the party." She mimes a glass. "You and those other Adler girls were always jetting somewhere. Churchill Downs. The Bahamas." Aurelia shakes her head like if it were her money, she'd be spending it better.

"Sorry? Churchill Downs?"

"The Kentucky Derby, sweetheart. Y'all went every year."

"Ah." It's all Iris can say.

A loud, drunk, southern socialite. Iris can't picture it. That girl must've been blown out of her head by the bullet. She understands the appeal of the glamor of this life. The diamonds. The cleanliness. The freedom. But the idea of flaunting such wealth while she wasn't even working feels wrong.

Aurelia moves towards the hall. "If you're hoping to jog your memory, I think it's best you first remember who you used to be."

"I'm trying. And Aurelia?"

"Yeah?"

"I'm sorry if my original question was prying."

"Everyone who's ever seen me on the grounds of Sweet Blood wonders it, so don't feel bad for having the guts to ask. In fact, I believe you might have asked me that before. If anything, it feels like a return of the Iris I know."

"Thanks."

Aurelia gives her a wink and walks off down the hall.

Iris sits a little stunned. She wants to get out of here. This sleepy plantation has always felt haunted, but now it feels like *her* ghost is here, too.

Mail

Iris resumes her notes. She puts aside what Aurelia had told her about herself, as if that might make it less real. She keeps going with her list.

Joseph Senior and Augusta had met working at the Adler Corp. She was an ambitious young manager and climbed much faster once they married. He was a decade or so older. The company has its hands in all kinds of agriculture. Thousand-acre farms, slaughtering, shipping. The Adler Corp., Iris read on its website, prides itself on being vertically integrated.

Iris's husband managed the entire meat-packing department. The slaughterhouses. They have separate plants in the region for the big three—chickens, pigs, and cattle. All told, he oversaw more than six hundred employees.

Jamie is in sales, and the youngest Adler son, Gideon, has a made-up job in operations to keep him out of trouble. Even then, his position changes every time he cycles through rehab.

Annabelle works for the Adler Corp. as well. Despite her pregnancy and the added wealth of being married to Jamie, she has no aim to be a southern housewife. She's currently the head of Exports, and her trajectory looks a lot like Augusta's.

Iris looks up from her phone as a noisy bird chirps and dives outside.

The window is open, and from the second story of the house, she can see out past the manicured lawn to the sugarcane fields. Sweet Blood is not the only plantation in Louisiana that's on the historical register that still farms, but it might be the only one where it's not for a gimmick. It got its name from some fable, almost biblical, about how the founder nicked his hand on a scythe, and after working with sugarcane all day, when he sucked his wound, he swore his blood was sweet. It's fiction because Iris knows no Adler had ever toiled in these fields. They used slaves and didn't shy from the fact.

The property is surrounded by sugarcane fields. A tunnel of oaks leads out the back door to the gardens but apart from an acre or two of magnolia trees and hedges, all the green around them is the eighteen-hundred acres of sugarcane. It's only a fraction of the tens of thousands of acres that the Adler Corp. owns between Baton Rouge and New Orleans.

They own the land right down to the banks of the Mississippi River, and Augusta laments that her husband's ancestors couldn't purchase the waterway itself.

Eight generations have lived on this estate. The first three of those owned slaves. This family has heirloom jewelry and furniture, and in the southern bubble of Louisiana, the Adlers are revered. This is an area of the country where old money is much more respected than new, and the way they earn it— sugarcane and livestock—is viewed as honest here. Far more so than if they were a banking family.

Iris watches her cursor flash on her phone. She's living in the heart of it all, and yet she only knows as much about the Adler family as any of their neighbors would.

This family has secrets. But if she was ever privy to them, she's not anymore.

Iris finally stands and goes to the table to pick up her mail. There are always letters from her insurer and the hospital.

Today, the largest one catches her eye. It's a foot-long envelope from St. Catherine's Hospital. She thinks it probably contains a pamphlet trying to sell her more physical therapy classes. Junk mail. But what leaves her curious is that it feels as light as a feather. She presses the letter with her thumbs. Feeling for what? A bomb? Anthrax? None of the above could fit inside. She feels what she thinks is a single sheet of paper.

She rips it open and looks in before reaching inside. There it is. One sheet of paper folded in two.

She plucks it out, and when she looks at the paper, she holds her breath

It's a printed picture. A picture of Iris.

She's a few years younger, sitting cross-legged, naked in a nest of tangled sheets. Her skin is flushed pink. Her hair is a mess. It doesn't take a detective to see this is the aftermath of hard sex.

Her expression in the photo isn't unhappy. It's somewhat surprised. Curious. Her eyes say, *"A picture? Now?"*

The paper it's printed on is almost translucent. She can see ink on the other side. Her heart lifts, and for a moment, she thinks everything is about to be answered. The affair. Her attempted murder. She turns it over and sees the words aren't handwritten. They're typed. Iris reads.

"You're being watched. You need to meet me. I'll be at the ruins of the Harvest Baptist Church at 11am this Tuesday. Walk there. Make sure you're not being followed. I can't say who I am in case they read this. Remember the Nile? Hopefully this photo helps you. You can trust me."

Iris's heart pounds. Is this the man she was sleeping with? The one the handkerchief made her remember? And who is watching her? Augusta? Annabelle? Why didn't the letter just say?

It's Sunday. She'll have to wait two more days for any answers. And that's if she even goes, Iris realizes.

How does she know this person isn't the same one who killed her husband and shot her in the head? She thinks it's just as likely this is someone trying to lure her away to finish the job.

She turns the paper over again to look at the picture. She peers into the younger Iris's eyes. Does she trust this photographer? Does she love him? She looks at the picture without blinking, as if it might help her remember.

And what was the Nile? Was it code? Iris pulls out her phone and quickly googles "the Nile Louisiana" but finds nothing. She puts her phone down and grimaces.

She always thought love had something to do with Joseph's death and her shooting.

This picture. The handkerchief. How likely is it that this secret lover was the same man who tried to kill her? And who did kill her husband.

"Iris?"

Augusta calls her name from downstairs. It's time to go to the police station. She rushes to her dresser and tucks the picture into the pocket of a pair of jeans. The picture is hidden, but the image of her naked and vulnerable doesn't stop playing in her mind.

There are answers in that photograph. That was its intention. But Iris can't remember a thing.

Unwelcome

Augusta accompanies Iris to the station. It's in the small town of Preston, just outside Baton Rouge, near Joseph and Iris's old home. They pass the highway exit that would take them there.

Iris has only been back to their house once since the incident. She walked through it like a medium looking for memories, but the place had been freshly painted and all the furniture removed. The gaps in her memory remain as empty as the rooms.

Augusta keeps her gaze out the window. Her eyes stay on the sugarcane they pass as if she's inspecting the crop. When they enter the town of Preston, she speaks.

"We sail out of here on Saturday." Augusta points to a gravel road that leads to a small harbor on the Mississippi.

"Sorry?"

"Our family's Labor Day cruise. That's where we board."

Iris has heard them talking about this event. Every Labor Day weekend, the Adler family rents a grand riverboat with a hundred rooms and parties until dawn. It's the biggest event of the year.

"I don't remember ever going."

"Don't feel bad. You only went to the one."

Iris leans forward in her seat to see more of the river. "Where's the boat now?"

"St. Louis, getting fitted. They're supposed to leave Monday and be here Friday. They better hope they're not late."

In another few minutes, they pull into a parking space out front of the police station, and three cops are already waiting for them on the sidewalk. The sheriff is in the middle. Two deputies in khaki uniforms stand on either side of him.

The sheriff smiles at Augusta as they get out of the car. "Mrs. Adler. So good to see you."

"Thanks for coming in on a Sunday, Fred." They shake hands briefly.

"I can always make it if it's after church."

"You're a better Christian than I am, Fred. I didn't make it this week and probably won't next week either. So much housekeeping with the business and the party and..." Augusta looks at Iris, as if she's another chore on her list she was about to mention.

"I read this morning that you were stepping down. How long you lead that company?"

"Too long." Augusta changes the subject. "Hopefully we can make some progress today." She gestures at Iris.

"Of course," says the sheriff.

This time he and Iris shake hands, and Iris has to resist the urge to wipe her palm. His hand is soaked. She can hear him breathing heavily from just standing in the sun.

He seems self-aware enough to be embarrassed by his sweaty handshake. "Let's get in that AC and go over what we got!" he says and turns.

They all head into the station. Iris expects Augusta to leave them, but she follows Iris and the sheriff all the way to a brightly lit conference room.

There's coffee, a box of pastries, and fresh fruit. The welcoming party outside, this little buffet, Iris can see that Augusta is treated like royalty. These cops are responsible for the investigation into her son's murder that has stalled, after all. They seem desperate to stay on her good side.

The sheriff pulls out two chairs, and Iris and Augusta sit down. "So what would you like to tell us?" He sits down opposite of them.

"Um," Iris starts. "I was actually hoping you could tell me some things."

"Is that right? And do you not remember the last time we spoke? In the hospital?" he says slowly, as if she's stupid.

"Not very well."

43

"Okay," he sighs. "Okay. So you want me to start at the beginning?"

"Please."

He clears his throat. Pulls a folder in front of him. "You and your husband were both shot on your property. You were both in the master bedroom."

"What can you tell me about the firearm that was used?"

"What about it?"

"What caliber was it? Do you have the murder weapon?"

"Now, there's a lot about this case that we can't disclose."

Iris pauses. "What do you mean?"

"This is an active investigation. It's important there is information only we as law enforcement know. Sharing facts publicly, even with a victim of the crime, could jeopardize the entire case."

"I mean, but don't you think these are unique circumstances? Being that my memory is what it is. Hearing about certain things might help me remember. I was conscious when this happened. If I can remember who did this, it's over. This is solved."

The sheriff leans back, and his chair creaks. He taps his pen and pulls nervously at his collar. "Unique does not excuse protocol."

Iris knows this means they're not desperate. They must have suspects. Maybe they've narrowed it down to one. If this case were as cold as it seemed, they wouldn't mind trying to jog her memory.

"So you're building a case?" Iris says excitedly. "You have a suspect in mind?"

He spreads out his fingers. *Slow now.* "Not exactly. I'm referencing a body of evidence. Only investigators know the sequence of events, placement of bodies, shell casings, etcetera. But if that information becomes public, it plays our hand before we know we've got the winning cards. You see?"

Iris doesn't think she can argue further. "So what can you tell me?"

"A few things."

"What about who found us?"

He points with his pen. "Augusta did."

Augusta shudders and shifts in her seat. She doesn't seem to have any desire to recount the event, but Iris doesn't give her a choice. She stares at her mother-in-law silently until she speaks.

"Joseph didn't come into the office that morning. He wasn't answering his phone. It was one of those times where a mother just knows. Something was wrong."

"You've never told me..."

"Because I don't like talking about it!" Augusta practically shouts. She is quiet for a moment. She breathes. "I'm sorry." She smooths her hands on her lap. "I'm sorry." The sheriff hands her a tissue, but she's not crying. She takes it and dabs her eyes anyway. "It's just a lot to remember."

The sheriff sighs, upset. "To be honest, I thought this meeting was because you had remembered something, young lady. I don't think you need to put Augusta through this again."

Iris wants to shout that Augusta doesn't even have to be here.

"It's okay, Fred," Augusta says to the sheriff. "It's fine, really."

The sheriff keeps tapping his pen. This time angrily. He stares at Iris like a dean would an unruly student. The three of them are silent for a moment and then he gestures at Iris. "You been to church since you got shot?"

Iris takes a deep breath. She knows she's lost control of the meeting. "I haven't."

"Young lady, if I were you, I'd throw my hat down and join the clergy. I've seen two men get a bullet to the noggin." He holds two of his fat sausage fingers in the peace sign. "One's moanin' in diapers in a group home, and the other was closed casket. Spend your days thankin' the lord. You leave catching the bad guys to us." He winks at her. It's a creepy little gesture.

This meeting is somehow already over. It's not that they don't have any information. It's that they won't share it. She scrambles trying to think of questions that might get her *something.*

"Mrs. Adler." The sheriff looks at Augusta. "You have my word that we'll be making an arrest any day now."

Iris watches the tendons of Augusta's hand flex as she crumples the tissue in her fist. Her tense body tells it all; she's bothered by these words. Afraid even, Iris thinks. But her face is a beam of sunshine. "Thank you, Fred."

Iris no longer cares about what the police have. Of course they have private information about the case.

But what does Augusta know?

Fertilizer

Iris isn't sure how to go about getting information from Augusta. She can't just ask her. Maybe she saw something when she first found her and Joseph, but there's no easy way to get that out of her. It makes Tuesday's mystery meeting all the more tempting to attend.

She has a lot to think about, and when they get home from the station, she changes into shorts and a thin T-shirt to walk in the heat. Iris would've gone crazy at Sweet Blood if it wasn't for its extensive grounds. She can pick a direction and just walk. This afternoon she heads out the back and follows the red brick path that's lined with old oaks.

It leads to the plantation's flower garden, and past that are the big metal pole barns where the farm equipment is kept.

There's a system of dirt roads that maze around the property. The paths they take are impractical. The point is to keep the tractors, trucks, and employees that are always moving around the farm hidden from the house. This is done with hedges and trees and great big, vined arbors. It all makes for a very lush walk.

She makes her way to the end of the flower garden, where there's an algae-covered pond. It's small enough to easily toss a stone across. She doesn't know its depth, but it's big enough to have life. Small turtles, about a half dozen of them, bask on a single log that stretches into the pond from shore.

A dirt road passes just past the pond, and Iris sees one of the turtles paused in the middle of the gravel. She changes direction towards it.

"Little guy, this is the second time now." She squats next to it. The turtle doesn't shoot into its shell. It takes a determined step forward. It has a crescent-shaped nick on its shell. She recognizes it from the last time she took a walk and found it in the road. "There ain't nothing for you in that sugarcane. Unless you eat the stuff."

A truck appears in the distance, and Iris points. "See? You're gonna get yourself run right over."

She picks up the turtle, and now it tucks in its limbs and head. She steps backwards towards the pond to let the truck pass. It's lifted and black, and the window tints aren't many shades lighter than the paint. She can't see who's driving as it rolls past towards the big metal pole barns at the end of the road.

It's a Sunday, and Iris knows it's only during harvest and planting season that anyone would be working the weekends.

She sets the turtle down near the pond's edge and walks across to the sugarcane. She rips a few leaves off the stalks and brings over an armful. She drops them next to it. The turtle is still in panic mode. It's all shell.

"Here. No need to for a suicide mission, buddy. If you're looking for the Mississippi, that's another story. It's that way." Iris points east.

She brings her arm back to her side suddenly and looks at the house. If Augusta or Annabelle knew she was talking to a turtle, they'd probably think she was crazy.

They seem like the kind of women who think talking to an animal is below them. They aren't pet people. They have all these acres and all this money, and Iris hasn't even seen a cat around.

Maybe Iris too, used to think the same way. But she hasn't had an honest conversation with someone since leaving the hospital. She's lonely. Friendless. Perhaps that's why she can't resist talking to critters.

She looks down the road to where the truck went.

Whoever it is must be at the barns. The longer of the two structures is half the length of a football field, and Iris has never gone in either before.

She walks down the road and sees a service door to the larger barn. She expects it to be locked, but when she reaches it, the handle turns effortlessly.

Inside, she's hit immediately with the sour scent of chemicals. Pesticides. Fertilizer. It's enough to make her head throb. It's not just the scent that assaults her. Everything is lit up in white fluorescent light. There are two tractors and two farm pickup trucks parked in the barn stalls, all spotless.

The floor is clean concrete, and tools hang on the walls in perfect alignment. It all has the look of well-oiled operation, and Iris expected no less from the company barn that sits only a few hundred yards from Augusta's back door.

She doesn't think anyone is in here. It's too silent. Iris's footsteps echo off the high ceiling as she makes her way towards the far end of the barn. There's a walled-off room with glass windows, and Iris finds herself walking straight to it.

She opens the door to see stainless steel tables. Six of them. Each is about eight feet long and four feet wide. They're set up in two rows of three. It's not so clean here. There are gloves, plastic bags, and empty fast-food bags littered around the tables. It doesn't quite look like a break room. There is no coffee machine. No lounge chairs or refrigerator. The tables are high, and it looks like whoever works in here does so standing up.

Iris opens one of the table's drawers. There are zip-ties, screwdrivers, and a spare deck of cards. She shuts it, and when she looks back up, something else catches her eye.

On one of the farther tables, there are three large plastic bags laid out in a neat row. They're not Ziplocs. They look like plastic packaging from a factory. The bags have been wrapped tight with clear tape so she can still see what's inside—a yellowish white powder. Iris walks to them and picks one of the bags up. Just as quickly as she lifts it, she tosses it down. These could be poisonous pesticides.

"Hey," someone suddenly says only a few feet from Iris. When she turns around, Nick is staring at her from the doorway. He's wearing a flannel shirt that's rolled up to his elbows. His arms are covered in forests of thick black hairs. He's holding a big cardboard box and looks at Iris with what she could only describe as amusement.

"Didn't mean to frighten ya."

"It's okay." Iris glances nervously at the bag she dropped and then back to Nick.

"What do you think?" He nods at the bags and steps forward.

"I, uh..." Iris freezes as Nick stops closer to her than he needs to. He sets the box on the counter and picks up one of the bags. He hefts it in his hand as if inspecting its weight. "This one's a phosphate," he says confidently and sets the bag down gently.

"Sorry?" Iris takes a step back. She looks at his sharp Adam's apple and then to his narrow eyes.

"Fertilizer. They just got these samples in for next season." He pats the box and then points to another one of the bags. "This one..." He picks it up, looks at its bottom, and nods. "Is nitrogen based. The Adlers will order this stuff by the ton. It's explosive, you know. It's the same stuff used in the OKC bombing. And enough comes through here each year to level New Orleans."

Iris ignores the bomb comment. *What is he trying to do? Impress me with danger?* "I didn't think you knew much about farming."

"I remembered a few things. It was my first job. Joseph Senior hired me. Farmhand. I only lasted one summer, but sixty-hour weeks will teach ya quick."

What Iris isn't sure about is what Nick is doing in the barn now. Was he told to keep an eye on her? Regardless, she feels like the one who's trespassing. "I bet," she says with a fake laugh.

Iris wants to remove herself as quickly as possible from being alone with Nick. She's seen the kind of eyes he has before, though she can't remember where. Some men just have them. His slight grin and narrowed, staring eyes. It's the same look worn by creeps the world over. He's undressing her with his eyes and wants her to know it.

She needs an excuse to go. Sundays also mean that the Adlers all eat supper together. "I should freshen up for dinner. I didn't mean to snoop or nothing. The door to the barn was open, and I just wandered—"

"Don't you worry about it," Nick interrupts her, and the moment he's done speaking, his sly little grin returns.

"Right. Be seeing you."

He doesn't move as Iris steps past him. She's forced to brush against his chest. She takes the opportunity to try to see if he smells like the cologne on the handkerchief, but the only thing she picks up is the sour, chemical smell that infests the whole barn.

When Iris is most of the way out of the room, Nick speaks again. "I'm sorry you had to see all that, by the way."

"Pardon?"

"That girl in the field. Nasty business I'm in, I'm afraid." He puffs out his chest, as if relishing the masculine nature of his job that requires him to deal with dead bodies.

Iris pauses. "Did you ever work on my case?"

"You know I didn't."

"And why is that?"

"Conflict of interest. You're family, Iris."

She takes another step out, but Nick keeps talking.

"But of course, you know as well as I do, not by blood." He winks at her.

Iris doesn't bother responding as she walks quickly across the barn to the service door she came in from. She can feel his eyes on her back the entire time, and when she gets to the door, she turns.

Sure enough, he's looking right at her from behind the glass of the room they were in. He waves.

Iris can't help but wonder what he meant by *you know as well as I do.* Is this the man? Did she have an affair with Nick?

She throws the door open without waving back and feels the warm sun on her face. Nick is about as far from her type as she can imagine. He had an especially lethal quality to him. Like it wasn't difficult to picture his veiny hands wrapped around a woman's neck.

Her mind keeps racing as she walks back towards the house. Why would she have slept with Nick? Why would he look at her with such knowing mischief? Cops have information others might not. That's the only conclusion she can reach. She would never sleep with him willingly.

But before Iris was shot, was she being blackmailed?

Scars

Dinner will be in the formal dining room downstairs, and in the time before, Iris maps out the route to Harvest Baptist. It still shows up on Google Maps, even though it's listed as permanently closed.

It's an hour away on foot up the river. It's not even three miles away, but she doesn't think she's ever been to the area. From what she sees on satellite, the old white rooftop of the church is surrounded by sugarcane fields.

Iris is physically able to drive, but both her car and Joseph's have been in storage since shortly after she was shot. She was told to come on foot anyway.

She takes plenty of walks around the plantation grounds. No one would bat an eye if she walked off and didn't come back for a couple hours. Perhaps whoever sent the letter knows this. Early morning on a Tuesday, both Augusta and Annabelle would be at work. Iris shudders. Perhaps they know it's the best time to get her all alone. It's dangerous. It's stupid. But Iris's craving for information may just lead her to do it anyway.

When she's done mapping the route she'll walk, she tosses her phone onto the bed. The windows in her room have big wooden shutters instead of blinds. She walks over and shuts them. As soon as the sunlight is shut out, the floor almost feels cooler on her feet.

Iris takes her shirt off and then her pants. She turns the fan on, and she watches it start to spin, ten feet above the top of her head, in the middle of the cake-frosting ceiling. It's French Baroque. The room is all whites and golds except for the cherry furniture that shines a whiskey amber.

The space around her feels massive. For all the rugs and furniture and ornaments, it still feels empty. It's like she's at a tea set placed in the bottom of an empty swimming pool. Sweet Blood isn't a plantation. It's a palace.

These rooms were built with the purpose of impressing company and the ego, but cozy and homey they are not.

She feels exposed in her nudity under the towering ceiling. Iris turns to her naked reflection in the vanity mirror. Even in this poor lighting, she can see the edge of it. She hooks her thumb in her underwear and pulls the elastic band down.

The scars from the bullet aren't her only ones. She has another on her right hip. Low enough to be completely hidden by her pants when she's wearing them. It's about four inches long and just as many wide. There are no other scars near it. The wound was contained. It's *almost* a perfect square. It looks like someone sewed an ugly patch of skin onto her hip.

Of course, she doesn't know where she got it. It resembles a burn, kind of, but it's in an odd place. It could be road rash. Maybe she was riding on the back of some hotshot's motorcycle when he crashed, but road rash wouldn't look even. She runs her fingers over the skin, and they bounce as they catch on the ridges and bumps.

It's just one more thing she has to figure out about herself. She knows she has to visit Memphis soon. Venomous family or not. Her half sister made it clear that she and their mom weren't going to come to visit Iris again. She texted her saying so after their complaints about Augusta. Iris could call, but it feels smarter to see them in person.

But she's not going anywhere before her meeting at Harvest Baptist.

She goes to her closet and dresses for dinner.

Iris doesn't think either Augusta or Annabelle believes brain damage and personal trauma are adequate excuses for Iris to dine in her sweatpants.

She hates the amount of dress-up she has to do. Being a socialite means having to wear a face-full of makeup for any errand out of the house and even for some errands in.

Iris is back at her vanity, and she tries her best not to look down at the crude carvings of slaves as she does her makeup.

She looks her face over. She's twenty-eight, yet easily looks a year or two older. Her best feature, the one that shows no age, are her lips. While the rest of her is small or flat, they have a healthy, full look. They're perfectly bowed, with a subtle dimple in the middle of the top lip.

If a man's eyes slip a little low when he's talking to her, that's where she'll catch them looking. Her chest isn't much of an attraction.

She has a triangle of three moles on her left cheek. Shaped like Dorito. They're little, black, ugly things that she has to shave, and if it weren't for them, Iris thinks she might be really beautiful.

This evening, she's doing something she hasn't done since her injury. She applies dark-red lipstick. It takes her from a pretty, but somewhat plain girl into a starlet. As she looks in the mirror, her eyes don't stay on her lips, however. And she doubts that many men these days will be entranced by them, either.

The scar on her forehead might as well shine. It's the only thing she looks at every time she passes her reflection, and she's not the only one. The sources of scars are so often banal, but not this one. There is nothing boring about a bullet.

She hears the high voices of people greeting each other downstairs. She stands and practices a few smiles. She's going to try to do something else at dinner that she hasn't done since the injury. She's not going to be loud like Aurelia said she was, but she's going to try to talk.

Guests

It's not your typical Sunday dinner. All twelve places at the table are set, and there are two hired cooks in the kitchen instead of just Aurelia.

Iris stands in the dining room. The floor here isn't marble like it is upstairs. It's buffed cherrywood that shines like a waxed car. There are two entrances—one that leads to the entrance hall and another at the back of the room that goes to the kitchen.

The massive table takes up most of the room. It's set for fine dining. The plates are thin china and stenciled with pink orchids. The silverware here is actually silver. Usually, Iris takes the last chair on the side of the table that is closer to the kitchen. Now she has no idea where to sit. Augusta whisks into the room while Iris stares at the table. She seems to read her thoughts.

"Iris, honey, you're between Annabelle and Gideon. Middle of the table." She nods at a chair. She's about to vanish into the kitchen when Iris feels her mouth open. She speaks without even thinking.

"Last night, whose handkerchief did you give me?"

"Pardon?" Augusta doesn't commit to the question. Her head is turned to Iris, but her body is pointed at the kitchen.

"When I was upset. Just before we went back inside."

"Why do you ask?"

The question catches her off guard. "Uh... I just still have it, is all."

"Keep it. I'm sure no one is missing it." Augusta hurries into the kitchen.

Iris should've waited for when she wasn't in motion. She picked the wrong time to ask.

Something important is going on tonight. Was she told? Dinner is usually just the Adler kids and their spouses. Sometimes Gideon brings a girlfriend, but never the same one.

Iris spots Annabelle coming in from the porch and walks to her quickly.

"Annabelle. Who are the guests?"

Annabelle leans back as if the question is a shock. "Dinner is doubling as a board meeting tonight. Don't you remember? Oh." Annabelle puts her hand on Iris's shoulder. "I don't mean to be rude. If you don't remember, that's totally fine. It's just, we talked about this all week."

Iris has to keep the anger from scrunching her expression. She thought her memory has been better. Why is it always Annabelle who's reminding her of things she is supposed to have remembered?

"Can you introduce me?" Iris points towards the porch, where the guests are mingling with their drinks.

"Are you sure? You've met all these people before. It can be a little uncomfortable for them."

"Can you tell me who they are, then, so I can at least pretend to remember?"

Annabelle motions with her head. They walk across the entrance hall to the door directly opposite the dining room.

It's the music room. A baby grand piano dominates the center of the space. There are two arrangements of chairs and coffee tables. The space in front of the piano is empty. The hardwood here is bare, as if the area is used for dancing.

What has always caught Iris's attention here are the watercolor paintings of a woman that hang on the walls. Her face isn't shown in any of them. They highlight her naked body.

They're modest—her nudity is mostly concealed. In one she cradles her legs in her arms with her bare breasts pressed against her thighs.

In another, the woman sits facing away from the artist. She leans lazily on one palm, and the long, gentle hollow of her spine snakes like a river through the middle of her back. It ends at the delta of her hips, where the bottom of her butt is mostly covered by a bedsheet.

These could be of Augusta. The body type seems right. Iris adds it to her list of things to find out as Annabelle points out the window. They have a good view of the front porch from here.

"The fat man, that's Jamie's uncle. Vernon Adler. His wife, Katie, is the little thing in lavender behind him."

Annabelle proceeds to identify several more people, all older, white and members of the board of directors. Two men are wearing cowboy hats and bolo ties. Cattlemen from Texas, probably, but Iris ends up regretting her request. Her memory is getting better, but names are sand between her fingers. She was too busy looking everyone over. Trying to remember faces from the past. She can't recall the names Annabelle tells her.

She sees Nick walk around from the back of the house. He must've had a change of clothes in his truck, because now he's wearing a tobacco-colored sport coat and dark blue jeans.

"How's Nick related to the family?"

"Oh, his mother was an Adler. She passed a few years ago."

"Were he and I friends before the injury?"

Annabelle looks at her funny. "Friends?"

"I mean... did we know each other well?"

"Course you did. He'd be with us every Sunday. Church and dinner."

"He hasn't been over for dinner in a while."

"He was here just a month ago? Don't you..." Annabelle starts but stops. "Oh, forget it."

Iris is about to confront her. She *knows* she met Nick for the first time since the injury just last night. Her memory of events since leaving the hospital three months ago has been more or less intact.

Annabelle is lying to her, but before she can speak, she hears Augusta call out to the porch.

"I don't mean to rush y'all, but today circumstances are a little different. Would everybody join me in the dining room?"

Everyone begins to shuffle inside.

Iris and Annabelle leave the music room and file behind them as the group heads into the dining room. Iris is surprised to see Joseph Senior at the table. He's in his wheelchair, seated to Augusta's right, while she's at the head of the table. The back of the house has an elevator that leads into the kitchen. It's a claustrophobic little thing with space enough for just two people.

Joseph Senior's hair is gray and wiry, and the skin on his face is so thin it shows an outline of his skull. His mouth is always slightly open, giving him a stupid look. Like you might expect him to start drooling at any moment. But his bright-blue eyes are alert and cunning, as if his expressionless face is only a curtain.

His eyes dart to each person entering the room with haste and then settle unblinking on Iris. She looks away quickly and keeps her head bowed as she takes her seat at the table.

When she looks up, he's staring at Jamie. There is debate whether Joseph Senior is still aware of his surroundings. Augusta is the only one adamant that he is.

Joseph Senior shares the same kind of dangerous look as his nephew, Nick. And for a moment, Iris can picture the past. She sees the Adler bloodline when they were still slavers.

She can picture those same narrowed eyes calculating the worth of men and women and children. Weighing the value of human lives like livestock.

The food starts to be brought out from the kitchen, and she's happy for the distraction. Nobody is talking.

Soon the table is filled with a king's feast. There's blackened catfish, biscuits, collard greens, and a crawfish etouffee. The smell is intoxicating, and Augusta bows her head to start grace.

Iris takes Gideon's and Annabelle's hands, but she's deaf to the prayer. She's saying her own, praying to God that her husband, the man she loved, was nothing like any of these people.

Business

When Iris is done plating her meal, she finds she has no appetite. The etouffee, with its brown hue and chunks of vegetables, looks like vomit. The collard greens are a soggy lump.

She moves the food around her plate to make it look like she's eaten more than she has. No one is watching her anyway. The subject of this board dinner is succession, and to Augusta, it's already settled.

When their plates are bussed away, there's a moment of silence as the room waits for Augusta to speak. Iris thinks those not on the board will be excused, but Augusta doesn't make any indication that will be the case.

She sits at the head of the table, staring at the far wall. There's an old oil painting of a sugarcane field hung there. She's still staring at it as she begins to speak.

"This business must stay in the family. Family is what started this company, and family is what grew it. I don't care what's modern. Or the benefits of selecting internally. I'm not going to give in to complaints of nepotism."

The table is quiet. No one disagrees.

"I want to stay on as CEO until the end of the third quarter. We're looking at strong revenues then. It's a safe time for a transition. Jamie, nothing has changed since the death of your brother. I'm going to nominate you."

"Now hold on," one of the cattlemen interrupts. "Don't you think it's prudent we discuss what will be done with Joseph Junior's shares of the corporation first?" The man looks at Iris as he says this.

"We will get there, Reggy. That is still being sorted with the lawyers. Jamie, we could vote tonight, agree on a date for you to start. Would you accept my nomination for Chief Executive Officer?"

The table looks at Jamie. He doesn't say anything. He bites his lip and leans back in his chair. Finally, he speaks. "No. I don't accept."

The room is silent. Everyone's heads snap to Augusta. She's trying to keep her composure. Trying to not look shocked. She lowers her brow and breathes.

"We discussed this privately. You accepted."

"We did. I did." Jamie clears his throat. He shifts like an uncomfortable child under her gaze. "I don't think I'm the right face. I feel like... a second choice. And everyone knows it."

Augusta huffs and stares at the table. She's not pretending to hide her disbelief. "And you're just going to fucking blindside me like this in front of the entire board?"

"I think it's a good example of why you may not want me as CEO," Jamie says.

"So who do you propose? Gideon?"

The room looks at the youngest son. Iris sees he was on his phone.

He looks up briefly. "I don't want that shit."

"It was rhetorical," snaps Augusta.

"Ah-hem," Jamie starts. "I propose the second most deserving person in the room and perhaps the most capable CEO."

"And who the hell is that?" Augusta's voice borders on a yell.

"My wife. Annabelle *Adler*." He puts emphasis on Adler, as if to say *she's family, too.*

Annabelle doesn't look awkward. She straightens up in her chair, confident.

Augusta's mouth opens, but she doesn't speak. She wears a look of genuine shock before her expression relaxes. "That's a fine idea and all, but the last thing a new mother needs is to be given the helm of a multi-million-dollar corporation."

"You had young children when you were CEO," Annabelle says. "The timing isn't perfect, I know that. But you just said it needs to be family, and who else is there?"

"Jamie," Augusta says. She's reddening with rage. "What the fuck?"

"She's perfectly qualified."

Augusta shakes out her napkin and lays it back calmly on her lap. "Everybody who is not on the board, would you kindly give us the room?"

"I don't think that's necessary," Annabelle says.

That's right, Iris thinks, Annabelle's not on the board, either.

"Stay. Let us discuss this with family." It's now Annabelle's word versus Augusta's.

Gideon chuckles and starts shaking his head. He clearly sees Annabelle's attempt to override Augusta's word as laughable. "I'm out," he says, tossing his napkin onto his plate.

Nick pushes back from the table next, and then Iris follows.

"I mean it, Annabelle," Augusta says with her gaze hardened. "Board members only."

Annabelle hesitates but pushes back as well.

They all go into the entrance hall and to the porch. Gideon is already striding across the driveway towards his truck. It looks like he's got someplace far more fun to be.

Iris and Nick pause on the stairs. The sun has sunk below the horizon. There's a jungle-red tint to the sky and already the bats wheel above the lawn, chasing bugs.

Annabelle brushes past them muttering to herself. She walks towards the guest house that sits about a hundred yards from the front porch. It's not an old, converted structure. It's newer construction, built sometime this century. It's white with black trim and surrounded by hedges.

"That was some drama," Nick says.

Iris watches Annabelle open the door to the guesthouse and slam it behind her petulantly.

"So," Iris says. "You're not on the board?"

He shakes his head. "I'm not a businessman. All that bores me to death."

"Law enforcement is more of a rush?"

"Sometimes."

It doesn't seem like Nick wants Iris's company. His gaze is distant.

Still, Iris takes the chance and speaks. "Can I ask you something serious?"

Nick suddenly looks uncertain, like he doesn't like where this is going. He doesn't say anything to Iris but glances at her sideways, waiting for her to continue.

"Do you think they're going to catch them?"

"The people who…" He gestures at her scar.

Iris nods.

"Hmm. Well, if I'm being honest with you, the odds of catching anybody don't look good. The first-forty-eight having long gone and all that."

"Do the police have anything? The sheriff made it sound like they did."

"They've conducted over a hundred interviews since the investigation began, and expect to do a lot more before this is done."

She wants to lead him away from generic cop talk. This is too formal. She's not going to learn anything new. "Do you know a lot about the case? I know you're not assigned to it, but I figure you know things."

"Of course. I'm up to date."

"So I take it you've heard my last memory before I was shot? The people coming across the lawn into the house, kicking down the door?"

"If I recall when you told the investigators about that when you were still in the hospital, you said you think it might've been a dream."

"I suppose. It does have a dream-like feel to it."

Nick nods. Something is distracting him tonight. If there ever was a history between her and Nick, he doesn't show it. He seems completely disinterested in this whole conversation. He's watching the bats dive with a frown, like there's something heavy on his mind.

Iris thinks of what else she can get from him while she has him here. "I'd like to have access to the text conversations I had with my husband. I know my phone broke during the assault, but have they been deleted?"

"No, you can get them from the phone company if you like, or I could have the sheriff's office email them over."

"That'd be great."

Nick pulls out his phone and makes a quick note. It suddenly starts to buzz while it's still in his hand. "I've got to take this." He stands and starts to walk.

Iris purses her lips as he walks off. Nothing is going as planned tonight. Her lack of memory is an annoyance to these people. It's like they've been humoring her, and at this point, they're growing sick of it.

Suddenly, her stomach sinks. What if Nick is so disinterested because she's asked these exact same questions before?

The thought makes Iris spiral. It makes her feel weak. Out of control. She starts to walk before it can pull her into a panic attack.

She takes off her uncomfortable heels and walks barefoot in the cold grass. She focuses on the feeling and the chirp of the crickets.

It's a warm southern night, and the sky has lost its scarlet hue. The horizon is now a weak purple bruise. It's almost dark. To her right, there's a very short hill with a line of trees planted in rows at its top. It's a footpath that leads around the property.

Iris walks towards it and up past the trees. The magnolias planted on either side of the trail make a kind of tunnel, and from here, she can walk a ring around the entire Adler property. She can even take this little path all the way to where the road starts that Harvest Baptist is on.

The trail turns sharply behind her, and she can hear the scritch scratch of footsteps on the dirt. Someone is coming. She looks towards the house to see another truck come around the gravel road. It's the same lifted black one that parked by the barns. It's Nick, and the call must be urgent if he's already leaving.

In her bare feet, her steps make no noise, and she moves off the trail and hides behind the branches of the magnolias. She keeps her eyes on the bend in the path. A dark silhouette comes into view. It's a man in all black with a long rifle slung across his chest.

Iris puts her hand over her mouth. Her heart starts to jump in her chest. She doesn't even bother to try to catch a glimpse of the man's face. All she can look at is the gun.

She's hidden where she is, but the man's head sways left and right like he's looking for something. She has to get back to the house. She has to somehow warn the others. The man stops and looks out towards the fields. Iris jolts as he talks.

"The east side is clear. Walking back south."

A radio squawks in response. *"Copy."*

The man keeps moving. The way he strolls appears almost leisurely. He's not trying to be stealthy.

He's hired security, Iris realizes. Not an assassin.

She lets herself breathe, but only for a moment. Her head keeps spinning.

Who is this family trying to protect themselves from? The wind blows, and by the time the air is still again, the sound of the man's footsteps is gone. It's just the crickets chirping again.

She wonders how the guards have been able to stay so hidden.

They must spend their days in the farm trucks, patrolling out of sight, pretending to be field hands, Iris thinks. But have they been out here stalking the grounds every night? Iris can't say. She doesn't walk after dark.

The presence of the guards is confirmation enough. This family is hiding something. Joseph's death and her shooting might not be the mystery everyone is saying it is. Augusta isn't in a fevered panic to catch whoever did it. No one is.

No, this family is no more moral than they were when they were slavers. They would do anything to keep their fortune.

She starts back towards the house. She's halfway across the open lawn when suddenly, she stops. She has the hair-raising sensation of being watched. It's the guard, of course, she thinks, but then she sees something.

A silhouette stands at a second-floor window of Sweet Blood. They're standing at *Iris's* second-floor window. They're in her bedroom, but the only light must be coming from the upstairs hallway because this figure is only a shadow. An outline. Augusta? Annabelle?

Her heart leaps as she watches the person's arm move. She can't tell what they're doing, but it looks like they're holding a finger to their lips as if in a shush.

Iris starts to walk faster. She passes where she dumped her heels and scoops them from the grass, and then she clomps onto the empty porch and across the marble of the entrance hall. She goes upstairs two at a time, and by the time she throws open her bedroom door and switches on the light, her lungs burn.

There's no one here. Her eyes quickly pass over the room. She walks to the attached bathroom and pulls back the shower curtain. Then she steps back out. Everything looks the same as when she was last here, but when she looks at the window she had seen the person standing at, the big wooden shutter is clasped shut.

PART II

Interviews

Daisy is dropped off at her trailer. She doesn't say a word as she steps out of the passenger seat of a red 90s Silverado and shuts the door behind her. She turns around and opens her palm. For some reason, she always has to be outside the truck for this last exchange.

The driver tosses something through the open passenger window. Before Daisy even has a firm grasp on it, the truck's tires spin in the gravel and it roars off.

She slowly unfurls her fingers. It's half a gram of heroin balled up tight in plastic. She puts it in her pocket.

The single-wide she lives in is on its own half-acre lot just off Highway 2. It's a seldom-used road. It existed before the interstate was made, and now it's used little more than your average avenue.

Her trailer looks disused as well. Grime runs like mascara-streaked tears from the corners of all the windows. The sheet metal siding bulges in places from moisture and rot. There are two more trailers just like hers a few hundred feet down the quiet highway. They have weedy, dirt lots for parking.

She waits for the truck's taillights to disappear in the dark, and then she starts walking along the shoulder of the road, away from her own and to one of the other trailers farther away.

When she gets to the stairs, a graying orange tabby meows and steps around from behind them.

"Hey, old man." She bends and scratches his chin. "Did Bree kick you out?"

He purrs and tilts his head into her hand.

"Follow me back to my place. I could use some company tonight."

He meows as if in affirmative. Daisy smiles and knocks on the trailer door.

It opens immediately, as if she was being watched from inside. A young woman her age stares at her seriously. She's wearing nothing but a bra and camo pajama pants.

"Hey, Bree." Daisy doesn't look her in the eye when she talks. "Can I use your phone?"

Bree doesn't ask why. She doesn't say a word. She only tilts her head to one shoulder and leans on the doorframe. She's bartering without a word. Her posture says she'll stay here all day until the deal is sweetened.

Daisy sighs and holds out the heroin. Bree plucks it from her palm and disappears into the trailer. She comes back with a disposable flip phone in a plastic bag and tosses it at Daisy. Everyone in her life is always throwing things.

"Thanks. Mind if I take Dexter tonight?" Daisy nods down to the cat.

"Whatever." She shuts the trailer door. Bree can be kind, Daisy thinks, but not when she needs a high.

Daisy paces in front of the trailer, and Dexter rubs up against her legs and slinks between them. She's glad Bree didn't ask her why she needed the burner phone. She could lose a lot more than her job for this.

She's scared but needs to do the right thing. She pulls out the detective's business card from her back pocket and dials.

Evidence

Nick wasn't expecting any more leads on the girl in the field. He thought the story was watertight. Girl goes off to get high. Girl overdoses alone or maybe with friends, but they don't want to get caught so they panic and dump her body.

It happens often enough. This isn't Oregon. If you get caught with Fentanyl in Louisiana, you are going to prison. There is no honor among thieves—or addicts.

As far as cases like this go, it should be wrapped up by now. Nothing to raise an eye over. But the phone call he got on the porch of Sweet Blood made it seem like there is a conspiracy going on.

Her name is Daisy. No last name given. He had volunteered to make himself the contact for the case, and she got his number from the station.

She wants him to meet her at a trailer on a rural stretch of Highway 2. "Cassidy's death wasn't an accident." It was all she'd say over the phone. Nick had her give a description of the body in the field. Daisy even knew what she was wearing.

He did a little research before going over. The area code wasn't local. He thinks maybe she called him on a disposable phone. He should make other calls. There are several people who need to know about this, but they might get worked up. No need for that until he finds out what's going on.

Nick keeps it to himself, for now.

Daisy seemed paranoid, but junkies often are. Still, it sounds like it could be a setup. When he arrives at the trailer, he keeps his hand on his holster and his head on a swivel. The trailer door opens when he's still several feet away.

"Hey," says a girl of about twenty. She's pencil-thin, and her face is boxed in by the bangs of her pixie cut. "I'm Daisy."

"Hi, Daisy. Nick."

"Sorry to sound weird, but could you park behind the trailer? So no one can see you from the road."

"Oh." Nick turns around. He's wary but not afraid. "Is there anyone else in the trailer with you?"

"No," she says quickly. "No, it's just me I promise. I just..." She grasps the back of her neck with one hand. "I've got an ex-boyfriend that drives this road. He's a little crazy jealous."

Nick doesn't question the lie. He knows her pimp might see his truck. "I'll move."

"Thanks."

When he reparks, he sees that Daisy has walked around the trailer to follow him. She stands with her arms crossed, and they don't speak until they're inside.

"Sorry about that. Again, I don't mean to sound weird."

Nick doesn't respond right away. She goes to the living room to sit on the couch, but he walks into the bedroom of the trailer, briefly checks the closet and then the bathroom. He walks back out to the living room and kitchen area to find her rubbing her hands anxiously.

"I'm alone. I told ya. I'm not lyin'."

Nick inspects her closely. She's a tiny thing. Maybe 5'1". A baby-faced blonde. Her cheeks hold some fat, even though the rest of her is thin. She doesn't have any visible tattoos or meth scabs. She looks clean. When he tries to look her in the eye, she turns her entire head sideways.

"You said her name was Cassidy?"

"I'd have to see a picture of the girl you found, but she went missing Friday night. From the motel."

"Was she reported missing?" Nick isn't looking at her. He's pulling up his photos.

"Not to the police, no. We kept hoping she'd show up. But she was wearing what I said she was, wasn't she? Pink tank. Denim shorts."

"Could you bear to see a picture?" he asks but doesn't wait for an answer. He steps to Daisy and holds his phone out.

71

She closes her eyes tight and spins away from the screen. "That's her. Fuck." She looks at the floor.

Nick puts his phone away. "How do you know her?"

"She lived here. She slept right here." She nods down at where she's sitting. "On the pullout."

Nick sits in a paisley armchair across from the couch, and Daisy makes herself smaller. She curls up cross-legged.

She looks completely vulnerable.

Nick wets his lips but then reminds himself this is business. "So, Daisy." He clears his throat. He tries to make his voice more inviting. Less deep. He can tell this girl is scared, and his demeanor isn't going to help him get the answers he needs. "You think Cassidy's death may have been a homicide?"

"I do."

"Did you see anything suspicious that Friday night? Or is this a hunch you have based on other things you know?"

"It's both."

"Let's start Friday night then. What did you see?"

"Me and Cassidy were... workin'."

"Prostitution?" Nick interrupts her to try to make her more comfortable. "I'm a homicide detective. I have no interest if you're breaking the law like that. Okay?"

She nods. "Well, there was this party, and it was supposed to be the two of us for four guys. The night starts off fine. The men are behaving themselves. Not breaking the rules. They have their fun, and then a lot more guys start showing up. Girls too. They're just partying, all doing crystal. I had to work again in a room next door. When I got back, I couldn't find Cassidy."

"How much time had gone by?"

"About an hour, but ten minutes later, she comes into the party and says shit is about to go down. There's a black sedan passing the motel real slow. She thinks there's going to be a gang shooting, something like that. She wants to leave and for me to come with her, but I know that's not what she was really afraid of."

"Was Cassidy high then?"

"No. That's the thing. Cassidy is sober."

Nick sighs, like he's not sure this bit of information is believable.

"I mean it. And this is the motive part. She wanted out of the life because one of her clients was abusing her. Breaking the rules and getting away with it. Making her life hell."

"Roughing her up?"

"All kinds of messed-up shit. Cassidy was going to go to the police. Out the bastard publicly. Apparently, he's some big name. I don't know who though. She wouldn't tell me."

"And this man, he was getting away with doing these things to her? Don't you have a pimp?"

"He was a big spender. They let him do what he wanted."

"Is that all you heard about this man? Do you have any kind of physical description?"

"Cassidy never said. But apparently this had been going on for years. She wanted out of this lifestyle. She has wanted out of it for years."

"And do you not want out of the lifestyle yourself?"

Daisy tightens her brow. "Of course I do. But if I quit now, I go back to being broke and homeless."

"You could get a real job." Nick is going off topic, but he doesn't care. This girl seems smarter than most in her position, and he wants to hear what she says.

"I've got a record, mister. They don't hire girls guilty of grand larceny. Anywhere. Meth and theft. You got either of those on your record, and you might as well be Charles Manson. Swastika on your forehead and all."

Nick stifles a smile. He's been politely avoiding eye contact. He can tell it makes her uncomfortable. Probably a tic she picked up from her trade. But now he looks at Daisy. She tilts her head down and starts playing with a string of fabric that sticks out of her sock. She's nervous. Fidgety.

"Can I ask you something?"

"Yeah?"

Nick leans forward. "Are you lying to me?"

"Excuse me?"

"There's something else on your mind. Why don't you tell me what it is?"

Daisy looks around anxiously, as if someone else might be listening. She stays silent and rips the strand of fabric off her sock. "Okay. We were going to take this guy down together."

"The abuser? The big shot?"

"Yeah. This other man, a journalist, approached us months ago. He showed us a picture of the client, the one that had been hurting Cassidy. Apparently, this journalist had been following him for some time. He offered us money if we got the guy on tape. Doing things to us. He showed us legal contracts that he said would protect us."

"What paper did he work for?"

"He never said. He wouldn't say. We asked."

"Isn't that suspicious?"

"I think he was just as afraid as we were. These are dangerous people. They're willing to do anything down here to protect their reputations."

"So you do know who this sadistic client is?"

"I could tell you his face. Maybe. To be honest, I was still using when this journalist approached us. He told us his name, but things are hazy then." She brings her eyes up to Nick and says proudly, "But I'm two months clean."

He doesn't pat her back. "So you don't remember his name?"

Daisy purses her lips. Obviously she's disappointed she didn't get any praise. Nick looks at her coldly, willing her to continue. He isn't about to applaud a whore for not doing heroin.

Daisy sighs. "No. But I met him. Never alone though. The only time was when it was him and three of us girls."

"You met him, but you could only *maybe* describe his face?"

"It was more than a year ago and I was fucked up. He was wearing a Mardi Gras mask. He took it off some, but it was on for most of it."

Nick doesn't respond.

"You believe me, right? This man exists. Why would I lie to you?"

"Would you recognize him if you saw a picture?"

"Definitely. I just... That night was a blur. I think it was meant to be that way. We were offered a lot of drugs, and we took 'em."

"Did he abuse you that night?"

"No. He seemed able to have regular sex, too."

"So where did things go with this journalist?"

"Cassidy and me stopped hearin' from him months ago now. He stopped contactin' us. The number he gave us was no longer in service when we tried callin'."

"Do you know any other girls in your line of work who had complaints against him?"

"Lots. Everyone who had to sleep with him alone."

"Do you have a specific number? Do you know who they were?"

"The journalist said there were four other girls who had been abused by him."

"Just to be clear, four other prostitutes?"

"Yes. He said they were willin' to come forward to accuse the big shot of rape. He didn't tell us names. He mighta just been sayin' all that so we felt more comfortable. Safety in numbers and all."

"And what did this journalist look like?"

"He was a black guy. Young. Shorter. Kinda handsome, I guess."

"And he didn't give you his name?"

"He said his name was Jay. I remember that."

Nick takes a deep breath. This is familiar. "Do you think he could've been a cop?"

"I mean, he coulda been anybody. But he said he was a journalist."

"Okay." Nick leans back on the sofa. "Now, we're going to have to get specific. What exactly did this sadistic client like to do?"

"Choke girls. That was his thing. And I don't mean lightly. They had to blackout for him to get off," Daisy curses under her breath.

"So we have a possible motive. Cassidy was going to rat on this guy, and you think he found out?"

"Yeah."

Nick pretends to write something down.

"What happened at the party?"

"I thought Cassidy was just being paranoid. I saw the car, too. It passed every five or ten minutes. It was a black sedan. A nice new Dodge. But I wasn't fixin' to leave. I was still making money. Cassidy left sober. *Dead* sober, I swear to God."

"Was she driving?"

"No, she doesn't have a car. She was going to walk a half mile to a bar in Hillsdale. Grouper's. I tried to get her not to, but she wasn't hearing reason. After she left, the car never drove by again."

"You didn't happen to see the plates, obviously?"

She shakes her head. "Black Dodge. The four-door one. That's all I saw."

"Charger?"

"Yeah."

Nick's heard enough. There's just one more point he wants to reiterate. "So, you don't know any of the other girls who had complaints about this abuser? What about the ones you met him with? When he was wearing a Mardi Gras mask, you said there were other girls there."

"I didn't recognize them, and again, that was a year ago. They weren't the usuals."

This isn't the best of leads. The information about the journalist is interesting, however. He'll have to get a list of field reporters based out of Baton Rouge and New Orleans. He might have to cast a net even farther out than that. Nick can find him. In the meantime, he knows what he has to do.

"Is there anything else you can think of, Daisy? Anything that relates to either catching this abuser or Cassidy's death?"

Daisy is quiet for a moment. An orange cat strides into the room and jumps onto her lap. It arches its back as she pets it. "Do you know about the body found near Port Vincent? The burned one?"

"'Course."

Daisy lets her hand rest on the top of the cat's head. "I think I know who it is."

Nick nods. "To be honest, we have more information on that case than we've released. A more useful tidbit would be who did it."

"That's not what the FBI said."

It feels as if Nick's heart stops beating. "What's that?"

"A few weeks ago, this lady came by, said she was FBI. Workin' on that burned girl."

"Did she show you a badge?"

"She mighta flashed one."

"What did she look like? You get her name?" Nick says quickly. He knows he needs to compose himself. He takes a breath.

"Her name was Long? I think. She was younger. I tried gettin' ahold of her to talk about Cassidy, but she wouldn't return my calls today."

"You have to be careful who you talk to, Daisy. Someone shows up at your door saying they're FBI... You make sure they are who they say they are first."

"You think she was faking it?"

"Maybe." Nick shifts. "I haven't heard about the FBI poking around. Did you talk to her about this abuser?"

"She only wanted to know about Sarah. She's the girl that might've been—"

Nick holds up a hand. "I know. Do you have anything else to say about Cassidy?"

"No. No, that was everything I could think of."

"Okay. I'll have to run to my truck for my kit first, but I want to gather some of Cassidy's DNA. Make sure it's a match with the body. Did she keep any belongings here?"

"The dresser by the door is hers. There ain't room for two in the bedroom."

Nick glances over to it. It's a tall white dresser with the paint chipping off. "Perfect. I'll be right back." He stands, and Daisy gets up off the couch.

He goes out and around to the back of the trailer and takes his briefcase out from under the back seat of his truck. He fucked up. He didn't think this interview would lead anywhere, and he left his usual tools at home.

A car is coming down the highway. Daisy doesn't want him to be seen, and neither does he. He waits for it to pass before walking back around front and into the trailer.

When he steps back in, Daisy opens one of the drawers of Cassidy's dresser. "I think these are all washed and clean." She points at a messy pile of shirts and underwear inside the bedroom. "Those aren't, and she's got a hairbrush in the bathroom, too. The pink one. If that would help."

"Let's start there." They walk to the bathroom. Daisy trails Nick with her arms crossed. He pulls the shower curtain back and inspects the clear liner. There's a layer of soap scum on the bottom. He takes a pair of purple latex gloves out of his back pocket and snaps them on.

"Do you mind if I take this?" Nick points and then starts to unfasten the shower rod from the wall.

"The shower liner?"

"These actually collect a lot of DNA. Dead skin comes off during a hot shower. It'll be easier to test than hair, but I'll still take the brush."

Daisy opens a cabinet and hands it to him. "Why do you need DNA, anyway?"

Nick pauses. "Cassidy's name is not on any kind of rental agreement, is it?"

"No."

"Does she have any mail here addressed to her?"

Daisy shakes her head.

"This will prove she was staying here. And your story. That's a step." He takes the rubbery liner off the shower rod and folds it several times so it fits under his arm.

"Will I get that back?"

"Yes," Nick says, and they step back into the short hall. He goes back to the living room and sets the liner on the carpet next to the sofa, then he takes a seat in his paisley chair again.

Daisy goes back to the couch. She perches on the armrest this time.

"What're you doing?" she asks as Nick opens his briefcase.

"I'm going to bag this brush."

The briefcase lid hides his hands, but Daisy still watches him intently as if she can see. The cat, too, stares at him skeptically.

The sounds that come from his briefcase certainly aren't congruent with pulling out an evidence bag. There's the squeak of metal as he threads the heavy silencer onto the pistol barrel.

Daisy senses something is wrong. She's perked up, nervous.

It's not until he chambers a round, and she seems to recognize immediately the heavy clank of the gun's slide, that she starts to stand. But it's too late.

Nick raises the pistol in one hand and shoots three times. All three shots hit her in the chest. She slumps off the armrest of the couch and onto the floor. She's coughing blood. Her eyes are unblinking. They stare at the ceiling in terror.

Nick quickly grabs the shower liner, shakes it out, and wraps Daisy in it. She's still alive but won't be for very long.

"Shh," he whispers. She shakes as he wraps the liner around her tight to keep the blood from dripping. "There's no use fighting it."

One of the bullets hit her in the lungs. He can tell from the foamy bubbles that seep through her lips. Everything up to this moment has felt messy. Nerve-racking. Now Nick can relax. There's something intoxicating, intimate, in being the last face this girl will ever see. This is better than Cassidy. Overdose victims don't have the same light in their eyes.

"It's nothing to be afraid of. I know you feel light. Let yourself float. Let yourself go."

Her eyes are still wide, terrified. They tick back and forth around the room like she's looking for an escape, and Nick is staring deeply into them as they finally go still.

Pedigrees

Iris stays in her room until the board dinner ends. The finish doesn't seem amiable. There is no chorus of goodbyes downstairs as people start to leave. She hears engines start in the driveway and more cars crunch on the gravel. She goes to the opposite end of the upstairs hall to look out towards the guest house. The lights are on, and she can see shadows behind the curtains.

She goes downstairs and back to the dining room. Aurelia is there gathering empty drinks onto a platter. Augusta still sits at the head of the table. Her legs are spread wide like a man's, and her posture is poor. She sits so her shoulders rest halfway down the chair's back, like she's melting to the floor.

"I'm not always proper." Augusta raises her hand and takes a draw of a skinny cigarette. When she exhales, its smoke smells sweet. It's a scent that Iris thinks she'd remember if she'd smelled it before, but she doesn't. This is new.

Augusta sits up some. "My daddy was a pipe fitter. A pipe fitter's apprentice, I should say. He was never sober long enough to run the show himself."

Iris sits in an empty chair immediately. It's unlike Augusta to be vulnerable. She could find something out from her now. She could get her to talk.

Iris lets the silence linger so she doesn't seem too eager to talk. "I never had a dad."

"You've said. I hope you don't think it's in bad taste for me to say you're somewhat lucky. One less man to let you down. One less man to *hurt* you." Augusta's gaze tightens as she says the word hurt. Iris doesn't know if she's talking about emotional pain or physical pain. Perhaps both.

"Was I open about my past?" Iris asks. "Or did I pretend to play it off like I came from money, too, when I first came into this family?"

81

"No," Augusta sighs, like she can't hide the fact that she's upset she has to remind Iris of every little fact of their relationship. "I liked you for that. Where you came from is not something you can hide these days. That is, if you ever could hide your pedigree in the South. But Annabelle..."

Augusta tosses her cigarette into her wineglass. "She thinks she's me. Her family were a bunch of lawyers in Baton Rouge. Her granddaddy was the Speaker of the Louisiana House. What she has on Jamie to pull this stunt, God knows. That girl has got his testicles on her mantle. Pardon my French."

Iris doesn't care about the business, but she doesn't know what else to say, either. "Is she going to be the new CEO?"

Augusta is quiet. It was a mistake. Iris should've just shut up or changed the subject.

"If she is, I'm the only one to blame."

Augusta seems content to let the topic die, and Iris doesn't try to fill the silence this time.

Aurelia comes back and takes the last of the dishes and then disappears into the kitchen.

"Aurelia says I used to be loud."

"Hmm," Augusta hiccups with a smile. "I was hoping someone would tell you eventually. This house is a little ghostly with you in it now."

"Come on." Iris tries a joke. "I'm not *that* bad for being partly lobotomized, right?"

Iris and Augusta both laugh. "Oh, Iris. You're getting better by the day." Augusta reaches out and takes her hand in hers. Augusta can only reach her fingers from where she sits, and she strokes them gently with her thumb.

"It feels like it," Iris says. "I'm dropping things less often. Talking more."

"So you *are* remembering more?"

Something about her tone prickles the skin on Iris's arms. She pulls her hand away from Augusta's instinctually. It was a mistake. Her face clouds with suspicion.

"Um, remembering? Not really, no."

"It will come, Iris."

"You could help me. There's a lot I'd like to know."

Augusta tightens her lips. "I know you have a hard time remembering things, but I don't want to repeat this every day. I cannot..." She closes her eyes. "I *will* not speak about my son." Augusta's voice quivers, and she stands abruptly. "Goodnight, Iris. I will see you in the morning."

Iris listens to her heels clack on the marble as she heads into the entrance hall and up the wide stairs.

She knows she made a mistake. She should've let Augusta keep speaking of her dad. Of her frustrations with Annabelle. She shouldn't have turned the conversation to her own past so soon.

Iris heads into the kitchen. Aurelia is not there and the room is enormous. There's two of almost everything. Two gas ranges. Two ovens. Two sinks. She walks to the commercial-sized fridge and takes out her probiotic drink. She does everything the doctor recommends. She takes walks. Reads books. Keeps her diet clean.

The drink tastes somewhat sour and chalky, but she's willing to stomach anything to get better. She pours it into a coffee mug and leans against the counter. She wishes she could down it in one gulp, but she'd gag.

When she brings the mug down from her lips, she sees the door to the basement cellar sway. She looks at it. Frowns.

Aurelia stands in the dark, and she's looking right at Iris.

Iris lifts her hand to wave, but just as she does, Aurelia turns and closes the basement door behind her. It creaks slowly before latching shut. And Iris is left in the kitchen, listening to the refrigerator hum.

Followed

Mornings aren't easy for Iris. Since leaving the hospital, she's yet to be able to get out of bed before eight. It's like there's lead in her bones. Her brain, too, hates to be pulled from sleep.

It's part of healing, she assures herself. Her morning lethargy won't last forever. Good sleep is just as important as a healthy diet. She doesn't feel guilty sleeping in, but she doesn't feel good, either.

Her body wakes up unrested. It's not until she takes her afternoon nap that she begins to feel like she actually has a clear head.

This morning, Iris is going to take a longer walk on the property. She still has a full day before the meeting. It's Monday, and the meeting at Harvest Baptist is on Tuesday, but she wants to try to establish a pattern before she's gone for a couple hours tomorrow.

She takes a book and a bottle of water. She wears running shoes and a baseball cap. She doesn't want to have to tell anyone where she's going. Since leaving the hospital and staying at Sweet Blood, she feels like she's lost all sense of autonomy.

Someone is always around to ask her how she's doing or what she's up to. She's supposed to be recovering here. Gaining confidence in her body, and just as importantly, her independence.

But she knows putting the creamer in the cupboard isn't the only thing she's been liable to do since her brain injury. She's put metal in the microwave. Crossed one of the farm roads without looking both ways and almost gotten hit. Her lapse in thinking is dangerous. But being treated like she's brain-dead doesn't exactly help either.

The weekdays are better than the weekends. Augusta, Annabelle, and Jamie all are working.

She slips out the service door in the kitchen where the groceries are brought in and walks to the path where she saw the guard last night.

A white pickup truck is parked near the front gate to the house. She knows now that it's security. They must stay in the air-conditioned cab during the day, out of sight, careful not to raise any suspicion.

Iris walks on the trail lined with magnolias. She sips her water and stops often in the shade. When she gets a half-mile from the house, the Mississippi comes into view. It's a brown scar amidst all the green. Its shores are not wild and lovely. Cranes stalk minnows with the crude tubes and towers of the oil refineries reaching into the sky behind them. The waterway itself is a constant stream of river barges and tanker ships.

The river gives off the constant stench of mud and rot and when the wind blows, she can smell the bowel-like stench of the crude oil being refined.

This is not a lovely place for a walk. She has her phone open so she can see her little blue dot on the satellite map. She's getting towards the end of the property.

Ahead is a dirt road. Its gravel shines blinding white in the sunlight. At the end of the dirt trail she's on is a little wooden gate with a padlock on it, indicating the property line.

Iris looks to her left. There's a camera not so carefully hidden on the tall limb of a live oak. It watches her like a black eye through the Spanish moss.

The gate isn't much of an obstacle. She can't open the padlock, but it's not much more than waist height and easy to climb over. On the other side, she turns to see it's plastered with "No Trespassing" signs.

She keeps walking on the gravel now. According to her phone, and the dusty street sign, this is Shoepick Road. Another mile and a half straight ahead, according to her maps, she'll find the old church. It's all green sugarcane fields here.

There are no houses. No signs of life. The fields are sprayed with pesticides, and it's eerily quiet. There are none of the insect calls she associates with late summer. There's just the bristle of the stalks rubbing against each other in the breeze.

When she looks left to where the road bends, she startles. The white pickup she'd seen by the front gate earlier is idling there. It was hidden from the trail she was on by the sugarcane.

The truck begins to move. It crunches the gravel as it creeps towards her. The windows are tinted smoky black. She stands still, waiting for it to pass, but it stops completely. The passenger window rolls down. There are two men in the truck. The one who's driving keeps his eyes fixed ahead on the road.

The passenger smiles. He has a bushy beard and matte sunglasses. He's chewing gum obnoxiously. He looks ex-military. "Hey ma'am, this area is private. You're going to need to turn around."

Iris ignores her annoyance at being called ma'am. She's ten years younger than this man. She looks at his black tactical vest before speaking. "This is a public road."

"Not anymore, it ain't. Farm access only."

Iris doesn't think this is true, but she's in no place to win a debate. "Look, I'm an Adler."

"We know who you are." He points behind her. "The trail you were on branches left about a hundred yards back the way you came. If you want to keep walking, it's best to stay on it. The farmhands aren't expecting any pedestrian traffic here no more. Tractor's got some serious blind spots, you know?" He snaps his gum. Smiles again. "It's a dangerous place to take a stroll."

"Sure," says Iris. "Thanks."

The man nods and rolls up the window. Iris expects the truck to drive on, but it just stays parked in her path. She turns around, climbs over the gate as gracefully as she can while being watched, and picks up her pace down the path.

When she's out of sight, she creeps back to Shoepick Road. This time walking off the path a little so she's hidden by the trees. She watches the pickup from behind a trunk.

It's begun to drive away slowly the way she wanted to go—towards Harvest Baptist. The guards must've been watching her from the beginning of her walk. They must've known she was on the move the moment she left the house.

He was lying to her, without a doubt. There's nothing unsafe about the road she looks at now. There's no farm activity or traffic of any kind, and she's almost certain the road is not private, as it connects to Highway 2.

The truck pulls into a U-turn, and Iris ducks behind the tree.

The fact that the truck was waiting for her the moment she stepped off the property line makes her feel claustrophobic. Were these guards keeping her safe? Or keeping her *here*?

Either way, she's not going to play damsel or prisoner. She starts back towards the house, already on her phone, looking up the number for cab companies.

Manners

Iris hasn't felt trapped in Sweet Blood before, but then again, she hasn't tried to leave. Every doctor appointment, every errand she's been on in town thus far, she's gone with either Augusta or Annabelle. They've been happy to keep her company. *Happy to keep an eye on her.*

Iris is afraid she's being paranoid. She has a brain injury, after all. She's shown some pretty serious lapses in judgement and memory. Maybe it's not all that strange that they want her chaperoned and don't want her walking on dirt roads alone in the heat of Louisiana summer.

She could get lost. Injured. Iris puts their motivations aside. She has her own. She has to get out of here, if only for an afternoon.

Sweet Blood is too rural for Uber. The little sonar pings will blink and blink until finally the app says there are no drivers available. When she's back inside, she makes sure she has everything she needs for a little day trip to New Orleans. Wallet. Fully charged phone. Water bottle. Sunglasses. Sunscreen. She's set. She decides to call the cab company before she runs into someone and they ask her plans for the day.

Iris calls and gives the dispatcher the details on where to pick her up. They tell her it'll be forty minutes, about the same distance the house is from New Orleans.

She goes to the kitchen and eats a protein bar and a banana. The blinds are always drawn in the kitchen, and the room faces north. It's dark and cool here, and since Augusta and Joseph Senior both have their meals brought to them, she doesn't have to worry about running into anyone but Aurelia here, no matter the time of day.

It's one of the only private places outside of her room in the house and she sits at the counter and scrolls on her phone. Nick still hasn't sent her an email with the old text messages between

88

her and Joseph. She wonders if it's best she calls the phone company herself.

Those texts will make her remember. Iris is sure of it. Thousands of messages. Hundreds of pictures. She'll find out the kind of wife she was and the kind of man she was married to.

There are more than just the texts with her husband. She'll get her messages with Augusta and Annabelle. Maybe even her sister back in Memphis. Iris is going to find out how she interacted with each of these women. What she said. What she cared about. What she thought was funny. The thought doesn't make her excited, however. Iris is anxious.

When it's close to when she's expecting the taxi, Iris heads towards the front door. She doesn't want to look like she's sneaking off. She'll walk right up the gravel drive and then text Augusta that she's heading to the city for the afternoon once she's already in the cab.

She slips her shoes on and starts across the gravel. She doesn't even make it ten steps out the door when she hears her name.

"Iris? Iris?"

She turns to see Augusta in the doorway. "I thought you were at work?" Iris blurts out. She suddenly feels guilty. Like she's a kid caught sneaking out.

"No. I've been upstairs in my office working from home today. I just have a few calls. Where are you going? It's terribly hot for a walk. You could get heat stroke."

"I'm going to the city, actually."

"New Orleans?" Augusta starts walking towards Iris. Her brow is arched in concern.

"Yeah."

"Why's that? Are you okay, darling?"

"I'm getting lunch with a friend."

Augusta stares at her. If she can see the lie on Iris's face, she doesn't show it. "That's nice, but honey, New Orleans is forty minutes away. You can't walk there."

"I called a cab."

"Oh." Augusta's eyes widen with surprise. Then she shakes her head. "Sorry. I didn't mean to make you feel dumb. I didn't think you'd do that is all."

"It's okay. I'll be back before dinner."

"Are you sure? Do you have your phone on you?"

"I think it's time I get out on my own, Augusta." Iris isn't even going to answer her question about her phone. It makes her feel juvenile.

"Of course. Sure. But hon, you should have Arthur take you. Our driver. He's on standby today since I didn't go into the office."

"I already called the cab. It's almost here."

"Oh, but the cancellation fee can't be more than what it would cost to get all the way to New Orleans. This'll be cheaper."

"That's alright."

"I insist. Arthur lives nearby." Augusta takes out her phone. "He can be here in five minutes. That way you have a way back, too."

Iris grits her teeth. She doesn't have a rational argument anymore. Augusta might think she's on to her and how she knows she's being watched if she pushes back more. Iris forces a smile.

"Okay. Let me cancel the cab. Thanks, Augusta."

"It's the least I could do."

Augusta turns and heads back inside.

Iris sits on the step, and several minutes after she's canceled the cab, Augusta is still not back. What's the line between being nice and being controlling? Iris knows it's much thinner when the object of another's control *doesn't* have brain damage.

No one will fault Augusta for being too protective of her daughter in-law, especially when the person who shot her is still out there and she lost her son.

"Here, sugar." Augusta steps back across the porch to the steps. Iris feels something cold on her shoulder. "Take this."

She's tapping her with a cardboard container of coconut water. It's cold and already sweating from the heat. "You should

90

stay hydrated, today. It's terribly hot," Augusta says again, this time staring out towards the road and fields as if the heat is visible and a thing that someone needs to keep an eye on.

"Thank you." Iris stands and cracks the plastic cap. "I won't be too long. I'll meet Arthur by the road."

"Alright." Augusta hesitates like there's something else she wants to say. Maybe she wants to force Iris not to go anywhere. But she steps back and walks across the porch. "I'll see you for dinner." Before Iris can respond, the big door clangs shut.

She starts across the gravel and takes a sip of coconut water. It's minerally. Sweet but salty. Iris can't keep it down and spits it into the grass. Did she always hate coconut water? She can't remember. All she knows is that it reminds her of having a mouthful of blood.

It's a quarter-mile walk down the main driveway to the road. There's a big iron gate at the end. This one is not so scalable, but before she even reaches the gate, it begins to swing inward. She looks down the road first, but Arthur and his black Cadillac are not in sight.

Iris turns. She can still see the face of Sweet Blood. The back of the house is prettier, with its garden and red brick path lined with oaks.

From here at the end of the road, the house's eight front columns look towering. The leaves of the live oaks in the lawn soften the sunlight with shade. Iris thinks she's staring at a postcard of the Antebellum South.

However, even without the bloody history of this place, this house seems venomous. The eight columns of the front look odd from this distance, like they're too close together.

A spider, Iris realizes. The house looks like a spider with all of its legs shielded in front of its face. Hiding its pincers as it waits for prey to pass.

Its appearance serves a warning, Iris thinks, of the arachnids living inside.

The City

Arthur does not arrive in five minutes. It's closer to twenty when she sees the column of dust rise in the distance.

He slows the black Cadillac when he gets in sight. When the car stops, Iris knows better than to step to it right away. She's made this mistake twice now. She lets Arthur get out of the driver's seat and open the rear door for her.

Arthur is bald, and his smooth, white head really does resemble a cue ball as it glistens in the sun. "So sorry for the delay, ma'am." He smiles, showing his big front teeth.

"It's okay." Iris figures he wasn't on standby. Augusta just wanted to make it seem as impractical as possible for her to take a cab.

Iris climbs into the car, and Arthur hurries to the driver's seat. "Where to? Temperature alright back there?"

"It's perfect, thanks," Iris says, but she's a little chilly. "The restaurant is by Audubon Park. You can just drop me there."

"Wonderful," he says in his thick southern accent.

Iris leans back and closes her eyes. She's afraid Arthur might try to make small talk, but he doesn't, and suddenly she realizes he may be a resource. She's the one who should be talking.

"So, Arthur." She tries to keep her tone casual, not inquisitive. "How long have you been driving for the Adlers?"

"It'll be sixteen years in September."

"Wow."

"It beats the hell outta drivin' a truck or a cab. Some guys, they'll moan about having to wear a suit in the summer and all, but I like it. I look nice." He pinches the knot of his necktie.

"You do."

"Thank you, ma'am."

"Pardon if I don't recall, but were you ever my husband's driver?"

92

"For nine or so years, I was Joseph Senior's personal driver. I didn't drive no one else. Now, 'course, I drive for everyone in the family and not just Mr. Adler."

Not just? Iris frowns. "Sorry, is Joseph Senior still driven places? I didn't think he left the house."

"Oh no, no," Arthur says loudly. "I only meant I drive for you others now. Augusta. Annabelle. The boys."

"Gotcha."

"Yeah." Arthur sighs. "I miss Joseph Senior. He was a funny man. Different from his three sons in that way."

"Was my husband a serious man?"

"More so than his daddy was, sure. But your husband was also a younger man. He had a lot to prove. His daddy had climbed the mountain. He could be whoever he wanted to be. I haven't had the chance to tell you, but I'm so sorry about what happened to him. And you, of course."

"Thank you."

"I hope they find who did that to you and string 'em round a tree branch."

"Hm." Iris nods.

"Teach 'em a thing or two first. You know?"

"Sure."

Arthur glances to-and-fro at Iris in the mirror, like he's hoping he said the right thing. "The Adlers are good at that."

"What?" Iris catches his eye in the rearview.

"Teaching lessons," Arthur says. "There are lots of old stories. Joseph's granddaddy once had the sheriff tarred and feathered for extorting the small farmers for crop taxes that didn't exist. This nasty old sheriff was going farm to farm where the folks couldn't even read and would invent some new law. Show them the paper it was supposedly written on. Fella had to run off to Texas to start fresh, but he never could. He done hanged himself." Arthur says this last bit proudly.

"That's a nice story," Iris says, somewhat sarcastically. She doesn't like hearing about violence.

"Oh yeah. They can dole out punishment. It's in their blood."

She doesn't respond to this. Iris doesn't know if she's imagining it or not, but she thinks Arthur is saying something else. Like the Adlers learned centuries ago how to hurt people with ropes and bullwhips and fists.

"The justice system is a sham. I mean, you read the news? Rapists getting a slap on the wrist. Murderers gettin' out of prison. Every day with that shit. Pardon."

"It's horrible."

"I tell ya, it's not complicated. I gots a solution. Hemp rope. Tree branch." He laughs heartily. "Oh, that's what Joseph Senior used to say. Gawd, he's a funny man." When he looks to see that Iris is not chuckling along, he quickly shuts up. "I don't mean to be crude, ma'am."

"It's okay, Arthur."

"I just don't like all the terrible things that are happening in the world."

"Neither do I."

Iris leans back and stares out the tinted window. Arthur keeps looking at her in the mirror. She can see his eyes darting to her and back to the road and it's beginning to make her uncomfortable. He can't stop searching her expression.

"I didn't upset you, did I, ma'am?"

"It's okay. I'm just not looking forward to going back into this heat."

"Oh, it gets worse every year, don't it?"

Arthur starts to talk about the weather while Iris watches traffic thicken out the window. Soon, the skyline comes into view. She's more nervous than she thought she'd be.

She's going to be alone in the city. She's convinced herself she was collateral damage in the murder of Joseph. Wrong place. Wrong time. He was the powerful one. The one with enemies, but now that she's alone and off the property for the very first time since the hospital, her mind can't help but play with the idea that whoever tried to kill her might be itching to try again.

Invitation

She agrees to meet Arthur back at Audubon Park, the same place he drops her off, in two hours. It should be plenty of time. She only has one errand in the city.

After three hot blocks, she reaches the shade of the campus green. Leblanc College is a private, four-year university and one of the most prestigious in Louisiana.

The campus is its own little neighborhood in New Orleans. There's plenty of green space, which keeps it cool on days like this. The sunlight doesn't get sucked into concrete, where it oozes out until long after dusk. Classes start in a week, just after Labor Day. The campus is only just starting to get busy.

Iris stares up at the stone buildings. She went to school here. It's where she met Joseph. This is where her life in Louisiana began. Everything—from the big plantation house she lives in now to the bullet that bounced out of her skull—can be traced back to this place.

Joseph was getting his masters when they met. Iris was a senior but wasn't the typical age of twenty-two. She would've been twenty-five her senior year. She knows from Augusta that she worked for two years out of high school to save up for school and then attended a community college in Memphis for another couple before transferring here.

She was ambitious. Smart. Now those are things Iris can't even picture.

She doesn't stroll aimlessly through campus. She looks at the map on her phone and keeps walking until she's back on side streets. Here there are houses with golden Greek letters above their doors. She's boiling in the heat, but she's too distracted to care. She suddenly looks up from her phone to the colonnaded porch of a fraternity house. The brick is orange, the woodwork all white.

Epsilon Delta Phi. This is it.

Not only was this Joseph's fraternity, but it's the place where they met. Interestingly, the place doesn't look entirely foreign. She can sense she has memories here.

Suddenly, the front door opens, and a skinny kid with a white polo only a shade or so lighter than his pale skin steps out the front door.

"I'm so sorry. I was expecting you later." The kid doesn't have an accent, and Iris is too stunned to talk as he speed walks to her, takes her hand in a shake, and starts pumping it enthusiastically.

"Charles Bradley. Vice President of Epsilon Delta Phi."

"Iris," she says, wondering how the hell Augusta knew of her plans all along.

He stares at her expecting her to say more. A last name or position title, and his mouth hangs open dumbly. He suddenly drops her hand.

"Are you not with the college?"

"No," Iris says with relief. He's mistaken her for someone else. "I'm sorry. I was just in the neighborhood. My husband was a member."

"A brother? Oh, what's your last name?"

Iris wants to shut up and walk away. She doesn't look at him when she speaks. "Adler."

Charles juts his chin forward. "You're kidding? Oh! Oh, I recognize you! Iris Adler. You were all over the news. I'm sorry about your husband."

"Thank you."

"Is there anything I can do for you?"

"I actually met my husband here."

Charles looks a little uncomfortable. He half turns and points to the house. "Would you like to come in?"

"I think I would, actually. If it's no trouble to you."

"None at all. Come."

Iris follows him up the sidewalk and into the house. When she steps inside, she actually recoils from the smell. There's the mothball-like reek of creosote. It smells like she's walking on

96

railroad tracks, and she can see why. Three railway ties have been carved into the Greek letters, E, D, and P. It's a rustic look but fits with the dark wooden trim.

Charles notices Iris is staring at the letters. "Would this have been here when you were? I understand it's only a couple years old. We're thinking of throwing it out this year. If you live here, you get used to the smell pretty quick. Guests don't."

"Yeah. It was here." Iris keeps walking into the house. The kitchen is to her left. She walks to its entrance quickly and then darts back across the small entrance hall into the living room. Charles can hardly keep up.

She hasn't blinked since she got in here. Iris can't believe it. *She remembers.*

Party

It was the beginning of 2022. Iris stood in a circle of a few others. She was one of the oldest girls at the party, but she didn't look it.

She'd had her eye on Joseph since she arrived. All the other boys at the fraternity house were baby-faced undergraduates, but the group he stood in were older brothers of Epsilon Delta Phi. Joseph and his friends were in grad school and were no longer allowed to live at the house, but they could still attend their parties to poach younger girls.

Iris didn't mind. She didn't think they were being creeps. She was just glad there were guys here who looked like men.

Joseph just looked like money. He wore a white button-down and a dinner jacket. Its lapels widened his already broad shoulders.

Shovel-jawed, his chin shiny with just a day's worth of blond stubble, he looked a little dangerous.

His eyes gave him away early. As soon as she arrived, he couldn't take them off her. She was nervous from this. She didn't know if he was looking at her because he thought she was pretty or not. It wasn't until they made eye contact and he gave her a wide, friendly smile. Disarming. Not everyone had a smile like that.

He was interested, but the night was young and everybody, Iris included, was happy to loosen up with a few more drinks before leaving their circles of friends and doing any flirting.

It was Iris that came up to him. She was told to be assertive, not play hard to get—some guys liked the confident type.

"Have I seen you here before?" Joseph spoke to her before she had a chance to say anything.

"If you have, I didn't see you."

"No?"

"No." She shook her head, tilted it towards one shoulder a little flirtatiously. "I'd remember you."

"I'm Joseph." He stuck his hand out.

She offered him only her fingers to shake. A true lady. "Iris."

"Pleasure to meet you, Iris."

"You know, I don't meet many Josephs. Plenty of Joes."

"It's a family name."

"A family name... Fancy. So you a freshman?" she teased.

"Yeah, don't you know these are the guys I pledged with," he said sarcastically and pointed at a row of boys by the beer pong table. They were young and not holding their booze well. There weren't enough girls here for everybody to try to get some action. Some guys were content to just get roaring drunk.

Joseph and Iris talked for most of the night. An hour passed like nothing. They flirted and joked. He was well-bred, but not a bore. They decided to leave to find a bar with a crowd closer to their own age with live music.

This was when Iris grew nervous.

She didn't want this to be a one-night stand. Not that the night felt like it was headed that way. She felt a connection. But it wouldn't be the first time a man showed a grotesque amount of interest just to ghost her after sex. Was Joseph a showman? Was that smile bullshit?

He went to say goodbye to some old fraternity brothers, and Iris walked towards the beer pong table. The floor was sticky from spills, and the boys were only getting louder.

She heard a racial slur, not exactly an anomaly at an all-white frat house. She looked the boy over. He was bigger than most. Tall but fat. She backed into him and felt a hand brush her butt. She thrusted her pelvis forward dramatically out of reach and spun around.

"What the fuck?" she yelled.

His wide dumb eyes met hers. His cheeks were lit up, burning red from booze.

"You think you can just grope my ass like that?"

"Shut your face." His head rolled in a circle as he spoke. "Bitch," he slurred.

"Did you think you knew me or something?" Iris shouldn't even try to give him an out, but he didn't take it.

"Bitch, no one wants to touch you."

"Fuck you!"

The boy stood straighter like he'd been able to end confrontations like this before. He thinks his size alone should shut things up.

Others have begun to notice. The party would've been quiet if it weren't for the music.

"Damn, Jeffrey, what did you do this time?" a smaller kid said.

"He didn't touch her," said another boy who came to his friend's rescue. "I didn't see shit."

"Hey, hey, hey." Joseph pushed his way through the small crowd. "What's up?" he asked the boys, but they said nothing. Then he looked at Iris. "What's going on?"

"This asshole grabbed my ass."

"You wish, bitch," said the culprit.

The big guy must've been too drunk to realize Iris and Joseph had been talking all evening, or he didn't care.

Joseph looked like he wanted a fight. He curled his big hand into a fist. The big guy was too drunk to notice. "Apologize to her. Now."

"Fuck if I will. Hey!" he called in no particular direction. "Bucky? Yo, who's this old dude at our party?"

Joseph looked at Iris with tight lips. His expression was apologetic, like he didn't really want to do this, but he had to. He launched a left hook right into the big guy's gut, and he toppled.

The guy's smaller friend, the one who was quick to come to his defense, grabbed Joseph's arms and tried to pull them behind his back. In one deft motion, Joseph twisted his back so the kid was swung to the floor. Joseph pounced. He landed a knee on his chest, and from there he started pummeling him.

He hit him in the nose. But didn't stop at one. The kid's head knocked back onto the hardwood with a clunk at every punch.

"Joe! Fuck!" Some of his older friends who hadn't taken interest in the situation until hands were thrown now raced to pull him off.

"Dude. Come on." They pulled Joseph up by the collar of his dinner jacket. "What the fuck are you doing? These guys are five years younger than you."

"They're groping the girls."

His friends turned to the beat-up boys. "This true? You harassing the ladies?"

The big one had gotten to his feet and was rubbing his belly in circles like a kid with an upset stomach. The one with his nose beat in covered the gore with his hand. The two looked at Joseph.

"Yeah," said the smaller, more sober one. His voice was nasally. Thick with blood. "It won't happen again. Sorry."

"We're out of here," said Joseph. He looked at Iris and gave her a nod. "Ready?"

"If you weren't royalty, you'd be in big fucking trouble, Joseph."

"Vet your fucking pledges better, Ricky!" Joseph was high on adrenaline. His eyes wide, he grabbed Iris protectively by her bicep, and they walked together from the living room to the little front hall. "I'm so sorry."

She stood on her tip-toes and kissed him on the nose. "Thank you, Joseph."

He smiled, no doubt feeling a little heroic now.

"I should wash my hands." He hid his knuckles, not wanting her to see the blood he had to wash off, but she could see it running along his fingers.

Iris didn't follow him to the kitchen. There were another dozen people in there, and she didn't want to jostle through the crowd.

Two girls left from there. They were walking towards the living room with fresh drinks. They were identical-looking blondes, even dressed the same as sorority sisters would sometimes do, in black jeans and black tube tops.

One of them looked over her shoulder at Iris and then whispered in her friend's ear. Both girls stopped and looked at her.

"Are you leaving with an Adler boy?" asked the prettier of the two.

Iris looked confused. "Are there more than one?"

"Unfortunately, yeah. There are three." The girls laughed.

"Should I ditch him?"

"If you know what's good for you." The girls kept walking towards the living room, but Iris wasn't done talking to them.

"So what are they? Players? Fuck boys?"

"No." The girl looked back at the kitchen doorway, making sure Joseph wasn't in sight. "They're all psychos," she said, and both girls disappeared, giggling, into the other room.

"Ready to go?" Joseph came back into the entrance hall.

Iris looked at his knuckles. They were clean, but the skin was still swollen and pink. His hands were large, but they weren't the long, spidery type of a pianist. They looked like they could inflict cruelty. A boxer's hands. A brute's hands.

Iris couldn't stop staring at them. Was she aroused? Afraid? She supposed perhaps both. "Yeah. Let's go."

They stepped outside into the night.

"Where to? You got any preference?" Joseph asked as they walked side by side. She could see how this man was dangerous, but he was beautiful, too—a dagger bejeweled with diamonds.

"Let's find a jazz band, baby," Iris said and leaned into him while she walked.

"Alright. Let's," Joseph said, draping his arm over her shoulders.

He was dangerous, sure. But at that moment, Iris didn't care. She had a feeling of victory. He was hers.

Bloodline

"How many years ago was it that you were here?" Charles asks.

Iris is slow to respond. She's looking out the window of the frat house's living room to the street, chasing the memory of the two of them walking away, but it fades.

They disappeared into the night. There is no memory of a bar or a band. No memory of sex.

"I don't know. Years," Iris says. "I should be going. I don't mean to intrude."

"You're not intruding. Not at all."

Charles isn't the kind of person Iris can relate to. He's like a personified number two pencil. Tall, skinny, preppy. Sharp yet boring. He reminds her of an exam room.

"Really. The smell." Iris points at her nose. "I should get going. I get headaches easily these days."

"Oh. I'm so sorry. As if I needed more confirmation to get rid of those railyard scraps."

Iris goes back through the entrance hall. There are dozens of photographs on the wall. All of them have about two dozen white men in them. They're posing on the steps of the fraternity house and the pictures range from black-and-white to modern day.

Her eyes pass over a few of the frames. She's not expecting to see anything of interest, when suddenly her eyes stop. There's a photograph. The little label at the bottom says '76.

Iris leans forward. One man in each photo is front and center. A president of the frat no doubt. It reads 1976, but the man she stares at now might as well be a spitting image of Joseph.

Charles must've been following her gaze. He speaks. "Joseph Adler Senior. You have a good eye."

"They look so alike."

"Strong genes."

103

"Were all the boys members here?"

Charles looks embarrassed. He chuckles like she asked something foolish. "Yeah. Gideon Adler lived here until he graduated just last year. Epsilon Delta Phi was founded by their grandpa, Clarence Adler. It's still owned by his son, your father-in-law."

"Oh." Iris defends her ignorance. "They don't talk about their college days that often."

"The brotherhood we form here isn't a topic of idle conversation for them, I'm sure."

"Right." Iris turns back to look at the picture of her father-in-law. The men don't smile in any of the pictures, but Joseph Senior's face is extra serious. The skin around his eyes is darker. His stare then was as calculating as it is now.

She's been so focused on her husband that she hasn't stopped for much more than a second to consider the man who raised him. Maybe it's the hazy 70s grain to the picture or the dark suit he wears, but Joseph Senior doesn't just look serious in this photograph—he looks evil.

It's nearing the time Arthur is supposed to pick Iris up at Audubon Park. She's stopped at a corner café for a coffee. It feels good to sit at a table alone. It's the first time she's done anything like this since before she was in the hospital.

The caffeine is too much, however. She can actually *feel* her heart rate begin to pick up. She used to like coffee. She knows that. She loves the smell of it roasting in the kitchen. But this is the exact reason she's avoided it.

Iris is extra anxious now.

The doctor told her to avoid things that affect her brain chemistry. Nicotine, caffeine, alcohol. She thought this little jaunt of independence meant she could ditch another rule, but she's now learning the hard way.

It doesn't help that storm clouds have rolled in from the Gulf. They're black and low, leaden with rain, but for now the downpour holds. She texts Arthur, telling him she's ready to go early, and starts towards the park.

The streets have cooled from the breeze, but people are walking quickly now with an eye on the sky. She's one block from the coffee shop when she notices a man on the other side of the street. They're almost parallel to each other. She's just a few steps behind, and his eyes keep glancing towards Iris. He's tall and in a black raincoat.

It's nothing to worry about, she tells herself. She's paranoid from the coffee. But then the man slows his pace so Iris is ahead of him. She'd practically have to stop for her not to pass him.

She tries to think. She doesn't want to walk with her back to this stranger. The park is four blocks straight and two to the left. There are enough people on the streets that she doesn't feel unsafe, but still, that could change fast if it begins to rain.

She does the old trick of taking three left turns to see if she's being followed. After she takes two, she doesn't need the confirmation of the third turn to know she's being followed.

The man has since crossed the street so he's on the same side as she is, and Iris doesn't even think when she suddenly turns and reverses direction. She starts walking directly towards him.

He's a professional, however. The man doesn't react at all. His pace stays steady and consistent. He does pull the hood of his black raincoat up so Iris can't see his face fully. Then he looks both ways, steps off the sidewalk, and crosses the street. Iris stops and watches him as he walks into an alley littered with food scraps.

He knows he was spotted. He seems to walk into the alley like a challenge. *Follow me here. Bet you won't.*

She can't tell if she recognized him from what she saw of his face. White guy. Buzzcut. He also had a little bit of an ex-military look. One of Augusta's minions. If he was actually trying to stay out of Iris's sight, it shouldn't have been that difficult.

He wasn't trying to be hidden. He was behind her to send a message, she thinks. *You're being watched.*

Blackout

The rain starts before Iris is back in the car. At first, she picks up the pace on the sidewalk, and then when it falls even harder, she ducks under an awning.

She doesn't want to arrive back to Sweet Blood in soggy clothes looking like an unprepared child. Iris gives Arthur her location and waits for him to arrive.

When he pulls up, he gets out of the driver's seat, opens the back passenger door, and unfurls an umbrella. He escorts her to the back seat like a celebrity.

He gets back in and sets the umbrella in the passenger wheel well. "How was your day in the city?" he asks as he starts to drive.

"Oh fine. Wasn't expecting this weather."

"I don't think any of us were. Forecast only called for a twenty percent chance this afternoon. And it's pourin'." He switches the windshield wipers to a higher setting.

"So how's your friend?"

"Sorry?" Iris leans forward.

"Mrs. Adler said you were here for lunch with a friend of yours."

"Yeah, it was fine. She's good. I just didn't know you were aware."

"Sorry. I'll mind my own business. She just tells me everything."

The two quit talking. She didn't realize just how good it would feel to get away and feel independent for once. Now she's heading back to Sweet Blood. Augusta will ask her a dozen questions about her outing.

She wishes she still had a home of her own. Maybe not a house, but a condo on a high floor with a single entrance, somewhere she'd feel safe would be nice. Iris wouldn't want to go back to her old house. The place where her husband was murdered and she was shot. She wouldn't feel safe, but at this point a condo may be nice. It's been two months, and it's time for a change. She needs out of Sweet Blood. Out from under the eye of others.

When they turn to merge onto the interstate, Arthur groans, and Iris looks up out the windshield. There's a sea of brake lights shining in the rain. Traffic is bumper to bumper. "Rush hour in the rain. Sorry about the traffic."

"It's okay. You can't control it." If anything, Iris feels relief. She needs more time to decompress before she's back at the gates of the plantation. Before she's back in the hands of the Adler family.

But as she looks around the leather interior of the Cadillac, she begins to feel uneasy. Getting out from under them might not be as easy as she thinks. Even this little trip has been nothing but an illusion. Ever since she left the hospital, she has always been in this family's grasp.

It was a bad accident that kept them in traffic for over an hour. By the time they pass the scene, the cars have already been towed away. There's nothing but the oil stains and bits of plastic and glass the collision left on the asphalt.

It's almost nightfall by the time they get back to the house. The Cadillac pulls up to the gate, and Arthur clicks a button on a little remote that's clipped to his sunshade.

"Huh."

"Everything okay?" Iris asks.

"My clicker isn't working for the gate."

He hits it a couple more times, but the big iron gate doesn't move. He can't just drive around it. There's a steep drop of a few feet to a ditch to prevent just that and hedges on the other side.

"You know, Arthur, it's fine. Can you drive me down a quarter-mile to where Shoepick Road starts? There's the short gate there where the trail ends. I can just get in that way."

"That trail gets a little dark. Let me call Augusta. I texted her to say we'd be late, but she didn't get back to me."

Iris doesn't want to sit in the car any longer. She's starting to feel like a prisoner.

"Look, I really, really have to pee." It's not a lie. Iris has had to pee for the last half hour.

"Oh," Arthur says, surprised. "Oh, okay. Sorry. I should've asked if you wanted to stop when we were driving. Um, lemme me take you to the path, then." The car lurches forward, and it's only thirty more seconds before they roll to a stop again. Iris tries her door handle, but it's still locked. "Be sure to tell Augusta the gate's not workin'," Arthur adds.

"Of course."

He gets out of the driver's seat, and Iris leans back in frustration. She hates this whole charade, where the rich act like they're above opening their own damn car door.

The door opens. "There you are, ma'am."

"Thanks." Iris slides out and stands. "Have a good evening, Arthur."

"Always my pleasure. You as well."

Iris walks to the gate and climbs over it. It's dark now. The sugarcane stalks are swaying in the evening breeze. She has half a mind to walk to Harvest Baptist just to scout it out, but Arthur isn't driving anywhere. The car idles where he let her out.

She's not allowed to leave the property unsupervised. That much has become clear. She starts down the trail, and once she's out of sight of the car, she hikes her pants down to pee.

She doesn't want to hold it while Augusta questions her about her day as soon as she's through the front door. When she's done, Iris keeps walking down the path. She scuffs her steps and clears her throat often. She doesn't want to sneak up on a trigger-happy guard with an assault rifle, but Arthur has already called Augusta by now. Iris's location has probably been radioed in.

But as she gets closer to the house, something is wrong. It takes her a moment to notice what it is. The house isn't where it should be. The black of night is unbroken. She has to blink several times for the columns of Sweet Blood to appear in the dark.

Every single light is out.

Iris stops in her tracks. Is this why the gate wasn't working? Maybe it's just a power outage. But the storm didn't hit here. The ground is dry. Her steps still crunch on the dry dirt of the path.

She can't bring herself to walk any closer to the house. Even if the power is out, she should see flashlight beams through the windows. Candlelight. *Something.*

But there's nothing.

The house is ghostly quiet. As much as she didn't want to come back here, this is worse than being greeted by a nosy Augusta. She pulls out her phone and turns the brightness all the way down. Iris feels vulnerable here in the dark. She doesn't want anybody to spot her.

She is going to call Augusta, when suddenly a light comes on. It's in the very top window of the house. The fourth floor. The attic. There's one round window looking out from the tippy top of the house like the eye of a cyclops. The window shines a warm orange. The light is only on there for a moment before the rest of the house suddenly bursts to life.

The windows fill with light, and Iris sighs in relief. She walks quickly across the lawn and towards the front door. When she steps onto the porch and reaches for the handle, the tall oak doors don't budge. The house is locked, which is never the case at this hour.

The doors lock at ten. That's the rule she's been told.

"Hello?" Iris knocks. With the warm light coming from the windows, she's less afraid. "It's Iris!" she shouts and puts her ear against the wood. She can hear soft voices on the other side, but there are no footsteps on the marble floor making their way to the door to let her in.

She walks around the porch and looks inside. She can't see the entry hall from outside, but she peers into the music room and then the first-floor study. There's no one in either. She's walking back to the other side of the porch to try to see into the dining room, when suddenly the front door opens.

"Iris!" Augusta says as if she wasn't expecting her. "So sorry to lock you out. We lost power here, and I was a little spooked."

"It's okay."

Augusta leans against the door to make room for Iris to pass. "Come in."

Annabelle and Jamie are standing near the foot of the stairs. They're both dressed casually in T-shirts. Annabelle wears sweatpants, while Jamie is in jeans with frayed cuffs. Usually, even if they're just stopping by the house to say hi, Jamie would wear a collar.

Augusta doesn't allow T-shirts in the house. There are exceptions for the sick, the pregnant, and of course the brain damaged. But there are no exceptions for her sons.

"We'll be getting back to the guest house now, Mama," Annabelle says, walking forward. "The power should be back on there, too."

"I'll see you tomorrow," Augusta says, as if making a point not to wish her goodnight.

Annabelle and Jamie smile tightly as they pass Iris.

"Goodnight, Iris," Annabelle says sweetly, but neither makes eye contact. They're embarrassed, perhaps about how they're dressed, thinks Iris.

"Goodnight," she calls after them.

The big door claps shut. It's still hours from ten, but Augusta steps over and flips the big deadbolt locked. The sound echoes in the entry hall.

"I don't know about you, but I'm just having one of those days. I'm calling it early, Iris. I'll see you tomorrow to head to the plant."

Iris is surprised she wasn't questioned. It makes her think maybe she's exaggerated the control Augusta wants over her. She doesn't have long to analyze it.

"I'm sorry. Head to the plant?" She hates asking questions about things she should know. From Augusta's tone, it's obvious she thinks this is something the two of them have discussed. Tonight, Iris doesn't care. She needs to be free tomorrow. She's supposed to try to sneak to Harvest Baptist to meet this mystery man.

Augusta turns. Her eyes say *poor thing*. "You wanted to see Joseph's office. We're going to clear it out." She pauses. "Together."

She had expressed interest in the past about wanting to see where Joseph worked, but they hadn't set a date. At least she didn't think they did. Now she's suddenly doubting herself. Maybe this was discussed. Did she really forget?

Joseph's office was one of dozens attached to the Adlers' slaughterhouse near Baton Rouge. It's a stinky place to conduct business, but he was in charge of the meat department. It was one of the most important jobs, according to Augusta. He didn't go to the same cushy office in downtown Baton Rouge where Annabelle, Jamie, and Augusta all worked. The slaughterhouse was the front lines.

This, Iris can remember. She wonders for the life of her why she can't recall Augusta making plans to visit the place.

She doesn't want to look like a fool and doesn't bother asking Augusta when this idea was discussed. "What time did you want to go?"

"Ten a.m."

"How about we go early afternoon? I still don't feel very well in the mornings."

"Mm, no." Augusta shakes her head. "I can only do the morning tomorrow."

"Another day, then?"

"I want this done. What I told you the other night about not wanting to talk about Joseph... I meant it. I know you want to learn more about the man you loved, but I won't hear of rescheduling."

The inconvenience of this timing does not feel like coincidence. She should've burned the letter about the

112

rendezvous at Harvest Baptist. She's certain her room has been searched.

She wants to argue that she could go to the plant alone, but she doubts she would win. "Okay. I'll be ready to go."

"Wonderful. Goodnight, Iris."

"Goodnight." Iris takes off her shoes and watches Augusta walk up the stairs. She waits a minute and then goes to her own bedroom. She opens her dresser and finds the pair of pants that she stashed the picture in. It's still folded neatly in the pocket. If someone found it—Aurelia or Augusta—they did a good job making it look like it hadn't been touched.

Iris leans back. She's okay not going to Harvest Baptist tomorrow. Maybe even a little relieved. Besides, if this man really wants to talk to her, she assures herself he'll find another way.

Cruel

The house is quieter than usual tonight. Iris hasn't seen Aurelia all evening and Augusta seems to have been telling the truth about hanging it up early. It's just her and 9,000 square feet of wood and marble. This place has gone from feeling like a palace to a prison in just the last day.

She has gone the last couple days thinking she is going to get answers tomorrow, but now she's back at square one. She's antsy tonight. She eats a late dinner and takes her medicine in the kitchen, and when she walks upstairs to go to bed, she stops on the second floor and looks down the hall, where there's a staircase to the third story.

She hesitates for a second, looking towards Augusta and Joseph Seniors' room, before going to the third floor.

It's a half story here. There are only a few rooms. There's a den with a sectional and a flat-screen on the wall. It used to be the Adler boys' playroom. First it was probably toys, then poker and video games. There's also a full bathroom and the servants' quarters. Aurelia typically drives home in the evenings, but she does have a place to stay in the house if she likes.

The bedroom door to the servants' quarters is closed. No light seeps from beneath it. Iris looks up to what she came here for.

There's a square in the ceiling—the entrance to the attic. She's never been up there before, but after seeing the light on this evening she realizes it might be worth a look.

There's an eye hook drilled into the attic door with a string hanging down from it. Iris isn't quite tall enough to reach it, but with a little hop, she catches the string and pulls. The sound of its hinges is so loud, the damn door practically screams.

Iris grits her teeth and pauses, but the damage is done. The door is already halfway down. She opens it the rest of the way and folds the little ladder out that is screwed into the inside.

She waits several seconds to listen and see if she disturbed someone, but the house is just as quiet as before.

She turns on her phone's flashlight and starts up. When she gets to the top, she's surprised to find the attic isn't a dusty, cobwebby mess. The wooden plank floor is clean. A brick chimney passes through the roof next to her and there's a metal light switch box on it. She flips the switch.

The rest of the attic is just as clean as the area around the entrance. There are cardboard boxes and plastic totes stacked against the slanted ceiling that runs down to the floor. There are only two windows. One looking out the front of the house, and another facing the back. The attic doesn't have the same footprint as the house. It's perhaps only 1,000 square feet.

Out of all these boxes, what catches Iris's eye is a piece of cut lumber. It's a wood board, a 2-by-4, about three feet long. It rests on the floor next to where the attic door is. It looks like there's a notch for the wood board to be inserted into the door so it can't be opened. It's a lock, she realizes. So this is the Adlers' panic room.

Iris looks around. Towards the end that faces the main driveway, she sees a large painting hanging on the wall. She walks over slowly, her footsteps creaking the whole way.

It's an oil painting. There's a sugarcane field and a full moon above it. The light from the moon is a sickly yellow, and it illuminates an unplanted field.

In the dead center of the field are slaves. They stand in a circle, holding hands under the moonlight.

Iris steps closer, and her heart starts to beat hard. It almost looks occult. In all the dark purples and greens, there's a bit of maroon paint. There's something in the center of the circle. Iris leans closer. It's a woman on her knees. She's white. Her skin is pale, and blood seeps through her clothes.

Iris stares at the painting for a long time. It looks old, but at the same time, she can see it as being something commissioned recently. *Why is this here? Who on earth would want to keep something like this in their house?*

When she finally looks away, her gaze becomes fixed on something even more ominous.

Close to her on the wall next to some boxes is a line of wooden pegs. They look like coat hooks. In fact, that's what they are, but instead of jackets strung around the pegs, there are links of gray metal chains. There are cuffs and collars made of solid iron among the chain links.

Her eyes are open a little dumbly in disbelief. She walks closer and is about to touch them, to see if they're truly real leg irons and not some plastic recreation, when she hears floorboards creak behind her. She spins towards the sound.

To her surprise, it's not Augusta or Aurelia. It's Annabelle. "Oh, I've never climbed a ladder with this belly." She pats her bump with both hands. "I think I've got only one more month while I'm still able. This thing is going to stick out farther than my arms."

"Hi, Annabelle." Iris puts her hands at her sides. She's nervous, and she doesn't think she can hide it.

"I was looking for Mama when I heard the attic open. It makes quite the sound, doesn't it?"

"She went to bed early."

"Ah." Annabelle glances, left, right, and up like a prospective home buyer while she walks the length of the attic towards Iris. "Whatcha doin' up here, Iris?"

"I was just looking for some of Joseph and I's things." Iris gestures at the many boxes to validate her lie.

"No. Everything y'all owned is kept at a facility off Highway 9. Were you looking for anything in particular?"

"Just something to remember him."

"Oh, honey." Annabelle finishes walking to her. "I can only imagine." She looks past Iris at the oil painting. "Admiring Duncan's work?"

"Um..." Iris stutters. She can't begin to pretend to like the painting. She won't.

Annabelle raises her brow at her, expecting some sort of answer. Maybe she's expecting to hear what the old Iris would have to say about it. "I'm kidding," Annabelle says, but it doesn't seem like she is. "Horrible isn't it?"

"What's it about?"

"The Southampton Insurrection."

Iris nods, but she has no clue what Annabelle's talking about.

"You probably know it as Nat Turner's Rebellion. Anyway, Jacob Fontenot had it commissioned after the massacre. He wanted to remember that his slaves were always a threat."

Iris is embarrassed for Annabelle. There's no hint of shame in her voice. This art feels criminal to be hung up in this house. It's hidden up here for a reason.

She keeps her composure. "I'm not familiar with the name."

"Fontenot?"

"Yeah."

"They were the original owners of Sweet Blood. Jacob had all daughters, and his son-in-law took over the estate. It's how we have the name Adler."

"I see."

"We used to lend it out to museums. No one seemed to want it around 2016 or so. Duncan White ain't the most fortunate name for a painter of Antebellum America. Apparently, it's in poor taste. Mama agrees—she doesn't want it in the house—but I had it hung up here."

Hearing "mama" out of Annabelle's mouth never ceases to make Iris cringe. She scratches her neck and turns from the painting. "It's a little dark." She turns to the chains. "Are these a museum piece that got sent back, too?"

As Annabelle gazes at the chains, Iris sees something like nostalgia gleam in her eyes. "No. We've never lent these out."

"Family heirloom?" Iris says sarcastically.

"Should we remember what this family used to do to people, Iris?"

"Sorry?"

She continues like Iris understands her. "Or should we throw these out?" She points at the chains. "Smash the painting,

117

too? Maybe I should just let this baby inside me grow up ignorant to the human suffering that first built this family's fortune. Is that a good idea?"

"Fair point," Iris says, but she doesn't believe this is the intention behind why Annabelle keeps these artifacts. She's simply smart enough to know how to defend herself.

"Between me and you." Annabelle nudges Iris's hip conspiratorially. "I think it's interesting. I'll admit it. The human history of control. I was reading an article the other day." Annabelle smiles. "Dolphins torture their prey, did you know that? God, they were my favorite animal as a girl. We used to boat on the bay, and I'd watch for them all day. Daddy would have to console me as I sobbed if we didn't see any. Now I learned they're just awful."

"Nature is often that way."

"Exactly. Oh, they'll even torture the weaker babies in their pods to death. They could just do it quick, but they'll beat them with their tails, even flip them into the air. They'll let them think they're going to escape before going in for the kill." Annabelle tsks. "Poor babies."

Iris is lost for words.

"Anyway, the point of the article was how self-aware creatures, things that understand pain, like to inflict it on others. Orcas and elephants. Chimps, obviously. They *all* torture. They all exercise control over weaker things. I just think it's fascinating that intelligence correlates to cruelty. When people are given power over others, they like to see what they can do with it."

Annabelle is looking at Iris seriously. Her eyes won't leave hers. They're drilling into Iris. *Why is she looking at me like this?*

"I don't know," Iris says. She's hardly even thinking as she speaks. "Isn't it the opposite? You may think of orcas and dolphins as smart, but compared to us, they don't even make it on the IQ chart. Right? They're still stupid, just smart for fish."

Annabelle squints, like she doesn't like her idea being contradicted. "Dolphins ain't fish."

118

"I know. I'm just saying..." Iris is afraid of this woman, but she can't stop speaking. Annabelle's little spiel about cruelty in front of these artifacts has made her too angry. "It's the dumbest of us humans that get convicted for violent crimes. So isn't it better said that stupid things with the slightest bit of sentience like to hurt others? And that *low* intelligence correlates to cruelty? People and animals too dumb to know any better."

Annabelle bites her lip. "You know Iris, maybe you're right. It's just... a little strange you should have that opinion now."

Iris doesn't like where this is going. "Why's that?"

"Because... Huh?" Annabelle hiccups with a little chuckle. "I didn't read it in an article. I heard that idea from *you*." She turns and starts back to the entrance. The way Annabelle talks, the way she walks, it all says that whatever trust she had left in Iris has just been severed.

Iris doesn't even know if they used to *actually* be friends. There are dozens of pictures on Annabelle's social media of the two of them hanging out, but they were sisters-in-law in a powerful family. Appearance in the upper echelons of society is always less likely to be reality. The pictures, their smiles, they all might've been for show.

"Annabelle, wait."

She turns and looks at Iris expectantly.

"Were we friends? Like close friends?"

Annabelle smiles sadly. "The best," she says with a kind of finality. Like the casket has just been closed on any chance of rekindling that friendship.

Annabelle descends down the ladder. She seems to believe that the person Iris used to be is gone, destroyed by the bullet.

But after hearing the kind of ideas Iris used to have, she's no longer just afraid of this family, but herself.

It's beginning to dawn on Iris that her worst fears were true. She was far from the black sheep she is now. The pictures aren't fakes.

This lifestyle didn't grind against her morals.

She used to fit in *perfectly*.

Menthol

Iris wakes up earlier than usual. She'd left the wooden shutters in her room open the night before, and dawn shines in. The marble floor looks ablaze with rich oranges and golds.

She has hours before they have to go to the plant, and she stretches in the sheets. The feeling is a kind of ecstasy. Nowhere to be. No one to wake her. This is freedom, Iris thinks.

When she gets out of bed, she doesn't feel so fresh. Her head pounds the same as it usually does in the mornings. There's that familiar haziness to the world. Every time she wakes, it's like she's hungover.

She showers and gets ready. At nine, she begins to feel anxious. It's not a light uneasiness. Iris wants to believe it's from the fact that she has to see Joseph's office and meet more strangers she's supposed to know. But it's not that.

Her anxiety branches from the idea that she used to be as cruel and calculating as any other Adler.

If she was like that, maybe her death wasn't just collateral damage for whoever killed Joseph. If she was an awful person, it leaves the possibility open that *she* was the target.

That maybe she deserved it.

Iris can't even sit still. She goes to the bathroom and throws open her medicine cabinet. There are at least a dozen prescription bottles. She plucks out one on the far right. Xanax. High dose. The doctor prescribed them in the case of panic attacks. Otherwise, she was to avoid mind-altering drugs. Iris takes the lid off. She feels like she's falling into a bottomless pit. Getting rid of the feeling is only a pill away. She's about to empty one into her palm, when she stops.

This will only make her memory more suspect. The last thing she needs is to lose the little lucidity she has. Iris turns towards the toilet and holds the bottle upside down. The scores of little pills plop into the water. She flushes them and starts to wash her face.

She tries to occupy her thoughts instead. She desperately wants to know who might be waiting for her at Harvest Baptist, but she doubts she can get there without being tailed.

Whoever wants to meet is trying to stay anonymous, but there's little hope of that now. Augusta knows about the meeting and she'll have the place staked out. Iris curses herself. She should've flushed the letter down the toilet, too.

It's telling that this person hasn't tried to communicate with Iris by texting or calling. They must not trust that her phone is not somehow bugged. She shared a wireless plan with Joseph, but Augusta wouldn't have access to her calls and texts, Iris thinks. *Would she?*

The police do. Maybe it's not the Adlers this mystery person is afraid of. Maybe it's the police.

In some way, she's relieved the decision whether or not to go to Harvest Baptist has been taken from her. There was always the possibility it was a trap. The intimate picture in their possession means nothing. At least when Iris can't remember the circumstances behind it.

At ten, Iris is waiting for Augusta near the foot of the main staircase. At five after, Augusta still isn't down. They were supposed to leave by now, Iris thinks. She wasn't misremembering last night. Augusta said ten.

Iris heads upstairs and down the hall on the west side of the house. There's an office at the end.

Iris knocks a few times. "Augusta?"

"Come in!"

The room is all wood, with bookshelves stretching to the ceiling. Augusta is at the far end of the office, facing Iris. She sits at a wooden desk the size of a small car.

"Everything okay, Iris?"

"Yeah." Iris points awkwardly over her shoulder with her thumb. "It's just already ten is all."

Augusta just stares at her, unsure what she means.

"We were going to go to Joseph's office."

"Oh!" Augusta rolls back in her leather swivel chair. "Oh, of course. I'm so sorry. Just give me five minutes, and I can be down."

Iris doesn't respond. She shuts the door and goes back downstairs. If Augusta forgot, maybe it meant she wasn't concerned with what Iris might've been doing this morning. Maybe they never found the letter.

It doesn't matter at this point. She's going to her husband's office, not the church. Arthur takes another five minutes to arrive once Augusta comes downstairs, and then they're driving to the meat-processing plant.

"I don't want to be more than an hour." Augusta looks at her smartwatch. "I arranged a meeting with the staff there for 10:30 that will have to end before noon. I have a one o'clock lunch. All the business items are removed from his office. It's just personal belongings at this point, and I trust you to go through those. We don't want some intern stuffing them into a file box."

"Okay." Iris sees that Augusta's keeping her composure by making this outing about business. She doesn't even want to say her son's name.

Iris smells the slaughterhouse before she sees it. The air in the car becomes fecal, gamey. Iris thinks the smell is sort of like standing next to a cow, only it's been turned inside out.

The processing plant is a massive gray building. It stretches for acres, and a multitude of steam stacks rise out from its roof. Big green letters on the side of the structure read, *Adler Corp.*

Iris can suddenly remember herself driving past this plant. She sees herself in a pickup truck. It's nighttime. There are no other cars on the road, and as she passes the plant, Iris can't stop looking in her rearview mirror. She was terrified. She remembers that—a horrible anxiety twisting her guts.

Was she running from someone?

She keeps trying to follow herself and the pickup, but as the Cadillac exits the highway, Iris knows she kept driving on that night. The memory is gone, but hovering right on the edge of her mind.

The arm of a security gate lifts, and the Cadillac bounces into the parking lot and comes to a stop in front of a pair of glass doors.

"You'll want to breathe through your mouth," Augusta says.

"What?"

Augusta doesn't elaborate. "It's worse outside the car."

Arthur steps out to go open their doors, and Augusta's voice becomes nasally as she holds her nose. "It's better in the building, but trust me, you'll want to cover your nose."

Iris's door opens first, and she stands. She does the exact opposite of Augusta's advice and takes a whiff of the air. The smell doesn't make her remember anything. She's too busy trying not to gag.

Augusta makes a beeline to the office doors and beats Iris. She shuts the door behind them, blowing a raspberry.

"I don't know how you lived with Joseph when he'd come home from here. The stench sticks to your clothes."

Iris is a little shocked by their surroundings. They're in a dim little hallway. She was expecting a grand lobby, something up to snuff with the Adlers' lavish style.

But that's far from what she sees. The dull colors, the stained carpet. The building they're in is Soviet.

A small young woman wearing a gray suit over a white blouse approaches them. She's 4'10", maybe, and of Indian descent. "So glad you decided to visit us, Mrs. Adler. I'm Becca, the new assistant administrator here."

"Oh, hi."

"We were all so sad to hear you'll no longer be leading us."

Iris watches Augusta smile in a pained way. She has a special talent of turning a smile into an expression of displeasure. "I'm a big believer in fresh blood."

"Yes! I've read your piece highlighting how CEOs, executives in general, tend to lose efficiency after the seven-year mark and become out of touch with the actual workings of the company."

"Ironic. I don't remember writing that one."

"I believe it was March 2009, in the Louisiana Journal of Business. You called it C-Suite Syndrome." Becca smiles, expecting praise for her memory. She's hoping an encyclopedic knowledge of all things Augusta Adler might impress the monarch.

"Well, I guess my resignation is more than a decade overdue then. Are they waiting for me?"

"Y-Yes!" Becca stutters from the abrupt change of subject. "We got your email a half hour ago, so not all troops are here. Nathan and Dominic are both out this morning."

"Where are we meeting?"

"Right this way," Becca says, a little stunned, and turns. The three of them start down the hall.

Business in the South moves slowly. There's no such thing as small talk here—it's all important. But Augusta doesn't seem to have time for it today.

Becca stops at a set of heavy wooden doors. "They're all inside."

"Would you take Iris to her husband's office? She'll be clearing out his personal belongings."

Becca looks at Iris for the first time. "Certainly."

"And give her a hand."

"Um..." Becca looks like she's about to protest. Iris thinks she's going to debate that she should be a part of this meeting, but Augusta is sending her to babysit. "Okay."

Iris frowns. Does Augusta not want Iris to be in this building unwatched?

Becca opens the door to the conference room for her, and Iris watches a round table of white men rise as Augusta steps inside.

A few fidget and flatten their ties on their bellies. None of them look past Augusta to Iris. Their eyes are all on her. Their body language makes it obvious—this woman is the boss. The scene makes Iris feel something. It's almost a little intoxicating. She keeps staring ahead, even after Becca closes the door.

It was satisfying seeing a room full of men stand at attention like that. And not your self-proclaimed *ally*, women-pleasing men of the coasts, who will stand pencil straight for a girl if she so much as looks at them.

These are good ol' southern boys with season tickets to see the Tigers, hunted birds with two-thousand-dollar shotguns, and vote Republican.

These men don't enjoy standing for a woman, but her authority gives them no choice. It makes Iris's heart flutter. She stands flushed, her cheeks reddening a little when she realizes what she's feeling.

She's turned on.

"Iris?" Becca leans forward and speaks delicately. "Are you ready to go to your husband's office?" She says each word like there's a period at the end. Like Iris is mentally challenged.

Iris realizes she hasn't spoken in front of this woman yet. That, combined with Augusta's request to watch, her must have Becca thinking she's severely impaired.

Iris smiles and speaks clearly. "Yes, let's get on with it."

Becca looks disappointed. Like maybe she was hopeful the reason Augusta ditched her was because Iris *needed* a chaperon. Now, Iris thinks, Becca knows she was scorned for something.

"Okay," she sighs. "Follow me."

They take a dizzying series of turns down halls lined with air fresheners that dispense a fruity smell. They reach an elevator and are both quiet as it ascends just two short floors.

"It's this one," Rebecca says as they step out.

They only need to walk a dozen steps from the elevator doors until they're there. It's a glass-walled office with big windows that look out over the distant sprawl of Baton Rouge. It's a stark change from the grim look of the first floor.

There's a big desk—also glass—and a seating area by the windows with a rug, coffee table, and a few chairs. That's all there is for furniture. The room is mostly empty, like it was originally designed to house big file cabinets that all went digital.

"Do you want to be by yourself?" Becca asks.

"I'm not sure," Iris says. What she really means is she might have questions and she wants Becca around.

"Okay. I'll get a box for you real quick."

Iris looks around the room. There are some old things written in Sharpie on the glass walls. It's all pie charts and corporate slang. There are a few pictures on his desk. One is of the two of them on their wedding day. She picks it up.

Iris sits on Joseph's lap, with a big beaming smile on her face. She's laughing so hard, her eyes are closed. It actually looks genuine, and like Joseph had good taste in wedding photos. This picture wasn't pomp and circumstance. This was a photo of the woman he loved, as happy as she was all night.

They were married at Sweet Blood, of course. The sugarcane fields made for a lush green background. That was just over a year ago now. July.

Iris sets the picture down and opens the desk's single drawer. There's nothing but a wireless keyboard, some pens, and a package of golf balls. She opens the golf balls to see if there's anything else inside but is quickly disappointed. There's nothing in here worth seeing. There's hardly anything for personal belongings. Did Augusta know this when she made this plan?

Of course she did. She's ignorant to nothing, Iris thinks. This is all a distraction to keep her from Harvest Baptist.

Becca comes back in with an empty file box. She sets it down and looks around. She's thinking the same thing Iris is most likely—there's nothing here to take.

"Becca." Iris licks her lips. "Could you show me the processing floor?"

Becca's eyes bulge like she didn't hear her right. "You want to see the plant?"

"I would, yeah."

"I really can't recommend it."

"But can you take me there?"

126

"Yeah!" she says, like she's been wrong to question an Adler. "Of course. I just want you to be prepared. It's not a nice place. Bloody, stinky, and noisy. You'll need booties."

"Fine by me. I'd just like to see it."

"Okay. Do you want to pack things away here first?"

Iris looks around. Her eyes fix on the wedding photo, but she doesn't reach out to take it. "No," she says and starts out into the hall. "Let's have someone else do it."

A couple minutes later, they're on the first floor in a tubular hall that connects the offices to the plant.

Becca rang the plant manager, and he's waiting for them there with his hands on his hips. He's about as large a man in height and width that Iris has ever seen.

He stands in front of the big white double doors, a beefy guardian to the slaughtering floor. His name is Buddy, and Becca explains Iris's want for a tour.

His orange mustache twitches. Branches of red veins curl and spiral on his wide cheeks. Iris wants to give it up. She thinks he's furious before she realizes this is just how he looks, like a pot brought to a boil.

"So you wanna see how da sausage gets made, huh?" he says in a thick drawl. "You'll needta suit up."

"That's okay," Iris says a little too eagerly.

He points at Becca. "You too, Becca."

"Oh. I think I'll just wait here."

Buddy looks down at her with his orange eyebrows brought to a point. "Mrs. Adler tolds you to look after Miss Iris here, right?"

"Yes, of course."

"Then you come along now, ya here?"

"Yes."

Iris is suddenly nervous. There was no one else around for that conversation. How does Buddy know what Augusta wanted?"

"We'll keep ya away from blood spray. I don't think you'll need full coveralls."

Buddy hands them both white rubber coats, hairnets, and plastic covers to slip over their shoes.

When Iris dons it all, he hands her a little circular container with a mint green lid.

"Menthol. We don't use it cuz we used to the smell, but you'll want some."

He unscrews the cap, and Iris puts some on her finger. She wipes it under her nostrils, and then after Becca does the same, Buddy opens the big white doors.

They're not done yet, because before they start walking, Buddy takes a few packs of disposable ear plugs from a dispenser and hands them each a pair.

The noise of the plant is muffled but still plenty loud after Iris puts them in. There's the hiss of steam, metal clanking, and somewhere more distant... screams.

Buddy holds a single finger up and tilts his head sideways. "You hear dat? Those is the hogs. This is pig plant as we call it. Smells worse here than where dey slaughta the cattle next door. Pigs is nasty. Smart, but filthy things. You want to see the slaughta part of the slaughtahouse? Or processin'? If you see the pigs gettin' kilt, it might make ya say 'no thank ya' the next time ya offered bacon."

A desperate pig wails, crying out louder than any others. Its cry goes suddenly mute.

Iris's heart is pounding. Despite the menthol, she can still smell the blood. Her body can sense the killing around her, and her fight-or-flight response has been activated.

"I know it sounds awful. But we don't bleed our hogs here. We kill 'em real quick. We gots a tool that shoots a lil' metal cylinder right to the brain, and it's lights out."

Buddy suddenly looks at Iris's forehead and reddens. "But no need for ya to see that kinda violence. We can see processin'. All the machines is being cleaned."

Iris is taken through a maze of stainless steel. The concrete floor is wet. All the equipment has been recently washed, as is protocol before a new batch of pigs comes through, Buddy tells them. The water that runs off the machinery is foamy and maroon and smells of iron.

She thinks this was a mistake. Neither the menthol, nor the smell of pig insides are making her remember anything. This whole outing was a waste of time. She should've gone to Harvest Baptist. Snuck as close as she could to at least *see* who it was. To hell if she got caught.

"And this is the grinder," Buddy says as they come upon a gigantic metal machine. It has a black conveyor belt that feeds into a mouth of four steel augers that look like rolling pins covered in razor wire.

"It takes all the parts of the animal we can't butcher for wholesale, trimmings, and turns them into one. We mix it with scrap we get from da cattle plant, some corn staach, and bologna is born."

Iris freezes. Suddenly an alarm begins to blare. Buddy sticks his hands out to stop them as pigs begin to come out of some washing apparatus. They're dripping wet and hung upside down from a track set in the ceiling. The pigs move like one big curtain of flesh and pass just in front of Iris.

She can see the red wet hole in their heads where the cylinder went in. Their eyes are all open. The wounds don't remind Iris of what happened to herself.

Her expression must be one of horror, because Buddy speaks to her with sharp concern. "Mrs. Adler?"

She's slow to speak, stuttering, "I-I'm good."

"Okay." Buddy looks over his shoulder. "Maybe we turn back."

Iris can't agree or disagree. She can't speak at all, not when her memory is playing like a film reel.

Disposal

It was nighttime. Late spring. Iris was behind the wheel of an old pickup truck. Vintage.

It had a single bench seat, and her stomach rocked and sank along with the entire vehicle over every little bump.

She was hot. Itchy. It was warm out, but Iris was in long sleeves and a stocking cap. Her hands sweated in black cloth gloves.

She couldn't keep her eyes off the rearview mirror, but she wasn't concerned with being followed.

The truck bed was uncovered, and every time she passed under a streetlight, she could see the body outlined under the sheet. It was wrapped tight with paracord, but the sheet still flapped in the wind. *What if the sheet flies out? What if I get pulled over?*

Iris couldn't stop the hypotheticals. Did she have what it took to get out of a traffic stop?

She opened up the glove box. The truck cab was also dark, and she had to wait for another streetlight to see the glint of steel. Then she wrapped her hand around the pistol's grip and took it out. She held the gun in her right hand while she drove with her left.

Its fully loaded weight made her feel secure. The two-pound pistol was an anchor. A paperweight on her stress. If she got pulled over, it wasn't all over.

The processing plant came into view. The stacks didn't steam. There was no scalding happening at this hour. The little digital clock on the dashboard read 3:22 a.m. She didn't have that much longer. She was racing against a deadline, and her heart kept kicking in her ribcage.

She hit the accelerator, and the old V8 roared, eager to eat up more road. Some exits later, the world around her was completely black.

There weren't sugarcane fields here. She was driving into the woodlands. She took a series of turns and passed a gray or black sedan pulled onto the shoulder, and that's how she knew she was close. Soon she could see ahead that the muddy road she was on dead ended.

There was a metal sign at the tree line that abruptly swallowed the road. Whatever it said had been lost to rust and bullet holes left by country boys.

Iris leaned over the steering wheel and noticed a camera angled towards the truck. She could see its black lens glint in her headlights. It might've been placed there to observe wildlife, abandoned by the DNR. Or perhaps it belonged to a hunter scouting deer. Either way, what mattered was that Iris couldn't be seen on the film. She didn't care if the truck was spotted.

She pulled to the shoulder where the camera could no longer see her and turned the truck off, got out, and walked around to the tailgate. Before she opened it, she turned around and stared out into the dark. It was still too early in the year for insects. The woods were deathly silent, but Iris wasn't looking to see if she was being followed.

She let her eyes adjust to the dark, but she didn't have to. There were two flashes. A signal from a flashlight. *All clear.*

Iris kept staring until she could see the outline of a person against the dark. A man was standing about fifty yards back, just off the road, keeping watch.

Everything was safe so far. She yanked the tailgate open.

The body was light enough for her to drag out on her own without too much effort. She didn't risk injuring her back by attempting to break its fall and let the body slap on the dirt.

Iris picked it up by its ankles that stuck out from the sheet and began to drag it.

She knew where she was going. There was a gap in the trees, a well-worn trail blazed by bucks and teenagers that took her to a clearing of tall grass. There was a fire pit dug into the dirt with stumps set up around it. A plank of wood stretched across two stones to make a bench.

She kept dragging the body past the bonfire where the trail continued. She took a random left into the grass wet with dew.

She set the body's ankles down gently and started to unwrap the paracord. The sheet was tied far too tight, and she had to pick at the knots with her nails to get them undone. When the last one was loose, she balled up all the cord in her hand and yanked the sheet off.

She stared down at a dead girl of about twenty-one. She was black, with full cheeks and full hair that stuck out onto her forehead in a devil's peak. Iris's eyes lingered just below it where two round holes shone glistened wet above her brow. Bullet holes.

Iris stood straight and started back to the truck. There, she opened the passenger door and took a canister of gasoline from under the bench seat. She couldn't drag it, and the full five gallons felt heavier than the body.

It sloshed back and forth as she walked back to the corpse. She twisted the safety cap off and began to pour. She took shallow breaths to keep the fumes from her lungs the best she could.

The canister seemed to go on forever, and at last when the stream turned to a trickle, Iris figured it was good enough and dropped the canister.

She walked backwards several yards, all the way back to the trail. She dug into her pocket and pulled out a Zippo.

She sniffed her hands and wiped them on her pants just for good measure before lighting it. She flicked it open and struck the flint. Iris watched the flame sway lazily, peacefully. It was about to become something far more violent.

She lowered her arm into an underhand toss position. She was afraid if she threw it too hard, the flame might go out. She needed to be gentle. She threw it up so it made a little arc.

The world flashed bright before she even saw it land. There was a whoosh, and the grass shook in the little shockwave. She felt the heat on her face and turned. When she looked back, the flames spiraled ten feet high, and the grass around them scurried back in retreat, crumbling black.

If it was a drier spring, she'd be afraid of starting a forest fire, but with little wind and everything as green as it was, she thought it unlikely.

She stared at the fire for a moment before turning on her heel and running back to the truck. She could already see taillights on the road. He must've seen the flames.

Iris turned the ignition and skidded off down the muddy road. She took her hat off and rolled the window down. The anxiety in her gut had begun to leave her. The flames were nothing but a light-orange flicker between the trees, and soon, they were gone entirely.

She didn't just feel relief as the warm night air tossed her hair.

Iris felt free.

Everything

Iris waits just inside the glass doors for Arthur to bring the car around. Her eyes are stuck in a thousand-yard stare.

The girl had to be the same body that was found by Port Vincent. She's trying to remember more of that night, trying to remember what came before the girl was in the truck bed and after, but nothing comes. She's left attempting to answer her questions. Whose truck was she driving? Who was the dead girl? Who was the man standing lookout?

Iris begins to convince herself the memory is manufactured. Her brain is making it all up. Taking tidbits of information she's heard and read about and putting them together into something false.

That had to be it, she assures herself. No matter who she was, Iris was never a murderer.

Iris is afraid she's going to start panicking, when she hears her name and startles.

"Iris?"

She turns quickly to see Augusta walking down the hall.

"Why don't you have any of Joseph's things?"

She's relieved for the distraction. She doesn't even fear being caught in a lie. Everything feels so little now. "Oh. He hardly had anything in his office. It had been gone through already."

"Ah." Augusta doesn't seem pleased with her answer. "Arthur's here." She gestures at the door, and Iris opens it.

"Wait!" someone calls from down the hallway. Iris looks to see a shorter black man in a dress shirt and slacks jogging towards them. It's Dominic, Joseph's assistant. The one who made a scene sobbing at his funeral. He must've been given a new position in the company.

"I'm sorry I was out, Augusta."

"Dominic," Augusta says very formally. Iris notices that Augusta glances at her briefly before looking back at him.

"I have, uh... the plant inventory reports you asked for."

"I don't remember asking for such a thing."

"Um." He pulls a folded sheet of paper from his back pocket and hands it to her. "You might want to see it."

Augusta takes the sheet, and Iris looks at Dominic. She has a tight smile on her face, but he stares back at her with such blatant loathing that she tilts her head back. His tears at the funeral might not have just been because he was a sensitive man. Iris makes a note that perhaps Dominic actually did lose more than a boss that day. She looks at Augusta and watches her study the paper to avoid his gaze.

"What's this highlighted item?" Augusta turns the sheet back to Dominic, and his face immediately resumes the expression of courteous employee.

"That's what I thought you should see. The plant is missing two containers of hydrochloric acid. Two liters total."

"And why is that a problem?"

"It's a fortified kind of acid. Very dangerous. It's only sold commercially. We could catch a fine."

"Is it missing or stolen?"

"That's what I'd like to figure out."

Augusta suddenly looks nervous. She turns the sheet back to herself and stares at it. "What's it used for?" she asks.

"When there's real bad blockage in one of the machines. It corrodes the product to liquid while doing little damage to the metal."

Product. Iris knows he means flesh.

"I see. Well, Dominic. Find it."

"That's the thing," says Dominic. "It's kept under lock and key. Only Joseph and Buddy have access to the locker it was in. He says he didn't touch it. So did the police find anything of the sort at his house?"

"No. There was nothing like that."

"Okay. Sorry for asking."

"We must be leaving."

"You two have a lovely afternoon." Dominic takes a step back, and Iris and Augusta step out into the heat.

Arthur stands next to the back of Cadillac at the ready. He opens the car door for Iris. She thinks Augusta is going to go to the other side of the car to get inside, but the door doesn't shut. Augusta is waiting to get in behind Iris.

"Oh. Sorry," Iris says and sits in one of the jump seats that is opposite to the back two.

Augusta is silent. She takes the seat directly across from Iris that faces the front. It's awkward having to look at each other the entire drive. Is Augusta going to interrogate her and ask her what she was really doing while she was in her meeting?

"Mrs. Adler!" Becca calls from outside before Arthur closes the door. She has a heavy file box in her arms. "This is everything that was left in Joseph's office. I thought you might want it anyway."

Arthur takes the box from her and disappears towards the trunk.

"Thanks, Becca." Iris says, but Becca is only looking at Augusta.

"I hope you had a good visit, Mrs. Adler."

"Oh yes. Thank you." Augusta smiles tightly, and when Arthur shuts the door, the expression immediately evaporates. She shakes her head and looks at her phone, and then Iris watches her nose twitch. "What the hell is that smell?"

Iris is silent.

"Did you go *into* the plant?"

"I had a lot of spare time while you were in your meeting."

"Why on earth would you go in there? They let you?"

"I asked for a tour. I wanted to see where my husband worked."

"He didn't work on the floor. Fuck, Iris. Not since he crashed my car high at sixteen and we put him to work for a summer. I mean... Jesus Christ. Take your shirt off. It's your clothes. They stink to high heaven. Arthur?" she says loudly, leaning her head towards the front.

Arthur has just sat down and pulls his seat belt across his chest.

"Arthur? Would you close the partition?" Her tone is suddenly sweet.

"Certainly."

The car is quiet apart from the shade's little motor. When it's closed, Augusta shakes her head.

"I'm not kiddin' you. Take your clothes off."

The car starts forward. Iris is holding her seat belt. She was about to buckle it, but now she's frozen.

"I'm sure you'll get used to it in a second," Iris argues. "I don't smell it anymore."

"Now," says Augusta. "Or I'll have this car pulled over and you can call yourself another cab."

Iris lets her seat belt slack back to the ceiling. She hesitates again but grabs the neck of her blouse and pulls it off. She balls it in her hands. She's unsure what to do with it, when Augusta pulls a little strap in the middle seat back. It opens to the trunk. She takes the blouse from Iris and tosses it through.

"Your jeans stink, too."

Iris starts shaking her head, but her fingers find the steel of her pants' button. She undoes it and yanks the zipper down. She slips her shoes off and then struggles to pull her pants off her ankles from the way she's sitting. She does so with a groan. She balls them up, too, and thinks of tossing them through the little compartment herself, but she wants Augusta to work for this. She hands her the pants.

Iris leans back in her seat and huffs, now mostly naked. Her head is craned towards the window.

"Everything, Iris."

"What?" The car is accelerating onto the highway now.

"Bra, underwear. This is my car. My rules."

Iris lets out a laugh. It's a short, awkward hiccup. It doesn't make her appear comfortable or like she's in control of the situation like she thought it might. "You want me to get completely naked? These don't smell." Iris pinches a cup of her bra and bends to sniff it. "They were covered by my clothes. They're clean."

Augusta pauses. She crosses her arms as if this was some elementary concept Iris was having difficulty grasping. She hits a little white button embedded in the door. It's the intercom. "Arthur? Would you pull over to let Iris out?" She lets go of the button, and Arthur's voice comes through the speaker.

"Certainly, ma'am." His southern accent is gone. His tone is cold. Orderly.

Iris looks out the window as the Cadillac pulls onto the shoulder. Cars race by them, and one truck honks. The shoulder of the highway is only a few feet of pavement that borders a swamp. The next exit is a mile or more ahead.

Iris doesn't move right away. Her heart is racing again. This is just a rich woman's power move, but then she realizes something else and begins to blush. It's the same feeling she had by the conference room door. Iris is *aroused*.

She blinks rapidly to clear her thoughts. It's not Augusta, is it? No, it's this control she has over others. This aura of power. It's the thought of being naked in this rich leather interior with the world oblivious just outside.

"Okay." Iris tucks both hands behind her back and deftly undoes her bra. She tosses it aside and hooks her thumbs into the sides of her underwear, and then she slips them off in one motion. She smushes them up in her fist and keeps them there.

Augusta doesn't look at her anymore. She stares out the window, a small, satisfied smile curls the corner of her lips. "Never mind, Arthur."

The car rolls forward.

Iris thought she'd feel uncomfortable—Augusta certainly hoped she'd be—but she's fine with being naked. She needs to remember she's not the helpless little widow she thought she was. She's learned something about herself today. She learned she wasn't just cruel. She was capable.

Iris lets out a quiet moan and wiggles her shoulders in her seat contently.

Augusta's smile fades. She purses her lips. Looks at her phone quickly. Now *she's* the one who's starting to squirm. And this is just how Iris thinks it should be.

This whole time, the Adler family has seemed dangerous. Iris spreads her legs, closes her eyes, and smiles as the AC tickles her skin. Now she's more afraid of who she used to be than she is of Augusta.

She thinks of the gun in her hand, the body in the truck bed. Those memories don't scare her like they did a few minutes ago. She feels something like relief. It all makes sense now.

As *dangerous* as these Adlers are, Iris is no different.

It takes a few minutes for Augusta to get comfortable. She starts to look at Iris, and the first time she does, her eyes find the scar on her hip.

They're taking turns like this is a tennis match. Now Iris begins to fidget. Augusta's eyes won't leave her side. She stares at the big square scar she has there. She stares at it like she knows exactly how Iris got it. Augusta has to have seen it before. There are pictures of them in bikinis together.

Iris wonders if she can ask her about the scar and still keep her confidence. Then she realizes she couldn't trust the answer, but she wants to hear what Augusta says anyway.

"Where'd I get it?"

Augusta doesn't deign to meet her eye. She keeps staring at the scar as she speaks. "Boiling water."

"Cooking hot dogs?" Iris teases.

Augusta makes eye contact. She pauses for emphasis. "Your sister poured it on you while you were sleeping."

Iris doesn't know how to respond to this. "Is that what I told you?"

"That is one of the many things you told us."

She says it like Iris has been feeding them lies for the past two years, and, Iris realizes, she's probably right.

The Nile

Iris waits in the car for Arthur to fetch her a robe once they get back to Sweet Blood. Augusta doesn't keep her company. She leaves her naked in the back seat, waiting, and the action acts as a last word to their little power struggle.

She won. Of course she did. Iris wasn't going to win a game like that against Augusta.

When Arthur returns with the robe, she takes it through the window but steps outside while still naked to put it on. Arthur spins and goes to the trunk. Once she has the robe tied, he approaches her with the file box of Joseph's things. "Here you are, miss."

"Thank you," Iris says, a little surprised. The clothes she took off are stuffed on top. Arthur and Aurelia are always carrying her things. Since her injury, Iris hasn't had to lug so much as her own purse into the house without someone offering to take it. This was an order from Augusta herself—Iris is done getting special treatment.

She hauls the box upstairs in nothing but her sneakers and a bathrobe. She sets it on her bed and shucks off the robe like it's an insult. Then she goes to the bathroom, showers, and comes back to the box once she's wearing clean clothes.

She takes the clothes she took off and walks towards the hamper, but halfway there she pauses. They don't even smell that bad. She holds them to her nose.

In fact, they don't smell at all. She was wearing a rubber coat when she toured. She'd only been in there for ten minutes. It makes sense the scent wouldn't stick to her.

She smells her hair, too. Nothing. There's a little shampoo scent if anything.

Augusta didn't smell Iris. She knew that she had been on the processing floor. Buddy or Becca had told her before she even went in. Iris's nudity was simply punishment.

"Goddamn it," she says aloud, and tosses her clothing into the hamper.

She goes back to the box and starts going through it. The box, too, is an insult. There's a fucking *stapler* in here. Iris takes out the golf balls, the pens, when suddenly she pauses.

There's a little tray filled with business cards. They're not Joseph's, but associates. She starts flipping through them slowly. Most are generic corporate titles of people in similar industries or other employees at Adler Corp. She's about to toss them down, when she flips to one that makes her jaw slack a little.

It's cream white with gold lettering. It reads, *Raymond Brady, Concierge, The Nile Hotel.*

Iris's eyes go to the bottom of the card. The address is for downtown Memphis.

She goes back to her dresser drawer just to make sure. She can't trust her memory at all anymore, but sure enough, when she pulls the picture out, the text on the bottom reads as she remembered.

Do you remember the Nile?

She thinks she's an idiot for not thinking of it before. This mystery man is talking about a hotel. She starts to feel the same fear she had in the slaughterhouse, but this time there are no memories to go with it.

She pulls out her phone. The Nile Hotel is a five-star establishment. It's just a few blocks from the Mississippi River. Her thumb hovers over the hotel's phone number. She thinks of calling, asking for Raymond, but instead she erases the search bar and types again.

She looks up flights from New Orleans to Memphis. There's one flight tonight—$700 a ticket.

She sits on the foot of the bed and thinks about how her evening will play out. She'll take a walk. Try to read. End up beyond bored with no new information to go on.

Iris goes to the airline's website and books her flight.

She's leaving tonight.

Personal Property

Iris packs as light as she can. She doesn't have a return ticket but doesn't think she'll stay in town for more than one night. She texts her sister, asking if she's free and in Memphis for the next 24 hours. Her sister is not a stranger.

Iris remembers her half sister, Lanie, as a mean, oval-faced, strawberry blonde. She doesn't remember her pouring boiling water on her. They would fight a lot, but Iris thinks that is an event significant enough to remember. The memories of her childhood are mostly intact.

Lanie texts back a single: *Ya.*

Iris goes on the Nile's website but can't find a room for tonight or tomorrow. It's short notice, and the hotel is sold out. She'll head there anyway, if not as a guest.

Iris then tries calling her mom, but it goes straight to voicemail. She hangs up on the automated message and sends a text to her instead, asking if she could stay with her. She got along somewhat better with her mom than with Lanie, but she wants to meet with them both regardless.

She packs her medications, her clothes, and a few toiletries. She keeps it as light as possible.

She can manage for a few days. She wants the freedom. Iris paces in front of the vanity, whispering to herself. She's rehearsing her speech to Augusta. It's leaving on such short notice that feels like it could be a problem.

If this is a game to Augusta, then she's going to retaliate.

As much as Iris doesn't like being here, she doesn't want to get kicked out of Sweet Blood, not when there's still so much she needs to learn. Leaving isn't as simple as getting an apartment.

Her and Joseph's finances have been taken over for the time being by the family trust. She uses a joint credit card they had, and the balance is paid out by a joint bank account. But the shared checking account is not stuffed with cash. She gets a transfer every month from the Adlers' wealth fund equal to her credit card balance.

She has money. Her husband's wealth is hers, but she doesn't have access to it. She's picturing being broke in her condition. Jobless. Clumsy. She couldn't get hired. If Augusta tries to keep Joseph's money, Iris will be in trouble.

A jury would side with her, the brain-damaged widow. But Augusta is not just smart, she's conniving. She could pull strings. Lie. Iris worries she might make it so there's no money to get.

Iris realizes if she's not careful, she could end up in a women's shelter while she lobbies for the money that's hers. And what infrastructure is there like that around here? Louisiana has many great things. A strong, social safety net is not one of them.

Iris will apologize, she decides. As genuinely as she can. She'll tell the truth—she's suffocated. Needs to see her mother. She'll be back in just a day or so when she's feeling better. She calls a cab again, and a little after seven, ten minutes before she's going to meet it at the front gate, Iris goes to look for Augusta.

She's not in her upstairs office. She might be in the master bedroom. A line of light shines from under the door. "Augusta? Are you in there?"

No response.

She turns the old ivory knob slowly. "Augusta?" she says again, louder. Iris is immediately surprised. Joseph is not in bed. She can hear the tub running in the bathroom. Aurelia or Augusta must be bathing him. But it's a little late in the day for that. And usually, baths are the part-time nurse's job. Joseph isn't bathed in the evenings as far as she's aware. But Iris is off about a lot of things, she thinks.

She's not going to barge into the master bathroom, so she goes back to her room and grabs her suitcase.

When Iris gets downstairs, she leaves her suitcase by the front door and checks the music room, the living room, the downstairs study, but Augusta is nowhere to be found. She's about to head back to the kitchen, when she walks by the front door again and smells sweetened cigarette smoke.

It's open a crack. She steps out onto the porch to see Augusta and Annabelle in rocking chairs side-by-side. Augusta is smoking. Neither is talking.

"Hello, Iris," Augusta says.

"Hi, I was trying to find you..." All the finely chosen words she had for this conversation leave her. Iris feels like a child. "I was going to—"

"That's an expensive ticket," Augusta interrupts her, blowing out smoke. "Seven hundred dollars?"

Iris is frozen. They're keeping that close of an eye on her credit card. "I think I need to see my mom. Get some space."

"That's a late flight, too. What's the rush, Iris?"

"I was feeling... claustrophobic. I want to see my mom."

"You hate your mom."

"You don't know that."

"What a foolish girl," Annabelle interrupts and talks to Augusta as if Iris is not there. No one says anything. A big beetle buzzes onto the porch and flies directly into a light bulb. *Ding.* It recoils and decides to give it another go. *Ding.*

It flies off, and the women are silent. The chirp of crickets is few and far between. It makes the night lonely. The pesticides from the sugarcane fields kill most of everything here, too.

Annabelle speaks again. "You're not going anywhere, Iris."

Iris feels her blood pressure rise immediately. "What?"

Annabelle keeps rocking. Her eyes are on the dark lawn. "You're not going to Memphis."

"And who do you think you are?" Iris sees headlights near the gate. Her heart sinks as she thinks it might be the security contractor's truck, but the headlights are low. It's a sedan. Her cab. "I've got to go." She goes inside to grab her suitcase, and when she's back on the porch, Annabelle is standing in her way.

"Look, I know things aren't easy for you, Iris, but you need to try to think your actions through. We still don't have the first clue who did this to you and murdered my brother-in-law. You can't just wander off. You're a liability. A threat to all of us."

Iris's hands sweat as she holds her suitcase. She keeps looking to Augusta to see what she has to say, but she isn't even watching them. She looks deep in thought and keeps rocking in her chair, seemingly oblivious to this exchange.

"I can't just sit in bubble wrap forever. It's been months. If you're so fucking afraid, why don't you have some of your hired guns follow me around?"

Annabelle puts her hands on her hips. She snickers like what Iris said was stupid, but she's just buying time. She doesn't have a retort.

"It's not for you to decide anymore. Do you even realize how brain damaged you are?"

"I've been a lot better."

Iris starts to move towards the porch steps, but Annabelle moves with her like a defender. "Oh yeah? Who was your driver today?"

Iris pauses. "What?"

"Who drove you to the plant?"

"Arthur did."

Annabelle smiles. "Yeah, that's what Augusta told me you were calling him all day. It was Richard. Arthur doesn't work Tuesdays."

"What are you talking about? I even heard Augusta call him Arthur several times." Iris is suddenly worried. She swore it was Arthur. "Augusta, it was Arthur, right?"

Augusta doesn't say anything. She flicks her cigarette over the railing, not bothering to save the butt.

"It was Arthur, right?" Iris is sweating. She didn't even know there were two drivers. This little bit of information alone makes her heart pound with doubt.

Augusta opens her mouth to talk, shuts it, licks her lip. It looks like it pains her to speak. "It was Richard, Iris."

Iris is silent. She loosens her grip on her suitcase. "Why didn't you correct me?"

Annabelle answers for her. "Because if we corrected you every single fucking time your brain slipped up, we'd never be done talking to you."

"Annabelle," Augusta says, warningly.

"You're not mentally well enough to so much as use a microwave, and you want to get on an airplane?"

Iris can't even respond. She's thinking of earlier today. She tries to picture Arthur standing by the back of the car, opening the door for them, but suddenly the memory of his face blurs. She never really *looked* at him.

Annabelle puts her hand on Iris's suitcase. "You're putting everybody in this family at risk. Now go inside and put the suitcase away."

Iris is getting angry. Annabelle is abrasive. Her sharp, jutted jaw and clumpy mascara aren't winning Iris over.

If Augusta was talking her down from this, maybe she'd listen. Augusta, in fact, doesn't seem to be very interested at all. Something is bothering her. She still isn't watching them.

Iris yanks her suitcase into her own hands and steps around Annabelle. She doesn't have any witty rejoinder. She's just trying not to cry. "I'm a grown woman. I can still go where I want."

Iris suddenly feels her neck twist sideways. Annabelle has grabbed her hair close to the roots and pulled.

"Maybe you don't understand. We weren't asking."

Iris's first instinct is to push Annabelle away, but with her head twisted, she's eye level with her pregnant belly. She drops her suitcase, and it goes clopping down the porch steps and hits the grass with a thump. She keeps her hands to herself. Instead of fighting back, she grabs onto Annabelle's hands to try to loosen her grip.

"Get the fuck off me! Ahh," Iris moans in pain.

Annabelle yanks harder and Iris is suddenly scared. Her neck has been twisted too far. It feels like if Annabelle twists another inch, her neck will snap.

"Augusta," Iris finds herself begging. "Augusta, please help me." Annabelle pulls again, and Iris yields and steps closer to her so she's not so twisted.

Iris can see Augusta looking at them now, but even with this entire altercation she's still not standing. "Annabelle," Augusta says, but Iris suddenly screams in pain as Annabelle tugs.

"Annabelle!"

Her grip loosens.

"Let her go."

Annabelle bends to look Iris in the eye. "Are you going to stay and behave?"

"I don't just mean let go of her hair," Augusta says sternly. "Let her *go*, now."

"But you said—"

"I know what I said," she snaps. "Let her go!"

Annabelle releases her hair, and Iris shoots up straight with the pressure gone.

She stumbles down the steps like a frightened animal and picks up her suitcase. The porch light is distorted into dozens of razor-sharp lines, and Iris realizes she's crying. She tries to keep her dignity by quickly turning from them both and starting up the road.

Neither of the women call after her, but Iris can feel their eyes on her back.

Iris is enraged. Her head pulses. For the first time since leaving the hospital, she thinks she can feel her scar throb.

She resolves that she'll never set foot in Sweet Blood again. She'll have her things boxed up and will pick them up from the porch. She's cooled down only a little by the time she reaches the gate.

The porch light is still on. She can see Annabelle leaning against one of the columns. Augusta is still in her rocking chair.

"Fucking freaks," Iris says aloud. She almost wants to flip them off, but she already feels like a teenager. The cab is idling just on the other side of the gate. But there's a problem. The gate won't open. She forgot the code again.

147

"Damn it," Iris groans and tilts her head at the sky.

Is this why Augusta let her go? It's all about humiliation, isn't it? Power. Control. She expects to see her goons come by in the truck any second to tell the cabbie to get lost. But no one comes. Augusta and Annabelle still haven't moved from the porch. They still haven't stopped watching her.

Suddenly, Iris hears a motor whine, and the gate begins to creak as it glides open. So, she gets to leave. Even so, she feels defeated, but it's not for the argument or her failure to win the fight with Annabelle. Iris looks over her shoulder at Sweet Blood one more time.

She's defeated because she knows she'll be back.

Red Eye

Lanie had agreed to pick Iris up from the airport and take her to their mom's house. She could use the directions. But when she lands in Memphis and checks her phone while they're taxiing, she sees that Lanie never texted her back after Iris texted her that she was taking off.

It's raining lightly here, and in the distance, there's a lightning storm strobing in a cloudbank. She can't see any bolts. It's just flash after flash after flash. Whether that weather has only just passed or is on its way here now, Iris doesn't know. She pulls out her phone. The Apple weather app flashes, too, with a dramatic lightning bolt—100% chance of thunderstorms for the next three hours and then rain all night into tomorrow.

She didn't pack a raincoat. She rationalizes that maybe this was the way she was before she was shot, too. She just doesn't know if she was forgetful or organized. Whether she liked plans or flying by the seat of her pants. These are questions hopefully her mom and sister can answer.

Iris goes to the arrivals area, even though she doesn't know what car to look for. She tries calling her sister. It rings and rings until a robotic voice alerts her that this number's voicemail box is full. Iris puts her phone away and starts towards the taxis.

Lanie must've fallen asleep, that's all. She's going to have to get a hotel. She's about to search for one when she gets a text. It's from Lanie.

Cant come to give you a ride. Mom address is 22826 Cole Street

So she's not asleep. She's high. Iris is annoyed until she looks up the address on her phone and the maps app shows the address in *West* Memphis, just across the Mississippi in Arkansas. She didn't grow up in Arkansas. She knows that much from her Tennessee-issued driver's license.

She clicks on Google Street View. 22826 is a teeny little thing. It's so narrow it looks like a long jumper could leap from one side of the house to the next. There's an overgrown lawn out front. Next door is a vacant lot. Iris knew she wasn't from a nice part of town, but this can't be right. Her mom must've moved.

She thinks she should head there in the daylight. But despite the hour she's wide awake. If her mom's expecting her, she's not about to settle for a hotel room.

Her connection in Atlanta made this a late flight. It's past one in the morning, and there are only a few taxis waiting for arrivals. Iris manages to get one. The cabbie wears loose jeans and an equally baggy T-shirt. He has a goatee and a diamond stud earring. He doesn't make eye contact as he opens the door for Iris.

"Where to?" he asks, getting behind the wheel. He sniffs and wipes his nose. It's not cold season. Or allergy season. He sniffs again. His fingers drum the steering wheel. A late-night cabbie high on some kind of speed. Of course that's her luck on this dark and stormy night.

Iris sighs. "Um. West Memphis," she says, and before she even gives the address number, the cab takes off.

They're quiet for the entire drive, and Iris pretends to scroll on her phone but is really making sure they're staying on route until they're only a few blocks away. Then she relaxes and puts her phone into her pocket.

She watches the houses go by. Most are falling apart. A few are abandoned, missing windowpanes. Their sides are graffitied with big bubble letters.

The cab starts to pull over. He looks at Iris skeptically in the rearview. His eyes alone say what Iris is thinking. *You don't belong here.*

At least not anymore. Iris remembers poverty, but it was when she was a child. She's since been removed.

The cab pulls up in front of a blue house. It's the same one from Google Maps, but it looks far more unpleasant in the dark and the rain.

"This is you," says the cabbie.

"Oh, thank you." Iris pulls out her Visa and holds the card's chip against the reader.

The machine gives her three angry honks. *Card Declined,* the screen reads.

Her brow grows hot as she blushes. She doesn't have another card.

Iris doesn't have to try her card again to know what happened, but she does anyway. *Fuck, fuck, fuck,* she thinks and starts to bite her lip. *Honk! Honk! Honk*! The card reader responds angrily.

"Try swiping it," The cabbie is staring at her in the rearview.

Iris opens her wallet, but she knows she has no cash. There's just the one credit card she shared with Joseph. If she could see how much the ticket cost, of course she could shut it down.

"I think my card stopped working."

"You got cash?"

"No."

"Alright, just Venmo me then."

"Uh-huh." Iris laughs nervously. She probably used to have a Venmo, but redownloading a cash app hasn't been a high priority since getting a new phone and leaving the hospital. "I don't have one."

He sighs. "Look, it's twenty-five-bucks. Can you go ask your friend?" He nods towards her mom's house.

"Yeah. Okay, just a second."

Iris gets out of the taxi. She turns towards the trunk, expecting the cabbie to pop it so she can grab her suitcase, but apparently it's collateral. It stays closed.

Iris ducks and walks quickly through the rain and up the front stairs. She knocks on the white wooden screen door, but the sound isn't very loud. She opens it, steps into a musty box of a porch, and knocks on the front door. Then she hits the doorbell. There's no sound from inside. No window in the door, either.

"Hello? Mom, it's your daughter. It's Iris!" She knocks again. There's no response from inside. Iris turns over her shoulder. The cab's wipers are at full speed, throwing the rain off the windshield left and right. She knocks again and tries the handle at the same time.

The door is unlocked and opens silently. There are no lights on. The living room is right in front of her, and the kitchen is just past it. There's the glow of appliance LEDs. The stench of cat litter behind it. The cabbie honks, and Iris starts fondling the wall for a light switch. She flips one on, and the living room lights up in a dark shade of yellow.

There's a cracked leather couch, an old box TV. Stained tan carpet and tan walls. The one thing Iris can say is that it looks somewhat clean. There's not much clutter. No old magazines or dishes left lying around.

"Mom? It's Iris." She can't hear the rain anymore. The room is dead silent, and she can hear the *thump thump* of her nervous heart. *What if Lanie sent her the wrong address? What if this whole thing was a set up?*

She senses something behind her and spins. She gasps as she sees the cab driver. He's looking around the place as if assessing it for valuables, or… Iris backs up. Privacy.

"This your momma's place?" He's holding her suitcase and sets it down inside the door. He must have heard her calling.

"You can't be in here. I'll get your money. Just get out."

"You're stealing from me right now. I don't have to go anywhere." He sniffs. "She home?"

Iris doesn't like his questions. He's tall but not broad. His narrow shoulders make him look sharp. Dangerous. "If she's not, she will be any minute. She gets off work at one," she lies.

"I don't have time for this shit. I gotta be back at the airport." He points a long finger at her. "This is comin' out of my pay. Give me something worth twenty-five bucks and we're square." He looks her over from head to toe. Telling her with his eyes that he might know something of equal or greater value.

Iris goes cold. She starts to back towards the kitchen. "I... I'll look." She walks in and turns on the light. What she looks for first is a knife. There's a block full of them at the end of the counter. When she turns again, the cabbie is even closer behind her. He's moving quietly on this carpet. She goes to the counter by the knives and turns so she faces him.

A knife won't do her much good. His arms are probably a foot longer than her own. He'll grab her wrist before she can get close, take her to the kitchen floor...

"This might work." The cabbie reaches on top of the fridge, where there's a line of liquor bottles. They clink as he paws through them.

Iris is silent. Is he looking for a weapon too?

Iris maneuvers her hand behind her. She takes a knife from the block and holds it behind her back.

He's taking too long. The tall cabbie is eye level with the fridge top. He can easily see what liquor there is, but he carefully considers each.

"Ah." He finds a tall bottle of vodka. Grey Goose. It's near the back and looks unopened. It's probably been saved for a special occasion. "This works." He doesn't ask if he can take it. He just plucks the bottle up and starts walking towards the front door. He vanishes without turning. Without even saying another word to Iris.

She remembers that this is how people treat you when you're poor. This is how you are. Vulnerable to the law. Vulnerable to everybody.

She hears him clomp down the steps, and she races to the front with the knife in hand. He jogs to the driver's seat, and Iris watches him uncap the vodka and tilt the big bottle up to take a quick drink. When he's done drinking, the car still doesn't move. Only once music begins to blare does the cab pull away with a swish on the wet road.

Iris relaxes. The drinking and the speed at which he pulled away all suggest he was no longer interested in her after finding the booze. Some cab driver, she thinks.

She locks the front door and looks around. There is no upstairs, and it would appear that there's only a single bed and bathroom, which are both behind a shut door just off the living room.

Now that the threat is gone, Iris feels a little more confident. She goes over and opens the bedroom door. It's lighter in here. The blinds are open, and Iris can see the shadows of everything. Bathroom door, dresser, nightstand, bed...

There's a lump under the covers. "Mom?" Iris says softly.

The blankets jostle. Whoever is under them is now staring back at Iris from the dark. A nightstand light is switched on, and for a moment, Iris doesn't recognize her mother.

She looks decades older than Iris remembers her. She looks like she could be in her seventies but she's twenty years younger than that. Yellow bruises splotch her face like continents on a made-up map. "Iris, my love. Is that you?"

Iris doesn't respond right away. She can smell the alcohol in the air. Iris knows for a fact that she is not her mother's *love.*

Either way, she goes over to the side of the bed and helps her tottering mother to her feet.

154

Down the Block and Out the Back

Iris tries to give her a hand, but her mother waves her off like she's being ridiculous.

Iris can smell how she slept through all her yelling. Her mother—Julie—smells ripe. It's like she's drunk so much, her insides are now fermenting.

"Your sister told me you were coming. I must've fallen asleep."

"You can go back to bed. We can talk in the morning."

"I need some water." Her mother goes to the bathroom. The faucet runs, and then she sits and pees with the door open while Iris stands idly.

Her mother shuffles out of the bathroom and passes Iris to the living room. "I'll make some coffee."

"It's two in the morning." Iris trails her. "I'd still like to get some sleep if that's okay?"

"Decaf, then." Julie stops and faces Iris. "You're not wearing your wedding ring anymore."

"Huh?"

Julie points to her hand. "You were wearing it while you were in the hospital. That big rectangular rock."

"Oh. Yeah. It didn't feel right anymore."

Julie looks away and keeps going towards the kitchen. "So, you're still staying at that plantation? I've looked at pictures online." She starts to fill the coffee maker.

"Yeah."

"You've come a long way from here. You get lots of money? Did you get your husband's?"

"Um, not quite yet. It's with the family account."

"Ooo. You might wanna change that."

Iris changes the subject. "I was still pretty out of it in the hospital. I don't remember you visiting. I'm sorry."

155

"I hadn't seen you for five years before that. Not since you came by here to steal from my purse." Julie fills the coffeepot with water and pulls out a tin of decaf.

"I used to steal from you?"

"Oh, you don't remember that? You little addict."

"I'm sorry?"

"Oh, how convenient for you to have forgotten. You don't remember shootin' heroin?"

"Mom—"

"We saved you. You're only still alive because of your sister and me. And what do we get in return? Nothin'."

"Oh yeah? How'd you save me?"

Her mom is stumped on this one. She can't give an answer. "You decide to waltz back into my life for the first time in half a decade to back talk me?"

Iris doesn't bother to respond. She's being gaslit, surely. Again.

A heavy sadness causes her shoulders to slouch. Is this what happens when you have money and a brain injury? The vault is open. The second people are able to question your reality they swoop in. Their lies like sharpened shovelheads. All hoping to collect their heap of gold.

She's not going to listen to her mom. Iris was a college student. Ambitious. She was not a heroin addict.

"When you dropped off the face of the earth, I figured you ran away with some asshole or overdosed. Imagine my surprise when I get a phone call that you were shot and find out how much money you had all along. You *owe* us."

There it is.

"I didn't even know you were married. Now you gots the guts to come into my house when we're starving, Iris."

Iris looks at the hundreds of dollars of booze above the fridge. Again, she's quiet. This is how she used to be with her mom, she can remember. Just let her yell it out. Iris can tell that her mom isn't just a little tipsy. She's still quite drunk.

"So what did you come back here for, Iris? Did you come back to see me and your sister? Save us from squalor? How much money do you have access to, anyway?"

Iris feels exhausted. It's too late for this. She throws it back at her. "I actually need to borrow a little cash while I'm in town. There's a problem with my card. It's not working."

"You think *I'm* going to give *you* money?"

"I was thinking... I'll pay you back more than triple. I can wire three times whatever you can give me once I'm home."

Julie crosses her arms and considers this. "Ten times."

"Okay."

"No. Twenty."

"Mom."

"Do you see where I live? While you live in a goddamn palace. God damn *you*. You never sent money back to us. You didn't even let us know you were alive."

There was a good reason for that, Iris thinks.

"Okay," Iris says. "Twenty times. How much do you have in cash?"

Julie walks to the bedroom. It's as quick as she's seen her move since she got here. She comes back fanning four twenties. "Eighty dollars. What will that be?"

Iris has to think. She still remembers her multiplication, but it takes a moment. Eight times two. Add some zeroes. She almost reaches for her phone before it comes to her. "Sixteen hundred."

Julie smiles at the number and gives Iris the cash. It's the first time her face hasn't been shrouded with hate. It should be enough for lunch tomorrow and cab fare to the airport. From there she'll have to make some calls. Beg Augusta to get home. That's what she wants, after all.

"Oh! I got some quarters in the bedroom. Let me fetch those, too."

"I don't need any change, Mom. The eighty bucks is fine."

"Oh screw you! Too good for anything less than a twenty-dollar bill, are ya?"

"I didn't say that. I can't buy things with coins."

"Imagine being so rich that you think quarters are worthless. I have at least another six dollars."

"Mom. Stop."

Julie shuts her mouth, and it twists in a grimace. She grabs a coffee mug, but the decaf is still brewing. She goes towards the fridge and pulls a little step stool out from against the wall with her foot.

She climbs up and wraps her hand around a bottle of brown rum, but then she freezes.

Iris watches her nervously.

"My vodka is missing."

"I was going to tell you. Like I was saying, my card wasn't working, and I didn't have any money for the cab driver. I was calling for you, but you weren't answering. I didn't think you were home."

"So you gave him my vodka?"

"I was afraid. He followed me inside. I—"

"You let a stranger into my house?" Julie's face is contorted with rage.

"Are you listening to me?" Iris is at the point where she could explode. "He followed me in."

"And stole my booze?"

"I thought he was going to hurt me!"

"I don't give a shit. You're a big girl. Go on. Go get me another bottle."

Iris grits her teeth. Breathes. If she has to walk out of here in the rain to get a motel tonight, she might not have enough money to get back to the airport. "It's the middle of the night. Nothing is open."

"Spoiled fucking rotten. How that happened with me raising you, I have no idea." Julie pulls the rum bottle down and starts to fill the coffee mug. The bottle glugs four times before she finishes pouring.

She takes a sip, but the alcohol doesn't cool her. "I let you stay in my home, and the first thing you do is ask for my money

158

and give my things away. You in your palace with your millions. You're a disgrace, Iris. Iris the virus. The *leech*."

Iris swallows hard and starts to sweat. This is what she remembers about her mother. Verbal abuse. The stench of booze. Lies. Louisiana wasn't far enough away from this shithole. But Iris is smart enough not to take the bait. Her mom wants a screaming match.

"I'm going back to bed." Julie storms past her, mug reeking of rum. Her bedroom door slams, and Iris listens to the coffeepot hiss and gurgle. She walks over, grabs the cord, and rips it from the wall.

The second she saw the address that Lanie texted her, she should've gone to a motel. But with her card canceled, she wouldn't have been able to get a room. All roads would've led to this dank little house.

Iris's only saving grace is that she's exhausted. She turns off the kitchen light and adjusts the pillows on the leather couch to get ready to go to sleep.

She changes into a pair of sweatpants from her suitcase and brushes her teeth at the kitchen sink. Then she gets settled down on the couch.

There's a blanket folded on the coffee table, and Iris drapes it over herself. It's raining harder now. She can hear it on the roof. She hopes it will lull her to sleep, but as soon as she begins to fade away, the memory of the truck and the girl and the fire begins to play again in her head.

She sits up, breathing heavily.

Is that why she's really here? Iris thinks. Is that why she jumped on a plane? She's really just running from that burning girl?

Before she can give it any more thought, there's a click in the kitchen. She turns toward it. It's even darker than it was when she first came into the house. She sees the clock on the microwave is dead.

The power is out, Iris realizes. She sits up all the way. Heart racing. She sees a motion light turn on in the backyard. It must be battery powered. She rises and goes to the kitchen window quickly, but when she looks out, she doesn't see anyone in the arc of light it casts. Just wet, overgrown grass and rain pattering into puddles.

Iris's gut is screaming that something is wrong. It's probably just from the stress. First the cabbie and then her mom's yelling. Her brain is primed to go into fight-or-flight.

She walks into the living room and looks out the front window towards the street. There are lights on in a couple houses on the block next door. The outage isn't neighborhood wide. It's just this house. Her gut is right.

Suddenly, something else catches her eye. There's a man in a long black coat walking away from the house. He crosses the street to a parked SUV and opens the driver's door.

She reasons it's just a neighbor, but then she thinks that the raincoat the man wears is too formal for a neighborhood like this. It's long, collared, and reaches past his knees. The SUV, too, looks like a brand-new model.

Okay. Iris takes a deep breath, trying to steady herself. If Augusta sent someone to spy on her, she'd probably make it obvious like the tail she had in New Orleans, but this car is parked towards the *end* of the block. There are plenty of spaces he could park just out front.

She watches the man twist something with one hand. He's rotating something round and round. He shuts the car door gently, quietly, with a slow press of his hand and turns back towards the house.

She watches him tuck something long into his raincoat. She saw it clearly, but she's too dumbfounded to even process what she saw for a moment. He keeps his hand there as he walks. Iris flinches away from the window. She realizes exactly what he's holding: a pistol with one of those long silencers attached to the barrel.

This feels like a nightmare. She looks back to the couch as if she might see herself sleeping there. The hair on her arms and neck stand on end. Her blood is buzzing.

This is real life.

She whips back around to face the window. There's no doubt the man is coming towards the house. He's only ten seconds away from the front door. Iris grabs her shoes, her phone, and even the money her mom gave her, and then she sprints into the kitchen. There's a little metal squeak just as she gets to the back door. She pauses and turns. It's too dark to see, but she knows what's happening. He's turning the front door to find that it's locked. Iris opens the back as quietly as she can and starts to sprint.

Prey

She didn't have time to put her shoes on, and when she's almost to the alley, she hears a bang. She thinks it's a gunshot but then thinks the sound was too wooden. She keeps running, realizing it must be the front door being kicked in. Iris runs until she gets around the corner and then hobbles as she quickly slides on her shoes.

Her soaked socks get balled down on her feet as she puts them on. Her heels are naked.

At the end of the alley, she stops and throws herself against the wall of a garage. She peers out towards the back of her mom's house. It's loud from all the dripping water. It races from downspouts and falls in a steady stream from the corner of the gutter next to her.

It's the man who shot her back to finish the job. Augusta and Annabelle were right. She never should've left Sweet Blood.

She reaches for her phone and panics. She pats her sweatpants furiously, but it's not in either pocket. She looks back the way she had run and sees it right away. The screen is a little black rectangle on the cement. It fell out almost as soon as she started sprinting. She didn't even hear it.

She wants to retrieve it, but just then a figure comes out of the black from her mom's backyard. He's wearing a blue surgical mask. One hand is still tucked into his coat, no doubt holding the gun. He sees her phone immediately and bends to pick it up. He suddenly whips his head towards Iris, as if he sensed someone watching. She ducks behind the garage. She thinks she was able to get back behind the edge before he saw her, but she's not about to look and see. She's sprinting again, dodging puddles, trying to make as little noise as she can.

She thinks quickly and turns left into the next alley.

She takes a sharp right into the little sliver of space between two garages, but the back is fenced. There's no way through, and

162

she'd make too much noise climbing the chain links. She turns to go back to the alley, but then her eyes go wide.

She hears wet footsteps clopping, getting closer. They slow, and Iris starts to hear plastic thud after plastic thud. She frowns. He's searching the garbage bins. He's probably looking in the spaces between the garages, too.

How'd he know I stopped? Can he hear my running steps?

She wants to scream from anxiety. She can't run out of here anymore. She's trapped. The decision is made for her. She has to climb the fence and the sooner the better. He'll hear her the second she sets a foot on it.

She gets a short running start and jumps up. It's only six feet, but her sneakers slip on the wet links. She can't get a grip. The footsteps resume pounding. They're running towards her now.

She scurries over, falls hard on the grass, and jumps to her feet. The whole backyard is fenced, but she can't run straight ahead. He could shoot her through the fence while she tries to climb another if she did. She turns hard left and climbs again.

She doesn't fall so hard this time. She lands on her feet in stride and starts towards the street. A dog erupts into barks behind her. She doesn't even turn. Her ass puckers and her arms pump. The next fence is shorter—four and a half feet. She can't clear it in one jump. Instead, she grabs onto the top bar while in motion and swings her legs over. The dog crashes into the chain link.

A light turns on in the house.

"Help me!" Iris screams as she starts to run. "Somebody help me! He's trying to kill me!"

That's as much breath as she can give to getting someone to call the police. She has to keep running.

The man can't take the same route, not now that the dog is already on alert. Unless he's willing to shoot it. But he's probably only been slowed by seconds. He's going to be faster than her.

She *can't* keep running and the problem is that he doesn't need to catch her. He only needs to have a shot. This is the only time she's going to be out of sight, and she needs to make use of it. The dog on the other side of the fence has run to the opposite side of the yard, presumably to bark at her pursuer.

She's in a strip of grass between two houses and sees an uncovered window well. It's right next to the last fence she hopped. It's so close to the yard, she thinks the man might not even consider she stopped to hide there.

She crawls into it and waits. It's only three feet deep, and she has to crouch down to not be seen over the top.

If Iris is wrong, this is it. There's no getting out of this hole. The window to the basement isn't large enough for her to get through. At least not quickly. If she tried to wiggle through, she'd get stabbed in the gut by the broken glass and shot in the back.

Iris begins to breathe. She's waiting to hear a door open or somebody to yell from the house, but maybe on this rainy night she wasn't loud enough. But she doesn't hear the man either. The dog gives off a few last barks, these ones less urgent.

The silence comes on fast. All Iris can hear is the deep thump of her heart and the rain pelting everything. The roofs, the grass, her head. The wind blows. The rain drum rolls, falls normally, and then drum rolls again. The thunder is over. It's just heavy rain that is left.

Iris peeks over the steel lip of the well and looks towards the street. She stares at it for a long time. Five minutes. Ten. No one passes.

She's starting to feel a little better. She thinks her yelling did the trick. He probably wasn't going to stick around to risk that somebody heard her and called the police. He took off.

Iris climbs out of the window well. She's soaked through now. Rivulets of rain pour from her hair. Her feet squish in her shoes.

She starts towards the street slowly, but as she nears the gap between the two houses where the front yards begin, she freezes.

She's being an idiot. The police aren't coming. There's no commotion in the neighborhood. Her killer would know this. He might not be here, but he's nearby.

He's waiting just like her. Waiting for Iris to get confident and step into sight. She shivers as the wind blows and goes to hunker back down in the window well. He wouldn't be able to see her head in the darkness she's in, but Iris can see the street. She watches it madly. Her eyes fixed, unblinking. She's going to win this waiting game.

It feels like an eternity before the sky begins to lighten.

Dawn

Iris has never been happier to see the sun. The storm blew off only twenty minutes before sunrise. The sky is all scattered clouds now. The sun shines on the wet pavement and puddles, casting everything in a lovely gold.

To Iris, it feels like victory. It's still not enough to get her to come out of hiding. She's waiting for people. The first commuters to head out to their cars. She's heard a few engines start around her, but none close enough to lure her out.

Finally, she sees a man in coveralls walk out of his front door with a lunch pail. Iris practically jumps out of the window well. She starts to run to him. "Hey!"

The man stops on the sidewalk and stares at her. His expression is skeptical. He leans back a little like she might be a threat.

Iris crosses the street, and it's only when she sees how angry the man appears that she realizes how much she must look like a junkie. Soaked in her sweatpants, crazed at dawn. This neighborhood probably doesn't have a shortage of the type.

She has to choose her words carefully to be believed. Assassin is a word she should probably avoid.

"I'm sorry," Iris says. "But my mom got drunk and locked me out in the storm. There's a man…" Iris pauses. "Her boyfriend's dangerous. I think he hurt her. Can you call the police for me?"

The man looks left and right like this might be a setup. Then he looks back to Iris before speaking. "You can't use my phone. Sorry." He starts to walk to his car.

"You call them! I don't need to touch your phone. Please."

He stops again. Sighs. "Fine. But I ain't stickin' around for them to get here. Could be a whole hour around here."

"Okay," Iris says like it's no big deal, but her stomach sinks. There's no one else out. If this killer is still waiting for her— watching her now—he'll have another opportunity.

166

The man in coveralls takes a few steps towards his stoop and puts his phone to his ear. She tries to follow, but from his hunched posture, she realizes he doesn't want her to hear.

A few things he says louder. "No, I gotta go to work." And then he turns to her. "Where's your momma's house?"

"A block over—228..." Iris trails off. *Fuck.* She can't remember the rest of the numbers. "It's a block over. Cole Street, but just have them come here."

He turns back around. His tone is hushed. Even if the police think she's an addict, they'll send a cruiser. It just might be a while.

"Okay," he says louder as he gets ready to hang up. "Okay," he says again and brings his phone down. He looks at Iris only briefly as he starts towards the street. "They'll be here in twenty minutes."

"Melvin?" A woman in her pajamas opens the front door. "What's going on?"

"Family problems next door. Police are on it. Don't worry."

"Girl, you are *soaked*." The woman steps outside quickly in her bare feet and goes to Iris. "Oh, are you okay?"

"I'm a little cold."

"Let's get you some dry clothes. Come on."

"Don't let her inside. Not when I'm not home," Melvin says.

"What would this young lady think we have worth stealin'?"

Melvin harumphs and walks on to the car.

"Come on, sugar." The woman takes her by the arm. She's older, of mixed race. Her hair is somewhat red. "We'll get you fixed up."

Iris starts to cry a little but keeps her expression composed. "Thank you."

"Of course."

When they're inside and the door shuts, Iris feels like she could melt.

"Let me get you something to put on." The woman disappears for more than a couple minutes and comes out with a neat stack of clothes folded in her arms. It's fresh everything. Socks, underwear, shirt, pants. On the top is even a hair clip.

Iris stands. "I can't thank you enough."

"I just hope someone would do the same for me. Bathroom is just to your left there."

Iris takes the clothes and goes to change. She lets her wet clothes ball and pool around her feet. She rings her shirt out in the sink and yellow-brown water drips into the drain.

She puts on a pair of jeans that are a little large and a baggy men's sweatshirt. She twists her hair back into the clip. She's about to assess herself in the mirror when there's a knock on the door.

Iris panics. It hasn't been long enough for it to be the police. "No," she says aloud. "No!" Iris throws open the bathroom door and turns towards the entrance. "Don't..." Iris starts, but she doesn't finish her sentence.

There are two cops on the stairs. One is bald and black and has one foot perched a stair higher than the other, like he's Captain Morgan. The other is pale enough to be his ghost, but not large enough. As relieved as she is to see the police, she wishes she could've gotten a woman officer.

"Hey there," says the bald one. "What's your name?"

"Iris."

"Would you step outside for us, Iris?"

She goes down the stairs, and the cops walk back onto the lawn.

"What's going on this morning, Iris?" says the one with the thin mustache.

Iris has to be even more careful with her story with the police. She hasn't slept in twenty-four hours. Her eyes are bloodshot. Her brain is misfiring. One wrong word, and she's in a hole trying to convince these cops not to take her to detox.

"It's my mom's house. Can we just go there? There was a home intruder this morning. I ran out to get help."

The cops both frown. "Dispatch says you spent all night in the rain?"

"Oh, not that long. No. It took a long time to find someone who would help me. I didn't have my phone to call you guys myself."

Iris needs to get her story straight. She can't just tell the truth of what she saw. Could she say she was shot in the head and her assassin is back to finish the job? No, Iris realizes. She'd be taken to detox.

"Let's just go there. Trust me, you'll see a crime scene. He kicked the door in. It's just on the other block."

"Okay." The bald cop nods his head back towards his cruiser. "Let's go."

Blood Relations

The cops let Iris get out of the backseat when they pull around to her mom's house. The place looks normal, nicer than it did in the storm. Birds chirp and flutter between bushes. The air is cool after the rain. The cops look disinterested. They walk so Iris is a little bit behind them.

When the officers reach the screen door, they immediately reach for their holsters.

"We got forced entry."

She can see the door has been kicked in, and it leans buckled in the frame like a drunk.

"Police department!" the cops yell as they head inside with guns drawn.

Iris stays out front. It's only a few seconds later that a woman starts yelling inside, and Iris rushes in to follow the police.

They're both putting their guns away at the kitchen entrance. Iris can see her mother sitting at the table. Another woman is in the chair next to her. It's her half sister, Lanie. She has her hair cut short. Her bangs hang down from her forehead like an ax blade. She's the one yelling, not her mother.

"Oh! And there she is! Get in here."

Lanie doesn't look happy to see her. "Who did this, Iris? Did you really come back home just to terrify Mom?"

The cops turn to Iris, but she doesn't speak to them. "Did you see him, Mom?"

"I woke up twenty minutes ago when your sister came over. What the hell did you do to the door? Who's this *him* you're talking about? That fucking cab driver you helped rob me came back here, didn't he?"

"Cab driver?" one of the cops repeats.

Iris considers what to say as they all stare at her. There's an active investigation into her attempted murder, and she could prove this easily, but she doesn't think her story is worth telling. What are they going to do about it? Put out an APB for a man with a nice raincoat who drives an American-made SUV? The taxi driver is a good out, Iris thinks. She needs to get out of this situation and on with this trip. She needs to get to the Nile.

"My card got declined, and I didn't have cash. The driver got pissed and followed me inside. He took a bottle of Vodka to call it even."

"Stole," her mother adds.

"Yeah. Stole. I saw him drink some behind the wheel. He must've come back here later looking for me. Kicked the door in."

"Why would he be looking for you?" the bald cop asks.

"Because he was… into me. Wouldn't stop undressing me with his eyes. I think he was high on something, too."

"And when he broke in here, you just left your mother alone with him?"

Iris stutters. She feels like she is staring at a jury. "He was after *me*. I mean, I was right, wasn't I? He didn't even wake you up, Mom."

"And what time was this?"

"I don't know," Iris lies. "Before sunrise. I couldn't say. I just ran."

"Did he take anything else?" The mustached cop looks at Iris's mom.

Julie pauses, thinking. "He took my MacBook! It was charging right on the kitchen counter."

There was never any computer on the kitchen counter. Iris knows this.

"That's two thousand dollars and the door is at least another grand. Who's paying for this, Iris?"

Iris is not about to debate the existence of a laptop in front of the police. She just wants to shut her mom up.

"I'll write you a big check, Mom."

"I'll be fixin' to sue if not." She leans back and crosses her arms.

171

Iris gives them the rest of the details about the cab driver, and the police give her and her mom a detective's information to get in contact with. At one point, Iris goes out the back to look for her phone, but the man must've kept it.

When she goes back in, Lanie is looking at Iris's hands. "Not wearing that big flashy ring of yours anymore?" Lanie asks.

"Hmm?"

"Your wedding ring. You didn't wear it?"

"Well, I'm not married anymore," Iris says coldly, and then she makes the connection. Her mom and Lanie both had the *exact* same question about her ring, and Iris realizes why—they had seen it in the hospital. They had wanted to steal it.

She can't spend another second with these women. Iris spins towards the police. "Could I get a ride? I don't really want to get another taxi if you can believe it."

"We're not a taxi either. We could take you to the station and have one pick you up from there if it would make you more comfortable."

"Sure."

"How can I know I'll be gettin' my money for this?" her mom asks. "Is there something we can sign?"

"I don't want trouble. I'll send you a check. Bigger than you've ever seen. You two deserve it. I'm just so sorry for this," Iris speaks sarcastically, but her mom and sister are too greedy to notice.

"I'll be expecting one. Or you can expect a letter from a *lawyer*."

"No need for threats, Mom."

They don't ask her if she wants to stay for coffee. Lanie and her mother look at each other nervously, as if they're wondering if they did all they could to get an egg while the golden goose was in town.

As Iris follows the police out, she looks back once more at her mom and sister. She has been furious at the way she's been treated, but now her heart sinks.

Greedy. Vicious. Iris can no longer pretend like she was the same good-intentioned person she is now before the injury. If she loved Joseph, Iris thinks she'd remember. No, she can see who she used to be here. She married for money. Status.

The apple didn't fall far from the tree.

She tucks her head, ashamed, and grabs her suitcase. As she walks out behind the cops, she doesn't bother saying another word.

The Nile

Iris spends the cab ride to The Nile looking out the back windshield to see if they're being followed. She's making the driver nervous. He clears his throat and starts looking in the rearview himself.

As far as she can tell, there's no one following. There's little chance this killer would've tailed her to the police station. She doesn't have a phone anyone could track. She hasn't told anyone other than the cab driver where she's going.

Maybe it's the lack of sleep or the bright, beautiful day, but she's not so afraid anymore. She has a plan. Go to the hotel and then the airport. Stay in public places for the next twelve hours. Then she needs to get back to safety.

She hates that what that means is to get back to Sweet Blood. She trusts she's safe there. The Adlers had plenty of opportunities to take her life when she was living on the plantation. If any of them were somehow behind this, why wait until Memphis? She has a track record of being clumsy since her injury. An accidental death—a run in with a tractor or a fall down the stairs—wouldn't be unbelievable. No, Iris thinks, she's safe at Sweet blood. Far safer than she is here.

She gets out of the taxi, and she's greeted by the doorman of the hotel while the driver grabs her roller bag. The building is seven stories of tan stone, the same searing color as the pyramids.

She has to get lucky. The name on the business card Joseph had was Raymond Brady, but if he isn't working his shift or got a new job, she'll be in trouble. Her plan doesn't account for needing to stay in town for longer.

Iris takes her roller bag and strolls inside. She's afraid of being underdressed, but this is the 21st century, after all, and not New York City. While the staff are all crisp and white collared, the patrons who idle in the big chairs in the lobby are in casual

174

clothes. Nobody looks at her twice in her baggy sweatshirt and pants that she has to hike up every ten steps.

The receptionist is a thin woman, midthirties. She greets Iris with a smile. "Good morning. Are we checking in?"

"Um. Yes," Iris lies.

"Could I get your last name?"

"Adler."

The receptionist pauses like that name means something here but quickly composes herself. She starts typing, and Iris interrupts her. "Raymond Brady wouldn't happen to be working, is he?"

"Raymond? Oh, I'm sorry, but he doesn't work here anymore."

The receptionist stops typing and stands straight up, as if this might change Iris's desire to stay here.

Iris tries not to let her disappointment show. "Do you know anyone who worked with him while he was here?"

"Are you of the Louisiana Adlers?"

"The same."

"I thought so. James was manager the whole time Raymond was on staff. I could go get him for you."

"That would be great!" Iris can't hide her enthusiasm.

"Just a moment."

The receptionist is gone for longer than a moment. Iris taps her feet. Neither the lobby around her, nor its citrusy air freshener smell, elicits a memory.

The receptionist doesn't appear again. The manager comes around from the back room. He's an older man. Fifty or so. His hair is dyed black and slicked back.

"Mornin', Mrs. Adler. My name is James, and I'm the manager here. I hear you're lookin' for Raymond." James walks to the end of the horseshoe reception counter. The two stand near the wall where they won't be in the way of other guests checking in and where others won't hear them.

"I am," Iris says. "I'm sorry, but have we met before?"

He pulls at his tie and chuckles. His cheeks redden. "I believe so? To be honest, I'm not certain."

Her heart starts to beat, hard. She feels like she's about to catch what she's been chasing. This man knows something, and it's making him uncomfortable, but she doesn't know what questions to ask.

"Did you know Joseph Adler?"

"Joseph Adler? Him I know well, yes. He stayed here whenever he had business in Memphis. He would always try to stay at an Elysian property when he traveled in the South."

"I'm his wife, Iris Adler."

"Oh!" James looks very surprised by this. "I'm sorry, I didn't know. You used past tense, I noticed. Did something happen to Mr. Adler?"

Iris decides to avoid the word murdered. This manager already seems shocked enough. "He died."

"Oh, my. I'm so very sorry."

"It's okay." Iris starts to play bereaved widow. She looks away sadly. Wipes an eye. She needs his sympathy to get answers. "What happened to Raymond? I know he was his connection here."

"We had to let Raymond go, unfortunately."

Iris bites her lip. She never realized how hard it was to ask delicate questions. She can't just ask why. An establishment like this has a reputation to protect. She'd get a generic answer. She has this manager on his heels already, and she needs to hit while he's still nervous.

"Did something happen here with my husband?"

"I'm sorry. I can't speak of our guests. Even if you are family."

Iris feels like she lost a round. This would be so much easier if she could find words. A whole day without sleep. Her brain rotted from stress. She forgets her questioning and pictures all the king-sized beds right above her. Their cool, down comforters. She needs sleep. She doesn't know how to use her words to get the answers she needs. She's not sharp, so she has no choice but to be blunt.

She uses what she knows. Something happened with her at this hotel. Her husband has the business card of a concierge that was fired. The current hotel manager is clearly uncomfortable. Iris thinks she understands.

Joseph was seeing someone here.

"Listen, James. I don't think my husband was good to me when we were married. I think he did things behind my back. I *know* he did things. He's passed, and I need to move on. I'm sick of missing him. Can you please tell me what he was up to here? Tell me about him and Raymond?"

"I can't say there's anything to tell you."

"There obviously is. Okay?" Iris gets louder. "So are you going to keep lying to my face about my dead husband, or can you tell me the truth?"

"Okay." He holds his hands out. *Down, girl.* He looks both ways to make sure no one is listening. "We had an incident a few years ago now."

"When exactly?"

"Oh God... I don't know—2021? Somewhere around there. Raymond was an old-school concierge. No request was too far. He knew people." James clears his throat and looks around again. "Paid women."

"Prostitutes?"

"Yes. Your husband... I'm sorry, but he would... partake."

Iris is sick of his careful euphemisms. "Fuck them?"

He blushes. "Yes. One night, something went wrong with the girls. If I remember correctly, he had two prostitutes with him that evening. There was a fight in an elevator with one of them. I can't remember the specifics, but he had to be restrained."

"Joseph had to be restrained?"

"Yes. Another woman showed up some hours after the fight. My shift had started by then. It was you, I believe. His wife. This is why I do think we've met before."

Iris isn't about to reveal her memory problems. She nods. "Right. No, I remember. Joseph was just never honest with me about that night."

"Ah. So, you see. We had to fire Raymond afterwards. I'm sorry about your husband. For both his actions that a former employee helped facilitate and his death."

Iris shakes her head. She's too sleep deprived to play along with the formal, corporate way he's talking. "Thank you, James. But what was the fight in the elevator about? Do you have any idea?"

"Oh, Mrs. Adler. I really can't say."

"Can you tell me what the prostitute looked like? Was she hurt?"

James looks exhausted. Like this painful memory that insults his hotel's name is killing him. "She was an African-American girl if I remember right. And yes, she was hurt. She was hospitalized."

Iris's eyes widen. *Hospitalized?* So her husband was a bastard. Iris remembers what those girls said about the Adler boys at the frat when she first met Joseph. *"They're psychos."*

If she wants to know exactly the kind of man her husband was, she's going to have to find this prostitute. "So Joseph went to jail that night?"

"Oh no. A young man showed up. The woman's brother, I believe. He spoke on her behalf. They did not want to press charges."

Iris is suddenly awake. "What? He was never charged?"

"It was my understanding there must've been an under-the-table settlement."

"So what ever happened to these girls, either one? Was there a police report at all? Do you know where I could find her?"

"No. The authorities were never involved. As for where they ended up, I don't know. The one that ended up in the hospital, her brother said something about Louisiana when I was speaking to him, I think."

Louisiana. Iris wonders if she's close to home. Either way, she's going to find her.

"Was my husband banned from staying at the properties?"

"No." James shakes his head. "We would never hold such a thing against our top guests. Good men sometimes make bad choices."

Iris is too tired to respond. Hospitalizing a woman is apparently just a bad choice. *Rich men get away with vile behavior* is what he's really saying.

"Is there anything or anybody else who might be able to tell me more about that night that works here?"

"No. Not that I know of."

Iris nods. She tightens her grip on her roller bag. She doesn't want to go out into the daylight on her wobbly feet. Suddenly she has an idea. "My credit card had to be switched off. Someone used my card number to buy a couple flat-screens in Little Rock."

"Ah, so sorry."

"Could I still stay here for a night, even if you can't charge me for the room right away? I've got my ID and credit card still. You know the Adlers are good for it," she says with a smile, playing on that wealth.

"Of course! We've just had a couple cancellations this morning," he says elatedly, as if happy to be able to help and get off the subject of Joseph. "Let's check you in right away."

"Great," Iris says. Of all the things this man has said to her, these are the only words she's able to focus on. Everything else can wait. Iris is going to get to sleep.

179

Visitor

She doesn't make it to the shower. Iris strips out of her clothes, stumbles towards the bed, and faceplants on the mattress. She crawls up towards the headboard after a few seconds and kicks her way under the covers.

The A/C whirls gently. The curtains leave the room mostly dark. Iris can't remember being this comfortable. She has a brief sensation of falling, a jolt that shakes her whole body. Then she's already asleep.

The room is pitch dark when she wakes. She perks up in bed with a start, forgetting where she is. Her mouth is dry and her stomach rumbles. Her heart beats hard and anxious, as if she's hungover. She leans over and looks at the clock—11:47 p.m.

She slept for more than twelve hours. She stays in bed for a few minutes, not ready to get out from the covers.

When she stands to go to the bathroom, she teeters from a head rush. Iris has to reach out to hold the wall to keep from falling. She's starving. Literally. Her body is probably running on nothing but fat stores by now.

She should've tried to eat something before going to bed.

This hotel might have twenty-four-hour room service. If it doesn't, she'll tip the concierge all the money she has left if he can get her a pizza. She can feel her mouth moisten just thinking of food.

When she's done in the bathroom, she goes to the desk. There's a leather-bound menu for room service. Hours six a.m. to two a.m. Iris could cry. She orders a cheeseburger, fries, and chocolate sundae and watches cable news until it comes.

She has them leave it at her door. She brings in the platter and demolishes the meal in little more than five minutes. She sits on the end of the bed, eating her ice cream slower than she did the burger and fries.

She's still deliriously tired. Her eyes begin to feel heavy again after the food. She only has one of the bedside lamps on, and the room is mostly dark. Iris is staring into space when she suddenly sees something disturb the line of light that shines under the door from the hotel hallway.

She thought it was just someone walking by, but now she sees that a shadow has stopped. In the light under the door, there are two dark spots, a shoulders-width apart. Legs. Someone is standing outside.

She puts down her spoon gently and stares. She thinks it's hotel staff, but after the shadow lingers for several seconds without knocking, that hope leaves her mind. Iris just waits to see what they do next. Eventually, the shadow moves on. She can hear heavy steps receding down the hall.

She hops off the bed and races to the peephole. She doesn't know what she expected. There is nothing to see, and she's not about to risk opening the door in order to look down the hall.

She checks to be sure the locks are in place and slowly makes her way back to bed. She leaves the lamp on as she curls up under the covers. She thinks she's going to stay awake and alert, but it's only a few minutes before her head slumps off to her shoulder, and once again she's fast asleep.

Trouble

Iris wakes up facing the window. The blinds are open now, and outside is the violet sky of early dawn. She moves a pillow in front of her eyes, and suddenly she feels a hand on her shoulder. She flinches and scurries back.

"It's okay," a familiar voice says. "You're safe now. It's me."

Iris tries to blink herself awake. What she sees doesn't compute. Right next to her, sitting on the edge of the bed, is Augusta in a herringbone blazer with a full face of makeup.

"You gave all of us quite the scare. Disappearing like that."

Iris is still fully clothed, but Augusta's presence makes her feel naked. Juvenile. She feels like a teen who's overslept for school. A runaway child who's been found helpless.

"What are you doing here?" Iris backs away in bed. "Who let you in here?"

"The hotel contacted me. They told me you showed up here lookin' like you'd had a rough night."

"And they just let you in here?" Iris leans forward, looking towards the hall that leads to the door.

"It was me or the police. They were very worried about you. Your card wasn't even working, Iris. You were staying on the family name."

"You deactivated it," Iris says accusingly.

"That card wasn't for traveling. It had a lock on it. We just thought you knew."

Iris almost wants to tell her to shut up. Quit lying. But she feels something else from Augusta's presence—relief. Rich, confident, strong. Augusta is here. Her worries are over.

Iris starts to untense. "A man has been following me..."

"I've already talked to the police. I've been in town since yesterday looking for you. I've been worried since your phone stopped sharing its location."

"You were tracking me?"

"Iris," Augusta says in a reasoning tone. "Can you blame me? You're not well. Look at how you ended up."

"Because there was this man, Augusta. He had a gun."

"The taxi driver?"

"No. It wasn't a taxi driver," Iris says in frustration and gets out of bed. "There was somebody else. They've been following me. I think it's the same person who killed Joseph. Now that I'm not at Sweet Blood, they're back after me."

Iris gauges Augusta's reaction. She looks at the floor then the window. Almost like she's embarrassed for her daughter-in-law. "Let's just get you home."

"Do you believe me?"

Augusta doesn't speak right away. Then she looks her in the eye. "Of course I believe you."

But she doesn't, Iris knows. It's plain as day.

"Don't worry. The room is already paid for. I got us a flight back home. It leaves in three hours. Let's get you showered and fed. Okay?"

Iris can't debate anymore. The room service didn't make up for more than a day of not eating, and her hunger has returned. It's already hard to focus. She nods.

Augusta stands and, to Iris's shock, gives her a strong hug. "You go freshen up." She moves her hands to Iris's shoulders and pats them.

"Okay."

It's been nearly 24 hours since she first lay down in this bed. She's slept for most of a day. Even though she was sleep deprived before, Augusta is right—being this tired is a sign that Iris is not okay. Her brain isn't fully healed. She's been reckless.

She goes to the bathroom, but when she sees the door to the hallway, she pauses.

"How were you able to get in here?"

"What's that now?"

"I had the door locked."

"Oh, Iris. Hotels have ways of unlocking those."

Iris doesn't even respond. She goes to the bathroom and puts her hands on the marble. She thinks about the man across the street in New Orleans and the fact that Augusta has always known where she is. Maybe her worries are far from over. She can't help the lingering thought that this woman is the source of them.

Guardian

Their flight lands on time back in New Orleans. They stand at Arrivals together, waiting for Arthur. Or Richard. Iris doesn't know or care to ask.

The black Cadillac pulls up, and after the door is opened, Iris hesitates to get in as she sees Annabelle smile at her from the back seat. To her surprise, she doesn't stay seated. Annabelle stands and gives Iris a hug.

"Oh, bless your heart. You poor thing. We were all worried sick. It's so good to see you. Let's put that little tussle we had behind us. I was just so angry something like this might happen."

Iris doesn't hug back or respond. She stands still like a limp doll, her arms hanging awkwardly at her sides, while Annabelle rubs her back.

She breaks the hug and looks at Iris. "So you're okay?" Then she looks at Augusta and asks her, too. "She's okay?"

"I'm fine." Iris isn't about to let someone answer for her. She already feels like a dependent.

"Oh, I heard you had some trouble with a *nasty* taxi driver. That's why I'm so glad we have Arthur."

"And Richard?" Iris quizzes her. She's still not sure he exists.

"Oh yes, of course. He just hasn't been with us as long." Annabelle suddenly waves them towards the back seat. "It's awfully hot out here. Come, come. Let's get back to the house and have some tea."

Iris is slow to get in. They're all silent until they get on the interstate. It's only three in the afternoon, but it looks like rush hour. Traffic is bumper to bumper.

"Ugh. Everyone wants to leave the office so early on Fridays. Get an early start to the weekend. Nobody likes to actually *work* anymore," Annabelle says, shaking her head at the cars in traffic around them.

Iris wishes she had her phone. She doesn't have any way to check the date, but it has to be Thursday. She left for Memphis Tuesday evening and spent most of Wednesday asleep. *Today has to be Thursday. Right?*

Annabelle is wrong, and Iris is confident enough to tell her so.

"It's Thursday, isn't it?"

Augusta and Annabelle both look at her. Augusta sighs, looks at her feet. She seems upset. Annabelle sits up in her seat. She brushes her pant legs with her hands awkwardly. "It's Friday, sugar. Friday the 30th."

"Oh."

"But that's okay!" Annabelle reaches out and touches Iris's knee. "We're going to get better about this kind of thing. Momma and I have been talking... We're going to pay for a neurologist to come to the house every single week. It's not going to be like the pointless little checkups you have now. His name is Doctor Reid, and he's renowned in the South. Only takes a new patient or two a year. He's not just going to prescribe you medications, but a whole regimen. Games for your mind, a stricter diet, that kind of thing. We're going to get you better."

"Thank you." It's all Iris can say. She wants to get access to Joseph's money. She wants to move away from these people, not spend another three months in Sweet Blood getting evaluated once a week.

Now that she's left Memphis behind, she knows there's information there she needs, but she's far out of her depth. She needs to hire a private investigator. Someone to dig into her past and Joseph's. But for that she needs money.

She needs to get her inheritance, and for *that* she needs a lawyer.

"We're going to have a little meeting when we get back, Iris. Just so you're not surprised," Annabelle adds.

"With this neurologist?"

"No, not quite. There's just some business we have to go over regarding the estate."

"Joseph's?"

"Yes."

Iris tries to hide her relief. *Speak of the devil.* "Okay," she says as casually as she can. She's relieved she didn't have to bring this up herself. She doesn't want to ask for the cash whenever she wants to buy things. She doesn't want it to arouse suspicion. Especially when what she wants to purchase most of all, Iris realizes, is a gun.

The gate opens for them at Sweet Blood. There are two cars parked in the grass—a black Mercedes and a nondescript Chevy Malibu. It's an undercover cop car. Iris can tell that from the two uniformed deputies that sit on the porch. They have on black pants and khaki shirts with red neckties. They stand up as the car slows.

"What's going on?" Iris asks, but no one answers.

Arthur comes around and opens the door. Augusta and Annabelle get out of the car, trying their very best not to meet Iris's eye or each other's.

"Afternoon, Adlers," says one of the police officers. He's wearing a wide-brimmed, black Stetson. Iris recognizes that it's the sheriff.

"Thanks for coming, Sheriff." Annabelle climbs the porch steps and daintily shakes his hand.

The sheriff greets Augusta, but she only smiles. Iris's stomach feels like it won't stop falling. Do they know something about her case?

There are two more men on the porch. They are standing farther behind the police. One is a man of about seventy in a tan three-piece suit, despite the heat, and the other is also in a suit—navy and without a vest.

The man in navy is a few decades younger, bald, and keeps a sweaty handkerchief crumpled in his fist. He keeps wiping the sweat from his forehead.

There are big fans spinning in the porch ceiling, and with the shade, the temperature really isn't that bad. Unless you are in a suit.

There's a table set up with tea and six wicker chairs around it. They all start to sit except for Iris and the deputy, who leans against one of the house's columns like he's not part of this business. He's younger and black. *Shorter*, Iris thinks. She tries to keep inspecting his face, but her attention is taken to the table.

"Sit, Iris," Annabelle says like she's a dog and taps a seat cushion.

When Iris sits, she begins to blush. Everyone is looking at her. She's the topic of discussion.

"Iris. This is our family's lawyer." Annabelle nods at the older man in the three-piece suit. "Marshall Walker."

He half stands, flattens his tie, and extends his hand across the low table. Iris does the same, and they shake hands but don't talk.

"And this is Dave Burns." She gestures at the bald man in the navy suit. He's sitting farther away, and he and Iris just wave to each other. "He's an examiner for the 27th District Court here."

"Okay," Iris says, expecting more information. She notices that Augusta is silent. It's strange to see Annabelle taking the lead and Augusta just letting her.

"Mama?" Annabelle says, "This was your idea. Would you like to let Iris know what this is about?"

Augusta lets out another sigh. "I suppose. I'll get right to it. Iris, we are extremely concerned for your well-being, especially after the events of the last couple days. We've submitted a request to the 27th district court for a curatorship."

Iris gulps. She has an idea where this is going. "Curatorship?"

"That doesn't mean support for the arts. Here in Louisiana, it's our form of conservatorship. Guardianship over an adult who cannot manage their own affairs. Both financial and otherwise."

Iris's mouth slips open. Her eyes start to water. This can't be happening. "What does that mean?"

"It means when an individual is no longer able to properly care for themselves, in the case of disability or injury such as yours, the ability to make decisions is handed over by the court to an adult who can make those for you."

Iris looks at the sheriff. What is happening right now feels illegal, yet the law is right here. The sheriff picks up a glass of sweet tea and starts to gulp it down greedily. Iris feels hot tears on her cheeks. Everyone looks away now, sparing her the embarrassment.

Iris wipes them away madly. She doesn't want to cry. "What decisions specifically?" Iris asks.

"Financial, relationships. Travel, of course."

Iris starts to laugh, but she knows how fucked she is. The tears pour without control. No one can look at her.

"So like... Financial meaning you have to okay any big purchase I make? Like if I wanted a house or car? Or would you control every single fucking cent I spend?"

No one responds.

Finally, Augusta licks her lips. "The limitations and powers are specific to the curatorship, but we've sent our requests to the court."

"It's closer to the latter," Annabelle says matter-of-factly while tapping her foot. The fake smile she wore in the car is gone. Her face is smug. Victorious. "That means the second thing in a sentence."

"I know what it fucking means."

"Okay." The sheriff sets his tea down with a clank. "Can we watch the language, young lady?"

That's what he's concerned about? Iris thinks. She's having her rights stripped away, and he wants her to watch her mouth?

"I want to fight this. I have to have that right."

"Of course, you do," Augusta says. She looks strangely pained. This *hurts* her. Iris realizes. She's not elated like Annabelle. That or she's simply the better actress. "You have that right. The court will appoint you an attorney."

"What if I want my own?"

"If you can find the money..."

"What do you mean?" But Iris understands. "I have Joseph's money..."

"That money fell under control of the family trust with his death. You signed it as such in the hospital."

"But I was practically brain dead in the hospital!"

"You were conscious."

"Well, what about our checking account? And then there's life insurance."

"Yes, and while you were in the hospital, you agreed to let the family office manage those as well."

"*Manage*. Not fucking steal."

"Young lady, you need to settle down." The sheriff makes like he's going to stand, but Augusta shoots him a glare.

"Sit down, Fred."

He looks at Augusta and hesitates, as if weighing who is the authority here. Unsurprisingly, he settles back into his chair.

Augusta turns to Iris. "Nothing is stolen. The money is yours. I won't be able to spend any of it, and that is a written part of our conditions. We don't want to steal your money, Iris. We just want what's best for you."

"If I may?" Marshall the lawyer puts his hand up like a kid in class. "Iris, your ownership stake of the Adler Corp is currently in limbo. It's been quite damaging to the company and brought uncertainty to this already... stormy leadership transition. It's important to take into account that your inheritance affects the Adler Corps' employees' livelihoods. There is more at risk here than money."

This is the first Iris is hearing of this. She's heard plenty of mentions about inheritance, but not company shares. "My ownership stake?"

"Well, yes. It's important you know the facts here. Your husband owned a considerable chunk of the company that is now, according to his will, half yours. The other half was stipulated to go to whoever the current CEO of the Adler Corp was in the event of his death, that being your mother-in-law."

Iris doesn't know what to say. It's starting to make sense now. These Adler women don't just get off on control. They want her shares. For that she needs to be their puppet. She looks at Augusta's five-hundred-dollar-an-hour attorney. His fine suit. His combed gray hair.

She will not be winning this battle with a public defender, but she has to fight.

"I want my attorney now."

"The court will provide you one in time," Augusta says.

"I want to call the court."

"Iris, hon. With what phone?"

"I don't know... Yours? Am I not allowed to make phone calls anymore?"

The sheriff clears his throat and looks at Augusta like he's asking permission to speak.

She gently nods.

"Young lady, if you would really like to fight this, it would be best to extricate yourself from the care of Augusta Adler as soon as possible. My understanding is that you lost your phone when you got yourself into some trouble traveling alone in Memphis."

Iris cringes. So they know about that. The court probably does, too. This whole thing feels like a coup for control of her life. She's already lost.

"No one owes you a phone call," the sheriff continues. "You don't *have* a phone. There's a women's shelter in Baton Rouge. We've already called. They're ready to take you in right now. You can stay there while they try to get you a job and set you up with a lawyer. It's a little dangerous. A lot of the ladies there are dealing with drug abuse, but it's a roof."

Iris crosses her arms and watches the pitcher of tea sweat.

The sheriff follows her eyes and starts to pour himself another glass. "As for a job, however, on account of what we've been told about your mental condition and what little employment history you have, you won't have much for options. There's a *Mac* Donalds owned by a nice fella from my church, and they hire slow people, criminals. People who need first and second chances. We might be able to set you up there. But things—"

"Thank you, Fred," Augusta says, like she's content with the point he got across.

The sheriff grumbles and leans back, creaking his wicker chair.

"I'll tell you the next steps, Iris. We already talked with your mom and sister in Memphis, and I'm sorry, but neither of them would like to have you."

Have me, Iris thinks. She's a dog.

Augusta gives her some grace. "Not that you'd like to live with them. I'm just making your options clear."

"Sure," Iris says quietly.

"We've already submitted a neurological report to the court."

"How's that possible?"

"Your current physician, Dr. Prager, put it together."

"Can I read it?"

"Certainly. Nothing is going to be kept from you during this process."

"But the report says I can't be independent? It sides with you, doesn't it?"

"There are no sides here, sugar. Just facts," Annabelle adds mockingly.

"Anyway," Augusta says. "The next step is an independent evaluation by the court. This is done by an examiner." She gestures at the bald man in the navy suit. "He's going to ask you some questions. See what a day for you might be like. That kind of thing."

"Right now?" asks Iris.

"The court prefers these questions to be a surprise. Think of it like a test. It's a pretty simple one, so if you had time to prepare, you could ace it, but that wouldn't give the full picture. These are questions anybody should know the answer to off hand."

Iris looks at the bald man in the navy suit. He's pulled out a pamphlet and put on a pair of reading glasses. He looks deathly serious.

"We will leave you to the examination if you like," says Augusta.

Iris only nods. She's too nervous to speak. Everybody stands and shuffles towards the other side of the porch, where there is another arrangement of chairs. Augusta lets her hand linger on Iris's shoulder for a moment before walking on.

A homeless shelter. A job at McDonald's. The sheriff was just scaring her, Iris thinks. If she wins the case against this curatorship, she gets her money and her freedom. Everything is on the line.

Iris's hands sweat. Her heart pounds. The examiner still hasn't even looked up at her from his pamphlet.

Finally, he scribbles something down, crosses one leg over the other, and sighs. "Okay, Iris. So do you mind if I ask you a few questions? Would you say you're in a proper state of mind at the moment?"

"Go right ahead," Iris says firmly, like she has nothing to hide.

"What is your date of birth?"

Iris smiles. She's happy to have such an easy one. "March 21st."

"Your birth year?"

Again, so easy. She smiles again and rattles off the year without pause.

"And can you tell me the last four numbers of your social security number?"

Iris's heart flutters. She can't, but she's quick with her answer. "Oh, I couldn't tell you that *before* I was injured. I've never been good with that kind of thing."

He doesn't react at all. He just scribbles something down fast, and she tenses at the scratch of his pen.

"Okay. What about the parish we're in? Do you know the name?"

"Sorry?" Iris says but curses herself. She knew what he meant, but she just doesn't know.

"Tennessee, other states, they've got counties. In Louisiana, we have parishes." He speaks to her like she's a toddler in Sunday school. "Do you know which one Sweet Blood is in?"

Iris has to keep a tear from falling. "No, I do not."

He scratches with his pen. She can't stand the quick way he moves his hand. It looks like he's writing her off. Scratching a big fast X every time. This was a setup.

She's failing.

"Okay, Mrs. Adler. What month is it?"

"August!" Iris says quickly, desperate for a win.

His pen scratches again. "And what day of the week is it?"

"Friday," Iris blurts out, but as soon as she says it, she wishes she could take it back. She watches him frown and scratch again.

"What is the final letter in the alphabet?"

"Wait." Iris leans forward slowly. "It's Friday, right?"

He sighs. He doesn't look at her when he talks. "I'm sorry. Today is Thursday, August 29th."

The way he says *I'm sorry* makes it clear—she's already flunked.

"But Iris, could you tell me what the last letter of the alphabet is?"

Now they're onto the brain-dead questions. Iris knows it's over. But that fact is already far from her mind. "Gaslighting bitch," Iris whispers under her breath.

"Pardon me?"

"I mean... Z." Iris holds a finger up. "Would you excuse me? Just one second." She grabs a glass of tea and strolls to the opposite end of the porch, where the others are sitting out of earshot.

Annabelle watches her approach with amusement. It's already over, and all Iris wants to do is humiliate this evil woman if only for a second. She's about to throw her drink in her face, when she gets smarter. Annabelle has a temper, and Iris has an idea.

She sits facing Iris. Her smug expression stretches her smile ear to ear.

When Iris gets close, she starts to wobble, she fakes a trip, and hears others gasp. The sheriff's deputy is still standing and makes a half-assed attempt to stick an arm out to stop her fall, but it's too late. Iris braces herself against Annabelle's shoulders, spilling her tea all over her breasts, neck, and face in a splash. Iris falls and intentionally makes it so her right hand sinks deep into the soil of a potted plant that sits on the porch.

"Oh my God. I am so sorry, sugar." Iris pulls herself up. "I am just such a klutz. Oh my gosh. I can't even walk right, can I?" Iris rubs the tea that drips down Annabelle's face with the hand that was in the planter. She smears her chin with the dirt, and with the help of the tea, it turns to mud.

"Oh my goodness. I'm just spreading it around." Iris takes her hand away, and her face stings hot before she even hears the sharp crack of the slap. Annabelle struck her in the face.

"Get off me, bitch."

Everyone quiets. Someone mutters, *"Oh my."*

"Annabelle!" Augusta says, drawing out the last syllable. She sounds like a parent scolding a child that should know better. "You apologize this instant. Are you okay, Iris?"

"I'm fine." Iris stands.

"Annabelle. Apologize," Augusta says.

Annabelle looks shocked. It seems like she's about to argue that Iris's fall was no accident, but at the last second her mouth closes. "I'm sorry, Iris."

"Oh, don't be. I'm so clumsy, and you look so nice. I'd be a bit peeved, too."

Annabelle looks like she's ready to combust. Her face has reddened with rage, her eyes bulge. "I'm going to freshen up," she says and spins, walking off towards the guest house.

Iris catches Augusta's grin. It was Annabelle who was humiliated by this situation, and Augusta seems to be reveling in it.

"Is she... Is she just going to get away with that?" Iris asks, rubbing her cheek. The action is no dramatization. Her cheek hurts. The others just look at her, and Iris turns to the sheriff. "She assaulted someone y'all have been arguing is mentally handicapped. Is that not a crime?"

The sheriff and the deputy look at each other. "You want us to arrest a pregnant woman?" The deputy chuckles a little.

Iris was just trying to see how rigged this was against her. She doesn't care about Annabelle being put in handcuffs. "I didn't realize they had immunity, but alright."

She fans herself with a dirty hand. "I should lie down. I feel a little woozy."

Augusta quickly steps to Iris's side and takes her arm. "How about I take you upstairs?" she asks, but it wasn't a question. Augusta starts walking. She's showing off her guardianship of Iris in front of everybody.

The men have all stood since the incident, and they part out of their way to let Augusta and Iris pass. The front door opens just before they reach it.

Aurelia stands with a concerned expression in the entry hall. "Everything okay, Mrs. Adler?"

"Oh, we just had a little fall. Could you fetch us some ice, dear?"

"Right away." Aurelia doesn't start back towards the kitchen, however. She lingers and stares at Iris's cheek until she and Augusta reach the stairs.

Iris watches Aurelia leave towards the kitchen and then speaks quietly in Augusta's ear. "You don't think I see what you're doing?"

Augusta doesn't say anything. She smiles tightly.

"Making me look like a helpless cripple to get control over your son's shares of the company."

Augusta chuckles. "You're a little off there, Iris."

"Yeah?"

They're quiet again as they get to the top of the stairs. Augusta opens the bedroom door, and Iris walks in. Aurelia is quickly behind them. She must've run to the kitchen. She hands Augusta an ice pack wrapped in a dishcloth.

"Anything else, Mrs. Adler?"

"No. Thank you, Aurelia."

She bows an inch and walks off, but Augusta stays in the doorframe holding the icepack.

"Congratulations," Iris says. "You control my life. Does that feel good to you?"

"I should've told you in Memphis." Augusta leans against the doorframe. She chews the inside of her cheek like she miscalculated something.

"That you were going to make a dog out of me?"

"No." Augusta shakes her head. "That I saved your life, Iris. Just now."

"What?"

Augusta tosses her the ice pack. Iris has to flinch to catch it, but she does.

"Freshen up. Tonight..." Augusta pauses. "Tonight, I tell you."

Memory Hall

Iris doesn't have her hopes up. Still, she's too excited to sit still. She spends the hours until nightfall pacing her bedroom, thinking. She knows Augusta is a liar. She has to be careful not to develop Stockholm syndrome. This woman is her captor, not her friend. Yet she can't help but want to please Augusta.

She's curious why her mother-in-law smiled after Annabelle took off.

It actually pleased Augusta to see that brat get what she deserved. For people to see her true colors. Maybe that glee was a result of the business feud they're having. It might have nothing to do with her opinion on Annabelle's manipulation of Iris. But Augusta *has* seemed more remorseful about the curatorship than Annabelle.

Iris needs to be careful. These women are experts in power. Control. This could just be part of the way they're playing her. Good cop. Bad cop.

Iris doesn't know how freshened up Augusta wants her, but she's not going to disobey, not when the offer of information is on the table. She puts on a khaki-colored dress with matching slingback heels and an appropriate amount of makeup, but not a full face. Her fingers hover over a line of a dozen different lipsticks. She picks a subtle shade of red, not much brighter than her lips already are.

After she's applied it, she rolls her shoulders back and takes a few deep breaths. Tonight, she's going to get what she wants. She's not going to let Augusta back out of it. Iris will tell her about Joseph and the Nile and the prostitute he put in the hospital. She will push Augusta until she gets the truth.

Iris goes back to her bed and lies on top of the blankets. She needs to get a neurologist of her own and start assembling the case that she can be independent. But even if she can live on her own, should she?

Iris thinks she'd probably be killed if she went to the women's shelter. This house, the protection of this family, is currently the only thing keeping her alive.

Augusta said she saved her life, but from whom?

A knock on the door never comes. Iris eats dinner out of the fridge alone in the kitchen, and it's nearly 8:30 when she hears the soft notes of a piano drifting upstairs. Only one person plays in the house.

Augusta.

Iris pretty much jumps from bed. She has to slow herself as she heads down the stairs, across the marble entrance hall, and into the music room.

Augusta has her back to Iris as she sits on the piano bench. Iris doesn't recognize what she's playing. Her fingers slip on the keys, and an errant note pings. She suddenly drops her hands and scoots to the side of the bench.

"Come sit." She must've seen Iris's reflection on the buffed piano.

Iris walks forward. The piano bench isn't all that big to begin with, and Augusta's wide hips leave her only a foot of space.

When Iris sits, their legs are touching.

"I taught all my boys how to play on this piano." Augusta's hands dance, and she plays a quick little riff. Then she brings her hands back to her lap again. "None of them play anymore."

Iris lets her talk.

"Do you know how to play? I'm not sure I ever asked you, even before..." Augusta raises her gaze to her scar.

Iris thinks the question is a bit out of touch. "When you were in Memphis, did you see my mom's house?"

"There wasn't a baby grand hiding in there?" Augusta smiles and shakes her head. "I'm sorry."

"We didn't learn any instruments."

"Of course. That's too bad. You have the perfect fingers for piano." Augusta picks up Iris's left hand without asking and turns it so her palm faces the ceiling.

Iris pulls it away. "I asked about Joseph at the Nile. The hotel."

"Oh?" Augusta stares challengingly into her eyes. Iris folds immediately. She looks at the keys and sees that they're textured with tiny cracks. They're ivory. Real ivory. But the piano looks new.

Iris stutters. "They, um... They told me he had a taste for certain women." Now it's her turn to use words delicately. "Women that weren't his wife."

"They told you he slept with prostitutes?"

"Yeah."

"I can tell you right now, my son would never."

"He specifically said Joseph—"

"Enough! I will not hear you speak about my son that way. Not when he was *nothing* but good to you. If anybody was unfaithful... Ha." Augusta shakes her head.

"What do you mean by that?"

"Is that what you care about? What about the armed man that chased you around Memphis? Doesn't that make you curious?"

"So you believe me?"

Augusta quickly leaves Iris on the bench and walks to the door. She peeks her head out and then draws the French doors shut.

"I used to be a bad person, Iris. I would do whatever it took to get to the top. I'd lie. I'd flirt..." She pauses. "I'd threaten people. People who were in the same situation as myself but weren't so capable of keeping secrets."

"What situation?" Iris begins, but Augusta raises her voice.

"I threatened people with violence before. And to be honest with you, I'm not sure if my repulsion comes from the fact that I've become a better person now or that I'm just seeing someone else use my own skill set to ruin me."

Iris knows what Augusta's talking about now. "Annabelle."

Augusta swallows. "She's just like me at that age. At least she thinks she is. Vicious. Ambitious. Oh, what's the difference? I actually worked. I proved myself to be the most capable leader. She… She stole it."

"What do you mean?" Iris hasn't ever heard Augusta ramble like this before. She's been drinking, Iris realizes. She looks around the room and sees a highball sweating on the coffee table. Augusta's purse is next to it. She must've just gotten back from somewhere.

She's analyzing this, when suddenly the next words out of Augusta's mouth stop her thoughts in their tracks.

"She killed him. You know that? You can quit all your searching, Iris. She killed my son, and she tried to kill you, too."

Iris watches Augusta closely. There is no lie in her expression. Her lip trembles, and so do her legs. She has to lower herself into one of the leather chairs.

"You really think that?"

"With Joseph out of the way, it's hers. It's all hers. And the bitch always wanted it. Just like me."

"The CEO position?"

Augusta nods.

It's starting to make sense. The control Annabelle wants over Iris. The hate she has for her. She survived. "So what, she hired someone to do it?"

"Of course, she did. But I don't know how to stop her now. I can't possibly tell the board my suspicions. I don't have proof, other than the answer to the simplest question. Who had the most to gain from killing my boy? And it's Annabelle. Every damn time. And the way she acted afterwards. I should've known she'd get Jamie to fold from taking the job himself. The way he couldn't even look me in the fucking eye."

"And she wants me dead because she's afraid I'll remember?"

"What?" Augusta looks up, confused. She's ranting in her own world.

"She's afraid I'll remember who shot me."

"Yes. Yes." Augusta suddenly stands. Now Iris thinks she's lying.

Augusta goes to her glass and picks it up, and then she heads to Iris and sits next to her again on the bench. She takes a long sip and places her glass on top of the piano. Iris can smell sugary liquor on her breath when she speaks. "It's why I brought up a curatorship, darling. I don't want to hurt you. I want to protect you. The second I told Annabelle about it, her expression changed. She realized there was another solution to keeping you under control. One that didn't involve ending your life."

Iris isn't sure she buys it. She looks away as if this is all too much, but really, she doesn't want Augusta to see the mistrust on her face. Maybe Annabelle did have the most to gain from Joseph's death, but the execution was sloppy. And why go after Joseph when Iris was home, too? Why make it a double homicide? This story doesn't add up.

She looks back at Augusta. "Have you told the police any of this?"

"I had them interview her. She has an alibi, but of course she would. Again, I don't think she was the one who pulled the trigger. It's hopeless. No DNA at the scene. No witnesses. This case was cold months ago. Her pregnancy was probably timed to be in tandem with this. A pregnant woman doing this? Preposterous. The cops couldn't disregard her as a suspect fast enough."

"So what are you going to do about it?"

Augusta's eyes narrow. She looks at Iris proudly. "We're going to stop her."

"Stop her how?"

"There's no way I can take her down without bringing myself with her."

"Why?"

"This company—not everything we do is... within the bounds of the law."

"Like tax evasion?" Iris says.

"You wouldn't believe how you ended up in this house if I told you, Iris. Your story. Your survival. It's all truly stranger than fiction."

"Try me." Iris says angrily.

"Hm," Augusta hiccups. "Maybe I'm exaggerating. Maybe there's not much to put beyond a person when money is their motive."

"Are you saying I was a gold digger?"

Augusta reaches for her glass but bumps it, and a wave of the liquor rolls out and slaps on the keys.

"Oh shit. Shit, shit, shit. Aurelia!" Augusta yells and walks quickly towards the French doors. "Aurelia!" she yells out again, but there's no answer.

Iris scoots so she's out of the way of the spill but still on the bench. "It's really not that bad. I can—"

"Oh, I'm such a fool. I'm sorry. One second, Iris."

Augusta goes to her purse and fishes out a handkerchief. She dabs it on the keys with one side, then the next, and Iris's eyes widen in shock as she watches the dark patch of moisture grow on the cloth. She reaches out and grabs Augusta by the wrist. She pulls Augusta's hand up to her face while the handkerchief is still in her fist.

A powdery scent wafts to Iris's nose. It's the very same one she smelled in the parking lot. The memory of the affair... The owner of the handkerchief. It was Augusta.

Augusta seems to know what Iris has just realized. She reaches out gently and cups Iris's cheek.

Iris is too stunned to speak and too stunned to move as Augusta's lips move closer to hers. "Do you remember who you were, darling?" she whispers and kisses Iris once before pulling back.

Iris didn't kiss back. But Augusta moves in again, and this time she does. She lets Augusta take her top lip in hers, but only for a moment before she recoils. She stares at Augusta's face. She looks suddenly scared. Nervous that she did something wrong.

Iris stands up from the bench so quickly that one of its legs screeches on the marble.

Augusta stands straight, too. "I'm sorry, Iris."

Iris still can't speak. Words are stuck in her throat. Her heart races. She looks Augusta over and leaves the music room quickly and without a word.

Guests

It took a long time for Iris to get to sleep.

When she wakes up the next morning, the very first thing she thinks about is Augusta. She can sense her presence like a ghost in the dreams she can't quite remember.

She had slept with her at least once. The exact memory the perfume scent brings forth isn't all that clear. She remembers a bathtub. Augusta was dry, clothed by her side. She got in the tub without undressing, stuck her hand under the bubbles...

That's all Iris can remember. Was Iris playing along? Manipulating her mother-in-law for something?

She wishes she kept her composure to ask questions last night, but she was afraid, she realizes. Afraid of getting naked on that piano bench and becoming Augusta's plaything. She couldn't let Augusta own her any more than she already did. To hell with what information she may have gotten.

Iris can hear voices from outside her bedroom window. They're down on the porch.

She tenses. It's probably the police here to take her away to the women's shelter. Augusta has probably changed her mind after Iris's rejection, and now she doesn't want anything to do with her at all. Then she hears laughter and calms down.

She spends twenty minutes getting ready. She puts on an airy white button-down and some loose-fitting black pants and then heads downstairs to the porch.

Augusta, Jamie, Annabelle, and Nick sit at the table. Joseph Senior is here, too, and she can't help but startle when she sees him. He's not in a wheelchair. He's been placed in a wicker chair.

His face is stoic, like he doesn't register anything that's happening around him. Sitting to his left, sharing the head of the little tea table, is a Hispanic man listening to Augusta talk.

He's young, around Iris's age. He has a short, well-trimmed beard and a full head of wavy black hair that contrasts well against his cream suit. He doesn't wear a tie, but his blue dress shirt is the soft color of the sky. He's breathtaking.

He's facing Iris and notices her before any of the others. He smiles, and his white teeth flash. "And who is the young lady?" he says with a flare to his tone.

Augusta turns and looks Iris over. "This is my son's wife. Joseph's."

Iris notices she didn't bother to introduce her by name. Iris crosses the porch to the table and extends her hand. "Iris."

The man stands. "Paulo." His name softly pops from his lips like a drop of water. He takes her fingers delicately. Runs a thumb over the back of her hand. "You have my deepest sympathies, *señora*. I'm so sorry for your loss."

"Thank you."

"Please." Paulo looks around for a chair. "Join us."

"I was just going to get Joseph inside," Augusta says, standing. "It's getting a little warm."

It wasn't warm at all. Under the silent ceiling fan, Iris wishes she had another layer.

"Aurelia?" Augusta calls.

A few seconds later, Aurelia comes out carrying a wheelchair, and she sets it down at Joseph's side. She unfolds it and then helps him in.

"A pleasure to see you, Joseph," Paulo says, reaching over to clutch his hand. Joseph senior seems to nod, but it is so slight Iris can't be sure. Augusta accompanies Aurelia and Joseph Senior inside, and Iris takes a seat.

She watches Augusta go, her heart pounding. What if *no* is the one thing this woman will not stand? Iris feels like she's in danger from all sides.

"I had a little cousin who had the same wound. Shot himself on accident in the head. Found his papa's gun. He lived too, but not so lucky. The only word he can say now is mama."

"I'm sorry," says Iris. She's a little disturbed by the story.

"Oh, it's okay. I'm only saying you are a very lucky woman. You stayed smart. Beautiful, too."

"Thank you." Iris bows her head a little, embarrassed. She changes the subject. "Are you in the States for business?"

"Yes. I got in from Mexico City this morning. I'm giving my input on the succession plans."

"So you're on the board?"

"Yes. Unfortunately, I couldn't make it to last week's dinner."

"How'd you get that position?"

"It was my papa's board seat. Our family business goes way back with the Adlers."

"Back to NAFTA," Annabelle chuckles and sips her coffee.

"Yes. Papa always had a picture of Bill Clinton in his office. Whether that was because of his policies or certain proclivities he could relate to as a leader, I... cannot say." Paulo smiles wryly.

"Ah shit," Jamie snorts, laughing. "Woo." He wipes his brow.

Iris shifts uncomfortably, sensing this is some kind of joke related to putting cigars where they shouldn't go or taking advantage of young interns.

"Proclivities," Iris says, "I'm not sure I even know that much English."

"You mind?" Paulo pulls out a thin cigarette, the same kind Augusta smokes.

Iris shakes her head, and he sparks it with a gold lighter. There's a coiled snake ready to strike embossed on the side. "I should hope you don't know more than me," he says while exhaling his smoke. "Not for the fortune my family spent sending me to private schools in England."

"Paulo went to Oxford," Annabelle adds, like she's proud of him. "And you went to boarding school with that prince. Was he English? Whose child was that again? What king?"

"Ah..." Paulo shakes his head like he doesn't wish to speak of this. "I cannot remember. It gets hard to tell one of those pudgy pale bullies from another. They were never very nice to the Mexican."

"That's awful," says Annabelle.

Paulo shrugs. "Papa said it would make me tough. Maybe so. But it also got me in trouble."

"So are you in the farming business, too?" Iris asks.

Paulo hesitates. Smiles. "Farming, butchering, but primarily shipping. Many crossovers with the Adlers. We used to be a small family business, too, but Papa swallowed the nearby farms one by one by one." Paulo scissors his forefinger and thumb like he's plucking berries from a branch. "Now we don't just have farms. You see the ships that come down the river?" Paulo points towards the Mississippi. "They fly the flag of Panama, but that's only for tax purposes. Those are Mexican ships. The bulk carriers taking grain, the container ships unloading goods. Many are our boats."

"What's your family's company?"

"Colinas Azules."

"Sounds pretty."

"It is in real life too. It is also the name of my father's ranch in Mexico. The Blue Hills. In the States, we operate under our family name. Delgado International."

"Does your family still own the ranch?"

"Oh, how about this weather? I think it's supposed to be one hundred degrees today," Annabelle interrupts them, as if wanting to change the subject.

"Still better than Mexico City," Paulo says politely and then turns back to Iris. "Yes, but it's no longer much of a ranch. More of an... estate. Not so many Vaqueros chasing cows anymore. Business has been good. *NAFTA* has been good." He smiles. "Augusta has been to visit us. We would love to have you all as well. Especially with you at the helm of the company, Annabelle. It would be good for you to pay us a visit."

"Of course."

The table quiets, and the silence gets to Iris first. "So where is your family's estate?"

Paulo raises his brow, as if this is something Iris should know. "Sinaloa."

"I'm not familiar."

"It's on the western side. It borders the Pacific."

"Oh, my." Annabelle looks at her watch and stands. "It's nine o'clock already. We should probably get ready to go into the office."

Because it's Friday, Iris thinks.

"Ah. It was a nice breather after all the travel, but back to business." Paulo taps his cigarette out in a small ashtray. He and Iris stand at the same time. "It was such a pleasure to finally meet you, *señora*."

"You, as well."

They shake hands lightly.

Iris starts back inside, and Annabelle calls after her. "Would you fetch Mama for us? I'm not sure she knew we were already running a little late."

Iris doesn't bother to return the fake smile Annabelle beams at her. She's too nervous to see Augusta alone after last night.

She walks across the entry hall and up the stairs. She's almost at the top when Augusta appears from around the corner.

"Hey, they're all—"

"I know. I'm coming." Augusta says but doesn't make eye contact as she passes Iris on the other side of the wide staircase. She keeps walking to the front door as she talks. "We're having dinner tonight outside on the porch. And don't forget the riverboat party is tomorrow. Make sure you're rested."

Right. Iris has forgotten about the party. At least she's still invited, she thinks.

"Okay."

Augusta hasn't turned around, but she's stopped at the front door. "One more thing."

Iris's chest rises. She takes a deep breath. Holds it.

"I picked you up a new phone. It's on the table just inside your room. Log in to your email, and you should have a message from my nephew."

"What about?"

"Nick sent you the texts between you and your husband. He wanted me to tell you."

"Oh." Iris is trying to think of something to get Augusta to stay. She needs to talk to her. Running away last night was a mistake. Now Augusta is making her pay, and she isn't going to give Iris the chance to corner her. She opens the front door, and Iris calls out.

"Augusta?" Her name trembles off her lips. Echoes in the entry hall. Her tone manages to say more than just her name. It asks a series of questions. Who *are* you? Who were *we*?

Augusta turns over her shoulder, but her eyes don't quite reach Iris. She steps outside without answering and pulls the big oak doors shut.

A Perfect Wife

Iris isn't so sure about the phone. It has to be bugged. There's not a chance that Augusta isn't able to listen to her every phone call, track her every movement. She should call the court for an attorney and then drop the thing in the toilet.

It takes her the better part of an hour to set up the phone. When she does, she logs right into her email and opens the message from Nick. It's a link to their wireless carrier with a username and password. In another minute, she's in.

There they are. It's a list of texts from the last six months. There are texts from a dozen or more contacts. She thinks she'll click on Joseph's first, but her thumb quickly taps the little tab that reads *Augusta Adler*.

Iris starts to read. The last conversation they had before she was shot was about when she and Joseph would be over for dinner that next Sunday. She scrolls through the weeks. The months. Their conversations are completely devoid of any interesting information. It's banal. Passive aggressive at times. The kind of back and forth between a young woman and a rich mother-in-law who probably doesn't think she's good enough for her son.

When Iris gets back to before the wedding, her eyes glaze over. They must've sent thousands of texts to each other planning the thing. When Iris gets to a part where they argue over the size of the cocktail shrimp they should serve, she closes out of the window.

She tilts her head back. She considers whether maybe what transpired between them happened *after* the accident. Maybe all her memories of Augusta, the control, the sex. It could've started back in July. Those hazy first few weeks of living here.

Iris finally has the texts of her late husband, the man she's been desperate to know, and all she gives a shit about is

211

Augusta. She opens the folder with texts between her and Joseph and begins to read.

The only text either of the two sent to each other on May 17th, the day of his death and her attempted murder, was *Where are you?*

It was sent by him at 3:47 in the morning.

Iris frowns. So she wasn't home in bed that night. She was gone, and Joseph was looking for her. She knows 3:47 isn't that far from the suspected time of the shooting. The coroner listed Joseph's death between four and five in the morning.

Iris chews her lip and keeps scrolling through the texts, and as she does, she loses her breath.

The first thing her eyes find is a picture of herself. Or, at least, her ass. The picture was sent by her. Her butt is bright pink, and her hands rest cuffed just above it in the small of her back. "Missing you, Daddy..."

Iris's face scrunches in disgust. *Daddy?*

Joseph responded with a picture of him holding his erect penis in his hand. The photo is mostly hand.

She scrolls up to see more pictures of herself naked. They're not from this same sexting session. She sends more than one every single day. Some are old nudes, like this spanking one that must be screenshotted from a video Joseph took. But most of the others were taken by her. Mirror selfies, under the skirt selfies. One photo was taken at the gym for a little bit of exhibitionism.

Iris has to stop reading. Her face burns. How many cops have read these? How many people saw this side of her private life? Dug into it?

Iris remembers how the sheriff couldn't even look at her when he came over. How quick he was to anger. He thinks she's a slut. Or his Christian conscience is racked with guilt because he didn't only view these photos of Iris for professional purposes.

Iris can't believe how much she and Joseph sexted. It's most of their conversation. There's an occasional break to discuss something like groceries or schedules, but for the most part it's Iris sending nudes and calling him daddy. She cooked for him.

Cleaned for him and lay on the bed spread eagle whenever he wanted. She was the perfect wife. They were rich newlyweds with little worries in the world. Maybe it was the honeymoon high.

She scrolls further to see pictures of her gagged and bound. Her mouth is stuffed with a pair of her underwear, but there's a smile in the corner of her eye. It looks like abuse. Snuff shit. Her skin is all pink and redder where the outline of hand marks still remains.

But the pictures were sent by *her,* and from the time stamps, she sent them to him when Joseph was at work. She *liked* this. She liked teasing him. Getting tied up by him when he was home and sending him pictures of the scene later to get him hot and bothered behind his desk.

Or maybe, Iris thinks, she didn't have a choice.

There are no more texts with Joseph after the seven-month mark. It's all been erased, but Iris doesn't think it matters.

There's a reason the police are out of leads. The text messages tell her nothing. Every conversation with acquaintances, friends, and family are what one would expect— proper, polite, brain-numbingly boring.

There is no bombshell. But it does leave a question mark that needs answering. The last text Joseph sent. *Where are you?*

Wait. Iris's spine tingles. There's something about this text that disturbs her, but she can't quite put her finger on it. She reads again before her eyes linger on the timestamp. *May 17th.*

That's only days before the article about the burnt girl's corpse was written.

It can't be a coincidence. She can't just ignore that memory anymore as uncomfortable as it makes her.

Iris stares at her phone. Her heart drums. The early morning of May 17th had to be the same day Iris had the body in the truck bed.

Iris pulls up the article on the burnt girl again. It's dated May 23rd. Why are there so few details about this? Iris remembers bullet holes in the woman's head, but the article has no mention of homicide. It had no follow-up. No news conferences. Nothing.

There was either that little information or, Iris realizes, they have their suspect already.

It doesn't matter how much she wants to ignore the memory of that night. She can't find out the truth without getting to the bottom of who the girl in the truck bed was. Iris has to face it, she realizes, even if it means revealing the monster she might've been.

She needs to discover her motive.

And someone in this family has to know it.

214

Parental Control

It takes an hour, but Iris has begun to calm down. There's another question she's not quite sure of. She goes back to her text conversation and pulls up some photos that Augusta sent her. They're of her wearing several different dresses. She wanted Iris's opinion on which she thought she should wear to her wedding.

The dresses all look stunning on Augusta. Her body fills out clothes the way Iris wishes hers could. She stares hard at the pictures. She zooms in and takes screenshots. Her heart starts to race a little, and her hand begins to slip down her pants, but then she stops herself. She sits up in bed, panicking.

She goes to the phone's system settings. There's an app that is installed that wasn't on her home screen—Kidkeeper.

It's a parental controls app. It grants camera access and microphone access to another device. "Fuck," Iris says aloud. She tries to change the setting, but it asks for its own password.

"Fuck." She gets out of bed and pitches the phone into the covers. Augusta can see she's taken these screenshots, surely.

Iris heads into the bathroom, strips off all her clothes, and runs a piping hot shower, but even as she lathers herself with soap, she still feels dirty.

She still feels *seen.*

Coercion. Control. Is this what turns Iris on? She paces back and forth in her bedroom before dinner. It certainly seems that was what she was into with Joseph. She liked being used. Being somebody else's.

And now that somebody is Augusta.

Iris feels shame, mostly. Some of it, she must admit, is from being turned on by another woman. But most comes from the shame of submitting to someone with so much power over her and shame for touching herself while that goddamn phone was on. It's getting dark already. She's since walked around the property and had a late lunch, but her anxiety has done nothing but build all day.

When she heads downstairs, Annabelle, Jamie, and Paulo are having drinks in the music room. Iris doesn't join them. She walks outside to see a table is being put together on the porch.

Aurelia has help tonight. Two groundskeepers in tucked-in polos are helping move the table in pieces from the basement. Iris goes to where she's out of their way and sits on the porch swing.

She stays there while they lay the tablecloth, light candles, and arrange the china and silverware. It's not long after that Augusta comes out the front door with Joseph in a wheelchair and the others trailing her. Nick is here. He wears a navy sport coat over a polo. He is the only one who looks over at Iris as the party comes onto the porch.

Iris stands but doesn't walk over as they begin taking their places at the table. She watches Augusta wheel Joseph Senior to the head of the table and sit to his right.

"Iris, would you join us please?" Augusta asks as she unfurls her napkin onto her lap.

"Yeah." Iris didn't even realize she'd seen her yet.

"We have you at the end." Augusta nods to a chair. It's not set up at the opposite end of the table across from Joseph Senior. She sits at the very end of the table and off to the side. No one sits across from her.

Another power play. Another reminder that she's the lowest on the totem pole. There's a place at the table set up opposite her, but no one sits in front of the plate. Everyone is paired off except Iris.

"Gideon was supposed to be joining us." Annabelle sits to her left and nudges her. "You know him. He'll probably arrive just as we're getting ready for a nightcap."

Iris just nods. The talk tonight is all business. Bushels and granaries and tariffs, and she tries to listen but opts instead to tune it out.

216

Iris's chair faces the lawn, at least. She has something to look at other than the side of the house. It's a beautiful night. Light and breezy. A few sleepy crickets call here and there. She tries to look at Augusta, but she won't even make eye contact with Iris.

Everyone, apart from Joseph Senior, has something to say about the business. They're all making inside jokes Iris doesn't understand, and she has half a mind to excuse herself and go upstairs.

Her attention only piques when Aurelia steps outside onto the porch quickly. "Mrs. Adler?" Aurelia says.

The table quiets.

"Your phone is on the dining room table. It's ringing."

"That's okay," Augusta says.

"I mean it won't stop ringing."

Augusta pauses. "Did you see who's calling?"

"I don't recognize the number." Aurelia says it like it's some kind of code, and Augusta tilts her chin up, realizing something is wrong.

"I see." She wipes her mouth with her napkin, although they still haven't even started eating, and sets it on the table. Then she smiles tightly as she follows Aurelia inside.

The table takes a second to talk again.

It's Paulo who breaks the silence. "So, Iris, how was your day?" They're sitting on the same side of the table, and he leans forward to make eye contact with her.

Iris looks at the others before she speaks, as if she needs permission. Jamie is being his invisible self and not paying attention while he sips his cocktail and scrolls on his phone. Annabelle isn't focused on them either. Her gaze is fixed on the front door. She's anxiously waiting for Augusta to return.

"Um. It was fine."

"Did you get outside? The weather ended up lovely this afternoon. Not quite a hundred degrees. I was staring out the office windows like a school child."

"I didn't, actually. The sun... It can sometimes..."

"Oh, sure. I imagine the headaches can be strong. A nine-millimeter bullet to the head is no bee sting."

The table is quiet again. Jamie sighs as he sets down his drink. Nick pinches his collar. But Iris is frowning.

"I don't think they ever said what kind of bullet it was."

"No?" Paulo says.

"No. Not publicly."

Paulo leans back in his chair. Iris can no longer read him. Annabelle sits in the way. She still just stares ahead, uninterested in their conversation.

"I just assume," says Paulo. "It's a common ammunition. And a bigger round from a Colt 45, or a revolver... You probably wouldn't be so lucky to be with us, *señora.*"

"You seem to really know your guns, Paulo," says Iris.

He chuckles. "I grew up a cowboy. Remember?"

"Hm." Iris grabs her water glass and takes a sip.

The door opens, and Augusta reappears. Her face is wide with fear, and the first thing her eyes land on is Iris. They stare at each other for a second before she keeps walking to the table.

"Joseph, darling. Let's get you inside."

"Who was it?" Annabelle asks.

"Paulo," Augusta says, ignoring her. "Could you help me wheel Joseph in?"

"Certainly."

Jamie looks up from his phone, realizing he might be needed. "I can help."

"You stay right there, Jamie."

"*Mama,*" Annabelle says louder. "Who was callin'?"

Augusta and Paulo start moving with Joseph Senior inside. Augusta looks nervously towards the road. "It was a neighbor. We're going to have company."

"What kind of company?" Annabelle looks toward the road.

"You just stay seated. I'll open the gate," says Augusta. She, Paulo, and Joseph Senior all disappear inside.

Iris stares at the road. She watches the gate open slowly. Who is coming?

218

She can see them before she can hear them. The close horizon is lit up with frantic flashes of red and blue. She feels her stomach drop as six police vehicles, three of which are black SUVs, race down the road. Their sirens are off while their lights whirl. All Iris hears is the roar of their engines, and they look more menacing for it.

They come to a skidding stop in the gravel, and the doors fly open one by one.

A short blonde woman flanked on all sides by tall officers starts marching towards the porch.

Augusta comes back outside.

"Augusta Adler?" asks the blonde woman. She's not in a uniform. She has a plaid dress shirt tucked into black slacks.

"Yes."

The woman produces a piece of paper. "Agent Long. FBI. We have a warrant to search the premises."

"Is this about my son?" Augusta's face becomes frightened. "Nick? Nick, do you know anything about this?"

Nick shakes his head with his eyes extra wide to show he's genuinely bewildered.

Augusta holds a startled hand to her chest. She's *acting*, thinks Iris.

"I'm sorry, ma'am. We're here for Iris Adler." Agent Long looks at Iris and walks up the porch steps. One of the officers around her pulls out a pair of handcuffs.

"What?" Iris blurts out. Her heart rate begins to rocket. The officers walk right up to her, and Annabelle stands from the table quickly to get out of their way.

Agent Long stops and stares down at Iris like she's something to pity. A criminal. A con artist. "You're under arrest in connection with the murder of Sarah Gray."

Iris opens her mouth but chokes on her words.

"Who?" shouts Augusta.

The cops are rough with Iris. They yank her up from the table by the elbow, spin her around, and clasp her hands behind her back. They clinch the cuffs so tight, her shoulder blades retract. The metal digs into the bones of her wrists.

"You can't just take her!" Augusta is yelling. This is not acting.

They're already leading Iris down the porch steps towards one of the black SUVs.

Another eight officers are coming towards the house now. Not officers. *Agents*, Iris realizes. This is an entire operation. They're federal agents with their windbreakers that have *FBI* printed in big yellow letters on the back. And they're here to search Sweet Blood. It all seems unreal.

Agent Long reads Iris her Miranda Rights, but she's too stunned to listen.

She sees herself driving the pickup. Sarah Gray—the body wrapped in a sheet in the truck bed now had a name. It wasn't a false memory. They've told her something she's felt was true all along.

Iris Adler is a murderer.

Questioned

Iris is left alone in the back seat of the SUV. There's a holey metal divider separating her from the front seats. A driver sits chewing his thumbnail. He doesn't look at her in the rearview. Once Agent Long shuts the door to the back seat, the man starts driving up the gravel road and away from Sweet Blood.

The other police vehicles stay in the driveway. It doesn't look like Iris is being accompanied. They drive north to Baton Rouge, while Iris is in shock.

In twenty minutes, the SUV pulls up in front of a nondescript office building. There are two officers in plainclothes, but they're not trying to hide the fact that they're cops. Their guns are holstered in plain view.

They take her inside to a conference room with a long plastic table. The metal blinds are drawn, and some are bent.

Nobody speaks. There are two chairs on each side of the table. One side for the detectives, and the other for defendant and attorney, Iris thinks.

They take Iris's handcuffs off, and she rubs her wrists.

"Your attorney will be arriving shortly," says one of the cops.

"Like a public defender?"

He doesn't respond. They turn and leave her alone in the room.

Iris pulls out one of the chairs and sits.

There's a clock high up on the wall, and Iris fidgets and watches it as the second hand slowly glides round and round. She's too stressed to even think. She breathes. Once. Twice. It's fifteen silent minutes before the door opens again.

An old man in a gray three-piece suit and an alligator-skin briefcase enters. "Mrs. Adler."

It's Marshall Walker, the family lawyer. The door shuts behind him, and he extends his hand. Iris half stands, and they shake.

"Augusta sent you?"

"She called the second she heard. I have good news. They can't possibly hold you or make an arrest with the flimsy amount of evidence they have."

"You know what it is?"

He nods slowly. Knowingly. Then he sits next to Iris on her side of the table. "They're just trying to scare you. They played their hand early, and they played it big. And they're going to pay because of it. You survived a bullet to the head, Iris. Your luck didn't just end there. I think we got the stupidest feds in the South on this case." He pops his briefcase open and pulls out a folder.

"Agent Long is based out of the Bureau's New Orleans office. I've had the displeasure of being on this side of the table from her before. She's a *mean* cop."

Iris grows nervous.

"But not a smart one." He wags a finger. "She can break you down, but not with me here."

"Okay."

"If they ask you *anything* I don't think you should answer, I'll let you know. If they ask you something *you* don't think you should answer because it may be incriminating, just say you don't know, don't remember... can't recall. Etcetera. You get the picture. I got a note from your neurologist being faxed here right now. You're special needs, okay? Mentally handicapped."

"Great."

He pats her leg with a smile. "Oh, don't worry. Not all lawyers are scumbags. But the best ones sure are." He winks. "Now, we need to get one thing clear. They're going to be askin' about the night you were shot. You were home. No matter what. They can dispute it, but we'll cross that bridge when we come to it. That's your story. Everything else you don't recall. Got it?"

"Who's Sarah Gray?"

"Exactly."

"I'm being serious."

"I should hope you are. They're saying you helped *kill* this girl."

The door opens, and in walks Agent Long and an older cop. Iris crosses her arms. The two get seated, and the man opens a folder, crosses his legs, and clicks a pen twice.

Agent Long puts her arms on the table and leans forward. "Hi, Iris."

"Have we met before?"

"We have not."

"Before we begin," Marshall starts. "I would like to know if you are aware of my client's mental state."

Agent Long looks ready to roll her eyes. "We got the fax, Marshall."

"I should hope so. I also hope you realize you just roughed up a twenty-eight-year-old widow with a mental handicap. Judge Precor isn't happy about it. Mrs. Adler has already called."

"I take it you mean Augusta Adler."

"The very one."

"Yeah. We talked to the judge. We won't be holding Iris."

"Good."

"That doesn't mean she can't cooperate in a homicide investigation."

"Are you talking about the open one into her husband's death and her attempted murder? Or the one about a girl neither of us have ever heard of until about an hour ago?"

Agent Long seems finished paying attention to Marshall. She sighs, looks at Iris. "Do you recognize the name Sarah Gray?"

Iris shakes her head quickly. "I honestly don't."

"Okay. I'm going to explain the events for you. Just a day after you and your husband were shot, a body was found off a rural road near the township of Port Vincent. No ID. She was so burned, we were lucky her pelvis bone was intact enough that we could at least identify the sex. I mean, there wasn't a strip of flesh to go off. You understand?"

223

Iris nods quickly, and she feels Marshall's eyes on her.

"We were able to ask around. We finally got the name of a girl that vanished around the same time the body was found. She wasn't all that missed. No one cared to report her missing. She was a prostitute. Born 2001. Sarah Gray."

"And what are you saying I had to do with it?"

Agent Long reaches over to a file that lies on the desk. She opens it and neatly lays a few big printed photographs in front of Iris.

The picture quality is terrible, but it clearly shows a two-toned pickup truck from the seventies, brown with a cream stripe running through the middle. It has big tires and a short cab. The driver's face isn't visible. The windshield is pitch black.

"Do you know what you're looking at here, Iris?"

Iris looks down at the photographs. "A pickup truck?"

"Do you recognize it?"

Iris shakes her head.

"It's your *husband's* pickup truck. It wasn't his daily driver. He kept it under a tarp nine months of the year."

Iris tries not to react at all.

"Did you know that he reported it missing around three a.m. the morning of the 17th?"

"No." Iris can't hide her confusion anymore. Her forehead crumbles like an accordion. "Nobody told me that."

"The state police didn't tell you that?"

"No. I just talked to them about my case. They didn't say anything about a stolen truck." Iris looks at her lawyer, hoping he'll confirm or deny this, but he won't meet her eye.

"Perhaps you just don't remember," says Agent Long.

"I think that's something I would."

"Okay. Fair enough. The truck did return to your property that same morning. It was there when your mother-in-law arrived and found you and Joseph."

"So, it was never really stolen?"

"Well, somebody took it for a joy ride. And your husband also mentioned that you weren't home."

"Did Joseph say it could be me? That I took the truck?"

The lawyer clears his throat and shakes his head. The message is clear; this line of questioning could be incriminating.

"No. He said he woke up to find the truck and his wife, you, Iris, missing. He didn't think you knew where the keys were. He—"

"I'm sorry. I'm sorry," Iris says quickly. "He said? He's dead."

"The morning he died, he called the police to report the truck missing. This is all from the transcript."

"Right." Iris settles back.

"He called 9-1-1 twice that morning. Once at 3:02 a.m. and shortly after at 3:06. He hung up the first time because he was getting another call. Then he called back to say never mind. He knew where the truck was. It was all a misunderstanding."

"So the truck wasn't stolen?"

"He didn't elaborate."

"Who was this other call? Do you have those phone records?"

"We can't disclose that."

Iris nods. She crosses her arms and cups her elbows in her palms as if she's cold, but if anything, this little concrete room is getting hot with the four of them in it.

Iris realizes they're building a case against her. They don't want her lawyer to know exact details because they don't want him to be able to wiggle Iris out of it.

"Another oddity... Do you know both of you were shot by a firearm belonging to your husband?"

Marshall taps her leg under the table. *Don't answer.*

"Well, the pistol's magazine holds fifteen rounds, but when it was found, there were only eleven bullets left."

"Maybe it wasn't loaded all the way," Marshall says, but Iris is thinking of the two bullet holes that shined in Sarah Gray's forehead.

"Either way. We're going to get you for this, Iris. Whether it's tomorrow or a month from now."

"Whoa. Enough," says Marshall.

"You're out of your minds," Iris says rather unconvincingly. "Can you even tell me why I would've killed her?"

"We can't," Long says casually, like Iris is already caught but they just haven't figured this part out yet. "We do know that Joseph's stolen truck was seen on camera. We do know that you and the truck both went missing from your home at the same time. And we know that genetic material found in the truck bed was just confirmed to be a match to Sarah Gray."

So that was the reason for the raid. This new DNA probably has them thinking their case is near solid, Iris realizes.

Long glares at Marshall and then glances back to Iris. "We're going to catch you. The state might go easy on you because of your mental condition. They could go even easier on you with a confession."

"My client's not falling for that shit. If you convict her, you'll stick her in the pig pen with all the real murderers." Marshall makes it seem like this statement is directed at Long, but really, Iris knows he's talking to her.

Iris spreads her hands on the table to steady herself. "How do you know the same people who shot my husband and me aren't behind this? How do you know they didn't kill this woman, and then drive to our house?"

Long is silent, but it doesn't feel like it's because she's stumped. She *knows* the answer to this question. This part is not the puzzle. "We're close to making an arrest in that case."

That case, she says, like it's unrelated to all this. But Iris knows that's impossible.

"Well, are they related?" Iris's voice is louder.

"We're not here to talk about that."

Iris wants to argue, but Marshall again taps on her leg. She takes a moment to calm down. "What else can you tell me about Sarah?"

Long pulls another picture of a woman from the folder and sets it in front of Iris.

She's a pretty girl of mixed race. Her eyes are big and dark, and her mouth is curved down naturally, like she's always a little sad.

Iris feigns nonchalance, but really, she wants to scream.

It took this long for it all to make sense. Who Iris was. What she was doing.

She understands her motive.

This must've been the African American girl the hotel manager was talking about. This is the Jane Doe Joseph beat at the Nile. The one who was hospitalized. Iris suddenly understands why she was out that night. She was cleaning up the mess.

Protecting her husband.

Protecting the family fortune.

She always had a hunch about the type of woman she used to be, but now that she *knows*, it feels like she could puke.

Girls

They recess while Agent Long takes a call. The cops leave, and Iris turns to her lawyer. The two chat in hushed voices.

"Did the police actually not tell me about the stolen truck?"

"I don't know. Your memory has been spotty. It wasn't private information, however. I knew about the truck being reported stolen, as did Augusta and Annabelle."

"What about my attempted murder? Joseph's death. Do you know who they're close to making an arrest on?"

"That's all bullshit. Long knows nothing. This whole Sarah Gray thing is a perfect deflection for them and I'm telling you, they're going to pay for it."

Iris bites her lip.

"Listen, I think it's best if you're done talking. We know what they know now. It's flimsy as fuck all. They're trying to get you scared. That's what they're doing."

"Okay."

"I'll get 'em to wrap it up."

"Wait. Could you ask them something? I don't want to ask it myself."

"What is it?"

"I need to know where Sarah was staying. Who she might've been friends with."

Marshall seems to consider this request before accepting. But he nods. "Okay, just keep your mouth zipped. I got it."

Iris leans back in her chair as the cops come back into the little room.

Agent Long explains that Sarah Gray was living at a bunny ranch off Highway 2. It's a settlement of half a dozen trailers turned into a whorehouse. There's technically a bar on the property, but everyone knows what really goes on there. It's a members-only establishment.

It's only four miles from Sweet Blood, but without a car and with the surveillance Iris is under, if she wanted to visit it might as well be the moon.

Iris doesn't answer another question. The interview ends, and when Marshall and Iris step out of the station, Iris sees Arthur is waiting for them.

Marshall must've gotten a ride here. He gets into the back of the Cadillac. When Iris doesn't follow, he leans out. "Come on now, Iris."

He can sense she's scared to return to Sweet Blood, but that's not what she's considering. She's thinking of confessing.

She has enough memory. The body in the truck bed. The accomplice standing watch on the side of the road. She needs to do what the woman she used to be wasn't capable of doing. She needs to be a good person.

Then she pictures prison, courtrooms. The actual consequences that would unfold, and she quickly gets into the car.

Sweet Blood is all lit up when they pull down the road. Iris feels a little ill. The FBI appears to be gone, but now everyone is standing on the front porch. Annabelle, Augusta, Jamie, and Aurelia. They all stand perfectly straight like a welcoming party. Paulo is not among them, Iris notices.

Iris gets out of the car, as does Marshall. She walks up the porch stairs, and no one says anything. Augusta just hands Iris a sheet of paper.

Iris doesn't ask what it is. She has a feeling she knows. There's a court seal at the top.

She looks down and reads. It's a document from a judge granting emergency guardianship of Iris to Augusta Adler. She starts reading what powers it gives to Augusta.

The first item reads, "control of movement." She doesn't have to keep reading to get the gist. Iris can't leave so much as leave the property without Augusta's permission. She can't spend money. She definitely can't drive.

"Congratulations," says Iris and hands the paper back.

Augusta says nothing. She doesn't look pleased. This isn't some kind of victory for her. Was she telling the truth? Did she really request this guardianship to appease Annabelle?

She glances past Iris. "Marshall, could we talk?" Augusta goes down the steps, and she and the lawyer walk off into the night talking quietly.

Iris starts inside.

"What did you tell them?" Annabelle stands in her path, her pregnant belly acting like a barrier.

"I didn't tell them anything."

"What did they want to know?"

"Just talk to the lawyer." Iris brushes past her inside.

She's in the entry hall when she hears another voice. *"Buenas noches, señora."*

She turns to see Paulo smiling at her. His dark-brown eyes look almost black in the poor light. She just nods and continues up the stairs. So he's staying here.

When Iris is in her bedroom, she turns to lock the door behind her, but her fingers find nothing. The little deadbolt switch is missing. She bends over, looks in the door. The deadbolt itself has been removed. Did the police do this? When would this have happened?

Her room doesn't look ransacked, but it's obvious the FBI turned the place over. Her dresser drawers aren't shut all the way. Her mattress is cattywampus from where they lifted it out of the bed frame to look underneath.

Iris is far too wired to try to sleep. She's not just going to wait to go to prison, living under Augusta's thumb. She's resolved to do something about it. Tonight.

She pulls up Google maps on her phone and switches the view to satellite. Agent Long didn't give an exact address to the brothel, just the general location. But it doesn't take Iris long to find. At the junction off Highway 2, she can see the roofs of the trailers that Agent Long told her about. Half a dozen of them sit in a ring around a circle of trees. She clicks the screen and sets a pin to the location.

It's only an eleven-minute drive, but it would be a three-hour walk along highways to get there. It's not the only place she wants to go. Iris has another destination in mind, and walking isn't going to cut it. Tonight she needs a vehicle, and she knows just where to get one.

She turns off the room's overhead light and goes to the closet. Her clothes are all wrinkled. Unfolded. The police went through them too.

She dresses in black.

Black jeans. Black long-sleeved T-shirt. Black trainers. Then she goes to the window and sits in the dark. She's going to watch the road and the paths all night. She's going to memorize the patterns of the hired security.

Marshall and Augusta come back into view after about twenty minutes. They shake hands, and he gets into the back seat of the Cadillac. After it drives off, Augusta heads inside. Iris hears her come upstairs and shut the door to the master.

She wonders what the FBI thought about the men on patrol. Ex-military hires with their long black rifles are suspicious. Suspicious enough to cause one to think that the Adlers have something to hide. Even if their son was murdered, it's strange behavior.

But after about a half hour, Iris realizes the security must be off tonight. She doesn't see anyone patrolling the property. No dark shadows wander down the path. The night is still.

Would Augusta have given them a heads-up that the police were coming and told them to hide? She probably didn't want the FBI to know about the guards if they didn't already.

The lights of the guesthouse are off. Jamie and Annabelle must be sleeping. Iris isn't sure where Paulo ended up.

He must be staying in a guest room. Perhaps the same one in the northwest corner of the house that Iris first stayed in when she came to Sweet Blood. Aurelia, too, must be in the house, staying in the old servant's quarters tonight. She wakes early to make breakfast. She's probably already asleep.

231

Iris knows there's a button to open the gate by the front door. The problem is that the gate sends alerts to Augusta's phone. Every time it opens, she knows.

She's going to have to take another route out of here. She memorizes the way to the brothel because she doesn't want to take the iPhone with her.

She gives it another hour, and it's still only midnight when she opens her door and creeps downstairs.

She heads to the kitchen and quickly out the back door. She doesn't walk on the red brick path. She stays in the shadows of the oaks as she makes her way past the garden. She passes the pond and is soon at the service door to the larger of the two pole barns. Before she tries the doorknob, she turns and waits.

She stares back at the house. She keeps expecting to see the back door open. All the lights to turn on and someone to shout and start to chase her.

She was certain someone was watching her. But maybe Augusta was banking that she'd take the bugged iPhone with her if she ever snuck out. The parental controls app probably has an alert feature that goes off if she gets a certain distance away from the house. It's possible nobody knows she's gone, and she doesn't want to give them the time to realize that she is.

She opens the door to the barn and finds the lights. The big LEDs overhead reveal the same vehicles that were here when Iris came in on Sunday—two tractors and two farm utility trucks.

The pickups have ADLER CORP printed in big green letters on their sides. Iris runs to the closer of the two and tries the door handle. Unlocked. She has to pull herself up into the cab, but she quickly sees what she's looking for.

The keys are in the center cupholder. She grabs them, puts them in the ignition, and slams the door. She doesn't start it yet. Her plan isn't fully formed.

If she wants to go out the main gate, she'll need to drive to the front of the house, park, run inside, hit the gate button, run back to the truck, and drive. That's her only option.

She's certain to wake someone. She's certain to leave an alert on Augusta's phone, but that's her only choice. The other gates that the farm roads take off the property are padlocked, and she doesn't have a key.

Iris looks around the cab to see if there's a remote for the gate. But there's only one remote that's attached to the sunshade, and Iris thinks it's for the barn door.

Iris starts the truck. The diesel engine roars to life, and then she hits the wide button on the remote. The stall door behind her begins to open. She puts the truck in reverse and hits the gas.

She skids onto the gravel and taps the garage door button again. She's driving. *Easy*, she thinks. She's doing this. If she gets caught, the Adlers could charge her with car theft, but with the murder charges looming, it's the least of her worries.

She takes the gravel road all the way around the garden to where it meets up with the house's main driveway. Iris drives all of ten miles per hour, staring at the house the entire time. Her heart pounds. If anyone inside is awake, they will no doubt hear the diesel engine.

When Iris gets to the front of the house, she puts the truck in park, throws the door open, and makes a run for the gate button, but she's stumped immediately. The front door will be locked. It's past ten. Of course it is. It's locked every night.

Shit. Iris hasn't thought through this at all.

She turns back towards the truck, when the hair on her neck stands on end. It wouldn't have mattered anyway. The main gate *is* opening. Only, it's not her. She can see a pair of high headlights at the top of the road.

It's the guards. Their truck starts to roll down the driveway, and Iris is just standing, stunned. It's over. Her escape never even started.

She really is a prisoner here. Any second now, Augusta is going to come out the front door with her arms crossed like an angry mother.

Iris isn't even thinking when she gets back in the truck and shuts the door. The guards slow to a stop. They're blocking the driveway so she can't get around them. There is, of course, another way off the property.

Iris puts the truck in drive and slams the gas. She feels the back tires spitting up gravel as they find traction. She rockets across the lawn and steers directly for the sugarcane stalks. She plows into the field, jostling in her seat.

The stalks slap the hood in a rapid fire. It's an angry drumroll that accelerates as Iris does too. The field isn't smooth like the lawn. It's rutted, and she bounces up and around in her seat so violently that the seat belt locks.

She grips the wheel for dear life and tries to think. If she continues straight, the field should exit on the public road. There's a steep ditch she'd have to look out for, but Iris can't see a thing through the stalks.

She tries to keep the wheel straight so she doesn't end up driving in a circle, but she's not sure how good of a job she's doing with the amount the truck is bouncing.

And as suddenly as the stalks started drumming on the hood, they stop. The sugarcane vanishes, and time seems to stand still for a second. Iris doesn't have time to react.

Ahead is the road, and with it a steep grade up to where the gravel begins. She tries to turn the wheel to ride up the shoulder, but she doesn't have enough time. The truck crashes against the ditch and then soars a couple feet into the air.

When she lands, the cab feels like it leaps from the frame before settling back. Iris brings the truck to a stop in the road, and a cloud of dust from her collision overtakes the headlights.

There are a few lights flashing on the dash and a hissing from the engine. Iris's hair is a mess over her face from how hard the truck pitched. She looks back at the hole she made in the field. There are no headlights following through the scar she left in the sugarcane.

She puts the truck in drive and starts forward. There's a plastic scraping sound. From where it is, she figures part of the front bumper must be hanging off and dragging against the road. She gives it a little more gas. Her teeth are clenched nervously. She keeps expecting to feel the tell-tale wobble of a flat tire, but the ride only gets smoother the faster she goes. Iris gets the truck back up to fifty miles per hour when she sees them again.

The guards elected to go back out the main gate instead of chase her through the field. They are gaining on her, quick.

She's in the slower truck. This thing is a diesel outfitted for farm work. The truck she's seen security driving is a similar size but not nearly as loaded down with equipment. Before she's done calculating how possible it is that she could beat them in a race, her eyes are scrunched from the glare of their high beams. They've already mostly caught up with her.

Their truck swerves aggressively out from behind her so it has a clear strip to pass, and they gun it. Iris keeps her head swiveling from the road in front of her and the truck coming up on her left.

Their passenger window is down. One of the men is leaning out with his rifle shouldered. He aims at her back tire. Iris tightens her grip on the wheel. She keeps her foot depressed on the gas.

Iris has the mind to try to attempt to run them off the road, but these men are just hired security. Desperate as she is, she *can't* crash her car into theirs. She can't risk their lives.

She's about to move her foot to the brake, when suddenly the man with the rifle leans back into the cab. Their truck starts to slow. It gets smaller and smaller in her side mirror until it turns, and then she sees nothing but its taillights.

They stopped. They turned around. Iris stops her own truck and continues to stare at the rearview. Eventually, when she's sure they're gone, she gets out and looks back at the road. The black is undisturbed. No one is coming after her.

Her own truck keeps hissing, and some fluid is dripping beneath it. The front bumper hangs on to only one side, and one of her headlights hangs out of its socket, but the light isn't out.

The truck doesn't look road worthy, but it still drives. For now. Iris is trying to think why they turned around. Augusta told them to. There's no other reason they'd stop right when they had her.

Maybe Augusta is sending the police after her instead. Or, Iris thinks, her eyes widening as she stares at the dark road ahead of her, a man with a silenced pistol.

Inked

Iris is afraid her memory failed her. When she gets to the turnoff where the brothel trailers should be, there's nothing but a dark wooded road. *Fletcher Road*, the sign reads.

She wasn't expecting a big flashing billboard advertising the place, but the road she stares at looks deserted. There is discarded trash—entire moldy couches and old appliances—littering the woods.

The FBI didn't say anything about a Fletcher Road when Iris had her lawyer ask about where Sarah was living. They were sparse with the details. A private trailer park off Highway 2. A semi-secret brothel.

Iris turns down the road and starts to drive slower. Her headlights catch critters' eyes that glow like jewels until they scurry back into the woods. She drives for maybe half a mile, when suddenly the road becomes a long strip, and she can see into the distance.

There are string lights hung all over oak trees. The shadows of people dance between the trees. Iris's chest thumps, but she's not nervous. It's from the heavy bass that plays in the distance.

It's a Friday night, holiday weekend, and this place is partying.

When she gets closer, she sees that there's a large space of lawn being used as a parking lot. She wants to hide the truck, not just park it. But in the end, she doesn't have a choice. If she drives any farther, the people partying might notice the damage. Then they'll notice her.

Pretty much every vehicle in the parking lot is a truck. Half of them are so lifted that it looks like they're driving on stilts. Iris parks and starts towards the string lights. They're playing Lynyrd Skynyrd. *Loud.* Perhaps it's to drown out the noise of the sex that's happening in the trailers or to keep the men drinking so they'll get loose with their wallets. Either way, the music shakes the leaves on the trees. If she had rolled her window down at the highway, she probably could've heard it rumbling in the distance.

A group of men comes stumbling towards the parking lot. They all have the same body type—average height, overweight. Two have bushy beards, and all three of them wear flannels, probably the nicest threads they own, to look good for the ladies.

"Uh-oh!" shouts one of the two with a beard as Iris approaches. She already starts to veer hard left to walk around them. "We got a wife!" He laughs, and the others chuckle.

Iris looks down at her outfit. Her all-black clothes do scream wife on a mission to find a cheating husband.

"Some men are just here for company, sweetheart, don't you know? If you find your man with a lady, be easy on him."

"No. Twist his balls!" shouts another, and they all holler.

"Hey, hey." One suddenly starts to whisper to his buddies.

"Are you serious?" Iris hears another say.

Do they recognize her as an Adler? They must.

"You have a good night. You hear?" they call after her, as if in apology. Iris keeps walking, and she can feel the trio's eyes on her back.

She stops when she gets to the edge of the oak trees. There are chairs and tables set up and even a painted plywood dance floor. The men dance with women in short skirts, and some are in no skirts at all. They're mostly naked in the warm August night.

The air buzzes with the bass of the music, and when she breathes in, Iris's nose stings from the smell of spilled bourbon. She needs to talk to one of these girls. She's about to go up to one herself when she's spotted. A short blonde in cowgirl boots with what is presumably their bouncer trailing her approaches Iris. The man wears a black T-shirt. He's barrel-chested and 6'5".

The blonde wears thick mascara and heavy eyeliner. Her blue eyes shine like sapphires in a coal mine. "You lookin' for your husband?"

"No." Iris has to shout to be heard. "I'm looking for someone who knew Sarah Gray."

The blonde and the bouncer look at each other and then back to Iris.

"Are you a fed, then?" The blonde holds a vape pen in her fist and takes a puff. "Your friends already came by earlier."

Iris can't find words for a moment. This girl has a tattoo on her neck. It's an eagle perched on a tree branch. Its head is turned to the right. The tattoo is familiar, but she can't place it.

"I'm not a fed."

"Well, who the hell are you, then?"

Iris didn't think about how she'd describe her relationship or interest in Sarah. Again, she didn't think this through. She isn't about to say she's a suspect in her murder. "I'm a friend of hers."

"A friend?" The blonde raises her brow incredulously. "You gotta do better than that." Then her eyes narrow as she looks at Iris's forehead. She's looking at the scar. "Wait, are you that Adler girl?"

Iris hesitates. Some man on the dance floor yells, and it takes the bouncer's attention away until he realizes it's all in fun.

"Yeah. I'm Iris."

"Shit," the blonde hisses, but it seems like it's more in surprise than fear. "Jack..." She pats the bouncer's chest. "We're good here."

He nods once and heads back towards the dance floor.

"Come with me, sugar."

The blonde starts walking towards the trailers and Iris quickly follows her.

"Where are we going?"

"Just somewhere we can talk."

They walk under the oaks away from the party and up the stairs into a doublewide trailer.

Inside, there's a row of three vanity mirrors, each ringed with lightbulbs. Only the stool in front of one is occupied. A black girl is dabbing her cheek with an egg-shaped makeup sponge.

Iris almost jumps as she notices another girl sitting on a loveseat across from the mirrors. She's smoking and has a 90s hairdo of massive curls.

"Uh-oh. Whose wife?" the girl asks.

"Nobody's wife. Iris fucking Adler."

"Whoa." The girl stubs her cigarette out. The one at the vanity stops applying makeup and watches them in the mirror.

"Do I know y'all?" Iris asks.

"No. I'm Lacy." The blonde who brought her in extends her hand, and they shake for a second. Strangely formal.

Iris is quiet for a moment, hoping to get more of an explanation, but none of them speaks. "Y'all just seem a little surprised to see me."

"You're practically famous, girl." Lacy laughs, but then her smile fades completely. "Is it true what they say about your memory? That you don't remember nothing from before you were shot?"

"Mostly."

"Well, you remembered one thing. You became friends with a few of the girls here."

Friends? With these girls? Iris has to keep herself from rifling questions off like she's crazy. "How close of friends?"

"More acquaintances, I guess. Look, do you remember coming around here with that reporter a few months ago?"

"No." Iris looks at the other girls, and they all look away. "Who was this reporter? Do you remember his name?"

"We weren't here. We heard it all from the girls that were. But let me get this straight... You don't even remember the man you came here with?"

"No."

Lacy puts her hands on her hips. The song outside changes and thumps so loud the glass rattles in the panes. "I'll lay it all out, then. Around April or so, you showed up here with a black guy. Girls said he was with some newspaper or website. I don't know. Kinda had a cop look to him apparently. Clean cut. You said you were doing some tell-all on the Adlers and needed witnesses. Girls."

"Witnesses to what?"

"Something about your husband being cruel."

"To girls?"

"Yeah." Lacy looks at the floor. "You wanted to catch the bastard in the act. Have him locked up. There were a few girls that agreed. The ones that had slept with him. We knew there was some rich sick fuck choking girls but never knew who he was until you showed up and said he was your husband."

"Who were the girls that were hurt by him? Was Sarah one?"

"Sarah was one, yeah. And there was Cassidy and Bree, and maybe Daisy. I know she knew all about it because she lived with Cassidy."

"Where are those girls?" Iris interrupts. "Are they here?"

The room goes silent. Lacy pulls on her fingers. "Daisy disappeared a couple days ago. Just after they found Cassidy OD'd dead in a field."

Iris's eyes widen. "Dead?"

"We lose a girl every month. You ain't no stranger to that. The girls said you were all open about being an addict yourself once."

Iris exhales a little laugh in disbelief. "I don't think that's right."

"I'm not going to argue. They were just sayin' that's what you told 'em."

Iris has to work to keep her mouth moving. This is no longer a coincidence. It's the second time someone has said Iris used to do *heroin.*

Lacy keeps talking. "Daisy might have overdosed, too. They split a trailer. Police are saying they had the same bad batch of drugs. It happens a lot down here. Especially now with all the fentanyl around... We gotta be careful."

"What about Sarah? When did she go missing?"

"We hadn't heard anything about her until those feds showed up this afternoon asking after her. She disappeared in May. We figured she got moved."

"Did the police say why they were looking for her?" Iris asks.

"No. Sure asked a lot of questions, though."

Iris doesn't want to break the news that she's dead. She doesn't want to distract from her next question. "Is there anyone I could talk to who met me when I came here with the reporter?

Lacy bites her lip, thinking.

"Bree," says the girl at the mirror.

"Right." Lacy nods. "Bree was there."

"Is she here now?"

"No. She's in the city tonight. But tomorrow, shit. She'll be at your boat party."

"What?"

"She'll be on the Diamond Lady."

Iris thinks they're pulling her leg. "There'll be prostitutes on a Labor Day cruise?"

The girls laugh softly. Lacy is the one to talk. "The thing's got seventy-five rooms. A lot of those men can't call it a party if they can't get laid."

"What about the cops? They don't shut you down here?"

"We don't like cops here," Lacy says, and the girl on the loveseat speaks.

"Yeah, they don't tip as well. They think they're doing us a favor by not putting us in handcuffs after fuckin' us."

Iris grimaces. This swamp is filthy, and not just the brothel. It's the corruption and the hypocrisy and the glossy exterior of cash that covers the rot. "Do you know anything else? About me? About Bree?"

The girls are all quiet again. They look afraid now. "Actually," Lacy says. "There's a lot of rumors going around that Daisy didn't OD. That she and Cassidy were murdered."

Iris pauses. "And you think it has something to do with me?"

242

"I don't know. Bree's been paranoid. She's afraid she's going to be next. I'd feel bad telling you this, only I think she trusts you. She's been wanting to talk to you."

Iris suddenly thinks of the missed rendezvous at Harvest Baptist. Was it Bree who had been trying to talk to her? Could they have been lovers?

Iris swallows nervously. "And what does she look like? Do I just ask for Bree when I'm on the boat?"

"I worked the party on the Diamond Lady a couple years ago," says the girl who's sitting at the vanity. She turns to face Iris now. "The sex all happens on the third deck. There's a presidential suite in the back of the boat. And yes, just ask for her."

"Okay."

"Be careful, Iris," says Lacy.

"I will be." Iris looks away, her eyes finding the coffee table that sits in front of the loveseat. She sees something else there. Something that takes her attention away from the girls entirely.

There's a plastic bag next to the ashtray. Inside is a yellowy white powder. A few syringes lie next to it. It's drugs. Heroin. But what leaves Iris breathless is that it looks exactly like the plastic bags she saw Nick with in the pole barn. *Fertilizer samples.*

She had fallen for it.

"Are you okay?" one of the girls asks.

Iris can't even tell which. Her head spins. "Yeah."

"Do you need to sit down?"

"I'm fine." Sugarcane isn't the only crop the Adler family sells. This family traffics drugs. Everything feels like it's exploded in size. Money. Motives. The Adler's secrets are not the petty subjects of everyday gossip.

They're fatal.

"Thank you. For everything," Iris mumbles as her hand finds the doorknob and she stumbles out into the dark.

243

Iris thinks she should stick around the trailer for a second. She should try to stand close to a window and eavesdrop on what they're saying in case the truth wasn't entirely being told, but the music is too loud.

Her thoughts swim too fast.

She's thinking of Paulo. Sinaloa. A cousin of his got shot in the head. His knowledge of firearms.

He's *cartel*.

It's simple. The Adlers must be using their ships and facilities on the Mississippi to take drugs in from the Gulf of Mexico. It's the perfect set up. They're the southern Christian conservatives that no one would ever suspect.

She starts back towards the parking lot at a brisk walk. When she gets to the truck, she looks under it first then walks to the window and looks in the back seat. It's all clear.

She gets into the driver's seat and fires up the engine. It chugs, turning over twice before coming to life. The dashboard lights up like a Christmas tree, and something beeps in warning. Tire pressure. Oil pressure. The check engine light flashes.

Iris puts it in reverse and rockets backwards. Then she's cruising back down the road towards the highway. If the police around here are corrupt enough to visit a brothel, what else might they be hiding about her attempted murder case?

They could all be bought by Augusta. Iris can't just tell the police her suspicions. If she's going to rat, it has to be to the FBI, but she's not there yet.

She still has to figure out what else this family is hiding from her.

She's not afraid of getting pulled over, not when she's heading to a police station. Cars pass her on the highway and linger when they're close to her front bumper to gawk at the damage. The bumper grinds against the asphalt. She's starting to feel one of the wheels wobble, but she's not sure if it's losing air or if the alignment is off.

When she gets to downtown Preston, she parks on the empty main street. She gets out of the truck and stares at the police station, where she met with the sheriff earlier this week.

There are still some lights on but no one inside from what she can see.

She gets out of the truck and looks both ways down the street. Downtown is dead at this hour. The only sounds are the breeze in her ear and an American flag outside the station snapping in the wind.

She had parked so the front bumper of the truck faces away from the windows of the police station. Not like it matters much anyway. If Augusta told the police to look for her, Iris is walking right into the trap.

She opens the glass door to the station and steps inside. The front desk is unmanned. There's a little bell left out like there would be at a hotel, and Iris steps forward and rings it.

She has a theory who would be working the overnight starting Labor Day weekend, and she's right. A young kid of about twenty-three comes through another set of glass doors. His orange hair curtains his forehead in a bowl cut.

He's a rookie.

"Um... evening, miss. Do you have an emergency?" he stutters and clears his throat.

"My name is Iris Adler. I'm actually here because I was hoping I could review some files from my case." She slides her driver's license across the counter, and he picks it up.

His eyes widen in surprise. He hands her license back to her. "Mrs. Adler... I'm sorry I didn't recognize you."

"It's fine."

"Um. To be honest, it's a little late. Um..." He looks around like there might be someone else to take charge of this situation, but he's on his own. "Look, I don't have access to case files. I'd have to call my superior for that, and it's a little late," he says, repeating himself.

"I don't mean to drop by in the middle of the night for no reason. I'm not sure you're aware of this, but the FBI just got involved. I've only just left an interview with them, and some of their questions jogged my memory. I'd really like to see the case files. Tonight."

This young cop recruit looks panicked. Iris watches his Adam's apple rise and fall as he gulps. "Okay. Let me just make a phone call."

He taps a little plastic keycard against a reader and goes back into the police station. She moves to where she can watch him through the glass doors and keep staring at him as he pulls out his cell phone. He puts it to his ear and starts pacing in a tight circle. After about thirty seconds, he puts the phone down and starts back towards the front.

Iris backs up to make room for him.

He opens the glass door but doesn't walk behind the counter. He stands with the door like a barrier between them. "I'm sorry. My sergeant isn't picking up," he says, as if this should end Iris's request.

"Then try the sheriff," Iris bluffs. "I need to see the files tonight. This is urgent." She is going to push this kid. If the police are conspiring with Augusta and keeping Iris in the dark, she doubts this baby-faced recruit is in on it. He doesn't know the sheriff wants to keep the case files away from her.

"Okay. Um…" he hums. His face is starting to turn red. "Come in, would you?" He opens the glass door more, and Iris steps around the counter and inside the station. He keeps walking past the desks towards a few offices at the back. He leads Iris to the same glass-windowed room she was in when she first tried to get details of the case.

She goes inside but doesn't sit.

"I'll have to try to call the sheriff."

"Okay. Try the sheriff."

He gives her a tight smile and shuts the door. Iris needs to think. If the sheriff answers, he's not going to let her see the case file. If anything, he'll come down to the station to put her in handcuffs himself for stealing the Adlers' truck.

The kid is on the phone again, but he's looking around nervously. No one is answering, Iris can tell. He brings the phone down and tilts his head up to the ceiling in frustration. Iris feels like cracking her knuckles. Her plan is about to work. Now she just needs to be a bitch.

She opens the door. "What's going on?"

"Sheriff isn't picking up."

She tosses her hands up and lets them slap on her sides. "I need to see those files. He knows this."

"I know, but I…"

"You know who I am, right?"

"Of course."

"You know my condition, don't you?"

"I've heard."

"Listen, if I don't see these files right now, I might forget the entire connection I'm remembering."

"Can't you write it down?"

"That's not how this works. I need to *see* the files. Do you think the sheriff would want you to keep them from me?"

"Okay. Okay, just give me one minute." He disappears into the back of the station, and Iris breathes. He comes back a minute later with the entire file box, not just a folder like the sheriff had the first time. He sets it on one of the desks. He starts peeking in. "Some of this case information is privileged. I can't share it all with you."

"That's fine."

"The thing is, Mrs. Adler… I don't know what's what."

Iris puts her hand on the side of the box. She's so close yet so far away. She's thinking of what to say next, when suddenly, the young cop throws his hand into his pocket. He pulls his phone out.

"Oh." His shoulders sink in relief. "Sheriff's calling me back."

Now it's Iris's turn to despair.

"Evening sir, it's Patrick. I've got Iris Adler at the station here. She—" The kid looks at Iris and then walks off a few steps. "Yeah. Mmhmm."

Iris isn't an idiot. They're not going to let her see these case files. She has to think fast. She pulls her shirt up to wipe her forehead, exposing her stomach and bra. The young cop can't spin away fast enough. He turns quickly and stays facing away.

She keeps dabbing her brow with the shirt and reaches into the file box. She can read the file tabs. One reads *Interviews*. Another reads *Timeline.* Iris grabs the folder with the tab that says *Forensics*. She stuffs it into her pants and pulls her shirt down.

The cop is still turned away from her, but she doesn't risk another look in the box. The bulge in her shirt and pants is obvious. She uses the file box to shield herself.

"Yeah. I can do that. No problem. Yes sir. See you then." He hangs up, and Iris raises her brow at him.

"That was the sheriff?"

"Yeah. He would like you to wait for him to come down to the station himself before taking a look at anything."

"I see." Iris realizes she has to keep her anger up if she wants to get out of here without raising his suspicion. "And how long is that going to be?"

"Sheriff said a half hour, tops."

"A half hour? What did I tell you about urgency? Fuck." Iris looks off, shaking her head. She walks quickly out from behind the file box and starts towards the glass doors. She moved quick enough for him not to see her bulging front. Her back is already to him.

"I need a cigarette," Iris says. She hasn't smoked one in her entire life as far as she's aware, but this cop doesn't know that.

"Um. Okay."

Iris looks over her shoulder to see that he's already peering back inside the box. When she gets outside, she picks up the pace to the truck. She's almost to the driver's door when she hears his footsteps clomping after her.

"Mrs. Adler! Mrs. Adler! Ma'am!"

She doesn't turn over her shoulder or stop. She clicks the key fob to unlock the door.

"Mrs. Adler, stop!"

She does and turns to see that he's about ten yards from her. His pistol is drawn. He points it at her chest but not confidently—the barrel is angled down. "You're in possession of police property. I'm placing you under arrest."

"Man, twice in one day?" Iris says as if in disbelief.

He doesn't know what to say to this. He just gulps.

"Listen." Iris reaches out and opens the truck door.

"Stop!"

She knows he made a mistake. He should've pulled out his taser and not his firearm if he wanted to stop her. This kid isn't going to risk shooting her in the back over a stolen folder of case files.

She actually feels a twinge bad for him. He's not corrupted, and he's not going to go unpunished for Iris's little heist, but she has larger worries. He did, after all, fuck up.

Iris climbs into the truck. She slams the door, locks it, and turns the key in the ignition. The engine chugs but doesn't start.

"Mrs. Adler! Mrs. Adler, step out of the vehicle!" He's already banging at the window.

Iris ducks her head and prays. She turns the key again, and this time the engine turns over. She backs out of her parking space and the kid runs around the truck the whole time. She accelerates and leaves him standing in the middle of the road, watching her go.

He's speaking into his radio. He's not going to follow her, but all nearby units are going to be closing in and fast.

There's only one road out of Preston, and Iris doesn't have a doubt there'll be a state trooper waiting for her. She can't run, but if she's quick, she can hide.

Murdered

Iris stays in town. She takes a quick series of turns to get off the main road and then sees a church. There's another road that leads around it, presumably to a parking lot that isn't visible from the street.

Iris takes the turn, parks the truck where it's hidden by the church, and kills the engine. Depending on how many cops are looking for her, she thinks she could have up to a half hour before she's found. Maybe.

They'll be surveilling the roads that lead out of town first. It won't be until they don't see the truck that they start canvassing the town.

She turns the key so the battery turns on and slaps on one of the overhead lights. Then she yanks the folder free from her pants. She opens it and spreads it on her lap. The first thing she sees are crime scene pictures, and she has to turn away.

It's what they denied her the first time at the station. There's a picture taken of their bedroom. Joseph has collapsed so he leans against the wall. His bloody head hangs towards the floor.

She doesn't have to look hard to see that he was also shot in the forehead, only the bullet entered lower, closer to his brow line. She can see exactly where it went in from the autopsy sheet. There's a drawing of a male body with its arms held slightly out from its sides.

On the head is a black X marking where Joseph was shot. One bullet. She puts this sheet on the center console and keeps looking through the folder.

Iris was taken from the crime scene before it was photographed since Augusta found out she was still breathing, but the police wanted to recreate the scene as best they could. There's a human outline made entirely of yellow tape stuck to the floor. From the writing in the margin, she finds out it's supposed to represent where Iris was lying when she was found.

She was halfway across the bedroom from Joseph. She was on her back, and one arm was tossed up near her face. Iris keeps flipping through the pictures and cringes as she gets to a close-up of Joseph.

The wound in his head drips blood down his face. His eyes are open, and so is his mouth. Even without the brutality of the gunshot wound, Joseph does not look peaceful in death. His face is still frightened. Disturbed.

Iris keeps flipping through the pictures. She stops when she gets to the gun. So they did have the murder weapon. There it sits, large and silver, in the middle of the marble floor. Even if a firearm is unregistered, it seems idiotic to leave it at the scene of a homicide. There's the risk of fingerprints on the gun and the bullets that were loaded into it. Plus, it still might be traceable. Someone could easily remember a silver pistol like that.

Iris rubs the scar on her head, and then she freezes. Her mouth creeps open. *She* remembers a silver pistol like that. It's the one she had in the truck when she was driving Sarah's corpse to the woods.

She goes through the pictures faster and faster until she reaches the end of the folder. One of the final sheets of paper is the full autopsy report for Joseph.

Toxicology discovered nothing unusual. There were no drugs or alcohol in his system. There were no signs of forced entry into their house. No broken windows. Kicked-in doors. The scene is nothing like Iris's memory.

The report mentions gunpowder residue on Joseph's hands, and Iris's eyes skip across the page until they reach the bottom. There's a short paragraph written by the medical examiner.

It summarizes the forensics. Bullet patterns, the placement of the pistol on the floor, gunpowder residue, but Iris can hardly read it. Her eyes have already found the last sentence. It stands spaced apart from the others.

Joseph Adler, cause of death—self-inflicted gunshot wound to the head.

Iris reads it again. And then again.

This is saying Joseph *killed* himself, but it's still not making sense. It's not until she turns the page and finds the same type of report, only it's not for an autopsy. It's the medical examiner's paragraph on Iris.

She reads the conclusion right away, and now everything falls into place. *Iris Adler was the victim of an attempted murder-suicide.* Iris notices someone had written in Sharpie below the conclusion paragraphs for both her and Joseph the word, *Inconclusive.* They've underlined it with a heavy stroke as well.

It looks like the word was hastily added. Like it wasn't part of the official report. The police were making their own narrative.

Joseph shot Iris in the head and then turned the gun on himself and according to this document, the police have known for months. They've been arguing against disclosure, Iris is certain. Saying it's inconclusive.

She shuts the folder. Her heart pounds so hard, it tickles the back of her throat. This is what Augusta and Annabelle have been so afraid of her remembering.

They're trying to keep it a secret that her husband, once heir to the company, is the killer they've been so worried to catch.

Iris's gaze darts ahead. She sees movement. She can see the windows of a few houses from the parking lot, and somebody was just peeking at her through their blinds. People in small towns can be paranoid. If someone sees a wrecked truck like this hiding out in a church parking lot in the middle of the night, the police are getting called.

Before she can even reach for the ignition, Iris sees a search light racing across lawns to her left.

She starts the truck and starts to pull forward, but right as she does a police cruiser appears blocking her way. They turn on their lights.

252

The siren wails once, and then the car stops. Both vehicles face each other hood to hood. There are no commands shouted from the loudspeaker. The police car just stays still.

Iris's hands start to sweat as she grips the wheel. Are they waiting for backup? Waiting to take her somewhere out of sight so they can dump her body in a swamp?

Lights come on in the houses around the parking lot. She can hear dogs bark.

She hears a staticky command issue from the speaker of the cruiser. *"Turn your vehicle off."*

Iris thinks about driving off, but here she has something she doesn't if they overtake her truck on a dark country road. Here she has witnesses. Another police cruiser pulls up, and then a third.

The parking lot swirls with the police lights. The cops exit their cars. Guns are drawn.

"Turn off the engine!"

Iris does as she's told and kills it.

"Now roll down your window and place both hands outside of the vehicle!"

Again, she obeys as slowly and carefully as possible.

"Open the door with the outside handle!"

The cops are walking up to her now. The second she gets the door unlatched and open, an officer appears. He grabs both her hands and wrestles them behind her back, while at the same time lifting her from the driver's seat.

"I'm cooperating!" Iris says, but they toss her onto the asphalt and tighten the cuffs tighter than the FBI. She's been arrested twice in six hours, and this time she pushed her luck. This is not the feds trying to frighten her.

These people are being paid to keep the Adler family secrets.

Iris doesn't recognize any of the officers. The sheriff isn't here yet. These are just the cops who were already on duty.

They put her in the back of a cruiser, and she watches them start to go through the truck. She needs to alert the FBI. She needs to get them those documents. But something tells Iris it's all going to be burned to ash before sunrise.

Custody

The cop car takes a series of turns that aren't the same ones that go back to the police station. They're driving out of town, Iris thinks.

"Where are you taking me?"

The driver says nothing. He doesn't even glance at her in the mirror.

She pictures a swamp. Another bullet to the head. This time not so inaccurate. They'd shoot her twice, three times for good measure.

Iris wants to start screaming until she hears the cop's radio squawk.

"Take her to the station."

"Copy" is all the cop says back.

They take their next left, and Iris's heart starts to lift as they pass houses and streetlights. They're going back to civilization. Not a swamp. When they get there, Iris feels like she could cry.

There's a black SUV double parked in front of the police station, and standing outside of it talking to the sheriff is Agent Long.

They must've had someone tuned to the police radio. The FBI is here, and they're not about to let these backwater cops take Iris away.

She could cry from relief. She wants to start yelling about the documents from the back seat, but instead she waits. Her driver waits, too. He parks, and Iris watches the sheriff and Agent Long argue.

Iris can't hear what they're saying, but she can see the sheriff's spit fly. She assumes it's the old rift—state versus federal power. The cops here probably want to hold Iris and charge her, but it's possible the FBI doesn't want them potentially muddling the case they're building.

Eventually, the sheriff storms off. It's Agent Long who comes over to the cop car. She opens the back door.

"Can't stay out of trouble tonight, can you Iris?"

She tightens her lips in a smile. "Apparently not."

"We talked to your mother-in-law, she said they let you borrow the truck... I hear you did quite the number on that thing. You hurt anybody?"

"No. No, I crashed into the ditch."

Agent Long nods. "Okay, well, this might not help her guardianship argument." Agent Long sighs. "But it does keep you from being charged with grand theft auto."

"Listen." Iris scooches so she's turned towards Agent Long. "I know you think I'm unwell, but the documents related to my case... I stole them for a reason."

Agent Long looks into the cab, puts one hand on the roof. She widens her eyes just a little, as if to say *go on*.

"They had been keeping them from me. They wouldn't let me see everything related to my case in the past."

"That's not unusual, Iris."

"I know. Just let me finish. Do you have all the documents related to my case? My attempted murder, not me and Sarah Gray."

"Yes. We made copies this afternoon."

"Here? At this station?"

"Yes."

"And did they bring you the documents, or did you walk in with a warrant and take them from evidence?"

"We requested access."

"So they showed you what they had? You didn't look for yourself."

"Yes, Iris." It sounds like Agent Long is getting ready to end this conversation.

"And did you read the original medical examiner's report?"

"Yes."

"Really, did you? The one that says it was my husband that shot me and then turned the gun on himself?"

Agent Long is silent. She frowns, and her eyes dart back and forth.

"They've been covering it up. Augusta. Annabelle. The police. They've all known who did this to me. They're trying to protect the family. The company. You have to believe me."

Long still hasn't said anything.

"Please. The files were in the forensics report. I stole that folder. I read it in the truck. One of the cops should have it."

"Iris," Agent Long finally says.

Iris looks up at her hopefully.

"I'm going to do you a favor tonight. I should put you in protective custody. You stole documents from a police station. You totaled a truck that I'm not for one second convinced you didn't steal. You're completely out of line."

Iris nods and sniffles.

"But you've had a rough night, and I know you're not an idiot. I believe that you don't remember things. I believe what you're doing, your actions, are you fighting for those memories."

"Thank you." Even if Long is only playing good cop now, the words still make Iris feel better. She's waiting for her to change the subject. To talk about what Iris just told her.

"Now, we're going to send you home tonight. The sheriff wanted to lock you up and throw away the key, but after a phone call from your mother-in-law, he seems to have had a change of heart. Apparently, it's all some misunderstanding." She drums her fingers on the roof. "You're lucky to have someone with so much influence looking after you. I'd be careful about trying to disparage the name of the only person you have in your court, Iris. If it weren't for Augusta Adler, the sheriff would've skinned you tonight."

Iris isn't going to debate that she wouldn't have been in this situation to begin with if it weren't for Augusta's lies. "What about what I just told you?"

Long ignores her. "If you fuck up again, there are no third chances. You're not catching a break from anybody. *Behave*,"

Agent Long says like a warning and leans away from the car. She shuts the door and walks towards the sheriff.

The sheriff gives a thumbs-up to the driver.

Iris didn't even have a chance to mention the drugs. But what would it matter? She wouldn't be believed.

Iris watches Agent Long and the sheriff speak to each other. Is she asking for the documents? Did Agent Long believe Iris but not want to show it?

The cop car suddenly starts to move before Iris can get a read on the situation. She panics for a moment and wants to ask where they're going, but she already knows.

They're taking her back to Sweet Blood.

Evening Wear

Augusta is the only one waiting up for her. The guards are nowhere in sight, and the lights of the guesthouse are out. The cop gets out and opens the door to the back seat just as Augusta steps down from the porch. Iris stands while the officer takes off her cuffs.

He gets back in the car and drives off without a word. Iris rubs her wrists while Augusta stares at her with her arms crossed. She wears a silk nightgown. Her hair is up. She's as underdressed as Iris can ever remember seeing her.

"I heard you had quite the night."

Iris doesn't respond.

"Don't worry about the truck. It's insured. Are *you* alright?"

She finally looks at Augusta. There's genuine concern in her eyes, but it doesn't make Iris feel like any less of a prisoner. Sometimes the captor falls for the captive. That's all her worry is.

"I'm fine." She's not sure she should play her hand and tell Augusta that she knows about Joseph. She'll find out eventually. The sheriff will tell Augusta what documents Iris got her hands on, if he hasn't already. Then her silence becomes questionable.

The game of keeping Iris silent might become too risky for Augusta. And she doesn't even know that Iris found out about the drugs.

"Get some sleep. We'll talk about it in the morning."

Iris starts up the porch stairs, and Augusta is right behind her. She's far from tired. She can't stop thinking. Why didn't Agent Long respond to what she told her about Joseph? Why didn't she question her about it more?

If Agent Long is bought too, it's over. And she very well might be. Long is based in New Orleans. She's well within the reach of Augusta's influence.

259

Iris turns suddenly to Augusta. "I want to go to the party tomorrow night."

"What, do you think you're grounded? Of course you're coming." Augusta shuts the front door, and the two square off in the entrance hall. "You think I'm going to leave you here all alone?

The words are on the tip of Iris's tongue. Joseph. Murderer. She wants to spit them out and watch Augusta squirm. That night in the music room, Iris was close to getting the truth from Augusta, but then she turned from her, and she's been banished to the dark.

"I have a dress picked out for you," says Augusta. "It's dark blue—Stratos, I think the woman at the shop called it."

"You dressin' me up?"

"Oh please, darling. Is it any secret you're my doll?"

Iris is too surprised by the words to respond.

"Do as I say, and tomorrow you might just get everything you want from me."

"And what's that?"

"Your life back." Augusta smiles, but it's a sad expression as if something horrible is coming that she doesn't have the power to prevent.

At the top of the stairs, despite the tension, they say their goodnights.

Iris lies in bed until dawn, staring at the ceiling, and only as her room begins to brighten are her thoughts taken by sleep.

Dress-up

Iris wakes to a knock on her door. She sits up in the pillows to see Annabelle walking into her room. Annabelle is just the type to barge in like this. Her knock wasn't a question asking if there was anybody there, but a statement. *I'm coming in.*

"Morning, sunshine. Or should I say afternoon?"

Iris is so sleepy she still has one eye closed. It's crusted shut with sleep. "What do you want?"

"I want you up. It's nearly two."

Iris is far from surprised. She's probably slept for about seven hours, but it doesn't feel like nearly enough.

"Come on." Annabelle yanks at her sheet. She pulls it to the floor, leaving Iris exposed and mostly naked in her bra and underwear.

"You should wear your pajamas to bed. It's more decent behavior."

Iris doesn't even bother to glare at her.

Annabelle still doesn't leave. She looks Iris over and then spins towards the door as if to look to see if anyone is listening.

"I heard all about last night. About what happened *after* the FBI arrested you."

"Uh-huh."

"Seems like you got yourself in a hole of shit. And you're fixin' to dig yourself deeper."

"Something like that, Annabelle. Yeah."

"Funny. You know the only person who stood to gain from Joseph's death was his mother and you. All those shares bequeathed to his wife."

Iris realizes Annabelle didn't just wake her up to be annoying. She's trying to tell her something. "What do you mean by that?"

"You're kidding, right? You heard about the shares from Marshall. He had more than any of his brothers. Eldest privileges. The Adlers are old-fashioned like that."

"Yeah. I know he owned some of the company."

"But haven't you read his will? That's what this whole curatorship argument is about."

Iris is quiet. She doesn't want to seem stupid, but then again, her ignorance is a result of all the things these women have withheld from her.

"Anyway. The shares go to *you*. The funny thing is, if you had died, the way someone intended you to, then the shares would've gone to Mama."

"Augusta?"

"Yeah. She's the next in line, so to speak. The shares always stay in the family."

"How much of the company is it?"

"Oh, nothing to scoff at. I believe he held just over twenty percent. That's some millions."

Iris trusts Annabelle even less than Augusta. She might not even be telling the truth. "Who's the third in line?"

"Excuse me?"

"If Joseph, Augusta and I were to die, who would those shares go to?"

"Oh. I'm not sure. Probably Jamie or split between him and Gideon. The shares wouldn't go to Joseph Senior on account of his condition and all. That's what Mama is really fighting you for, do you know that? She doesn't give a shit about you. She wants power over those shares."

Iris doesn't want to appear easily manipulated. She isn't. At least not anymore. "Interesting."

"I'm not saying she tried to have you *killed* or nothing. Although she did have quite the falling out with Joseph. The two hardly spoke right around the end."

Annabelle is not one to give out information without a plan. Iris decides to be blunt. She stands in her underwear and gets close to Annabelle.

She shifts her gaze away from Iris uncomfortably.

"And why are you telling me all this now?"

"I just thought with all the legal trouble you're facing it might be good to have something up your sleeve. Something to give to the police."

"What exactly would I be giving the police?"

"Something they've been desperately searching for since all this began..."

"A motive?" Iris asks.

"See?" Annabelle smiles. It's a nasty fake thing. The corners of her mouth curl up sarcastically. "You're getting smarter every day."

She leaves the room without shutting the door, and Iris storms over and closes it. Annabelle is not completely wrong. It does feel like Iris is getting smarter. She's smart enough to understand Annabelle's motive.

If Augusta got embroiled in the investigation into her son's death, it might be enough to make her step down as CEO immediately, or Annabelle might press the board to remove her themselves.

The motive Annabelle just laid out might have been enough to convince Iris that Augusta *did* have something to do with Joseph's death and her shooting, if she had told her yesterday. But after what she read last night, she knows it's false.

According to the medical examiner, there isn't any mystery as to who killed Joseph and shot Iris. It couldn't have been Augusta. Iris starts towards the bathroom but freezes.

Augusta admitted to being the first one on the scene. She could've staged things. It wouldn't take that much. Move the pistol close to Joseph, deposit gunpowder residue on his hands. There was no sign of forced entry. Augusta would have a key.

Iris supposes it could've been Augusta. The medical examiner's report might not be lying when it says *inconclusive*. But would she go through all that just to own more of the company? The motive Annabelle told her doesn't hold weight.

There could've been more to it, Iris thinks. Joseph could've been against the drug trafficking. A rift like that with the cartel involved could easily mean murder. All Iris knows is that she's not much closer to figuring out what happened. Bree probably isn't the missing piece of the puzzle, but Iris can't think of any more leads to pursue, short of tying Augusta to a chair and holding her feet to a fire.

Iris showers, gets dressed in sweats and a T-shirt, and heads downstairs. The first floor seems completely empty. If Paulo was staying here over the weekend, there's no sign of him now.

Iris finds Aurelia in the kitchen. She's seasoning a pork shoulder wearing a pair of latex gloves.

"Hey, Aurelia."

"Oh, afternoon." Aurelia flips the meat over and starts dabbing the other side. The pork is making Iris think of the slaughterhouse. Of Sarah.

She fidgets. "Is Augusta here?"

"She's already onboard the Lady."

"Oh."

"Has been since six in the morning. She's crazy about this party. Every year, she spends *days* planning the thing."

"She mentioned a dress..."

"I have everything you'll be wearing upstairs. I can drop it off in your bedroom now if you like."

"I can just grab it. Is it in the hall closet?"

"Yes. It's all in the back left corner. Dress is hung up. It'll be hard to miss."

"And... Do you know how I'll be getting there?"

"Arthur will be picking you up at seven."

"Okay." She pauses for a moment. "And Aurelia?"

Aurelia stops touching the meat. She looks up at Iris, sensing the seriousness in her tone.

"This may seem a little silly, but does the family have another driver? One named Richard?"

Aurelia looks down and starts shaking her head. "He was fired a couple years ago."

"Gotcha."

"Don't tell those ladies I told you."

"You know they've been lying to me?"

"'Course I do."

Iris licks her lips. She's eager for information and sees the opportunity. "Can you tell me what my relationship with Augusta used to be like? Before I was... you know."

"You used to come around the house a lot. Alone. Sometimes late at night."

"So we were friends?"

"Sure. Probably. You acted like it, but who knows who's being their true selves."

"You mean I might've been pretending?"

Aurelia sighs. She seems disappointed in herself. Like being privy to everyone's secrets in Sweet Blood is her job and she's not supposed to share them with others.

"I don't know who you were, Iris. You certainly weren't the nice woman I see today. But I do know one thing. Augusta liked you. *That* she wasn't pretending."

Aurelia picks up the pork again. The way she focuses on her work says enough—this conversation is over.

"Thanks, Aurelia."

"Don't thank me. It's the least I can do."

She knows more, and she's not trying very hard to hide it, but Iris knows better than to ask.

Iris walks out of the kitchen and heads upstairs. She stares at the clothes in the closet. There is not just a dress to wear left out, but the accompanying diamond jewelry.

A doll. Is that what she is to Augusta?

She feels rage build in her chest. All her searching has left her with answers but no solution. Maybe Iris has been going about this investigative business all wrong. Her life shouldn't be Augusta's to give. It's Iris's to take.

Suite

When Iris is done dressing, she must admit she's a little blown away. The dress Augusta left for her is not a bouffant ball gown, some gaudy call back to antebellum. It's an off-the-shoulder sheath dress. Dark blue. Almost black. It's sleek and hugs her frame. It widens perfectly at the hips.

The diamonds Augusta left her to wear are brilliant. Necklace, earrings, bracelet. Even a brooch that doesn't really go with the dress. It's shaped like a flower, and Iris pins the brooch just below her shoulder. It's small enough not to ruin the outfit.

At seven o'clock sharp, Iris heads downstairs. The house is empty. Annabelle, Jamie, and perhaps Paulo must've gone to the boat separately, because there is no one else waiting on the porch.

At 7:05, Iris feels a little panicked. There is still no car in sight. She could find Aurelia, have her call someone, but as soon as Iris starts to feel like the forgotten child, she sees the gate open and the Cadillac glide down the road.

It stops just at the end of the porch stairs, and Arthur steps out quickly and opens the back door. "You look lovely this evening, miss."

Iris bows her head an inch. "Thank you."

She stares at the open door to the car like it's the trap it might be. No one is here to watch her get inside. He could take her to the riverbank, where she'll be shot and dumped into the Mississippi.

She pictures the riverboat party in full swing, sailing over her body that floats just above the riverbed.

She takes a deep breath and gets in the car.

They stay close to the river the entire drive. Iris remembers how Augusta pointed out the boat landing when they were driving to Preston. They don't deviate from course, and it's not long before they meet a line of traffic on an otherwise rural road.

The cars are not typical, however. It's all Mercedes and Porsches and other Cadillacs. It's the line of guests waiting to park and board.

When the river comes into sight, Iris is confused. There's no boat waiting on the pier. People in evening wear queue near the dock. Arthur stops the car at the back line where other cars are double parked as well to let their passengers out.

Arthur goes around and opens Iris's door. He lends her his hand as she stands.

"I'll be here all night, miss. The Lady will dock twice to let guests off. Once at midnight and again at three in the morning. I'll be here to take you back to the house at either time."

"Thank you, Arthur." Iris steps past him onto the dock. She's surrounded by men in tuxedos and women in dresses. There's nothing to do while waiting for the boat, and *everyone* steals a glance at Iris. Some of the women are not particularly subtle about it.

She doesn't have anyone to mingle with. Annabelle and the others are presumably already on the boat, but there are a few faces she recognizes.

Gideon stands on the end of the dock. He actually looks startlingly put together, as if this is the one event he knows better than to half ass for his mother. A tall blonde stands next to him. Augusta will be less pleased with his date.

Her dress's deep V shows the sides of both her breasts, showing a mole that Augusta will probably say only a lover should know the location of.

Iris glances down the riverbank and sees someone else. Dominic, Joseph's old assistant, is walking up the gravelly beach. He's not wearing evening wear. He has a plaid shirt tucked into khakis. His pant legs are rolled up like he's had to wade into the water.

It looks like Augusta has recruited him to help with the event, rather than attend as a guest.

Iris is too busy looking at his rolled-up khakis to realize he's also looking right at her. He doesn't look at her as hatefully as he did at the plant. He gives her a little nod, and she gives one back.

Suddenly, Iris's attention is taken to the water. Everyone on the dock has begun to hoot and clap.

Coming around the riverbend from the north is the Diamond Lady. Iris is a little stunned by her size. It's a floating hotel. A small *cruise ship*, only its first deck sits just above the water. The red paddle wheel spins, kicking up mist, and the white body of the ship is adorned with row upon row of orange string lights that are starting to glow in the dusk.

The boat toots its horn twice, and the dock goes even wilder. It takes them five minutes to dock. The deckhands are wrapping lengths of rope the width of boa constrictors around the dock cleats.

The boarding ramp is set up, and the guests begin to file onboard. The line is slow going, and Iris realizes why when the crowd ahead thins enough for her to see.

Augusta is there, greeting each guest individually. She's flanked by porters in white tuxedos. Iris can tell that if someone lingers and tries to speak with Augusta, it's the porter's job to see them away and keep things moving.

Soon, it's Iris's turn.

"Iris, dear… You look stunning."

Iris could blush from the way Augusta is staring at her. She's unabashed in her interest. "Thank you."

"Join me for a drink in the Captain's Bar later."

"Okay."

Augusta wears an emerald green dress that shows off her body. Her white hair curls past her shoulders.

She has already turned her attention to the next set of guests. Iris walks up the staircase into the main hall of the ship. The ceilings are lower than she'd have thought, but the décor is breathtaking. There's white wood paneling, Tiffany lamps, and a grand chandelier glittering only a few feet above her the size of a minivan.

268

Iris realizes now is probably her best opportunity to find Bree. It's before the men get drunk enough to seek out her services. Iris shudders. How many married men are going to sneak off tonight for twenty minutes with a girl a fraction of their age?

Iris starts towards the back of the boat. The ballroom isn't huge, and Iris can see Annabelle and Jamie standing and chatting with others near the bar. There are doors on either side of the room that lead outside to the second deck, which is a story above the water.

Iris goes out the door to the right quickly. She's on the river side of the boat. The water reflects the string lights that line the railing. It is, Iris must admit, a beautiful place for a party.

She heads up a spiral staircase all the way to the third deck, but the deck doesn't continue to run along the length of the boat here. It's been turned into private balconies for the rooms.

Iris heads inside and walks down the hallway. There isn't anyone around. All the deckhands and porters are towards the front of the boat helping guests. Iris sees the presidential suite. It's the one room where the door doesn't branch off to either side of the hall. It sits importantly, directly at the end.

The golden placard reads *Suite #1*.

Iris knocks and takes a step back so she can be seen through the peephole. A few silent seconds go by, and she knocks again. She doesn't know what to say. Even if Bree is in the room, she might not be alone. "Hello?"

The door suddenly swings open so fast that Iris flinches. A young girl of maybe twenty-four is looking back at her. She has a square face and wide-set eyes. "Iris?" she says like she can't believe it.

There are two other girls in the room who stand behind her. All three are dressed in stockings and are wearing sweatshirts that cover their upper bodies. They're in the middle of getting ready for the evening.

"I'm looking for Bree," Iris says awkwardly.

"You found her. Baby, you remember me?"

"No. I was just—"

"Come in, now." Bree looks past Iris, pulls her inside, and slams the door. "Girls, we need a minute. Can you say Tristan's name loud when he comes back here?"

One of the other girls nods. "We'll give you a heads-up."

Bree takes Iris's hands and rushes off to one of the bedrooms. She shuts the door and locks it. "Lacy texted me sayin' you came by the other night. She told me to expect you. I knew you'd be here, but I heard rumors. I didn't think you remembered a thing."

"I actually don't. It's why I'm here."

"Did anyone follow you back here?" Bree starts chewing her bottom lip. Even with her wide application of eyeliner, Iris can see the bags under her eyes. She looks like an addict.

"No. I came as soon as I got aboard."

"They're killing them, you know that?"

"Who is?"

"The Adlers. They're killing all the girls that were going to testify against your husband. I'm the last one, Iris. Other than you."

"Can you prove it?" Iris isn't sure she can trust Bree. She seems fanatically paranoid, like she's high right now.

"You came by the ranch with a reporter. You said you wanted to expose Joseph."

"For being rough with the girls?"

"Sadistic is the better word, yeah. That was part of it."

"What's the other part?"

Bree looks at her skeptically. "You're not trying to entrap me? Did they get to you?"

"No," Iris says, frustrated. "I don't remember anything. I'm serious."

"Anything?"

"Not in the last few years."

"You wanted to stick him with sexual assault charges, sure. But more than anything, it was about taking down his ring. You wanted to get him with sex trafficking charges."

"What do you mean, ring?"

"Like *prostitution* ring. You think we're all just independent contractors?

"I haven't thought—"

"We have pimps. The pimps got bosses. It's structured. As orderly as a business."

"I don't get it. How is it sex trafficking? Why don't you just leave?"

Bree starts to look angry. "So you forgot how society works, too? They get us hooked on shit. They get us a rap sheet. I couldn't get hired at a goddamn Waffle House if I wanted. I ain't got no choice but to sell a fuckin' trick. And you didn't either."

"I'm sorry..." Iris says.

Bree starts taking her shirt off.

"Whoa. Um," Iris says, looking away.

"Is this familiar?" Iris looks back to see Bree standing in her bra. She points to a tattoo of an eagle just below her left breast.

"Your husband helped sell girls, Iris. Memphis. Nashville. New Orleans. There were little sex rings in each city. And you know what you told me?"

Iris's eyes are watering, and Bree steps closer.

"You told me you were one of 'em."

"One of what?" Iris asks. Her voice is quivering. But she already knows.

Bree puts her hands on Iris's shoulders. She starts to flinch away, but then she lets Bree take control. Bree slips the dress off the sides of Iris's arms, so it falls, exposing her breasts and stomach.

Iris winces as Bree touches the scar above her hip with her cold fingers. "You told me you used to have a tattoo just like mine. His mark. Adler. You know what Adler means in German?" Bree laughs, like she's disgusted. "Eagle."

Iris looks down at her scar. She remembers the pain as Bree touches it. She remembers standing in a mirror. She used the oldest method of tattoo removal.

Rock salt. Hydrogen peroxide.

Iris scraped her own skin away with sandpaper.

"And you know what else you told me?"

Iris can't respond.

"You told me you'd make him pay."

There's suddenly a burst of commotion from the other room.

"Tristan, what took you so long?" one of the girl's says loudly.

There's a pause, and then Iris hears a deep voice muffled by the door. "Where's Bree?"

"She's in the other room."

"Go!" Bree whispers in a hush, opening the door to the room's balcony. She throws her shirt on, and Iris gets her dress back on her shoulders.

"Hey! Why is this door locked?" The man is shouting and trying the handle.

"I'm changing, Tristan! Give me a goddamn minute!" She leans close to Iris. "Get to the other balcony. I'll come back out for a smoke and talk to you."

Iris steps outside, and Bree disappears as she closes the glass door and draws the blinds.

Iris goes to the railing. Thankfully, there are no gaps between balconies to the deck below. Iris doesn't have to worry about falling. When she's over the railing and on the next room's balcony, she can feel her pulse in her ears, but she's not afraid of being caught.

The Nile Hotel makes sense now. That's where this all began. In her hometown of Memphis.

But the hotel manager was wrong. He did recognize Iris, but not because she came to the hotel as Joseph's wife. *She* was the second prostitute.

She was Joseph's whore.

Used

Iris is alone on the balcony. She wasn't the college student she thought she was. She's almost certain now that she never actually attended LeBlanc. She feels duped. Little.

A prostitute?

What kind of life was she forced to live?

Was her marriage to Joseph some kind of revenge plan? Something was missing. If Iris was just some addict, how'd she infiltrate this family?

Her attention is taken from her thoughts. She sees something that bothers her. There's a small skiff in the river behind the boat. It's too far for her to make out many details, but there's one man in it wearing a black sweatshirt despite the heat.

He sits on the skiff's back bench with the motor's arm in one hand. It looks like he's waiting to follow them. Something about it fills her with fear.

Iris sees a black bag in the boats' bottom. Paparazzi? Media? Or, Iris realizes, it could be Augusta's security. Her attention is taken away as Iris hears Bree yell something muffled from in her room, and then the sliding door opens. She comes out lighting a cigarette.

She looks over her shoulder and then turns to face the water. "I can't look at you, okay? In case he comes into the room."

A part of Iris doesn't want to ask anything else. She may not have been the soulless social climber she feared she was, but a prostitute? A heroin addict? "When I met with you when I was with that reporter, did I tell you my story?"

"You told me everything. It's how I know this. You laid it all out."

"And you're certain that Joseph operated prostitution rings?" Iris figures it's not a long step from trafficking drugs. The

Adler family probably knows all the right people. It's just another revenue stream. They were already breaking the law. They already had the right network.

"You were certain. But you didn't have evidence other than word of mouth. They were smart about it. The tattoos were the only dumb thing they did. The only paper trail, so to speak. Joseph Adler used middlemen. They'd pay him cash. He communicated with them from an encrypted email address, and no one ever used real names. You had *nothing*, baby. That's what you told me."

"Did I ever mention a Nile Hotel?"

Bree purses her lips and grabs on to the railing. "Yeah. He paid for two girls. You and another. He wanted to choke your friend. Said he'd pay thousands extra for it, but he took it way too far. He was drunk or high or both, and when you tried to stop him, he beat the shit out of you, too. But she got the worst of it."

Iris is confused. "And this was years ago?"

"Three. That's what you said when I met you in April."

That would make it only about six months before she and Joseph started dating. "Why would he marry me, then? After all that?"

"Because he didn't know who you were, Iris. That was your whole plan. He met you once while he was sky high at a hotel. You were his type, though. You said he picked you and the other girl out specifically. You already knew he'd like you."

"Who was this other girl?"

"You met her that same night. You weren't close, if that's what you're wondering."

"But did I say her name?"

"I don't remember if you did."

Iris curses. "Okay, so, so," Iris stammers. She can't get her words straight. "Who gave me the tattoo? Joseph? Was he a pimp?"

Bree shakes her head. "God no. He was just a pretty boy who wanted to play Scarface. Rumor has it he has cartel connections.

He was the finance behind it. That pussy never did anything but abuse the girls."

There's an inkling of a memory forming in Iris's brain. She thinks of the night she met him at the fraternity party. She was nervous because she was afraid he'd recognize her. She pretended to get groped so he could play hero for her. She was trained. She knew what he liked.

"I'm sorry," says Bree, and this time she looks over at Iris. "You look sick. Are you disappointed to learn you were once a tart, too?"

Iris doesn't want to admit it, but she's struggling with her feelings. A prostitute from the streets of Memphis. Is that all she was? She can't stop feeling small. Stupid. Her mother wasn't lying. The last time she saw Iris, she probably was stealing from her purse.

"Don't feel bad. You might've been smart. I'm sure you met the wrong asshole and he put a needle in your arm. Next thing you know, you'd claw your own eyes out for the next hit. That was the kind of racket they ran. That was Joseph's business. Make the girls as dependent as possible on fuckin' for a livin' so they can't just run away." She wipes her eyes.

Iris takes her words to heart. Who cares if she was a sex worker? She was abused. Manipulated by men. What's important is that her identity of being a good person was the same then as it is now.

She wasn't the cruel woman she thought she was. She wasn't the socialite obsessed with status. It was all for show. Part of the plan. "So I married for revenge?"

Bree smiles slyly. "Look, I don't blame you one bit, but you married him to get his money. Revenge was maybe part of it." There are suddenly voices from Bree's room, and she turns. "I should probably go back in."

"Wait, wait, wait." Iris holds a hand out desperately. "There's something else. The FBI is saying I killed someone."

Bree seems to understand. "Sarah." Her voice cracks.

"Yes! Sarah Gray."

"I can't talk about her." Bree is shaking her head. She seems to be too upset to care if she's being watched from inside.

"Were you close?"

"We were bunkmates in one of those shit stain trailers. We were best friends."

"And are they right? Did I kill her?"

Bree pauses. She looks Iris straight in the eye. "She was one of the girls Joseph would abuse. She agreed to help you. Fuck, she was *excited* to help you. But Sarah had a big mouth. Not long after you showed up with that reporter, she started tellin' more and more girls that she was going to take down Joseph Adler. He heard about it through someone, and a few days later, I find her overdosed cold and dead in her bed."

"Overdosed?"

Bree nods. "It's how they've been killing the girls. I know it is. All these ODs when we've been so safe for years. They do it with a syringe filled with a drop of fentanyl. I found an empty one. Makes it look accidental."

The gears are turning in Iris's head.

"I don't go anywhere without Naloxone. The anti-overdose shot. But fentanyl right in the blood is so strong, I'm not sure it would even work."

"How'd I end up with Sarah's body?"

"I called you when I found her. And you know what your plan was?"

Iris does. "I wanted to frame my husband."

"Yeah. It was a pretty good idea. Sarah wouldn't have minded. She would've been so onboard with the idea. Using her body to get revenge on those fuckers." Bree smiles genuinely. "You had his truck, his gun, enough to pin him with. You told me you had nothing else. You told me you kept trying to catch him hurting a girl, but he smartened up. He must've started using other women. Ones outside of his little ring."

A breeze rolls off the river. It's warm, swampy, but Iris shivers. "So we shot her after she was dead?"

"Yes. In my trailer so no one would hear the shots. Look, I gotta go in. I don't know what good telling you all this does. You'd be better off not knowing. They won, Iris. I don't know if someone higher up the food chain in the family or the cartel decided Joseph was a liability and killed him or what, but it's over."

Iris realizes what happened the night she was shot. Joseph caught her. He woke up when he wasn't supposed to and found his truck missing. He must've found out the truth about her that night and shot her when she got back home.

But why did he shoot himself? Did he think he was going to get caught?

Bree moves to go inside, and Iris blurts out, "I'm sorry I didn't meet you, by the way."

Bree squints, confused.

"At Harvest Baptist. I was able to get the letter you mailed."

"Honey, I have no idea what you're talking about." Bree opens the sliding door and steps in. "Be safe," she whispers to Iris as she closes it.

Iris can't even mumble a response. She has to figure out what to do now. Bree said the Adlers won, but that's only in the eyes of the law.

She has to find Augusta.

Dance With Me

The balcony door behind Iris is unlocked. Inside the room, the bed is perfectly made. The Diamond Lady has been rented out for this event, and Iris doesn't think any of the cabin rooms are in use, other than the one the girls are using.

She collects herself in the bathroom for a minute. She can't cry. She can't let her makeup run, but the relief she feels to not be a murderer is enough to rack her with sobs. The anxiety that's kept her insides in a vise-grip is beginning to loosen.

She pulls down her dress again to look at the scar on her hip. It's this one, not the mess on her forehead, that mesmerizes her. She thinks of the strength it must've taken. The pain she must've endured. All so Joseph wouldn't recognize the tattoo when she slept with him. Wouldn't recognize that she used to be his property.

But the questions still swim. How'd she get free from prostitution? How'd she get the money to go to New Orleans and start dating Joseph? She thinks of the letter she got. The man on lookout standing on the shoulder of the dark road. There's someone else helping her. Someone on the inside. A man was helping her. Presumably someone who would get something in return for Joseph's fall.

Augusta might know. Right now, she's Iris's only lead. And she's going to get the information from her if it means threatening her mother-in-law's life.

She takes one of the water glasses that is placed upside down by the sink and quickly strikes it against the vanity.

It shatters, and the glass that's left is razor sharp, but it would be awkward to conceal. She can't use it as a weapon because there's no way she could conceal it in her stocking. She needs something better.

She heads out of the hotel room and back down the hall. She hears the boat's horn sound twice and then the muffled sound of cheers from below deck. The boat is leaving the dock. They're heading out onto the river.

Iris finds the stairs and takes them all the way to the bottom deck of the boat, below where the party is happening.

There's nothing ornamental here. No woodwork or chandeliers. The walls are metal and lined with pipes. The lights overhead are caged in metal cylinders. She walks confidently, as if she belongs down here. If anyone asks her where she's going, it won't matter. She's an Adler, after all.

She finds a toolbox with wrenches and chisels and screwdrivers, but there's nothing sharp enough, nothing she can conceal well enough under this near skintight dress.

Suddenly she pauses. She hears hissing, clanking, and shouting, but ahead of her is not the engine room.

She walks towards the end of the hall and into the boat's kitchen. She stands still in the doorway. Everyone is too busy to notice her. There are at least a dozen workers preparing food.

Iris looks around. In between two prep counters, there's a magnet strip hanging high that's riddled with black-handled knives. The steel shines. The problem is they're placed in the middle of everything.

She could play authority and take one, but that's suspicious. She thinks fast and walks forward confidently.

"Hey! No guests!" a man shouts.

Iris keeps walking, reaches high over her head and plucks a sharp-looking paring knife down from the strip. "Oh," she says. She turns to see a red-faced man trying his best not to explode on her.

"I'm sorry, but we have a bit of a wardrobe malfunction upstairs."

He looks ready to argue. To shout, *Find your own fucking knife!* But he seems to know better than to question the need of a woman fixing clothes at a party.

"Give it to a busboy to get it back here!" he shouts over the clamor of the kitchen and walks off quickly.

279

It's that easy, Iris thinks. She walks out of the kitchen and steps into a utility closet. The knife is light enough to be held upright by her tights. The blade is close to her skin. She needs to be careful. One clumsy step or trip, and it'll end up in her thigh.

Iris goes up one deck to the ballroom. The second she opens the door, she's hit by a wave of party noise. Laughter, music, and the raised voices of everyone trying to be heard over it all.

She walks steadily towards the bar, careful not to bump into anyone. It's a little early to speak to Augusta. Iris can see her still standing near the entrance where the ramp was pulled up. She hasn't made it more than ten feet since they started letting guests aboard.

The line for the bar is a dozen deep, and when it's finally Iris's turn, she stutters. "Um, one vodka tonic."

The bartender grabs a glass.

"Actually, make it two."

He nods and after some impressive sleight of hand, has two sweating highballs on the bar top just several seconds after she ordered. Iris takes them and finds an empty table near the edge of the room by the windows. There are no chairs. There's nowhere to sit at all. She's at one of those high tables that people are just meant to mingle at.

Iris remembers the first alcohol she had after leaving the hospital. The glass of champagne at the memorial dinner. She had downed the thing in two gulps and then wanted another. The addictive personality has always been just under the surface, but how'd she get sober the first time? Surely she wasn't still using during her years with Joseph.

Iris finishes her first tonic quickly. She needs to cool her nerves. Numb her senses. She sets the empty glass on the windowsill and plans to nurse her second one. She's only taken a sip when someone approaches her. Tall, dark, and handsome. It takes her a moment to realize it's Paulo.

He's striking in a black tuxedo. *"Señora,"* he says, his white teeth shine against his black coat and hair. "You look gorgeous."

Iris looks away. "Thank you."

"I'm sorry about the police last night. How have you been?"

"My head is still kind of spinning, if I'm being honest with you."

"Hmm. Augusta told me the kind of questions they asked you. Ridiculous."

"Yeah. They seem to think this family has something to do with drug trafficking," Iris lies. "Can you believe it?"

Paulo's eyes bulge out of his skull for a fraction of a second before he composes himself. "No. Augusta did not say that is what they asked you."

"She didn't? Huh. Maybe she's afraid. They said something about paying and selling girls, too."

Paulo's eyes look Iris over. They linger at her breasts and glide down her legs. For a second, she rolls her shoulders back, offended, but then she realizes he's looking for a wire.

He leans close to her ear and whispers, "They're after you, too, Iris. The FBI. They are not your friends. They want to... how you say? Lock you up. Throw away the key."

"Maybe," Iris says at regular volume. "But maybe I don't care."

Paulo's face has gone white. He looks right and left like he's trapped. Like the feds are going to burst out of the woodwork.

"Come to Mexico," he says suddenly. "They won't find you at the estate. In Sinaloa, they can't even come looking."

"Am I in that much trouble?"

"You are in far more trouble than you think, señora."

"I'll take my chances."

"You have options." He leans into her ear. "Don't trade your life for a slightly nicer jail cell, because that's all you get if you rat us down the river."

Iris raises her brow. "I wasn't planning on that."

"Good." Paulo takes a step away. "Because the FBI... They are telling the truth."

"How's that?"

"You are a murderer." He winks and walks off.

Iris watches him go and downs the rest of her second drink. The alcohol burns in her empty stomach. She wants a third.

She starts towards the bar line when suddenly the music starts to play louder. People are clapping, and Iris senses somebody has crept up behind her. She spins to see Augusta extending her hand to her.

"Can I have the first dance?"

Iris can't find words. She needs to get Augusta alone. Below deck. But she gives Augusta her hand almost out of instinct, and the two start towards the dance floor. Iris reaches down with her free hand while they walk and feels for the knife. Brushing it, just to make sure it's still there.

When they get to the edge of the dance floor, Augusta lets go of Iris's hands and steps to a microphone.

"Hello. Hello."

The room begins to quiet.

"This is the first time I've hosted this without my son." Everyone who was still chatting is silent now. Augusta takes a deep breath. "Before we get crazy, which is definitely what he'd want us to do..."

Everyone laughs.

"I want to remember him. So, to open this, I'd like to start with the song we played for our mother-son dance at his wedding. But this time..." Augusta looks at Iris. "It's mother-daughter. And I'd like you all to join us."

The crowd claps, and Augusta walks back to Iris.

The music begins to play. It's a sweet, melancholy country song. A cover of Dolly Parton, Iris thinks, but she's not sure. She's too shocked by this surprise. Augusta puts one hand on Iris's waist and another on her shoulder, and it takes Iris a moment to do the same. Once she does, the two start to two-step and sway to the music.

They're both silent for several seconds. Tonight, Augusta herself smells of the same perfume she'd spritz her handkerchiefs with. It makes Iris woozy. The powdery scent reminds her of sex.

Iris is done being her plaything. She speaks just loud enough to not be heard by those dancing around them. "I know everything."

Augusta keeps her expression the same. A tight, slight smile. "Do you really?"

"More than you imagine."

"I suppose you know you're gay, then?"

Iris blushes. The blood rushes to her cheeks in an instant, and she has to look away. She hasn't thought about it that hard, but it's true. Men do nothing for her. But Augusta... This woman... Iris composes herself. "I know who I used to be. I know what your son did to me. What he did years ago at the Nile Hotel, and what he did again in May."

Augusta is trying to keep a straight face for those who are watching them dance. But Iris sees the cracks starting to form in her expression. "I always knew you'd remember eventually."

"You're monsters," Iris says. "You know I saw the files. I stole them from the station, and I told the FBI about them. You've been working with the police to cover it up. Your son tried to kill me. He killed himself. Maybe your family business sex ring doesn't get exposed, but the whole world is going to know what your son did to me."

Augusta looks at her feet, and when her eyes come back up, Iris is a little surprised to see they glisten with tears.

"Iris. I'm not protecting Joseph." Augusta bites her lip suddenly, like something hurts.

"It says in the report clear as day. Murder. Suicide," Iris says, shaking her head. People are starting to watch them closer, but she doesn't care. "You're not gaslighting your way out of this."

"And the police report isn't wrong, Iris."

"No?"

"No. But it was you."

The music gets louder. The singer is hitting her solemn solo.

"What are you talking about?"

"It *was* a murder-suicide. But I'm not covering up the fact that it was my son. I'm covering up the fact that it was you, Iris."

283

Iris has stopped swaying along to the music. She stands still, shocked. She's thinking of the truck. The body in the bed. The weight of the handgun in her palm. Suddenly, she remembers pulling into the driveway of her house. The porch light turning on.

Augusta stops dancing, too. She brings a hand to Iris's cheek and rubs a tear away.

"It was always *you*."

284

Gun Smoke

Things didn't go according to plan. Joseph must've woken up. The lights downstairs weren't on when Iris took the truck, but they were when she got back.

Iris ditched her black hat and gloves. She pulled off her sweatshirt and put the handgun in the back of her pants.

She got out of the truck, shut the door, and started walking slowly to the house. The front door opened long before she reached the stairs. Joseph stepped outside. He was barefoot. Blue jeans. White T-shirt.

"I didn't think you knew where I kept her keys," Joseph said, pointing to his truck.

"Oh, yeah."

"Something wrong with your car?" Joseph leaned against the doorframe. He looks at his fingernails briefly, casually. It made him seem all the more sinister.

"No."

"Something wrong with my car?"

"No."

"I reported it stolen." Joseph chuckled. "I thought maybe you heard something in the night. Heard the thieves and didn't wake me. I thought you went to check it out and got kidnapped. Isn't that crazy?"

Iris wasn't sure she wanted to step any closer to the house.

"I mean, why else would my wife be missing from the house at three in the morning, driving my vintage truck that she ain't never drove before?"

Iris was still quiet.

"Then I noticed my gun was missing, too. But funny thing, I put a little tracker on that truck a few years ago. My line of work, which I guess you know by now, I have to run a tight ship, Iris. You can never be too careful."

Iris thought she'd be able to talk herself out of this, but she never even considered the truck was being tracked. He must have noticed the despair in her expression, because he laughed, genuinely this time.

"I open the app, on my laptop and I'm about to give the coordinates to the police, when all the sudden, I realize you're parked at a couple of trailers I happen to know."

Iris was silent.

"This whole thing felt like a nightmare. It's like I woke up still dreaming. I was in a panic thinking you were kidnapped, and next thing I saw my truck was off Highway 2 visiting some whores. I couldn't get my head around it. Why would my wife do that?"

Iris reached around to the back of her pants for the gun. *Does he know yet? Was his question rhetorical?*

He looked up at her, expecting an answer.

He *didn't* know. He still hadn't figured it out. Iris took back some control. "Do you remember the first thing you ever said to me?" she asked.

He threw his hands up in frustration, as if to say *what does that have to do with anything.* "Not a clue."

"*Don't I know you?* That's what you said."

Joseph was the quiet one now.

"You did know me. You should've known me. We met in Memphis, remember?"

His eyes searched the ground as he began putting the pieces together.

"I didn't spill boiling water on myself when I was a girl." She yanked her shirt up, exposing the top half of the scar on her hip, and started walking closer to him. "There was a tattoo here. A shitty little thing of an eagle, once upon a time."

He stared at her with his mouth agape. His eyes were wide. It looked like he was having a stroke.

Iris was able to take some satisfaction in the moment. She walked closer. "Maybe you should fuck your whores more sober. You might avoid this problem."

286

His mouth closed. His wide eyes began to tighten with hatred.

"Who helped you?"

She pulled the gun out and took a quick step forward.

Joseph didn't flinch. He didn't say a word.

"Inside. Upstairs. Now."

"You're making a mistake."

"I already made it. Inside. Upstairs."

Joseph turned, and Iris quickly closed the gap between them, so she was only a few steps behind.

"It was Jamie, wasn't it?" Joseph spoke over his shoulder.

"Enough of that."

"Oh, don't worry. I give you credit. You're a clever bitch, but you needed money. You needed to know things to do what you did. Someone held your hand."

"You don't have as many friends as you think, Joseph."

"Who helped you?" he shouted, trying to throw Iris off guard.

"Upstairs," she said coolly and closed the front door.

"You've got a few seconds still. The boys are on the way. The sheriff's coming to make an appearance as well, and just a heads-up—we don't plan on charging you."

Iris ignored the threat as the two marched upstairs. "Shut up."

"Unless you're planning a hostage situation, I think you should try your hand at a head start."

"In the bedroom." Iris directed him with the gun to his back.

He opened the bedroom door and stepped in. She turned and closed it behind them with her foot.

For the first time in months, Iris didn't have a plan. Truth was, she was trapped. There wasn't going to be anyone to protect her after this. Joseph was right. The gig was up.

"So you hoped to frame me for murder? Take all my money?"

Iris was trying to think, but a new plan wouldn't come.

"You're a gold digger. A prostitute who pretended to be some perfect wife. How'd you know all the shit I liked? My brother told you, didn't he? I'm sure you think you've got a great big heart, but no one goes this far just for revenge. You're a money-grubbing bitch." He wiped the spit off his lip. "But lucky for you, I can give you more than you ever dreamed if that's what you want."

Iris looked out the window. There were headlights approaching from the road. One set. Then another. Joseph wasn't bluffing.

"Two million dollars. Wired. Soon as the banks open today. Fuck." He looked at his watch. "In three hours. Give me a routing number, and it's yours. No need to panic. No need to shoot me. Let's work this out. I mean clever…" He was looking at the gun in her hand. "You were clever."

Iris wasn't an idiot. He was buying time. She could've started crying. It *was* over. She couldn't drive out of here. Their cars would block her way. If she ran, there was nothing but knee-high sugarcane in the fields around her. Even if she somehow got away, past the open acres, they'd find her in the woods. The only thing she could do was call the police, but she didn't have her phone on her. She left it at home so it wouldn't be traceable.

The question was futile, but she asked anyway. "Where's my phone?"

"You think I'm a fucking idiot? The one thing you could fuck me with is that phone. It's in a million pieces in the kitchen sink. Mine too, so don't ask for it."

"Fuck!" Iris said aloud. She shook the gun in her hand.

"Just give it up."

"Shut up!"

"I didn't tell them it was you, you know?" He motioned his head towards the window. "I just said we got a problem. I can call this off. No one will ever know."

Iris didn't know who Joseph called. Drug dealers or crooked cops. People who get paid to pull a trigger. She was going to get herself into a hostage situation. She had no phone. No way to call for real help. They were going to kill her, and they weren't even a minute away.

"I'm going to run for it." Iris hoped he didn't think much of the tears that began to thicken her voice. "Tell them I went west."

"Okay," he said, satisfied, like they'd reached a deal.

"Close your eyes. Turn around. And count to one hundred."

He hesitated for a moment and smiled.

"I fucking mean it! I want to hear each number nice and loud, or I'm not going anywhere."

Joseph turned to the wall. "One... two... three..."

Iris walked silently closer to Joseph. Her steps didn't make a sound on the marble.

"Four..."

He didn't know she was a foot away from him. She pulled the silver hammer of the pistol back.

"Fi—"

"Joseph," Iris said coldly.

He thought she'd already left the room and spun around in surprise. She gave him half a second—just enough time for him to realize what she was about to do, but not enough to react to it.

His eyes flashed wide as saucers as they met the gun barrel. They were filled with pure fear. And, Iris had to admit, she found satisfaction in that terror.

Then she pulled the trigger.

He fell faster than she'd thought he would. He dropped hard to the floor, and his back hit the wall so his body stayed somewhat upright.

Over the ringing in her ears, she could hear the cars coming down the driveway. She could try to shoot her way out. Try to hide. But what she wanted more than anything was for Joseph to pay for his crimes. As he lay now, he just died a golden boy. All his sins concealed.

Even if she escaped these men, made it to prison, she could holler all she wanted about what a horrible man Joseph Adler was. All she would be was the crazy wife who killed him.

She bent to Joseph and started rubbing her hands all over his palms and wrists. It was plenty to transfer the gunpowder residue.

She heard a car door shut. She had seconds.

Without a defensive wound—a black eye, a cut lip—this scene of husband killed wife didn't look very believable. The men coming inside might stage it, too. But there were some wounds that couldn't be covered up. There was one way to make it look certain she was the victim.

She got to her knees, transferred the gun to her left hand, and held it so her thumb was on the trigger. Then she raised her right hand in a defensive gesture in front of the barrel, as if to shield herself from the bullet. From the inevitable.

It all depended on where the gun fell. When she went limp, the pistol should fall easily from her hand, but what if it ended up too far from Joseph? What if the opposite happened and her hand flexed and clenched onto the gun when she was shot?

Nothing was certain, other than the men who were coming into the house now to kill her. And the prison cell that would wait for her if she somehow got away.

She was thinking too fast to focus on the fear of death, but the tears wouldn't stop. She had this one chance to make Joseph appear to the world like the monster he truly was.

She started to depress the trigger. Suddenly, the muzzle flash shined pink through her closed eyelids, and before she could even feel the pain, the world went dark.

Partners

"Iris?" Augusta says urgently through clenched teeth. "Iris? Try to act normal. Please?"

Iris hasn't been moving to the music. Her mouth hangs open in dumb disbelief. It takes her several seconds to begin to move again. She blinks rapidly to clear her head and looks at her feet as she wills them to dance.

The two sway silently for an entire minute. Iris is just trying to hold herself together.

"So everything you said about Annabelle being behind it was bullshit?"

"Quieter," Augusta warns.

"Why lie?"

"To protect you. It was brave to do what you did."

"Brave to try to kill myself?"

"Brave to do whatever it took to ruin my son's name."

"You don't hate me for what I did to him?"

The song ends, and another starts to play. The music turns far more upbeat. Iris doesn't even care. She matches its pace.

"How could I hate you?"

And there it is, Iris thinks. She's found the final piece. "It was you. You were the one helping me."

Augusta doesn't respond.

"You got to the scene first. Did they call you? Joseph's goons?"

"They thought Joseph killed you. I sent everyone home. I was kneeling next to you when I saw the slightest little rise in your chest." Augusta smiles at the memory. "You were *breathing*. I staged things right... Called the police."

"And before that... How long were we working together?"

Augusta takes a trembling breath. "Joseph called me to Memphis one night... He was having a panic attack at a hotel. He messed up, he said. When I saw what he did to you and that

291

other girl... I promised it would be the last time I ever cleaned up after him. And you were so beautiful, Iris. Not just beautiful. I got talking to you and you were smart—truly smart."

"Why didn't you tell me everything in the hospital?" Iris says loud enough for the couple next to them to hear.

Augusta dips her chin. She speaks towards the floor. "I thought I could protect you. Like you couldn't be guilty of anything if you didn't even remember doing it. It was my fault. Your injury. Joseph's death..." She leans close to Iris's ear as they sway. "We made an agreement that night. At the hotel in Memphis, when Joseph called me to pick up the pieces of his mess. I looked into your eyes, and before I even knew your name, Iris, I promised you I'd ruin him."

The song ends, and Augusta takes her hands off Iris. "I need some air," she says at normal volume. "Would you like to join me?"

Iris nods, and the two go out the side door and onto the deck. There's no one outside.

There are a few tables and deck chairs set up for guests, but the wind has picked up. It blows little white caps on the river.

Augusta looks pained. "I need to be clear about something," she says loudly. "I didn't like what Joseph was doing, but I knew. I knew about his little side project with the girls only months after he started it. Him and Paulo, and Annabelle, they went behind my back."

"Annabelle was part of this?"

"It's why she wanted you dead. She thought you had discovered everything and confronted Joseph. I let her believe he killed you and then himself."

Iris remembers the *inconclusive* written at the bottom of the medical examiner's reports. It wasn't a lie. It was the truth.

"I know about the drugs, too."

"This family has been doing *that* since before I was CEO. But then Paulo took over his dad's business a fear years ago. He got in Joseph's head. Trafficking drugs? Why not girls? More money. They did it without me. I couldn't shut it down without exposing the company. I wanted to get Joseph locked up. Ruined. Especially once I found out what he was doing to the girls. You have to believe me, Iris. I'm not a monster like that."

But you let heroin flow into the streets. Iris doesn't want a fight. She wants the rest of everything she doesn't know. She lets the wind fill the silence. She parts her hair out of her face. "Why did I marry him?"

"To divorce him."

Iris raises her brow.

"It was our whole plan. Joseph was going to be the next CEO. He had the largest single shareholder stake in the company. Twenty percent. I wanted him out. Divorce was the only way to get those shares back. *Without* killing him.

"You never wanted him dead?"

"My own son?" Augusta's voice cracks. "No, Iris. Horrible as he was, I didn't want him fucking dead. You took everything into your own hands. You aborted our fucking plan. It's like you stopped caring about the money. You just wanted revenge."

Iris looks away. "Maybe because I had to live with him."

Augusta just shakes her head. "We had the whole thing primed for a cause divorce. Prostitution. We were going to catch him with a girl. We cooked the pre-nup with Marshall. You were going to get ten percent of the company no matter what. It was a good plan, Iris. It ruined Joseph without putting anyone in prison."

"How is that ruining him, then?" Iris is realizing this is where she had qualms. She was never on board with Augusta's plan. *She* was using Augusta.

Augusta's voice turns desperate. "His voting power would be halved. I'd be able to bully him. That's why you agreed. If he didn't stop with the girls, I'd make his life hell at the company. I couldn't do that if he was the largest shareholder. He had more sway on the board than any of us."

Iris turns and looks off towards the Mississippi. Augusta isn't even telling the truth. She starts walking down the deck.

Augusta follows her. "I'll burn it all down."

293

Iris doesn't respond. She reaches the back of the boat and looks over the railing at the big red paddle wheel. It spins noisily, whooshing the air. A few stories up is the presidential suite. Iris feels tricked. Augusta is still lying.

She keeps her eyes on the windows of the suite as she speaks. "If you were so against Joseph's business, why are there prostitutes on this boat?"

"That's not about making money. It's about pleasing guests. There are important people who expect there to be girls here."

Iris looks at her in disbelief. "And that's something you're fine with providing?"

"Okay," Augusta says. "Okay. I'll blow it all up."

"Blow what up?"

"Every crooked cop. Every hypocrite politician. The Adler Corp. Myself. Everything, Iris. I know everything. I keep files, hard drives, under the fireplace in the study. It's hard evidence. Enough to stop Annabelle."

"That's what this is about for you. Isn't it?"

"It's not just a vendetta. She wants to keep Joseph's side business going, while I want to shut it down. She wants to increase drug trafficking while I think it's time to quit. We used to move cocaine and pot, and I honestly thought it wasn't that big of a deal. But do you know the shit we're moving now? Fentanyl. Meth. We're not helping people have a party anymore. We're killing them. I can't incriminate her without incriminating myself, but maybe it's time I'm as selfless as you."

"It's her. The one killing the girls that Joseph abused. Covering the tracks. It's Annabelle."

"The man in Memphis... I know it was Nick."

"Your nephew?"

Augusta nods.

"But what about the girls? The ones I was trying to get to pin Joseph. She's the one ordering their murders."

"I don't know what you're talking about."

Iris stares at her furiously.

"Iris, I swear."

"I know why you're doing this." Iris jabs a finger at her chest. "You hate Annabelle. You think I believe you had a sudden change of heart about being a fucking drug trafficker after two decades?"

"That's not it," Augusta says quietly. Her green eyes begin to glisten. "Do you remember...us?"

"You mean when you fucked me?"

Augusta closes her eyes tight like the vulgar word stings her. "I just thought..." She looks away. "That maybe..."

Augusta is crying. She won't meet Iris's eye. Iris reaches out and holds her shoulder. She *makes* Augusta look at her. "That maybe what?"

"Oh." Augusta laughs, but it's all tears. "That maybe you actually loved me, too."

Iris's heart pounds. She feels shame. "No, Augusta." Iris's stomach sinks as she speaks, and even as she says the words, she can't be completely sure. "I never loved you."

Augusta looks away and nods. "So was always screwing me in the music room a metaphor for you? Because you were just playing me?"

A memory flashes in Iris's mind's eye. She and Augusta are naked in the music room. Laughing. Plotting. Augusta is telling her all about Joseph. His likes and dislikes. How to fit his idea of a perfect wife. "I'm sorry," Iris says. She takes her hand off Augusta's shoulder.

She realizes she's not Augusta's pet. Far from it. Iris has this woman in the palm of her hand, and little did she know, she always has.

"I'll still keep my word." Augusta sniffles. "The files. I'll hand everything over, even if it means a life sentence."

"You should."

Iris can't console her. She's too angry Augusta left her in the dark.

"Come on. Let's go back in."

Augusta wipes her eyes. They start back down the deck side by side, towards the ballroom.

They get to the door, and Augusta sets her hand on the handle but doesn't pull. "Can I ask something? Why'd you wear my brooch tonight? Is that supposed to be an insult?"

Iris frowns. "You left it out for me."

"What?"

"It was with everything else. The earrings, the dress, the necklace. It was all together."

"I never left out that brooch." There's fear in Augusta's voice. Fear that Iris doesn't understand.

"Okay?"

Augusta reaches for her breast and pulls off the brooch.

"Hey," Iris complains, but she's ignored.

Augusta is too busy inspecting the thing. She looks at it from the front and then flips it in her fingers. There's a metal back that the pin is attached to. She wiggles the metal, and the whole back pops right out.

"Oh, fuck."

"What? What is it?" Iris leans closer, and Augusta turns the brooch so she can see. Coiled inside is a ball of wires, and at the end is the little foam windscreen to a microphone.

Iris was bugged.

Overdose

Augusta tosses the entire brooch over the railing and into the river and keeps staring out at the water.

"Do you think someone was listening?" Iris asks. "Like live?"

"If not, it's all stored somewhere."

"Well, what if it was only a recorder? It was a small bug. Maybe it didn't have a transmitter. The FBI, they might've thought they'd get it back. They probably didn't think I'd notice it. It was well hidden."

"I don't think so."

"Come on. There's no way they thought you'd just toss how many carats into the Mississippi? They figured they'd get it back."

"I need my phone. I need to move those documents."

"I thought you wanted to give them up."

"Yes!" Augusta shouts. "*Give* them up. Turning over everything voluntarily. Striking a deal with a lawyer present... That's one thing. This is another. Without leverage... Oh honey."

Augusta opens the door to the ballroom, and Iris follows. She's trying to think about everything she said with the brooch on.

There was enough said that insinuated Iris killed Joseph. But it was windy on the deck and the music was loud inside. The only thing crystal clear they'd have was the conversation with Bree. All that does is make Iris look innocent in the murder of Sarah Gray. Bree said it loud and clear. Sarah overdosed.

Inside, a few heads turn to watch them, but most people are having too much fun. The conversation is boisterous over the music.

"I suggest you get another drink," says Augusta. "It will probably be your last in a long time." Iris doesn't listen. She stays by Augusta and tails her to one of the tall white tables, where there's a porter in charge of looking after purses and other valuables.

Augusta asks for hers, presumably to make a call.

"Why do you need your purse?"

She won't even respond to Iris. It's not just the bug, Iris can tell. It's that she told Augusta she never had any feelings.

Iris huffs and turns away. The police are probably already waiting at the boat landing. Will they call the ship back early, or will they wait until they dock at midnight to come aboard?

Iris does take Augusta's advice and finds herself at the bar. She orders just one vodka tonic this time. She posts up at the end of the room where there's a lone chair. She takes off her heels and leans lazily with a posture that says she doesn't have a care in the world.

It was a hell of a story, she must admit, but it suddenly feels concluded. The Alders were crushed, but so was Iris. She might not get life, however, and prison might not be the hell she thinks it will be.

Perhaps she can write a book about this when she's locked up. Everyone loves a conspiracy. But Iris pictures the press. They'd call her a whore. A gold digger. She might be famous, but she wouldn't be taken seriously.

Plus, she was from the streets. She was an addict and a prostitute. When the story gets around prison of what she did, she might be respected by the inmates. She takes a long sip of her drink and sighs. She's thinking about Augusta.

Maybe she did like her. A little. She wouldn't quite call the feelings she remembers love, but there was something genuine between them, and now Iris has made her feel like a foolish old woman. If Augusta was being honest about her intentions to end the trafficking, to blow the company up, she deserves a chance.

Annabelle suddenly comes into sight. She weaves through the crowd, and to Iris's chargin, she plops onto the floor next to her. Did Augusta already mention the bug? Does she know the gig is up?

Iris sighs. "What do you want?"

"Can't your sister-in-law say hi?"

Iris says nothing and finishes her drink.

"I always thought y'all were a little too close."

"Who's that?"

"I could always have pigeonholed you as a dyke. You never really could dress yourself, but Augusta? I guess she had decades of experience hiding it."

Iris looks at her with disinterest. She's not going to give her the satisfaction of getting under her skin.

"You must really have been desperate in life to end up a whore, huh? I mean, can you imagine? A prostitute who doesn't even like men. Sounds like a late-night bit. I guess it made good practice for all your acting."

She didn't think Annabelle knew that she used to be a prostitute. She starts to straighten in her chair. "How'd you figure it out?"

"Oh, because you thought that big ugly brooch was a gift from your lover."

Iris starts to stand, and Annabelle pulls herself up with the help of a chair.

She puts her hand on Iris's arm. "I just wanted to pay my last respects, sugar. This family has been moving drugs for forty years. Girls for four. It's had many enemies, and you of all people nearly brought it down. All by makin' a silly old lady fall in love with you. It's impressive. Sorta. But anyway, it's a shame it had to come to this. Don't take it personally, okay?" Annabelle lets go of her arm and starts to walk into the crowd.

What does she plan to do? What did she mean by last respects? Iris has to find Augusta.

She starts to cross the dance floor.

She has to sway to dodge a tall man that's coming towards her. He's in a black tuxedo, same as everyone else, and Iris is too focused to look at his face. As soon as she passes him on the crowded floor, she feels a sharp prick in her butt.

"Ow!" Iris spins to look at the man she passed. It's Nick. She sees him slip something into his pocket. A syringe. She's about to yell, but her blood already feels thick in her veins. Her head already swims. She stumbles off the dance floor and catches herself on one of the tables.

She grips on to the tablecloth. She holds her breath, thinking the vertigo will pass, but the world only begins to tilt more.

Instead of anyone coming to her aid, an empty circle appears around her as guests give her space. "Augusta," Iris calls as loud as she can.

She feels the need to vomit but manages to keep it down. She's trying to find her voice. She's been drugged. Just like Bree told her. *A drop of Fentanyl. A syringe.* She didn't realize the drugs would hit her brain as fast as her blood courses through her veins.

"Hey, hey." Augusta suddenly appears at her side. "Iris, are you alright?"

She manages to shake her head, but that's all.

Augusta looks over each of her shoulders. "Let's get you some fresh air. Back outside. Okay?"

She puts her arm over Iris's shoulder and lets her lean on her for support. With a weaker woman, Iris would topple, but Augusta holds her up firmly as they walk the twenty feet to the door that leads to the deck.

Augusta uses her foot to push it open, and once it shuts and they're alone outside again, she spins Iris by the shoulders so she faces her.

Everything is refracted for Iris now. Light stretches into sharp streaks. Augusta's face is still, but to Iris it sways like a buoy in rough water. She leans towards the deck and lets out a stream of vomit. The vodka tonics clog in her nostrils.

"Iris!"

"There's Naloxone... A shot..." The puking helps her think for a moment, although there's no way for her body to get the drugs out of her bloodstream. "It's with the girls upstairs. In the suite. Nick stuck me."

"Stuck you?"

Iris can't respond. The world spins again, and she's hit with another wave of nausea. She leans and pukes, but this time it's just a dribble before it turns to dry heaves.

"Oh shit. Shit, shit." Augusta is undoing the straps of her heels. She tosses one off and then the other. "Come on. Come with me." Augusta lets Iris lean into her again. She practically drags her up the metal spiral staircase to the second deck, but before they start the stairs to the third, Iris pushes herself out of Augusta's arms.

"Augusta," Iris says. "Go. I'll be here."

"I don't know what I'm looking for."

"Bree. Bree will. Go."

"Okay, stay here!" She's no longer next to Iris. She's running up the next set of stairs towards the presidential suite.

It becomes hard for Iris to stand. She stumbles over to the end of the deck and clings to the railing. Luckily, she's too short to topple over it.

The river hisses past the hull beneath her. She pulls herself with both hands along the railing, as if it's a rope in a game of tug of war. Iris isn't thinking. She just wants to move like death is something she can get away from, and she pulls herself along all the way until she's near the back of the boat, just above the paddle wheel.

The mist it throws is blown back on her in the strong wind. In August, this stretch of the Mississippi is at its warmest and filthiest, but the tiny droplets feel like snowflakes on her face. She thinks she must be running a fever already. Her body is in overdrive.

She lets go of the railing and collapses onto the deck. There's a brief pinching pain in her leg. It's so subtle and she's so drugged, she's able to ignore it, but only for a few seconds.

Her leg suddenly feels wet. She looks down to see a pool of blood expanding beneath her.

She's dreaming. She's dead, Iris thinks. Then she turns her leg over and sees the paring knife she had concealed is stuck into the underside of her thigh all the way up to the handle.

"Oh no," Iris says and puts her hand on it. Someone is coming, running towards her. "No!" Iris yells. She throws her hands up uselessly to defend herself. It takes her a moment to recognize Augusta's voice.

"Oh, Iris, what did you do?"

She can't find an explanation worthy of words. She is trying to say something else.

"Augusta."

"Shh." She can hear Augusta mumbling aloud, reading the drug's instructions.

"I was lying..." Iris says but can't finish her sentence.

Augusta is silent for a second. Maybe she understands what Iris was lying about. Iris cringes, twists her head away to dry heave. "I liked you, Augusta. I'm not sure what it says... about me. But I did." She tries to breathe to find more words, but she can't keep any air down. It's like her lungs won't fill.

Her brain can't talk to them.

Augusta doesn't respond to her. "It's a shot, Iris. I need your other leg." She pulls her non-bloody leg straight.

Iris glances up. There's a shadow coming towards them. Augusta's back is to this figure. She thinks it may be one of the girls from upstairs come to help, but they're too large. Iris tries to point and scream, but she thinks of doing both and ends up doing neither.

There's a blunt sound. A kick. Iris hears Augusta yelp. Someone is holding her in a headlock. Nick.

He twists her in her arms and towards the railing. He's trying to throw her over.

The Naloxone clatters to the deck and rolls out of Iris's reach. She throws her hand out to it anyway, but it's too far for her to even see. It might've rolled right into the river.

Augusta yells, "Help!" But then her voice is cut out. She's being strangled. Iris can hear them both grunt. He pushes Augusta a little more over the railing.

Iris feels mist rise from the paddle wheel. She glances over her shoulder. He's trying to throw Augusta into the propeller.

A smaller woman would be over the railing by now, but Iris can see Augusta has her legs wrapped around one of Nick's. But with his hands around her neck, it won't be long before she's unconscious.

Iris pats her leg until she finds the handle of the knife. She doesn't hesitate. She pulls. The opiates are doing their intended purpose—she can't feel a thing, and the blade comes out weightlessly.

She doesn't adjust her grip. She can't. Iris holds the knife in her fist and swings her hand over. There's the thud of metal on metal. She missed. She's seeing double, triple. Nick's legs multiply like an object between two mirrors. They stretch for eternity.

She pulls her arm back and tries again. Iris can't apply much strength to the stab, but the steel is sharp, and this time the only sound is Nick's scream.

He kicks Iris in the stomach, and in doing so, he lets go of Augusta. Augusta doesn't run. She doesn't scream. She drops down to the deck, like she's looking for something. She forces the Naloxone shot into Iris's hands.

"Stick yourself, sugar."

Then Augusta throws her arms around Nick, and by using her weight to take herself with him, she heaves the both of them over the railing.

Iris tries to shout. There's a sickening thud of flesh hitting the big barrel propeller.

She turns over her shoulder in time to see two splashes erupt in the water.

There's muffled screaming from inside. The back of the ballroom has big windows that look out to the propeller, but the side deck where Iris is isn't visible.

Iris keeps staring at the water. The boat's wake is a streak of white in the middle of the black river, but nothing surfaces.

The night is now silent apart from the wind.

"Augusta," Iris cries. She holds the shot in her fist, but she can't move her arms. Again, it's like she's asleep in her own

303

body. Her brain can't speak to any part of her. Soon, her organs will shut down. She'll suffocate.

Iris hears the dull sound of fast footsteps on metal stairs. A woman is running towards her. Annabelle. It has to be. But instead, Iris looks up to see Bree's square face. She pries the shot from Iris's fingers and tears off its plastic cap with her teeth.

She raises both her arms over her head and brings the shot down hard into Iris's thigh. Her whole lower body is numb, but there is a sensation where it went in. Something that feels like hot light shoots through her veins.

"She's going to need another!" Iris hears Bree shout.

There's all kinds of commotion now. The deck doors are opening. She hears chatter growing as guests come out to gawk.

Iris lets her head roll back so she can watch the boat's wake. The river is blurry, but even if her vision were perfect, Iris knows that Augusta is gone.

She closes her eyes and lets herself fall asleep as the mist gently falls on her face.

Legal

Iris wakes up feeling more brain dead than she has since getting shot, but her body is fine. Limber, even. There's an IV stuck in her arm, but she's not wired to any serious medical machinery.

For a moment, before she's fully conscious, she thinks she's in her bedroom at Sweet Blood, but then the marble in her mind turns to linoleum.

She's in a hospital room. What looks like late afternoon light seeps through the blinds.

To her surprise, there is no doctor waiting in a chair next to the bed. No family, either. It's the lawyer. Marshall.

He wears a brown three-piece suit. He's standing on a chair and tinkering behind the TV that hangs in the corner. Then he steps down, opens the back of the TV remote and takes out the battery.

He's looking for bugs.

"Good afternoon," Iris says.

"Oh!" He startles. "Good afternoon." He clears his throat and sets the remote down. "Just makin' sure it's just you and me in here."

Iris sits up more in the hospital bed. "Um, would the doctor like to talk to me?"

"They already have. Don't worry. Memory loss is to be expected with the drugs that were in your system. They said your leg should heal fine. It might be stiff, but the knife missed anything serious."

"What about the police?" Iris's heart pounds. She's scared she talked to them when she was still high.

"That's why I'm here. No law enforcement will be speaking to you until you're singing and dancing again."

Iris nods.

"I have a list of questions here. I think it's everything they'll ask you. We're going to do a little rehearsal when you're ready. Is now a good time? Or would you like more time?"

"Can I ask some of my own questions?"

"'Course."

"Augusta?"

He shakes his head. "Two guests on the second deck caught a glimpse of a man and a woman going overboard. The sheriff's office has a dive team out, but that's a lot of river to cover. Current's strong there. Finding anything gets real difficult when they could be in the Gulf by—"

Iris holds her palm up.

"I'm sorry."

Iris knows this lawyer was Augusta's henchman. He probably knows everything from the drugs to the girls to Joseph's death. "And how much do you know?" Iris asks.

"Everything," he says knowingly while looking her in the eye.

"Nick stabbed me with a fentanyl shot."

"The doctor said you had quite the dose in your system. Lucky to not have brain damage. It took three of whatever those shots they gave you to keep your heart beatin'."

"Nick was trying to stop Augusta from reviving me. He's getting paid by Annabelle. Other girls have been overdosing. Ones that were going to help me put Joseph away. That could testify to there being a ring."

"I'm going to have to stop you there. Let's keep all that between us. Okay? It's not going to do you any favors."

Iris pauses. Leans back. "Are you retained by Annabelle, too?"

"Annabelle? God, no. Augusta and I had a shared disdain for her daughter-in-law. But I'm telling you, all this does is get *you* in trouble. The FBI wants to interview you after Labor Day. They want you at their offices in New Orleans on Tuesday. If you're able. They're leading this investigation. Oh, and it's Sunday, by the way. You were out for a while."

306

"You want me to lie? About the drugs? About the girls? Somebody has to pay for all this."

"I think you'll find there's not a lot of evidence to back anything up. Augusta likes her guests to have privacy on board the Diamond Lady. Many of the cameras are disabled. Even if they have Nick sticking you with a syringe on camera, how are you going to prove Annabelle had anything to do with it?"

Iris bites her lip. "There has to be a money trail."

"I can tell you that's one of the easier things to hide. Even if the feds find questionable transactions, there ain't going to be a memo accompanying it saying, 'payment for murder.'"

Iris shakes her head like she can't just stay silent.

Marshall reaches out and rests his hand on her blanketed knee. "I want you to know that I despise Annabelle as much as you do. Augusta's enemies are my enemies. Her friends..." He pats Iris's knee. "My friends. I'm telling you this as an ally. She won, Iris." He sighs, like this truly bothers him. "The bitch won. Pardon my language."

"She's not going to be..."

"CEO? Oh yes, she is. Nothin's in her way now."

"What about the drug shipments? What if they catch her using the ships?"

"There's about a dozen low-level employees who are paid to take the fall if anyone catches them trafficking drugs. And I imagine Annabelle is smart enough to stop shipments while the FBI is still investigating."

"Augusta said she had notes. Files hidden in the study."

"I tried to get my hands on those this morning. Somehow, Annabelle knew where they were being kept. There was nothing."

Iris leans back, defeated. Marshall doesn't know about the bug. "There has to be some way to pin her."

"Look, it's my job to think of things like that, and there ain't nothin. She's dotted her I's and crossed her T's. This company is careful. Your husband was too. Remember what happened the first time you got frustrated with not having evidence and got sloppy?"

Iris looks away.

"I do have good news for ya."

"What?"

"With Augusta gone, the curatorship argument has dropped. I'm going to help assist you with the financials, but I reckon in a week's time, you'll have access to Joseph's capital and control of all his shares. That being said..." Marshall leans forward. "It's going to make you a target. Annabelle knows you're no longer ignorant. She could come after you."

"So what do I do?"

"Talk to her. Play to her ego, tell her she won. And then, sell her all your shares."

"What?"

"I'm not going to convince you if you don't want to. I don't want you to think for one second I'm on that woman's side. But if you want to not worry about losing your life, sell her the shares. She'll make an offer, and we're talking many, many millions."

Iris doesn't say anything. Right now, she feels nothing from the idea of having many, many millions.

"Now, I think it's best we start rehearsin'. The FBI's going to have quite the list for you."

"Okay," Iris says and sighs. She's not all present. Her mind is elsewhere, thinking over and over how she can get Annabelle. But with the pregnancy, violence doesn't feel like an option. And with so little evidence, neither is the law.

Iris is coming to terms that the lawyer is right.

Annabelle won.

Like an Epilogue

"So, where'd you get the heroin that night?" Agent Long tilts her pen up when she asks the question. Iris knows she doesn't believe a word she's been telling her. She's past annoyed at this point—she's pissed.

The metal table they sit at is scattered with papers and empty cups of coffee, but this interview has so far gone along as Iris and Marshall have planned. It's gotten the FBI nowhere.

"I don't remember. You know how my brain injury is," says Iris.

Marshall nods along sagely.

"So let me get this straight, Iris." Agent Long extends her hands. Moves them erratically as she speaks. "You expect us to believe that you ended up with enough Fentanyl to kill three grown men in your bloodstream, somehow sat on a knife, and while all this was happening, Nick and Augusta had some argument that led to both of them falling overboard into the river?"

"I can't really tell you what happened. That's just the facts. I was so high. I was seeing stars."

"And what were they fighting about? I mean humor me. If you had a guess."

"The succession of the company, I believe. Augusta and Annabelle had been feuding, and Nick was trying to get Augusta to give it up, hand over the reins to the company."

"And why would Nick be so heated about that topic? He doesn't work for the Adler Corp."

Iris shrugs. "You'd have to ask him, but I think he and Annabelle were a little too close. He was family, but he and Annabelle weren't related, if you see what I'm sayin'?"

Agent Long crosses her arms. "You think they were having an affair?"

"Something of the sort."

"Any evidence of that? Or is it just a hunch like everything else you've said?"

"Call it a hunch. But can I ask *you* something?"

Agent Long looks like she's about given up at this point. She raises her brow. Crosses her arms.

"Did y'all ever do a toxicology report on the remains you found burned? I was readin' that you've got such high-tech equipment, you can do it on just ashes now."

Agent Long sighs. "Not quite ashes. But there was enough material to do toxicology. Sure."

"And did that turn anything up?"

"Funny you should ask. We detected Fentanyl in her system, too."

Iris frowns. "So maybe that's what killed her. A drug overdose, not the bullets. Not, you know... me."

"Sure, Iris." Agent Long smirks like there's something up her sleeve after all. "You know, I just wanted to thank you for calling our attention to the documents about your attempted murder case that you stole from the station. There are several discrepancies we're very concerned about."

Iris tries to keep her expression calm. They know. She can see it written all over Long's face.

"What kind of—"

Long interrupts. "Oh, you know. Gun placement. Gunpowder placement. Bullet trajectory... It's all a little wonky. Wrong. You said murder-suicide, that you think your husband shot you, correct?"

"Ah-hem," says Marshall. "I think we've gotten a little off topic. Do you have any further questions about what happened onboard the Diamond Lady?"

"No." Long smiles, and Iris's blood runs cold.

They've got her, she thinks. They're probably putting the finishing touches on the case. Making it rock solid. Then they're going to bring the hammer down.

"We'll be in touch, Mrs. Adler."

Iris is stuck in her chair as Agent Long stands and leaves the room. She's quiet as she and Marshall walk to the elevator. Iris would probably be more comfortable on crutches. Her wound throbs if she walks too long on it. The pain has been a helpful thing to be able to latch her focus on, but right now, it does nothing to stop her anxiety.

When the door shuts, Marshall speaks. "I wouldn't worry if I were you. If they go after you saying you shot Joseph, we'll take it to court. They'd need a hell of a body of evidence to get a conviction. And I'll find out what they have. A jury would *want* to side with you, remember that."

Iris doesn't say anything, not when the elevator doors open again or as they walk across the wide lobby and outside into the blaring sun.

There's a young man in a suit with his hands clasped behind his back waiting on the sidewalk. He holds out a pair of car keys to Marshall.

"Ah. Here you are, Iris. Just as you asked," says Marshall. He passes Iris the keys. They're to the shiny black Cadillac that sits parked at the curb in front of them. "You can send me a wire when the cash hits your account on Friday. I know you're good for it."

"Thank you, Marshall."

"Enjoy."

Iris walks around and gets into the driver's seat. It's the same model the Adlers were driven in, only without the custom interior. Now it's Iris behind the wheel. She puts it in drive and pulls away from the curb. The car is silent and the ride so smooth it's like driving a ribbon of silk.

When she gets off the interstate and onto the back roads, Iris accelerates. The engine purrs. The speed on the digital speedometer ticks up in increments of several miles per hour at a time. Soon she rolls to a stop in a cloud of dust in front of a gate.

Sweet Blood sits at the end of the drive. The trees are still on this breezeless September day.

Iris rolls down her window and stares at the camera fixed to the gate's stone post. There's an intercom button, but she doesn't press it. She just stares at the little lens. It's only a few seconds before there's a buzz, and the great big gate begins to swing open.

She takes her foot off the brake and drives slowly down the road. Annabelle is already waiting for her. She stands at the top of the porch stairs.

Iris pulls up in front of her and kills the engine. She steps out of the car.

Annabelle doesn't move and doesn't invite Iris up to the porch. She's wearing a black blouse that billows out with her pregnant belly and stretchy black jeans. Her bare feet shine pale on the wooden porch.

"You in mourning?" Iris asks sarcastically and shuts her car door.

"How was your meeting?"

"It was more of an interview."

"Did you get the job?"

"What would that be?"

"Of being a rat?"

"I'm not working with them."

"Oh, so they didn't give it to you?" Annabelle makes a pouty face. "But you have such good previous experience, don't you, Iris?"

Iris lets Annabelle get the anger out of her system.

Annabelle pauses. "So whatcha ya here for? A memento of your lover? I'm sorry about Mama. The two of you would've been the cutest couple of dykes in the parish. But so you know, she didn't have any love letters lyin' around. There ain't an epilogue for your little love story."

"I didn't come here to talk about Augusta."

"No? So what, came to rub your newfound fortune in my face. Looks like all the gold diggin' finally paid off. Or you *did* get hired."

"I'm not an informant."

Annabelle tilts her head. "Prove it, then."

"What do you want me to do? Sign something?"

"Lift up your shirt."

"Come on," Iris scoffs.

"You just came from a meeting with the feds. You think I'm an idiot?"

Iris lifts her shirt up, spins, and then pulls it down.

"Pants, too. Open 'em up."

Iris looks around. She knows this conversation isn't going any further without proof she's not wearing a wire. She unbuttons her pants and lets them fall just before her knees.

"Okay, you can button up, sweetheart."

Iris lifts her pants back up and stands as straight as she can. She tries to keep her dignity.

"So whatcha want?"

"I want to talk about my shares."

"Yeah?"

"I want to sell."

"For as much as you own, you'll need board approval. Something you're not likely to get without my support."

"What if I want to sell to you?"

Annabelle narrows her eyes at her. "And why would you want to do that?"

"So we're square."

"Square?"

"Uh-huh. Settled. Done. I don't want anything more to do with you or this family. You won."

"But what makes you think I'm done with you?"

Iris is silent. She glares at Annabelle.

"I'm just kiddin', sugar. We can settle up. Tell you what. I'll make you a deal. I won't ever share the recording I have of you saying you shot Joseph if you keep your mouth shut about everything you may have heard about me. And how our company makes its money."

"You still have that on tape?"

"All of it."

"Alright. Deal."

"I'll tell you what. With Augusta gone, I believe all twenty percent of Joseph's stake goes to you. At our most recent PE valuation of three times revenue..." Annabelle looks to the sky doing math in her head. "That would come out to around... seventy-million dollars."

"Draw up the documents." Iris is about to turn back to her car.

"Wait." Annabelle scrunches her face like something doesn't sit well. "I deserve a discount. For all the shit you put this family through. Plus, you don't have much leverage over me. Full price doesn't sound right. I'll pay thirty."

"Thirty million?" The sum is still unfathomable to Iris, but the insult of the discount makes her stomach churn. She has to watch her mouth.

"I think that's only fair, sweetheart."

"And wouldn't that devalue the company?"

"Doesn't really matter. Revenue and assets tell the truth."

Iris is out of her depth. "Let me talk to Marshall."

"Don't you bring that three-piece, two-bit son of a bitch into this. Thirty million. You've got no ground to stand on. I should ask for them for free if it wouldn't raise eyebrows."

"You know I can say things, too."

"And have no one believe you."

"Paulo's in the cartel. I'm sure the feds would love to hear all about that."

"Doesn't mean we work with him in that capacity. His family owns a legitimate agriculture and shipping business. Look at the paper trail. That's all we know. You're not very good at this, you know that?"

Iris grimaces. She puts her hands on her hips.

"Thirty million," Annabelle says and she spins back towards the house. "Who knows... Maybe you can buy yourself a new brain. Now run along, Iris. Keep an eye on your email. We'll set up a meetin'."

"What about my things?"

"Pardon?" Annabelle leans out of the doorway.

"My room. My clothes. I need my stuff."

"Ohhh." Annabelle puts her hand on her chest. "I'm so sorry, hon. When you were in the hospital, we didn't think you were gonna make it. I was just so overwhelmed with Mama's death... Seeing that room all cluttered was too much. We had the help take it all to one of those donation centers. It was all in pretty rough shape anyway."

Iris doesn't respond. She opens her car door and climbs in. She holds the wheel in a death grip as she drives, but her face is calm. For a moment, she debates the merits of murdering a pregnant woman, but she can't even entertain the thought. Marshall was right. Annabelle won. The world is just cruel like that, and Iris of all people should know.

Still, she can't help but wipe her tears with the back of her hand as she drives. She looks at the house in the rearview. She pictures Augusta sitting on the porch swing, that white waterfall of hair blowing gently in the breeze.

Now a real monster lives in Sweet Blood, and there's nothing Iris can do about it.

Think, Iris

Iris moves into a townhouse in New Orleans. It's an old brick building with a wisteria vine crawling up all three stories.

The inside is modern. White granite countertops. Cool white walls. She likes the idea of having neighbors on either side of her, but the thought does less than she assumed it would to make her feel safe.

She picked this place partly because its first-floor windows are eight feet off the ground. It's a little fortress in the French Quarter. A place she can actually sleep at night.

She has cameras facing every possible entrance, which she can access on her phone, but it gives her little solace.

She thinks about Hawaii. Maine. Far-flung places where she thinks she'd be safer from a paranoid whim of Annabelle's. But if Paulo wants her dead, there's no place on earth she'd be safe.

Iris has spent too much time online reading about the hitmen the cartel uses. Sicarios. Their best are ex-Special Forces. Often even Americans, Russians, or British. The most expert killers in the world trade in what was left of their morals for the hundreds of thousands they get per contract.

She hasn't bothered to hire security, but only because she's being surveilled by the FBI. She's calmed down about getting charged with Joseph's murder. They still haven't arrested her. Maybe they can prove that the forensics don't add up, that maybe Iris was the shooter, but they're still absolutely puzzled as to what the motive would be.

Iris is sure they're digging into her past in Memphis. They can't be that far from the question, *How did an ex-prostitute end up marrying into the Adler family?*

But the FBI isn't alone in Memphis. Iris hired a PI firm through Marshall. The best in the country, or so he said. They're all a bunch of ex-intelligence contractors themselves.

She wants old high school papers. Math tests. Anything that could help her see if there was a trace of an intelligent girl before someone stuck a needle in her arm. Her identity shouldn't rely on this image of who she was in the past, but she can't help it. *Prostitute.* She can't help it. The word still makes her feel small.

That's only step one. Step two is gathering the name of every street scumbag, every client, and nearly every person she talked to regularly since she was fourteen. She's going to map out her entire life before she came to Louisiana, and perhaps when necessary, pay to dole out punishment along the way.

They promised her a 100-page report by Christmas.

It's a rainy afternoon in October when Iris gets her first knock on the door.

She doesn't try to sneak a peek at them out the window. She immediately pulls up the camera app on her phone. It looks like the postman is standing at her door, but it could just be an outfit. It's not until she sees the mail truck with its hazards flashing that she thinks this person is who they appear to be.

She opens the door.

"I need a signature from ya."

Iris doesn't look at him right away. Her eyes are focused on a gray SUV parked on the far side of the street. There are people in the driver and passenger seat. Feds.

She doesn't think she ordered anything that would require a signature. "Okay."

The mailman turns his little device towards her, and she scribbles on the screen. "I've got your other mail here too." He hands her the package she had to sign for, which is just a thin cardboard envelope, and the rest of her mail.

"Thank you."

"Have a good day!"

Iris shuts the door and turns the deadlock.

She walks to the kitchen counter and spreads all the mail out. The package she had to sign for is too small and flat to be a threat. She's not so paranoid she thinks she has to worry about anthrax.

She rips open the top and pulls out a large card. The paper is embossed with gold lettering. It's an invitation.

An invite to a ceremony. *"Please join us as we introduce Annabelle Adler as our next Chief Executive Officer."*

Iris has heard about this. There's another ball. It's at the same converted armory that Joseph's memorial dinner was held. There is no mention of Augusta on the card. Her memorial service was a few weeks ago, although the river search turned up neither her body nor Nick's.

Augusta was swallowed by the Mississippi and never spat back up.

Iris throws the invitation down on the counter with a slap. It's clearly from Annabelle. It's a thumb in Iris's eye. *Come watch my coronation. There's nothing you can do about it.*

The deal to sell her shares still hasn't been finalized. Iris could still back out. She thinks this invitation is a strange gesture, and why was it sent via priority mail with a signature requirement? So Iris would notice it?

She doesn't care enough to decipher Annabelle's games. She taps the trash bin's "open" lever with her foot and tosses the card in, but she keeps her foot down. She keeps staring at the invitation. There's a little label, a *printed* return address on the card itself and the cardboard envelope it came in.

Iris takes the card out of the trash. Sets it back on the counter. Her eyes narrow and her breath quickens. The return address isn't for Magnolia House. It reads, *Harvest Baptist Church. 24726 Shoe Pick Road.*

This invitation isn't from Annabelle. There's something she's missing.

She reads when the event is being held. Tonight. Friday the eleventh.

It starts in four hours.

Iris decides it's worth it to be an hour late. She doesn't want to show up a mess to one of these balls where the women have

318

been getting ready since yesterday. It'll be a rush but she can make it.

The dress code is formal, and Iris needs a dress. She's surrounded by boutiques, and after an hour out, she has everything she needs. The gray SUV doesn't tail her on her errand, and when she gets back to her townhouse, it's gone.

By seven p.m., Iris is ready to go. She's chosen an emerald-colored split-thigh ball gown. It's something Augusta would've worn. It shows a little too much skin for this crowd, but Iris isn't attending to make friends. With matching gloves that reach up to the middle of her biceps, she looks the part of Southern Belle.

She goes out the back door and gets into her car.

It's a long drive to Baton Rouge. When she arrives at the event, the valets are smoking cigarettes. They're not expecting any more guests.

She hands off her keys, takes her ticket, and walks inside through the doors and into the big lit ballroom. People are mingling and chatting. It's getting towards the end of cocktail hour. According to the invitation, speeches will be starting soon.

Iris has already been noticed, and people don't look at her the same as they used to. She's been dubbed a drug addict by southern society. The rumors range from she always used heroin and her dealer killed Joseph, to she only recently got hooked on painkillers when she first got out of the hospital.

Whichever side one takes, Iris can tell it's not proper form to have a conversation with her. People shun her with their eyes. The couple nearest to her actually takes a noticeable step back.

Iris ignores them and scours the room. She's looking for Paulo. She thinks he has to be behind the card. It wouldn't be Gideon or Jamie. It can't be Joseph Senior. Maybe there's someone she's forgotten about entirely. Someone from before her injury that she doesn't even remember.

She can't find Paulo, and it makes sense. He wouldn't be here in the States. It's still too hot, with the FBI investigating. Annabelle is near the stage at the front of the room. She's staring at Iris with juvenile disgust. Her lips are curled and her nostrils flare, as if Iris has just crashed her birthday party.

Iris gives a little wave. Annabelle just turns away. She's very pregnant now. Even though her dress is altered, it only does so much to conceal it. Iris does the math. She's eight months. Only a few weeks from her due date now.

She stares at her bump, picturing the child she's going to bring into this world. It could be spoiled rotten like Annabelle, or it could see through it all. It could be a good person, as stacked as the odds are against it.

Iris gets a drink so she doesn't look so damn awkward, and once it's in her hand, she stands in the back corner of the room. The drink doesn't help. She smiles tightly, alone, as everyone speaks to one another.

She looks at her phone for a moment but decides not to hide behind a screen. She rolls her shoulders back and stares out at the crowd.

Thankfully, she has an excuse to be quiet. Someone taps a glass with silverware, and Annabelle takes the stage. She waves, blows a kiss.

Everyone claps, and Iris opts to sip her drink instead.

"I'd just like to thank everyone for taking the time to come out this evening..." Annabelle begins, but Iris quickly quits listening. Someone is approaching her.

Dominic, she realizes. He's wearing glasses this evening.

"Good evening," he whispers and stands by her shoulder.

She takes a steady breath. "Hello."

"Glad you got my invitation."

Iris tries not to react in surprise. She just nods. "You're the mystery man?"

"I take it Augusta never told you?"

"No."

Annabelle's speech is loud enough to give their conversation cover. Iris doubts anyone can hear them.

Dominic sighs. "That's where she and I had disagreements. I wanted you to remember everything, and she... She had other ideas."

"So you're the one who sent me that naked picture of myself? You're the one who wanted to meet me at that church?"

"You don't remember me at all, do you?"

"Don't be offended."

"Believe me, I'm not."

"So, were we intimate? Why the picture?"

"It was taken by Joseph, hours before everything went south that night. I was trying to get you to remember."

"Remember who I was?"

"Partly. More so to remember what you were doing."

"Taking down Joseph?"

"Not just him. Jamie. Annabelle..."

Iris steals a look at Dominic. There's fury in his eyes.

"Everyone at that goddamn company who treated girls like another product."

"I thought you hated me."

"I do hate you."

Iris widens her eyes. "And why's that?"

"Because you shot him in the head," Dominic says coldly. "A man we agreed would suffer for hours. Days. A *lifetime* if we could somehow manage it. You shot him in the fucking head. Lights out. No pain."

Iris swallows uncomfortably. It's not just what Dominic is saying. There's an undercurrent of craziness in his tone. "Why does that matter? Who was he to you?"

Dominic turns to face her. "All that running around, and you're still in the dark."

Iris is annoyed at the game in his tone. "Just answer the question."

"You knew my sister."

"Did I?"

"You were coworkers."

Iris pauses. "The other girl at the Nile... Sarah Gray."

"Sarah Gray was just another call girl. My sister is in a home taking her meals through a straw."

"I'm sorry."

"I was in college. I had to be away," he says through gritted teeth, like he's explaining himself before God. "It was the only way I could one day make enough to get my mom and sister out of that neighborhood. I was almost done. My senior year, and I get the call. She's in the hospital."

"Why didn't you press charges?"

Dominic smiles and shakes his head. "So there wouldn't be a motive."

"If you were to kill Joseph, you mean?"

"Exactly. I lied to the hotel, saying she was conscious. I lied to the hospital, saying she was randomly attacked on the street. No one second guesses what happens to *whores*." He says the word bitterly, like that's the only thing society thought of his sister as.

"Did Augusta know about you?"

"Of course. She helped me lie to the hotel to settle them down."

"She never mentioned you when we were talking about this."

"She would've got there. Augusta recruited both of us. She *did* want to ruin Joseph for what he did—she wasn't lying. We just had different definitions of the word. She moved me to Baton Rouge, got me hired as Joseph's new assistant. Found an excuse to fire the old one. She wanted me to snoop. Collect evidence. I was going to supply the blackmail while you were the vessel that would receive the shares after his divorce or, as we planned..."

"Imprisonment?" Iris asks.

The two have to be quiet for several seconds, as there's a burst of applause to something Annabelle said.

"So you do remember?"

Iris isn't sure she does. "We went behind Augusta's back, didn't we?"

"She didn't want to see him killed or in prison, just broke and powerless. You and I... We knew what needed to happen to him. We knew what he really deserved."

"So we went to the girls ourselves, and you posed as a reporter..."

A waitress with a mask on suddenly walks past them. She and Dominic make eye contact the entire time. He doesn't speak until she's gone. "Glad to see that brain of yours is back. Yes, we were building a legal case, not just blackmail. I didn't just want to kill him. I wanted the world to know who he was. But we were having trouble with evidence. He got smart, and Sarah Gray's overdose was an opportunity. You knew where Joseph kept his gun... You thought fast, but it was hasty, and we paid for it."

Everyone in the crowd claps again. Annabelle is spouting business platitudes about formidability in the face of the future.

"Is that why you cried at his funeral?" Iris takes a sip of her drink. "Because he didn't get what he deserved?"

Dominic grins wryly. "I didn't want him to be remembered as Joseph the Great. You know how you do that here in Louisiana? I put on a pink tie, and I *cried*. Everyone thought the same thing when they saw Joseph's younger, black new assistant bawling harder than his own mother at his funeral. You should've seen their southern faces."

Iris actually smiles. "Okay, so why invite me here tonight?"

"You have more mail."

"Do I?"

"I don't know if the FBI is reading your correspondence, but it's at Sweet Blood. Go there after this. As soon as we're done talking. Aurelia will receive you."

Iris isn't sure she trusts him. Not after his admission of hating her. "If you don't like me, why are you telling me this?"

"Because I still owe someone a favor." Dominic looks at his watch. "And there's one more thing, by the way. Something rather obvious you're missing."

"What?" Iris is annoyed. Dominic is acting like a know-it-all.

"I want you to think, Iris."

"I don't want to play a fucking game right now."

"I'm not giving you a choice. Think. There's something you've forgotten about. Something small, perhaps forgettable, but one thing has still not been accounted for."

Iris shuts up and plays along. She senses this might actually be important. Whatever it is, it must have to do with Dominic. Suddenly she remembers the last time she saw him.

"You were in that boat..." Her mouth opens. "You were in the little skiff trailing the riverboat. I saw you."

"Well, that's not what I'm referencing, but you're full of surprises. Yes, I was in the skiff."

"What were you doing?"

"I was planning on finishing this."

Iris remembers the black bag in the bow of the boat. "You wanted Annabelle."

Dominic nods his head forward at Annabelle while she speaks. "She's the next best thing to getting Joseph. She knew about it all. And she's the one who wants to keep it in place, do you know that? The girls. The drugs. She talks about trafficking human beings like they're products."

"So, what were you going to do? Shoot her?"

"I don't play with guns. Just look what happened to you."

Iris suddenly perks up. "Were you behind the boat when Augusta fell in? Did you see her?" Her heart pounds.

Dominic is slow to respond. "I saw her fall."

"And she never came up?"

There's a great big burst of applause, and neither can hear. Dominic's eyes sweep the stage nervously. He's waiting for something.

"We don't have time to get off topic. Me in that little boat isn't what I was talking about," Dominic says harshly. "When you saw me at the slaughterhouse. There was a list."

Iris frowns. She knows what he's talking about. "The liters of acid that were stolen."

"Exactly."

"So what? You burned off my tattoo? We disposed of some other body together?"

"Oh no, no, no."

Iris anxiously touches the scar on her head. Her palm is clammy. What if he's behind this scar? For a moment, her stomach drops out from under her. What if all her memories are false?

The speech is nearing its end. Waiters whisk around with trays full of champagne glasses. Dominic plucks one from a platter. He's smiling wide. Iris is too distracted to take one herself.

Annabelle is speaking louder now, and it's harder for their conversation to continue without raising their voices.

Dominic leans in to Iris's ear and whispers, "The acid... I never used it. I never got to."

He can't stop grinning. What is she missing? She feels like there's a conspiracy happening in this room but she's not in on it.

Dominic has shut up.

"And I'd just like to say," Annabelle belts into the microphone. "To the Adler Corporation, and all its friends and private shareholders, thank you. Thank you for this opportunity to lead! To the future!" She smiles, and Iris realizes Annabelle had been brought a glass of champagne by a waiter, too.

But she's pregnant.

That can't be what it is. The liquid's color is too clear, Iris thinks, and then her heart stops.

The speech has reached its climax. The crowd is shouting.

"Oh fuck," whispers Iris. "Annabelle!" she shouts, but in all the noise, it just sounds like another shout of support.

Annabelle raises her glass, she perches one hand proudly on her pregnant belly, and then she downs half the glass in a single, victorious gulp.

Iris jolts forward to run to the stage, but she's violently stopped as Dominic pulls her elbow. "Tell her to lie on her back if she doesn't want the acid to eat through the baby."

He releases her with a push, and Iris stumbles forward. The room is muttering nervously already. Iris hears the sound of shattering glass. Annabelle drops her glass. Falls.

She disappears from view in an instant as people rush to her aid.

"Hey! Hey!" Iris yells. She's elbowing her way through everyone, sending champagne glasses spilling left and right. She crawls onto the stage and pushes the others away. "She ingested an acid!"

Jamie already holds her head in his hands. Someone fans her as if she's only fainted. Annabelle's eyes are so wide in fear and pain that it gives her face a skeletal look.

"Lay her on her back more! Keep her on her back!" Iris shouts.

"Someone get her out of here," Jamie says of Iris and motions with a quick jolt of his head, but then Annabelle spits up blood.

"Annabelle? Annabelle?" he shouts. Suddenly, steam rises up from the stage. There's a hissing noise. Some of the acid has already burrowed its way out through her back.

"Oh my Jesus Christ," someone says breathlessly.

Another person is already holding a phone to their ear calling 9-1-1, and Iris shouts to them. "Tell the paramedics she needs an emergency C-section!"

"Annabelle," Jamie says. "Can you talk?"

She's still staring at Iris, and when she opens her mouth, Iris is frozen in shock.

Where the back of Annabelle's throat should be, Iris can see straight through to the floor.

The Living and the Dead

Iris stumbles outside into the night as the firetruck and paramedics arrive. They rush past her, and she hands her ticket to the valet.

"What's going on in there?" he asks, but Iris is silent.

Her mouth is stuck in a tight line. Her expression is distant.

He takes the hint and jogs off to fetch her car. Iris sits down on the curb until it's pulled around.

She drives to Sweet Blood in silence. She wasn't able to see where Dominic went after Annabelle went down. She has no desire to rat to the police. She would've saved Annabelle's life if she could, if only for the child.

The baby.

Annabelle stopped breathing when Iris was still by her side. She knows the kid couldn't have fared better.

When Iris gets off the interstate, there's a red glow in the distance. Her expression of shock morphs to concern.

Fires burn in the fields all around her. Then she remembers it's October, harvest season. They're burning the sugarcane. The flames get rid of the leaves and leave only the stalk.

There are vehicles on the roads with their hazards on. Farmhands making sure the burns are managed with order.

When she reaches the gate to Sweet Blood, the grand plantation stands like a haven in the center of all the flames. There are no guards around as far as she can see. Annabelle and Jamie have moved into the main house since Augusta died.

Iris has heard Joseph Senior is now in the guesthouse with his own full-time nurse.

Dominic doesn't seem to be lying. Aurelia is expecting her. The gate swings inward, and Iris keeps driving until she's parked in front of the porch.

The air smells like fall. Crisp air. Burning leaves. Some of the fires are less than a hundred yards from the house.

Iris knocks on the heavy door, and it opens only a few seconds later.

Aurelia looks out past Iris and waves her inside. "Get in here, quick."

Iris steps in, and Aurelia locks the door behind her. "Oh, if it isn't good to see you, sugar. You go have a seat in the music room. I've got to fetch somethin' for you."

Before Iris can respond, Aurelia is walking upstairs.

It's only been a month since she's last been inside, but the place already feels foreign. She walks to the music room, if it can still be called that. The baby grand is gone. So are the watercolors of the nude woman that lined the walls. It looks like it's been turned into a tearoom. There's a round table set near the windows and another sitting area with red velvet chairs.

Iris sits in one of them and looks out the window. There are farm hands in the front yard. Two are walking behind a tractor with a large water tank holding hoses. Here to make sure the house doesn't catch on fire from a stray spark.

Aurelia comes back with a standard envelope. "This is for you."

Iris takes it but doesn't open it quickly. She's still mute as she pulls out a card.

It's textured, cream-colored paper. Even fancier than her invite to tonight's dinner was. Two big words are written in Spanish on the top of the card. They're powder blue. *"Colinas Azules."*

It's Paulo's family estate. Iris is expecting this to be a threat, but at the bottom is handwritten text in cursive English.

"Iris, it would be my pleasure to have you join us at our estate. It would be lovely to show that we are still very much cowboys.

I promise. Yours truly."

The letter is left without a signature, probably in case the FBI got their hands on it, but there is an address for a town in Sinaloa, Mexico.

Paulo.

He had offered Iris a place to hide. He's staying true to word, but something still bothers her.

She stands. The cabinet Augusta used to keep her music in is still where it was before, despite the redecorating.

Iris opens the cabinet doors and quickly pulls out some sheet music. She paces in the middle of the room as she reads.

She doesn't have to look hard—in the margin of the music is the same cursive handwriting that the letter is written in.

Iris doesn't quite believe it. "Augusta?" she whispers aloud.

She looks up to Aurelia. "Do you know anything about this?"

Aurelia clearly doesn't. She takes the letter and music from Iris and studies them for a moment before handing them back. She looks far more shocked than Iris does. Perhaps, Iris thinks, because she didn't just watch a woman burn to death from the inside out.

"They can fake this kind of thing. The cartel. It wouldn't be hard for them," Aurelia finally says.

"You're saying it's a trap?"

Aurelia sits down, deep in thought. "On the other hand, if you were wanted dead, you probably already would be. But I don't know."

Iris goes back to the red velvet chair and sits next to Aurelia. They both watch the fires flicker out the windows. "Annabelle's dead."

Aurelia only nods.

"How much were you in on this?"

"I'm only ever the messenger, love. I ain't an actor in any of this. I don't know things till they happen. But I always know *why* they happened."

Iris starts to crumple the card in her fist, and Aurelia stands and crouches down in front of her.

"You go if you want to go. But if you decide you will, I'll come with you."

Iris looks up with a frown. "Really?"

Aurelia rubs her knee and smiles. "I'm not as much of a homebody as I look."

"You miss Augusta, too, don't you?"

"Compared to Annabelle, she might as well have been Mother Mary."

Iris can't respond. Her brain is occupied by a single thought. An image.

"How about you get some sleep, Iris? I could put you up in your old bedroom. We can figure things out over breakfast."

"Okay."

"Sleep on it. But if you want to go to Mexico, you've got a buddy."

"Thank you, Aurelia."

Aurelia gives her hand a squeeze, and Iris looks back to the fires. She's still expressionless. She's still in shock.

Tell her to lie on her back if she doesn't want it to eat through the baby. Iris knows it probably wasn't enough. The child likely fared no better than Annabelle.

She can't stop picturing her gaping mouth. The foul-smelling steam of her flesh being burned to a gas. All these months she spent trying to remember, and now Iris would give everything to forget.

"I'll sleep on it," Iris says suddenly, trying to force other thoughts into her head. What is there to sleep on? Iris thinks.

What waits for her in Sinaloa but more greed? More violence? Iris is already haunted by both.

But her skin has begun to itch. What is she supposed to do now? Go back home to her quiet, friendless life?

After all the high stakes of living in this house, how could she possibly just disappear? Iris looks at Aurelia, and she thinks she sees the same thing in her eyes—a *need* to go to where the action is.

Iris can't help it. As disturbed as she is, there's something else burning in her. A feeling that isn't at all unfamiliar.

Iris is addicted.

She pictures a rolling estate far larger than Sweet Blood. A palace with gardens and fountains and an entire house staff. And a body behind every brick of its foundation.

330

Iris is going.

In fact, as far as she's concerned, she doesn't even have a choice.

To be continued...

From the Author,

I hope you enjoyed my fifth book This Family Lies! One of the best ways you can support me is by leaving an Amazon review!
Contact me at https://jmcannonwrites.com/
And stay tuned for Part 2!

Made in the USA
Monee, IL
05 June 2024

59443650R00198